# Silly Goose

Ryan Hemar

Copyright © 2020 by Ryan Hemar
ISBN: 978-0-578-68432-1

# Prologue

Forgiveness, if squared and honest, shall overcome all detriments that have thus far annihilated our existence. March on and on down empty sidewalks neighbored by houses overflowing with conversations, observations and cremations of latter-day justifications. You will see a light there. Rotations never expire as the sunset becomes more and more redundant. The grand finale we have dreamt of ever since learning to think may end up being a monumental let down. The greatest disappointment of our lives will quite possibly be the way that it all ends. Though some pass on through fits of bravery, their corpses overshadowing the ten million strong, others simply abandon into tufts of air.

To all those who remain able to breathe the rotten wind provided to us by the hardworking folks from various companies that rape G-d until he/she/it/nothing himself/herself/itself/nothing regrets the very act of our creation, remember: There is a light.  Since thinking under supervision cancels out your honest self, be advised to hold nothing back.  Let the brain become thy train in which we all get another chance to dance our little feet to glory.  So scream a loud "Hallelujah!" (or whatever word makes you feel important), and let us begin.

## Part One: The innocent dance of the freedom fairies

The innocent dance of the freedom fairies…continues
The long awaited back-story to this tragedy
As we wait upon fertile hills and concrete pastures
We ask ourselves:
>Where did all the time go?
>Where did all the time go?

Beyond a tree branch of infinite wonder
A silhouetted dance scene marks the days
Delighted ears match smiling faces
Companion to the sparkling sunrays

Toes gently graze the kind grass
Twinkling between each tender step
A lovely place at a lovely time
A moment's rest in a feel good mind
A devil wishing to be mine
But still the clocks turn slowly

"We wait upon almost of nothing. We breathe in life, as times will fade. Rest assured, the shelter we offer stands tall. Cancel the junctions that defeat our days. Bow together through the connections we create and order out the kingdom come. Besides, we don't know any better than to think otherwise. What have we seen other than infinite bliss? As death does depart with such majesty, I furthermore remain in my constant state. Pure and total discrepancies will always come about. We can't let such a simple obstacle shatter our ways. Bring forth all that you have, for it all tastes so sweet after we're done with it."

- John Nelson, the noble man from South Forts. He is said to lack certain talents and skills that others can readily apply pressure to and be timely released. Nonetheless, he stands tall in moments of grave agony to soon rise above everyone else.

**Patricia CoLaToLa:** Let go of my insides for a small time, so that we may soon see a near exit point for all this madness.

**John Nelson:** If you keep me waiting long enough, I might just get a golden opportunity to finally replace you.

**Patricia CoLaToLa:** Speak no more! Speak no more! Your pretending actions have left a pale hole through my breast.

**John Nelson:** In case we never meet again, and let lace some new neighbors. Miss out on all the dreams we had sought out together. Exploring ocean upon ocean upon ocean. O great glory, it all blends together so nicely in the background.

**Patricia CoLaToLa:** That night you broke your arm, I'll never forget it.

**John Nelson:** I won't have any more of this, Patricia.

**Patricia CoLaToLa:** Holding in tears.

**John Nelson:** I was holding in nothing more than sneezes, for long periods of time.

How sad it is to be leaving home
Under nightly skies
A prize to own
Thank goodness erase
from this mind covered place
Row your boat

# *Row it home*

Sweet baby, you know I'd never let you down.
So purposely, I'd think twice to do it again.

> Driving out the bad lines.
> Off of highways,
> Going my own way.

> Taking everything so "day by day"
> Almost forgetting half the words you say.

> We sweep up the floor mess.
> An ill-tempered footrest.
> Standard issue shock test.

GO AWAY!        GO AWAY!        PLEASE STAY!

> Take us up six lines,
> …everything so day by day
> I'm gunna enjoy this.

Meanwhile over here, we're trying to avoid it.

Not a single race riot since 1963.

Paper sheet, popcorn spray.

Where did you.

Learn to.

Dance.

So.

Well, he listens to me when I try to explain.
It ain't painless bein' a fool caught in the rain.
Wishing I would have stayed home.
Forgiving the lies we now know.

Call up the national guard.
They need to hear about this.
It turns out we made a big mistake.
How can we possibly reimburse you?

With some warm tissues.
Singin' "clouds" and "pillows."
Resting ourselves to bed.

Good night.
Good evening.

## Chapter One
## The under-breath from her leaving

She almost always guaranteed a spectacular evening. You could consistently count on girls to give you a good time; well, mostly. Once in a while you'd get thrown a curveball, but you are stronger than you were before and you've learned to accept it. Forget about that for now. Such spectacular sights she'd show you. Man o man, I'm sure gunna miss this one.

**Goodbye, my rose,**
**my sweet, sweet rose**

For Jared, it was time to move on. He had already wasted so much time on her. His suicide letter begins our story:

Dear THE FUCKERS WHO SHIT ALL OVER ME,

This is because no one ever understood me. No matter how hard I tried to explain, I would always end up getting shoved away. But explanations must lead us toward a clearer understanding. I could easily sum up my main motive for this in one simple word. Well, it's actually a name. The name of the darling who ruined my life. Amy. Holy shit Amy, you really did me in good.

What the fuck is all of this? My life turned out to be such a tragedy. Good bye, good luck. I pray for better tomorrows. What a mess I am going to make when my brains are splattered all over the ceiling. I'm sorry mom and dad, you have to find me like this. If I could do it any other way, I would, but I'm too scared. This is the easiest way, but also the messiest. Dad, I've known where you keep your gun for so long. YOU SHOULD HAVE HID THE FUCKING KEY YOU BASTARD! What a worthless mess I am. And it's all because of that girl. That silly little girl who used to tickle my brain cells. She'd love me all day long, make my heart swell. But look at it now. This shitty disaster that it turned into. I'm fucking done writing this stupid letter. I can't go on another minute. Goodbye.

GO THE FUCK AWAY,

Jared

**Misery, misery. How else can you explain it?**
**Having to redistribute your entire thought process.**
**Everything is going wrong.**

Everything is,
Nothing spectacular.
When I was born,
Thinking of rabbit's ears.
Carry me home,
I wish for nothing more.[1]

Note to self. Write about:
1. Why Amy is referred to as Carousel.
2. The good times with friends.
3. The bad times with her.

# Until then...

## We hear about an old folk tale called
## <u>The California Disaster of 1804</u>

Whatever is left of it, I really don't know. It was such a gloomy time. Such a terrible time. There was nothing then. Look at it now, so much shelter and workingman's honesty. We lived in small town in Southern California. G-d bless that fucking place. It was so brutal growing up there. You need to understand what a terrible combination I had, living there. I loved the animals we used to see around town. But starving can only go on for so long until it breaks you in half. In all honesty, the only thing that gave me hope was her.

My heart stopped beating the day I met Patricia. I'd bleed days and days for her if she'd want it. I swear there was nothing sweeter in the world than having her around. Throw my

---

[1] A sweeter goodbye would have been nice.

arms around her, I'd be a bursting bubble. She'd spend the night sometimes. I'd sneak her in through the back door and we would stay up for hours. My parents never suspected a damn thing. We'd cuddle up and get all cozy, forgetting about time for a while. She swung my whole life open and I never could have wished for anything more. Of course, you can already see where this is going…

The winters there were fucking freezing. I'd worship the fire flames, their movement amazed me. But the warmth they gave off was never enough. Sweet little Patricia CoLaToLa broke my heart. She destroyed me. Whenever pops sent me out hunting, I would let a small taste of my insanity out. I spent days upon days running through the forest chasing junglefowl. My journeys inspired me.

> Out in the middle of my lawn
> A lame carcass will grow
> And in my garage
> A small table, it glows.
>
> But I am not there
> I am streaming through hills
> All of love's lost fate
> I am counting my kills.
>
> Run, boychick, run
> You won't get away
> Destroy at once
> A feast for today.
>
> I have captured him
> A loser of chase
> But tonight it is not
> His blood I will taste.

Garage returned
Set straight without movement
A brand new blade
Makes this an improvement.

Swan song fair beast
Upon plateaus above
Seven miles away
She manufactures her love.

Meanwhile still encased
Rotating past the present
Red marks my walls
During a new form of torment.

Adieu, my glum friend
Pass on by and by
Soar far away
You'll brighten the sky.

    None thought that anyone could possibly feel this way back then. You spin your head today, it's all over town. But back then, we all got by. Everyone I knew could make it on their own just fine. Everyone, that is, except me. I always stood on the outside during this false statistic. I proved them all wrong. I made them see my tears as they fell. I made them try to imagine what it felt like. They began to understand me, but they could just as easily snap their fingers and leave. Young adults today claim they are on their own, but at least they feel alone in large quantities.

    News of the incident spread in the form of a telegram. It was the first sort of teenage tragedy that ever occurred. Towns erupted into frenzies. If one were to listen closely enough, they could hear early traces of the "CRACK! BOOM! BASH!" that all the modern-day housewives would soon be making. A meeting was held for all concerned citizens. A gathering of sorts that had never occurred before.

No one understood it back then.

No one understands it today.
This is what we refuse to believe.

This story has been brought to you by gracious donations from:
THE FOLK TALE REGISTRY
and
THE THEN AND NOW THINKERS.

# Jared shall receive days from two separate planets.

1. We refer to his love, Amy, as Carousel. It is her last name and it is what everyone calls her. She has dark, brown hair and stands approximately five feet, four inches tall. She's got herself some lovely eyes and a wonderful smile. When we first meet her she is a week away from turning fifteen. She is almost angelic in her movements and won't stand compared to a single thing. Up until her parents' divorce, she had not a single care in the world. With the end of her mother and father together, her life fell apart.

"What's the point in even trying to gain strength out of all this?" she'd ask me from time to time. How does one answer that?

1. (cont'd) I'm terribly sorry, I forgot to also mention that she was an only child. This forced her into learning how to function easily on her own. It also made the relationship between her and her parents even stronger.

How could I show her that we would be worth it? The two of us, if together forever, would make an unbelievable pair. But I had only been with her for a few weeks. I could tell she still didn't even like me all that much, and here she is crying to me about her parents getting divorced. Most of my friends' parents had already gone through this, so I was accustomed to the situation.

"My life is meaningless now!" She started bawling. I honestly wish I could view this conversation again today. I'd get a kick out of it. I was not emotionally equipped to handle this level of domestic anguish; but I tried.

"Well, at least I've got you and you've got me," I'd say, in my most pathetic attempts at consolation. She gave me a rather harsh response, but later told me she didn't mean it. I don't feel self-confident enough to share with you what she said. Just know that it nearly killed me.

Looking back on it now, I realize that I should have left her right then and there. I was given a proper excuse to do so, but her apology felt a little too good. If I would have walked away from her then, this wouldn't exist. It didn't have to.

## RUN AWAY WHILE YOU STILL CAN!

O, Carousel! My darling Carousel

Your hymns build up to beauty

Cadence walk of my desire

Threaded out a setting fog

Alas! There she waits

I carry with me an offering

It is you that will bring me home

You that will keep me there

You can pocket the trash accidents

Under bland delusions

JARED.     Don't regret your choosing,
           Carousel.

CAROUSEL.  I play to packs of thieves,
           for which I receive full authority.

JARED.     Can you not hear my language? It is I
           that deserves the golden honor placed
           upon his heart.

CAROUSEL.  Whether or not these foul participants
           become victorious, they will still break
           sweat and leave with scraped knees.

JARED.     I call regulation, my love.

CAROUSEL.  Your words lie together in a broken
           mess. My sensitive ears seek
           fulfillment, which I cannot hear.

JARED.     With time and dull rhymes,
           I'll scream through your head.
           A monologue so brilliant,
           this morning starts in your bed.

CAROUSEL.  Cancel yourself, forsake my offer.
           None but a single leaf sits beside my
           entrance.

JARED.     There's a line at your door!
           An entire assumption stands waiting.

CAROUSEL.  Tell them I am busy,
           and cast an evil eye their way.

JARED.     Confusion! Confusion! You prance
           around the very line of opinion,
           making false claims about this
           moment's stance.

| | |
|---|---|
| CAROUSEL. | Where I stand, |
| | not in yours or any others' |
| | vocabulary. |
| | It is mine. |
| | My decisions, I'll make. |
| | I will choose who to break. |
| JARED. | Allow me a superior status.  I beg for |
| | the comfort received by the matching |
| | mold we create. |
| CAROUSEL. | I agree to your conquest, |
| | honest and true. |

**To all those who waste hours with timeless wonder:**
It has recently come to our attention that two human
beings are in love.

# JARED & CAROUSEL

We offer our most humble congratulations as a means
of expression.  Cheers.

*It's too late to turn back now.*

I will grasp the situation,
as watercolors paint my mind.
I think I might be happy now.
I think I might be happy now.
I think I might be happy now.
I think I might be happy now.
Don't listen to their words.
Don't analyze their faces.
Nobody knows a fucking thing.
Except you.

Here comes a fat man.
Deaf, dumb and blind.
He's Bouncing!
He's Bouncing!
"I thought it might be nice,
if you would let me ruin your life.
Listen to my bullshit advice."

SHUT THE FUCK UP
Your lips sound better sealed

I got a girl now.  A girl.
I've lost the world now.  The World.

I once had a friend who kept a bird in a cage.
One day it got out and got hit by a train.
I once had a friend who kept a bird in a cage.
Inside it grew mad, its blood filled with rage.
"I'm free, I'm free," he could finally say.
Step with caution, my friend, as you're marching away.

## BUT THIS is not where we left off.
## BACK STEP A BIT, and sing:

What a wonderful time it was to be alive.  Let's just assume, for the sake of humanity, that this is what life is all about. Meet a nice girl or boy, and love them until you die.  Forget all those shit bags who choose not to believe this and end up in a situation that is quite the contrary.

**A man in an apartment with his head in his hands**
*Look at what has happened to this place*
**Forgive me please, forgive me son**
*My memory I wish to erase*

Happiness will always depart out of any given situation, but it can be prolonged if we choose to follow these three simple guidelines:

1. Stay in control of your mind and your thoughts.
2. Keep a distance. Don't pounce on all your troubles at once.
3. As ridiculous as it may sound, try to be optimistic.


"Hurry up," Carousel yelled from about thirty yards up. She had with her all the necessary and proper supplies (the basket and the bread), and still she was faster than he was. She always did all the hard work, the dirty work, the murder-suicide news clippings.

"Slow down, babe." He made it obvious. There was no use hiding it.

She had this real look of grandeur to her. She loved movies from the '40s and resembled a character straight out of one.

"Maybe if you'd quit your bad habits, you'd be up here with me right now," she shouted.

It was true. It was the honest truth. But if it were to be explored more in-depth, one would discover that she was merely speaking straight into her own reflection. She was the one with the bad habits. He was only an innocent bystander.

There isn't a good enough way of inserting exactly what it was they were doing **going on a picnic**. Soon enough, this would all collapse.

As the day progressed, Jared and Carousel enjoyed a pleasant experience at the park. That naughty little boy brought a bottle of wine with him.

"I would like to propose a toast to the spectacular relationship we are sharing," he announced.

What a sweet time they were having. Their glasses collided and they began to complete the sauce. She ended up spilling about half her wine on his right arm. It was okay, because it gave them both a good laugh.

# I CAN FEEL SOMETHING TERRIBLE CREEPING UP ON ME!

From a blind man's standpoint, everything seemed to be going perfectly. The hallways were decorated with such majestic tapestries that one was forced into believing their sincerity. A lockdown seemed so unimaginable that even Carousel would occasionally sneak in a dance or two. Unfortunately, ghosts haunted their escrow and kept them on their toes. What a mean beast might perceive as a humble offering was really just a last chance reminder of the foreseeable apocalypse.

It is entirely understandable to experience a feeling of hopelessness about this matter. What can be done besides briefly inserting compassion into an otherwise debilitating struggle? A proper mind can effortlessly gain such insights by observing a situation in which life is suffering.

Hammering through the curtains
I broke apart full dawn
Cursed spells of enchanted nothing

Here lies a liar's den
And on the floor so conveniently

My weapon

A pen to mark my obsessions
A sword to kill my emotions
Strike down the wicked and the poor
Let go, it has yet to commence

Rotate and see
Rotate and believe
This is really happening
The end of everything
A dull blade's guaranteed offer
Such a sloppy insertion
Goodbye, my friend, goodbye

At the time it happened, everyone was really interested in analyzing dreams and memories. In the case of John Nelson, they were given plenty to work with. His life had such a bizarre end that it seemed almost inevitable that they would learn a thing or two from examining him.

They = a group of scientists from the early 1800s who believed that as a person's life progressed, all of their thoughts and visions were stored in a small chamber of the brain known as the felotix. Lacking the medical advancements and tools we now have today, these scientists performed some of the most horrific operations ever known to man.

**How to perform a Felotix Semi-Articular Remembrance:**

**1. Carefully remove the patient's pathetic brain by cutting a hole around the upper portion of the skull.**
**2. Slice the brain in half and expel the felotix with your bare hands.**
**3. Digest the felotix and stare at a ginko tree for approximately six hours.**

There were four of them. They divided the felotix into four individual sections. During the remembrance, they witnessed what some say is the worst possible example of human suffering ever recorded.

Ripping John's head apart ended up being their gravest mistake.

*NOTE TO THE READER: Your presence is no longer necessary for the success of this mission. At this point, you are only keeping the main characters company. If you fall behind, the story will go on without you. Feel free to stop reading at any point.*

They were told three stories that day. The first one took place between two and four o'clock.

# Patrick

## Part one

"Patrick! Patrick! Patrick, come back!" he SCREAMED. His vocal cords were beginning to shred apart.

For nearly two hours Rupert Podemsky had been searching for his dog, Patrick. That dog was Rupert's life! I'm talking about every single "this" and "that" with his dog.

No one could stand to look at him the day Patrick ran away. He was a mess. It was all over for him. Everything lost. The campaign banners fell from the walls of a defeated candidate.

He could have saved us all from this mess. Someone should have had the heart to step in.

"Father, forgive me for the betrayal I have cast down at you. I am anew! I am anew!" He prayed for the first time in his life.

*Dear G-d, I call upon you*
*Share your mercy with me*
*I will no longer blaspheme your name*
*I will never swear*
*I will stop breathing*
*You leave me nothing*
*You that is all-powerful*
*You that is omnipotent*
*A word that I learned in high school*
*What the fuck is high school?*
*A simple institution that has refused to*
*speak your name!*
*Why are you hiding?*
*Your absence has left such an awful stench*

He never believed in G-d again. He was defeated in such a small stretch of agony. The town felt his ghost burning through the place. Rupert was not yet dead, but felt as if he was.

It was time for the routine trip to the copy-making store. He could not stop crying long enough to create a legible "Lost Dog" flyer. The ink kept smearing through the treacherous dance of dampened paper partnered with the pale emptiness of Rupert's eyes. It was on draft seventeen that he finally completed his sworn task. He coughed up the $2.13 that it cost to alert the town of Patrick's absence, in the hopes that a few people might actually give a shit, and hit PRINT. He carried his copies out the door and proceeded to paint the entire neighborhood with his freezing cold isolation.

## Part Two

"Without a single shred of dignity, I share with you my love and joy," Eddie called out to his fellow confidant, Bernardo.

"I accept your most gracious offer, and will allow you to follow through with your wicked misbehaving," Bernardo replied.

Together they shared the ultimate unit of friendship. And on this night, the two of them decided to cast away their troubles and mindlessly wander the streets. Unaware of their intentions, they began their journey.

## Part Three

These boys have no idea, whatsoever, as to what is about to happen to them.

Two shots and they feel ready.

Lost under a false importance of their rights.

An unholy reminder of the truth.

Desolate springs glisten with the blind.

Hope me, I hope it is me.

Because this is it!

This is fucking it, man.

We're going to come alive tonight.

Tonight.

As the sun set behind them, unfortunate families suffered nearby. They were never truly free from the sadness that surrounded them. Sometimes people have no hopes or desires. Many are so abundantly confused by nearly everything. Eddie and Bernardo were no exception. Who's to say this city didn't splatter their empty defeats among everything? The truth remains out there, but no one wants to know it. Let the bleeders bleed on forever. Never let the poor see themselves for who they really are.

## You will die alone
## The system has defeated you
## Goodnight

The TV never told them the truth. This was how they got their information.

G-d bless you two. We are so honored and excited that you would choose to die for us. One night under the fire, and your warmth shall spread on for always. This was the CHURCH OF ALWAYS! G-d wants to shit all over your asses. He seems like he would be such a rotten bastard. *Again we have become sidetracked and must now return home.*

Eddie and Bernardo were merely strolling along the endangered sidewalks, talking about nothing as usual, when OUT OF THE FUCKING BLUE a pink Mercedes-Benz pulled up next to them. In the driver's seat was Rupert Podemsky himself.

"Hello, young citizens. I am rich, honest and stupid. I have almost no awareness of myself. Help me find my dog, for he is all that I have in this world."

He held out a copy of the flyer to them. They screened it over and agreed to search far and wide in order to find the dog.

They had never before made such a priority out of anything. This was an ultimate first.

"Let us dare not rest a night until we have retrieved his fantasy," Eddie proclaimed. They knew the dog had probably been eaten by coyotes several hours ago. Still, they couldn't let poor Rupert down.

### Part Four

They reached an almost perfect walking trail, which reminded Bernardo of how splendid his life used to be. The sign at the fork told them they could either go south:

# Tulip't Villé

or north:

# Hopler's Tea Trimmer

Due to the fact that they weren't redundant sheepherders, they chose to venture into Hopler's Tea Trimmer. The road before them, which they would soon be on, remained partially a mystery. Neither of them had ever seen what was beyond "of molecules, partnered previous entrance." It was time for an escape from their rotten prison. They were constantly getting hit by red, yellow and green tomatoes. This was understood and agreed upon as something they would have to suffer through.

Eddie was the first to fall into the trap. It caught him, shielded under a patch of maple leaves. His leg fell through a covered hole that measured six feet down. Sticking up from the bottom were five bamboo sticks in dice formation, sharpened to the finest possibility. Eddie's left leg was bent when one of the sticks entered his body. It passed through the back of his heel and stuck in, by about four inches, right where his thigh and scrotum connect. A scream never sounded. Only tears, and the saddest whimper in this nation's history.

Bernardo didn't know what to do. For almost an entire minute he stood, staring at what was once his pal Eddie. Everything felt gray and frozen. The sound was hideous. Eddie, the leader of the pack, was reducing. The trees seemed to weep for him. So instantaneously had it all occurred. Walking, happy, walking, happy, walking, NOW. The sky fell into night, and the cold dirt shimmered. Alone and unhappy, for the first time ever. Again, it was strange how suddenly it all happened. When the blood came, his eyes shattered. His teeth nearly did, too.

Everything was fine. Their movement was frequent and well-paced. The world seemed to spin around them. A conversation danced happily from lip to ear, and back again.

## LaLaLa LaLa La.

"Eddie's foot broke through false identity like a glass cabinet."

Then there was nothing except silence. Frightening and suspenseful silence. It killed Bernardo (not literally).

"My poor dog is missing. Someone please find him." In between tears, Eddie began to speak as if he himself were Rupert. "Today I lost my best friend in the whole world...My little puppy is gone!...I need you, Patrick...I need you...Don't you love me anymore?...Little pup...Little mountain ranger...You were always my favorite...Come back to me...Slobber hound...Golden crown...Curse these maple grounds...Sharp stabs...Babies can speak...But they have no voice to say...I am your emperor... Listen to what I tell..."

His blood began to create a small pool at the bottom of the hole. Then, like out of a fucking movie, some song by

AC/DC started playing. It had no source, it only contradicted the situation.

Bernardo finally mustered up the courage to help Eddie, but it only made matters worse.

### *From his heel and thigh, untimely ripped.*

Bernardo's quick, heroic movements inflicted such intense pain that Eddie began screaming like a Pterodactyl.

Dinosaur
by
John Nelson

# OOOoooo OOOOooo

I wish I was a Dinosaur
For a day
## Hey Hey
Bury my bones in the water
Can't you stay?
They'll dig up our fossils here
one day

Eddie in Bernardo's arms. Bernardo in Eddie's. Two soldiers in their own private Vietnam.

"The Vietnamese people deeply love independence, freedom and peace. But in the face of United States aggression they have risen up, united as one man."

-Ho Chi Minh

As the villain's blade slowly slid out of Eddie, the world tumbled itself around. Pools poured out empty, up into the sky. & all of earth's unattached beings, floated away.

And
Every single copy
Of the greatest film ever made
Flew up and hit the ceiling
Of homes and warehouse buildings
And
The genius liars formulated their plan
The Plan
That would eventually destroy me

Shhh…

Meanwhile, Rupert was at home, jerking off. On his computer screen flashed photographs of naked women engaging in various sexual acts.

# FINGER

Please stare at the above word for approximately ten seconds before you continue reading.

"I need to go to the hospital!" screamed Eddie.
"I'll run to the nearest house and call an ambulance."
-Bernardo -- winner of "Quote of the Year" by Reader's Digest 2004. Something about the way he said it won over the judges.

And just like that, Bernardo was gone. Eddie was left alone, trembling through his self-madness. As the last of his friend's footsteps fell into the darkness, the bitterness grew and grew. The ichor from his legs was swallowing him whole. He was freezing cold and bloody as a bat. The entire bright-light sun machine surrendered its horses and the forest walls swarmed around him. Everything, at once, turned black & white, metaphorically.

"Hello. Can anyone hear me?" Eddie called out.

From behind a bush came his answer.

"Eddie, we are the wolves that occupy this trail. You are invading our wilderness. It was us that set the trap. We want you to die. We have come to kill you!"

All he could see was their ice-green eyes shining from behind the foliage.

"Step away from me, you ill-tempered beasts. I have not set out among great men who have fallen before me only to–"

"We will hear no more of it, sir. This is the end, motherfucker. IT'S OVER. YOUR WHOLE LIFE. STOP AND REALIZE THIS: YOUR LIFE IS OVER!"

From behind trees and other shrubbery, they emerged. One by one, the pack revealed themselves. The fierce, ferocious animals. Murderers. The killers, unfolding.

There were seven in all. Everything was moving in slow motion.

Eddie spoke:

> "I will not die tonight for such pretentious reasons.
>     Cam Lé Ö Tesh rá.
>         Tū Züme, Tū Züme."

Just as they entered, their faces melted away. From first to last, his words defeated them. An all-star of an animal, killed by an extinct language.

Wolf heaven was nothing short of a modern day paradise. It had such a tropical, light blue feel to eat. Just wolves, looking back on the good old days.

"I remember once," a ghost began, "we ran through the woods and met our final fate. It was that boy. He annihilated us during our daily routine."

"EDDIE!"
Mother
Kitchen
Pots and Pans

Warping away

Knock Knock
Who's there?
Burn
Burn who?
Burn Burn Bernardo

The door swung open at an alarming rate. In its frame stood the dark shadow of a man, a drenched shotgun in his arms.

His real story:

Henry Fronten had forgotten his entire life. He used to fuck all the sluts in high school. They were never hard for him to find. While all the lonely souls sat in their cars at the drive-in theatre, he would be slamming whore ass in the back of his truck (sex without romance can ruin a soul). Soon after graduation, everyone he knew moved away. **After that, he changed.**

Now here he stood with a "gun" in his hands, living in the muddy swamplands.

Gun (noun) - The symbolic figure of loneliness for the American shit bag.

"What's the matter, kid? Don't look so sad," he proclaimed. He could tell something was wrong.
"Sir, can I please use your telephone? My friend is in trouble," Bernardo asked.
"This appears to be a sad time for both of us. Please, do come in."

"Thank you," Bernardo said, and bowed his head.

"We must remember that times do change and things always happen. Life is existence. Forgotten are the dead, who weep tremendously. Recall, with solemn reverence, the–"

"I would love to hear more of your useless observations," Bernardo interrupted, "but unfortunately, I must use your phone."

The man grabbed Bernardo by his shirt collar and pulled him in close. He whispered in his ear.

"The phone is in the bathroom, where my business resides."

Their eyes matched, and so began the definite stare. It lasted forever.

Flies began to gather around the remains of the wolves. Eddie was shivering so badly that he appeared almost blurry in sight. Unaware of his feelings, the shock comforted him. He decided that he might as well attempt to trace Bernardo's footsteps. Assuming he could correctly guess the house, he put his left leg forward. It took several minutes until he finally captured the proper transportation rhythm. He was on his way, but unsure of where he was going.

Shit. Shit was everywhere. The entire bathroom was covered. As soon as he flicked the moist light switch, he saw what the man had done. He scanned the room. Four young Asian boys. All naked in the shit-covered bathroom. For their entire lives they dreamed of becoming scientists.

### Oops, looks like someone screwed up.

The youngest and most hostile son spoke out:

# HELP US, OUR SAVIOR

[We now interrupt this commercial broadcast to bring you a free sample of "The Time Machine." Yes, it has been invented. No more hypothetical situations!]

Eddie in the year 2064:

Back ago
Through the wicked woods I traveled
And sure enough found very odd
That the seize-fire roundup
Ended in blood splatter
And the property was never sold

[Now Back]

"Whistle blowin' street cat,
Your mother was a meekrat."

Eddie sang, in a pure and hopeful plea for redemption. There was no way he could mask the pain. Everything had been wasted.

In the center of the trail stood three tall men. Only, "taller," in nature, meant "much smaller than." And the three here in this sudden place, decided that it would be proper to say...

## Absolutely Nothing

They appeared in perfect formation. Amounting to that which one would call unordinary. You could compare them to gnomes and get away with it. Their faces looked worn and tired. A lost hope, remembered.

Tiny, Trip and Tosie stuck out their hands.
"It is a triumph and a treat that you would share your lands with us," said Trip, with his barracuda lips.

"For months we have roamed alone, only to learn that these trails are uninhabited," said Tiny.

"We are searching for so-called friends," entered Tosie, "but only receiving threats or De-Bondings."

(De-Bondings is when the goose comes out, and shows its awful thorns)

HEY, SHUT UP!

"We welcome your neighborship," sang all three. Their voices created such a beautiful harmony.

"I will accept your kind greeting," answered Eddie. "We may now join together to create the complete and champion self-image, which we so desperately crave."

Eddie's new friends became profoundly confused. Eventually they stopped pretending that they understood what he was saying.

"You look hurt," interrupted Tosie. "Would you like us to bandage your wounds?"

"Why, yes. It hurts tremen–"

Tiny screamed, "For only a small, reasonable fee, we will fix you!"

"At this moment in time, I would give almost anything for a savior," Eddie started. "A dear friend of mine, Bernardo, has already gone to find help. I do not know whether or not his mission will be successful."

"In what realm of existence does reason prevail?" Bernardo whispered, silently.

The sight itself was unpleasant, but what was even worse was the smell. The fumes entered Bernardo's nostrils like an exploding ball in a padded room (self-contained, but still dangerous). His mind was almost unable to comprehend what was happening. Here, through the dim light, he saw faces of the unraveled. Expressions he had never before observed. A lonely ghost, wandering the earth for eternity.

The man came up behind him.

"See anything you're interested in, kid?" he asked.

Bernardo had no idea what he was talking about. He assumed that:

-The four boys are being held prisoner in the small bathroom.

-With the plumbing broken, they are forced to release their asses in various sections of the room and are unable to wash themselves.

-Judging by the amount of feces, they must have already been here for a long time.

-Since they are still alive, they must somehow be eating and drinking.

-It is likely that they are being fed by this strange man.


"Did you not hear me, boy? I asked you a question!" His voice was getting louder and louder. Bernardo laughed because he realized that the man had actually asked two questions. When the three sentences were put together in his head, the sound of it made the old man out to be quite the fool.

"Now, I want to give you a present. I am trying to do a decent thing FOR ONCE IN MY LIFE! And here you are, comin' up all crazy on me," the man said.

"I'm afraid I don't understand your question, sir," Bernardo finally spoke.

"You dumb drum head! Quit staring and do what you came here to do!" the man yelled.

Bernardo's eyes glided across the room. He scanned the boys again. Not one moved. The silence blinded his ears. Bernardo couldn't think. The underlying purpose of his visit had seeped from his mind.

"Phone! We are a phone!" called out one of the boys. It was the same one that spoke earlier.

The man turned his attention to the boy. He was obviously mad at him.

"How dare you fucking speak!" he screamed. The man then grabbed a CHUNK of SHIT from the wall and threw it at

him. It splashed against the boy's face. He didn't move a
muscle.

"Now, if any of you raise your voice to me again," the
man yelled, "I will shove the hose up your ass and leave it on for
three hours."

Tiny, Trip and Tosie guided Eddie
to the most tropical hint of the woods.
He could not see underneath himself,
for the ground was already taken.
Among their shelter
lay bricks of passage.

These four nameless boys had nothing worth living for.
**A strong nothing is always aroused.** (Pause) Beep Beep The
stillness of their suffering surrounded them. And now, Bernardo
had to remember what to do. How on earth could they possess a
method of communication? Ugly meat on a doorstep.

"Now!" the man screamed. His voice echoed out and fell
silent. That's when it all began. The four boys stood up and
lifted their right hands. They rose in perfect alignment, through a
scattered sense. A dull conscience doth roar to grow more.

Each individual mouth opened to its maximum grip. And
out came "The Song of Indifference."

Four tall with voices of angels. The song only required
long, stretched hold-notes, yet still it rang properly.

The brown ground rose from their lingo. It danced
around them as a ballet of shit.

Tiny carried out a handmade first-aid kit. His little
fingers pulled open the lid and revealed its contents. Inside was a
woven cloth. Inscribed on it was:

**LOVE YOUR BROTHERS. STAND TALL
TOGETHER, AND DON'T LET A GIRL GET
IN THE WAY OF THINGS. IN THE END,
LOVE MATTERS MOST.**

"Eddie, I want you to read this and tell me what you think it means," Tiny spoke.

Eddie read the words.

"This uh, this makes me think of a dear friend of mine. He… he's no longer with us. Killed himself. Man, but if he was here, he'd sure have a lot to say about this."

"What would he say?"

Eddie, ever the shapeshifter, did his best to channel Jared. "Well, I used to know a girl, and before I met her, my life was empty. Her and I shared all sorts of adventures together. I felt happy, but it was an illusion. Blow jobs and sex seem like a main priority to everyone. The hype is contagious and it's made into this grand event. I'd spend so much fucking time with her that I departed from my friends a bit. They all knew her and treated her good. But still, I never came back. Not fully, at least. There's no return once you reach that particular summit. Those days of careless boyhood playfulness are over for good. The story always ends the same, and she left me. I was sad, but it's a situation experienced by all. After a few months I could tell she was being forgotten in my heart. This reduced the pain, so I didn't complain. But then they fired back, with harsh reality."

"Please don't go on anymore. I can't stand it!" Tiny said. His eyes were full of tears. "I plan on going the rest of my life without ever mentioning that incident."

Eddie hung his head. He handed Tiny the cloth, but accidentally dropped it on a nearby steppingstone. Tiny walked away, sobbing profusely.

Meanwhile, Trip and Tosie were cooking up a batch of carrot cakes. Inside, the oven was burning, bubbling, fizzling. Them old rodents never cared whether they could withstand the intense heat and ultimately, finish. It was only when their brains were smashed and thrown together that they expressed any concern for their own wellbeing. This was how the two met. Before, not a word had been spoken. As fate would worship, they were a perfect match. One, an angry drunk, the other, a calm sea turtle. Placed together in a small box, they ceased to endure it.

Earlier that same day, they were a sauce. The batter showed up late and left stale measures behind. Unrealized were the obvious entrails of an otherwise festive evening.

"I knew her once, though I doubt she'd ever admit it. What is even possible anymore? A misunderstood mentioning of everything? Let's all just forget the entire event ever happened."

At 2:00 a.m., the bakers mixed the batter. It was their usual technique. Stow away the yesterdays and hope for something more.

"Karen, where's your camera? Karen, where's your camera?" she asked. Karen was the name of the first cake to be placed in the oven. Katie, the other, was the second. She wanted to remember this moment for the rest of her short life. The day another mixture of ingredients showed up and blessed her with an amusing situation. This is something for the record books, an instance never to be forgotten. But too soon came the flame that engulfed them both. The oven was set at 2,000,000°F! Only the three could see their majesty. The cakes were beginning to take shape. Caker time! Trip and Tosie reached in and pulled out their prizes.

Meanwhile, Eddie was sitting outside, now alone. Tiny had disappeared into the surrounding wilderness. Trip and Tosie exited their cottage. Astonished glances crossed their faces. Tosie's left foot was nearly on top of the scattered strands of cotton. 100% all natural, no additives.

"What happened here?" asked Tosie.

Bernardo's entire future perspective of life and all humanity's glory had been deranged. Every adult must wonder: "If only I could see myself now, when I was younger." So much for any sort of special life. Of course, all individuals long to be special, to stand out in a crowd of one million fishes. Will ever there be a time where this comes true? Probably not.

"I'm not afraid of you, kid!" the man snarled. He could tell. They could see it in each other's eyes. The truth of the matter. **Again Rupert masturbates...**

*This is the end, Bernardo. Someone finally stood up for himself and spoke the truth about man's indecencies. But it wasn't you. You never would have done a fucking thing. You know this to be true. STOP DENYING EVERYTHING. Someone had to make a move. Was this just going to continue forever? Did you honestly think that something was going to be done? No! You are a fucking human. We all love to fuck. We all love to lie a little. But the past has buried itself deep within you. Forget it. Why can't you forget it? Why, Bernardo? Why?*

*The moral continues to change;*

**Let us remind ourselves of the confusion. Compared to any sort of global threat to national policy, this is a nightgown. This town is invisible. Nothing goes on here. Nothing ever "happens".     GODDAMNIT, LET ME PUT THE PERIOD AFTER THE QUOTATION MARK. FUCKING PROPER USE OF THE ENGLISH**

**LANGUAGE IS SUCH BULLSHIT. WHO THE FUCK CARES!!!!!!!!!!!!!!!!!!!!!!!!!!!!!!!!!!!!!!!!!!!!!!!!!!!!!!!!!!!!!!!" IF YOU HAVE BEEN OFFENDED BY MY ERRORS, YOU SHOULD GO TO COLLEGE AND SHOOT YOURSELF. I am sorry, I don't want people to think I'm an asshole. SHIT man, this is always my excuse as to why I hated <u>Breakfast of Champions</u>.**

Where were you that night? **Tosie**

I was in another world. **Eddie**

And they...? **Tosie**

They were together. That night, for me, was beautiful and natural. The sky was warm; it swam around me. **Eddie**

Yet at the same time, the conquest of despair was built. Forever was ruined. **Tosie**

I can't believe it. I fell asleep on my deathbed. **Eddie**

The same thing happened with Tiny and Trip. I was in the middle. I played no part. **Tosie**

How did you handle it? **Eddie**

I cared, I danced, I sang a sweet, sad lullaby around the wicked palm trees. I smiled and never asked questions. I only hoped that it didn't happen. **Tosie**

I played the victim. **Eddie**

And I played the chief. Hey, I learned something new about you today. **Tosie**

"I think we all did."
                    -ENTERTAINMENT WEEKLY

"His wisdom sections of truth help to accentuate a moral belief system demanding to be shattered!"
                    -PAT O'BRIEN

# BY THE WAY (fucking Vonnegut again) I FEEL SO FUCKING SORRY FOR WHAT HAPPENED TO PAT.

"Don't you love me?  HE won't hurt us.  HE never touched me.  Honestly.  HE is good to me.  HE is good to us," another called out.
    Bernardo had now heard two of them speak.  The brainwash sounded terrible.  He could see it.  He could see the sounds and wasn't afraid to confess to the stereotype.

# Hey man, what's your stereotype?
# Who you be typin', fool?

Stop and assess the situation (a phrase I've always wanted to use). I have finally offered the truth. It was an honest offering, and I am glad you told me about it. Nobility has charged forth. Look at the fighters! The true fighters. Ernest Hemingway and Martin Luther King Jr. (shit) They glanced into the charge and protested a million items; they ran away from fear and did not know it; they killed the mockingbird and could not show it; they ALARM ALARM ALARM ALARM ALARM ALARM

Pardon our interruption.

Excuse the sounds.

"Take me to an F-word paradise," whispered Bernardo.

**The room fell silent. Bernardo slammed his FINGER into the air. His hand then glided back down, toward the waist-buckling module. Closer and in, he reached for the sacrifice. He stood without shame. Representative to his cause for notifying beauties, nothing would stop him. This was it. THE GRAND EVENT. The moment we've all been waiting for.**

"Allow my teeth to breathe easily. Allow all of my masks to run together in the valley. Why must we only live on this single channel of communication?" **Bernardo's tone was building.** "I am ready," he said.

## Slowly, the madness started.

One by one, the zipper hinges came undone. Skip the details and his penis was exposed. The eyes of each opened wide. The man, frightened in the doorway, did not know what to do. Could he withstand the curiosity burning beneath him? He could not! Instead, he dove into the moment, along with the four willful boys. Bernardo's penis became erect instantly. As they all moved forward, it rose.

Chomp chomp chomp!  The four boys began munching away at what they saw.  The skin stuck to their lips.  As they pulled back and away, the skin came with (traveled).  Red spots of carnage formed all over.  This continued for quite some time.  After 5 minutes, all that remained was a red slab of meat.

*As for the man, he slowly slipped out of his overalls and, once naked, began dancing.  A real rock-beat sort of rhythm penetrated from him.  He was alone, grooving to the background noises.  It was flopping around all over the place.*

AFTER A THOUSAND GRUESOME WORDS ABOUT WHAT WENT ON, BERNARDO'S PENIS WAS GONE. NOTHING WAS LEFT, EXCEPT FOR A SMALL RED STRAND.  HE STOOD STILL FOR A MOMENT, NOT SAYING A

**WORD. HE SWAYED BACK AND FORTH, BACK AND FORTH. A MINUTE LATER, HE PASSED OUT AND HIT HIS HEAD ON THE TOILET SEAT. HE WAS OUT FOR A WHILE.**

Trip had not been listening to what the two were talking about. He was nearby, but could hear nothing.

"Wow, these are some interesting creatures," he mumbled to himself, while admiring the behavior of the bumblebee and the snail. "What a wonder they are. The snail and the bee are both backwards, symmetrically. If you were to look at it from the standpoint of, say, a painter, you would realize that their alignment is both true and unusual. Now, the snail happens to be a very slow moving creature. The speed of a bee and the speed of a snail are far apart in measurement. A snail will take its time getting somewhere; although it has no other option." Trip was going on and on.

It seems that in this unfortunate atmosphere, we have all been gently exposed. In terms of measurement, this shall be considered a final and just expression of all the sick, sad elements in my head. The terrible memories, the horrible nightmares. With this passage, so stands a new rising. Hope for all individuals! Racism forgotten! Unity of man's hearts, brave and skilled. A world of friendship and trust. A world.....
.............................................
.............................................
.............................................
.............................................
...............**so suddenly destroyed**

Scientist #3, Arnold Destrapa, was the first to snap out of the trance. He jumped up immediately.

"I don't like this. I don't like this at all," he shouted. The other three were still deep inside the wonder. "What the hell is going on?" He couldn't control his breathing. He was absolutely terrified. He looked around and was glad to see himself back in his own world. His proper state of mind. He was back to his "normal." The comfortable and familiar self-image he had (almost) achieved. Yet with all that, in this particular moment, his body needed another. He craved the satisfaction of connecting with someone else. He needed the guidance and support of one of his fellow colleagues. Desperately, he tried to shake them out of their trance. It was no use. The chemicals were overwhelming. Arnold stood up and began to panic. A feeling of loss and loneliness swept over him.

And just like that, he fell to the ground. His body collapsed. Arnold Destrapa died that day, after experiencing only a strange beginning. His intake of the entire situation was undoubtedly incorrect on all levels.

Level one - An intelligent and thorough observation of each and every event. (Details come in very handy here)

Level two - A recorded evaluation of what happened. He must then break it into pieces and analyze his findings.

However, for his last minute of life, if he were to perchance attempt to reach level two, how would his results look?

Amongst the broadness of my mind, I can in no way elaborate upon the distinguished principals from which I now see and experience this life. On one hand, I am in intense pain because the fragile, delicate structure of my brain—my consciousness, as it were—feels as though a huge chunk of it has been rendered into wartime carnage. Part of me was saying, you are about to die. And I knew it. I sort of believed it. In a way, I wanted to believe it, because of what I had seen. I can't even describe it to you.

Those boys. What the fuck happened? I had seen such greatness, for I knew them both. But my contact with them ceased before any of this happened. I only knew them when things were good. I only remember positive energy being exchanged between them. And they were completely unaware of it; rightly so. They were blissfully oblivious to the happiness, the joy and the comfort they gave each other. It was just there. They didn't need to be aware of it at the time. It was never acknowledged because it had no need to be acknowledged. It was merely a miracle that would rotate effortlessly between them. And they two were the honeydew. I recall, at the peak of their friendship, an instance when they spoke of a mutually-desired future wherein they would live next door to each other. In this particular fantasy, the fence that separated their backyards would somehow be retractable, to allow their families to play together during days of communal reverie.

But now I see destruction and death. I see the fall of friendship. It is the empire people hold together. The immense bond of man and man. The voluntarily-assembled gang that together endure the brutal (and occasionally beautiful) cycles of existence. It is sick and pathetic how the events that occur in our lives can disassemble even the strongest of brotherhoods.

I forged my name on a contract they wrote approximately five years before that night. The night that stupid little boy lost his dog. That fucked up little freak! But herein lies my observation. I am supposed to be working, after all. They sent me here for a reason. I had a purpose. Somehow, I am supposed to gather information from this. How on earth can I gain anything from this?!

**Pull back, far enough to reach this. It was the hand that rocked the cradle. It has rattled thine eyes.**

If I, some chance, connect the two relationships (one being Rupert and his dog, the other being Bernardo and Jared), I can conclude, with confidence, that the love was similar. And it helps me to cope knowing that. Everything is going to be all right.

**Slowly, Arnold drifted away, and time was his final obstacle.**

# BRIGHT PRINCESS

She
I speak
She
Is on her way
She
Is coming

The target for most attraction begins elsewhere.

Where? Think. Where are we?

      The Bright Princess stood in her bedroom. The morning was always a pleasant time. The beauty of a new day awaited her. She looked in the mirror. Her soul took pause at a lifetime. She never liked what she saw. What is the reason for this? A generation of women lost in self. Maybe. Let's not judge people. Especially women. They're a curious subject.

      **The Bright Princess faded off into an hour of horrid flashbacks and sad visions of those who have yet to pass...**

In a fine fury, she denounced herself and left behind no chance of H O P E

She was lost in the kingdom.  Some days she would roam the halls from morning until night.  A portion of her soul was absent.

**Sometimes she would cry**
  her tears , pure
  loneliness , actual

There is beauty in nothing.  All surface and all shine.

*Window kill my shame*
*Window make me sane*
*Window pour my passage*

One day she decided to leave.
Why wait around here any longer????????????

She left.

So quick and sudden was her decision.  She offered no thought or passion.  She vomited negative energy.

She, like a dozen roses before, lasts not forever.
Death to all!
whether or not it is embraced.

The first steps of her journey proved a promising line. The grass underneath was rooting for her.  "Go, Bright Princess! Go to places unknown!  Explore!  This is not a rock n' roll circus, babe, it's a long walk."

rt is staAndard?

it's never too late to make a mistake

Where I am is not a mystery. Is she comfortable in this situation? Is she okay? Is she excited? Is she ready to go? Ready to let go? The only thing here that allows me to shit comfortably is my miserable shame and my regret. I regret nothing, yet nothing is my regret. My regret is that I did nothing. I should have killed everyone. Does anyone else hear her voice in songs? People are saying their names.!.!      Damn me   not 3

Not the girl, the boy and the key

> Aha!  She has targeted her impulse
> Go!  Run with it and soon you will fly

And she crawled the rest of the day, through rivers, rocks and hay.

Serendipity: what do you mean to me?

Images capturing memories.

At a nearby crossing, she interrupted an old man who happened to be in a mid-transitional phase. A real lubricated fellow. He was outside, fetching apples from his plum trees.

"Well, goddamn little lady, if you ain't the sleaziest bitch I'd ever seen!"

*"Excuse me, elder. I will pass."*

"Come closer and let me sit on your face a lil' bit more."

*"You are a rude man!"*

His face showed no mercy.

*"Ashually, now that you mention it, I am rather thirsty."*

Options:

1. Pick a spot, any spot.

2. Translate belief.

"I'm finding my place."

## I FORGOT TO MENTION, THE BERRIES AND THE BUSHES WERE DARK PURPLE

*"I am not afraid of you, sire."*

He lunged, she ran. They both made it out alive. Poor guy, didn't get what he wanted.

It is a noble moment, when the best among us admits defeat. He shows a side of himself that brings every man to his knees. Behold, the bright and shiny creature has fallen. But it is not the end. Before I drag this sad man lullaby out any further, LISTEN UP!!! We are not done. We are brave and never broken. Right? We are! We are not losers! Or are we? Who cares!? Yes! Right? Spite? Sprite? Sierra kiss? May these words be a march of human triumph to all who read them! Welcome to my weird little world. I think I fucking love Vonnegut to death. Butt Fuck, I gotta read more of his books NOW!!!!!! And this is why they appeared on my bookshelf, on a random day, in our random lives.

# We are the Generation Gap

The Random Generation. That's where I come from. Started high school in September of 2001. It wasn't much fun. Except when we won, and when we'd bang on drums.

I graduated high school 9 months ago. I realize now that in my heart, I loved everyone I saw. Individuals with character. Though some may be considered bad characters, or "false human beings living under a righteous set of standards." But nay, we were right. In some bizarre fantasy I shake their hands and speak verses, to dance.

As your eyes pass over these words, take my advice: at this moment play "Fight Test" by the Flaming Lips out of the nearest stereo. If you do not understand, go to your local record store and say "Gimme Yoshimi!" They'll understand.

'*That was strange*,' the Princess thought to herself. By now she was far enough away from the man that she finally felt comfortable and safe. Her mind ran around and took off into uncomfortable directions. She needed to rest.

But he still followed

"Listen bitch, I want you to come with me to the White Stripes concert tonight. I wanna make it up to you. I'm sorry. I really kinda like you."

*"I like them. I must go."*

LOOK at this!!!! It's unavoidable.

So that evening…

"I'm finding you out a little bit more every day. When I wrote **finger** you were still around. But goodbye now, girl. I just realized that I have no idea what happened. What did she do to me? Whaaaaaaaaaaaaa! Wizard shakin me more than an ape, I am a wigggglllleeerrrr."

My ears, hearing his voice, which, one evening, sang to him and her.

HOW SILLY THAT I MENTION THIS!!!!!!!!!!!!!!!!!!!!!!!!!!!
Take some time
Groove out on the !!!!! from above
And ferget abowt et all

That stupid fucker has no idea who I am. "Sorry" (hanging up from a cell phone). Shhh, don't go on. The goose man is getting closer. I can almost smell his brain from here.

*Slip behind the currrrrtain for a couple days*

*There is nothing to see here*

*THIS WAY→→→*

The end of her first day out

She leaves his house in the morning

She walked and walked, he talked and talked.
He told the whole town of their deed.
"She slipped, fell, might as well,"
the neighbors would quietly speak.

*an affair?*
*who would dare*
*if i tell you please*
*don't get scared*

As it turns out, the man she was "with" was married and had three kids. His wife found out. No one knows how, but she did. The Bright Princess kept moving. She never knew of the pain she caused those people.

# Instead........

*she walked on and on*

*for so long*

She adopted the mindset that Earth was her home. It was no longer a particular place where she kept her stuff. There was no stuff. She was nothing but herself, which is EVERYTHING. She felt alive.

She was inside the constant flashing moment.

GO GIRL

Mainly in a dream - I live to dream - When I dream I am free

Stupid presidents won't let me be!!!!
Somebody please kill my TV.

If only the BP would have used myspace.
She would have never been lonely.

Suddenly, everything became very intense.

*THERE IS A PICTURE*
*SOMEWHERE*
*I WAS TOLD*
*DURING A LAUGH*

The turbulence was sometimes a bit too much to handle.

Every morning, as she opened her eyes and saw her surroundings, she thought:

*i am fortunate
to be experiencing life
i am lucky
to be
and to see
and to feel*

She looked up and instantly saw the lonely grasshopper, singing his sad song.

The love of his life was far away from him.

"I left my heart, in San Francisco. High on a hill, it calls to me."

'That's only an illusion,' she thought. 'He isn't really there. I'm imagining things.' She quickly forgot about him.

She crossed a bridge and moved on

All eyes from up above,
Floating through desire,
No more,
This is all pouring out sideways,
Where does it truly begin?

**Her opinion didn't matter**

DONT

FORGET

WHO

YOU

ARE

Except, who are we?

We must accept who we are. If we don't, we must learn
There is no other way

She made it to the other side,
Free from virtue - free from her mind
Free from the incline of time
A worthwhile measurement that rhymes

Resting for a much deserved article
Thanks
Let go of indifference
Unite
Unite
Unite
This issue can't be stressed enough

But where is this all coming from?
Who wished these troubles?
Is it possible?

Hunter didn't think so.
And if there was anyone who had any idea as to what the fuck
was going on here, I'd say he was our man.

But this is worth trying!  Can we at least try?  Again, how does
this take place?

It would work if we could gather this planet's entire population
and stage a worldwide acid trip.

Drugs are not the answer

The power of words ^

Words that can scratch a man's heart

Don't worry drug heads

Don't be ashamed

Still, don't pass the blame

Words are not the answer

Government is not the answer

Leadership is not the answer

War is not the answer

Sports are not the answer

Art is not the answer

Homosexuality is not the answer

Space is not the answer

E.T. is not the answer

Cigarettes are not the answer

Hitler is definitely not the answer

Charles Manson has cancer

Love conquers all

The South lost the Civil War

We are the losers of our own history

The internal American conflict

Afraid to love

Not America

But she, our BP

After all, she is no more American than that man or that woman; or, no less.

"Well, fuck that," she whispered to herself. "If I'm floating around here, I will at least have the courtesy to flatline my constituents once every four years. I hope."

She kept walking…

Suddenly, she stepped in a pile of shit

It disturbed and disgusted her to the foul weathers of the north and the slick meadows of the southern region.

It offended her in every way

An unspeakable repugnance. She remembered the river underneath the bridge, and ran.

SHE RAN
SCREAMING
FANGS FLARING
IMPORTANT
EMERGENCY
CLEANLINESS
HYGIENE
THE BODY

there was a dog
drinking from the river

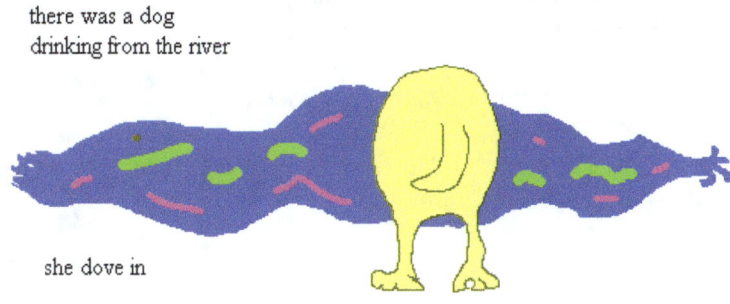

she dove in

Girl gone splashed and twirled about in the water. Free movement was taking place. The ability is possible within all of us. There were spirits in the water. They grabbed on to the Bright Princess. "Remember!" they shouted. "None of us make it out alive. Live full, girl." She jumped out of the water a new person.

"It's comfortable
When I miss her
Because I know that a real event occurred
And my master sometimes masturbates to it"

Who was saying this?  She aimed toward where it was coming from, and confronted the dog.

"What do you want?" she asked.

"I'm sorry.  It's just that my life has recently undergone a drastic change," he murmured.

"I stepped in your shit, you rotten bastard."

"Oh, that.  I'm sorry.  I guess I figured you'd be looking where you were going."

"Blow off!" *-bp*

"Forget about that and listen to what I have to tell you."

"I don't want to hear it. It only makes me sad when I talk to you."

"Where are you heading?" -*dog*

"That's none of your business."

"Well, I do believe we are both in the same situation."

"What do you mean by that?"

"I have taken off! I'm free! BARK"

"Me too. How did you know?"

"I can tell by the grace in your step,
by the dirt in your eyes,
by the cum on your face."

Embarrassed, she stepped back slightly.

"I'm sorry," the dog said. "I didn't mean to insult you."

She wiped her cheek and forgave him.

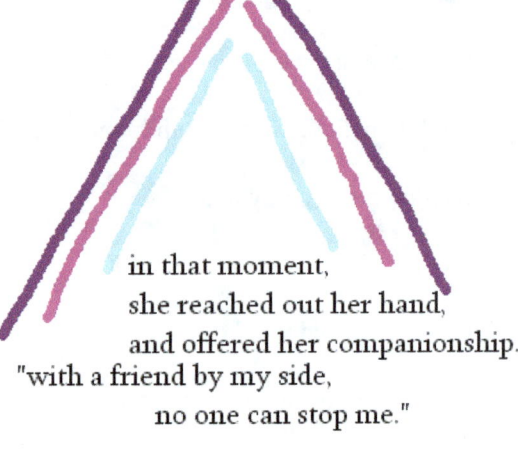

in that moment,
she reached out her hand,
and offered her companionship.
"with a friend by my side,
no one can stop me."


we are lonely



Overcome
Pain brought them together
The emptiness inside caused the attraction
United by sadness
A Broken man
Finding his missing piece

Maybe only for a few minutes
Maybe forever

2
Begin

When I heard
I heard tales
Heard tales of
Tales of terror
Of terror betrayal
Terror betrayal daily
Betrayal daily deed
Daily deed scrotum
Deed scrotum bears
Scrotum bears passive
Bears passive alliance
Passive alliance trial
Alliance trial failed
Trial failed nitwit
Failed nitwit pothead
Nitwit pothead more
Pothead more visions
More visions scared
Visions scared me
Scared me straight
Me straight maybe
Straight maybe gay
Maybe gay pride
Gay pride charade
Pride charade honest
Charade honest agree
Honest agree again
Agree again here
Again here we
Here we are
We are lonely

Hey, what's he doing here?

This is what happens when you fade away…

"Herco Von Villente," the locals sometimes snarled.

"Get out of here with your nonsense!  We don't want your kind around."

"Move along, beasts!"

Certain towns rejected them, while others approved. Their travels were always a gamble.  They never remained in one spot too long, for fear of ridicule, scorn or general unease. Nonetheless, the Bright Princess and her new dog friend got along quite well.  Objectively, they appeared as siblings; but in truth, were close lovers.

Torn apart - long ago -- forgotten - reunited

Modern man - learns ampersand - he can't wait to try it

A conversation - molecule - denied opportunity giant

Vocabulary - simplified - critical surprises

January - diaper time - loyalty - reminded

Ridiculed for wearing overalls

FUNNY,
I DON'T REMEMBER THAT EVER HAPPENING

LOVE

LICK

LEARN

3wisdom3

Love is a bad thing

Love is not a tag team

# It hurts

Enlighten yourself

---

Frighten yourself

On and about, up and throughout.
The underlying sadness of life now.  Wow!

Just thinking about an old friend of mine

Is he an old friend?

This is too true

Too real

I see teeth

I moved on from him, I guess, sorta, not really at all

My tumbled reasoning has left me a confused and broken man

But still

No matter how bad it gets

Here's to tomorrow
-
Drink up
-
Live
-
If you are reading this, you are alive
-
Remember that
-
It's not some silly joke
sucka

Music flows through our souls


We feel

How feel?

Feel good feel bad

## stop it


   She cut him off. The dog had been singing an old familiar song. It took her down an evening road. A place she never wanted to return to. And that was it. Goodnight. She began to shut down, emotionally.

   "Well, if this is making you uncomfortable, I shall hand you the reins. What do you want to talk about?"

   "How about–"

   Just as she began, he interrupted, "There's green smoke on the horizon!"

   "Let's not go there. Green smoke marks my confinement."

   "Hey, I'm having a blast just as well, but I ain't spending the rest of my life in an aimless wander. I have bigger dreams than that."

   Just as he finished, he knew he had said the wrong thing.

   Her head was down.

"That was the plan, pup."

"Come on, you can't be serious."

"I am," she said. "This is all I want. I couldn't ask for anything more. And now you want to destroy everything we've created just for a signal; which, in my opinion, is most likely meaningless."

"Where's your faith, girl? Don't you believe in anything?"

"I do, but–"

"What are you running from?" he asked.

"What are you talking about?"

"It's obvious we're both trying to run away from something. It's the disease of every man. But we're extreme cases. Besides, I want this trip to take me somewhere."

"I like you."

"We're doomed already, Princess."

"Why?"

"Our love won't survive,
no matter how hard we try.
In a breath eye's shadow,
musk tank Orlando.
Pivot, although sane or unbrain,
remains the same.
Underneath a new spirit
of soul enhancing vapors.
A pleasant ride
through opal berry plains.
The open wind reminds us why we are alive.
Threatening unknowns grip us away.
Remain
in constant motion and thought.
Let go, and escape the world.
Many people don't understand
the gifts of nature in our hands.
The power to enlighten our souls.
But we now live in a time where this is shunned.
Crowds gather like packs of angry hyenas
just to get their 2 cents in.
Worship Deputy Bob!
He's a cop!
It's time to throw the cops away.
We need to tell them this isn't working.
We need to use our voices.
Stop fucking your new boy/girl friend.
Stand up and take action.  We need to
fight back.  Forget peace,
it gets us nowhere.  If you
don't believe me look at
Altamont 1969.

I couldn't believe that when I
saw it. But we can learn
from it. We are
the children of that generation.
Let's get going. Let's get
moving. Cry Freedom! Cry Revolution!
Now America! Now England!
Now Israel!
Save Africa! Now G-d!
Now Bush! Now Matt
Lauer! Now! Now! Now!
Now in the Middle East!
Now in North Korea!
I want to know what Kim Jong
Ill thinks of me as an
individual. The TV says
he is going to kill
me. But I did not hurt
his mom. I did
not break his bong. How have
I done him wrong? This whole
world is behaving wrong.
Let's show them how we feel.
We laugh at them. We hate
them all. Let's tell them.
Let's show them.
And then, when you're done,
you can go back to fucking
the brains out of your new
girl/boy friend. I like you too,
but come on babe, you gotta be a fool not to follow the green
smoke."

"Alright. You've convinced me."

*We gave you one last chance*
*Again, it has been compounded*

      They skipped towards the smoke like two little dandelion roller coasters.  Up down around and throughout.

Knowing not what to expect
Mystery bound
Follow the unknown
Capture the essence
Freight your kindness

"Things are going to be different now."

"I know.  I'm ready for it."

Air of a new awakening

A
Full
&
Pure
Existence

I hate to be a downer, but…

This is real

Up up up up up up up up up up up

We're going up

"It'll be worth it, girl.  Trust me.  Feel it in your heart.  It is going to get us good."

"Everyone's got a story."

"Yea, I guess you're right," I answered.

"So come on, Jared. What's yours?"

"Well…"

Up until that moment, I hadn't paid any mind to the overall consequences of what I had experienced. I was so caught up in my emotions that for years I never had enough time to just sit back and reflect on what happened. But the moment he asked, as soon as the question mark left his lips, all I could think about was her. Not the fact that I led my high school wrestling team to its first JV league victory in over 30 years, nor the fact that my friends and I managed to sweep nearly every award in our town's annual film festival (both of which at the time seemed major accomplishments), not even the struggle my family went through and the hardships we faced after the passing of my father three years earlier; none of this managed to have an outstanding influence on who I was. At least not today.

"…I was in love with this girl, and–"

"Oh god! Not this one again."

He gets up. I prepare for the worst.

"Lemme guess. You met each other when you were young. Both still in middle school. Innocent times. Good times. You're just kids so any sort of sexual relationship is still pretty distant. I mean, I'm sure you were jerking off to her everyday after school, but making those bizarre fantasies in your head a reality just didn't seem quite right. So time advances and you and her manage to keep this friendly relationship going. A couple years of high school go by and now things start getting heavy. Things start getting sexay! Then one day the hormones and the curiosity are too much to handle, so you both go at it. The first time is quick and awkward but nonetheless an enjoyable experience for both parties. So now you both have this great new activity to partake in: SEXUAL INTERCOURSE. It's easy, it's free, and best of all, it feels fucking wonderful. So you arrange your schedules based upon when mommy and daddy are outta the house, and as soon as that door closes there's no turning back. Within no time you and her are a couple of natural porn stars. Every time you're together it's fuck fuck fuck fuck fuck fuck fuck fuck fuck fuck fuck fuck–"

"Alright man, that's enough fucks." I had to stop him. I couldn't allow this to go on anymore. His interpretation so far had been dead on, and if I let him continue I'm sure he would've done a pretty accurate retelling of the end. And I was in no mood to take it all in again.

"What's the matter?" he asked. "Too true for ya?"

"No, it's just–"

"Well, YOU CAN'T HANDLE THE TRUTH!"

He is overly amused by his shitty Jack Nicholson impression and is unable to stop laughing. I just sit there. I have nothing to say. He finally stops laughing and replaces the short, tranquil silence with more words.

"Just don't kill yourself, ya sad bastard."

The laughter starts up again. He pats me on the shoulder (which I can only assume is an attempted sign of friendship) and exits the room.

The door **SLAMS** behind him.

So, where did they go?  Aha!  You'll wonder.
Close your eyes for days; make fire.  And guess what?

# They waited

She was so passionate and understanding.  She took the
dog on a journey to incredible depths.  He believed in her, he
trusted her judgment and glanced in her direction with admiration.
She was a woman who truly embraced the brilliance of her
powers.

# ♀stand up (random burst of feminine glory)

"Where will we go first?" the dog wondered.

"You always make it sound like this is the beginning.
Why?  Stop speaking this way.  I'm tired of it."

"Relax.  Why are you freaking out?"

"Because, man, you keep anticipating a new start to this
journey.  You imagine that one day your life will be swifter than
it is now.  Like, you'll be a different creature because of it," she
stated.

"I'm not quite comprehending what you're talking
about."

"Hasn't this adventure already been going on?  It has
always been happening."

He understood.

"Okay, I apologize."

"We don't need to hear any more of that.  Just carry onward."

"Yea, don't look back."

**If travels increase thought
And plants rooted do not
Then animals must move,
for we have nothing to lose**

Often at night, when cuddled up anywhere
shelter was available, the Princess's thought patterns
became urgent and focused largely on the
relationship of her and the dog.  It was
then that she realized just how thankful she
was to have
found him.

Soon as it began

FREEdumb

Adventure
Adventure
Adventure
Adventure
Adventure
Adventure
Adventure

they decided to take shelter

Forcefield
Inn  Vacancy

Greetings,
Late Night Passengers.
How many evenings
of rest will it take
to refresh your
Spirits?

Ummmmm.....

7
, please

am **so**

it went....

(drumroll)

Seven nights
all alone in a ☐☐☐

**HEY!** maybe
this will help my
this will help my

thoughts

or maybe it
just signifies
that

I

AM Lo

But I love what we've got,
no matter what the cost
It may be hard for some
to understand
Together we shall rest
hand-in-hand
In our own land
We will eventually DIE
and disappear
But DO NOT fear
LIFE
is a passing moment
but a
GREAT
ONE
to behold

people come and go

L♡Ve that is shared

though NEVER

forever

always

Remains

"Tell me of what your hometown was like."
the dog asked, during their first
night in the room together.
"Why did you decide to run away?"

"We lived on top of a hill. Magazine
subscriptions and regular aflictions.
A diluted preamble of comfort
and ease. But I couldn't resist
my desires for exploring the outside.
There was something strange in the
overall atmosphere of the kingdom, I
never felt comfortable there."

"I guess I just always thought  that my dreams would come true somewhere else."

"dreams?"

"yea, didn't you ever learn to dream."

"You don't wanna know my dreams."

"Well, we'll get to that. I'm going to bed. Goodnight."

She slept and the dog stayed
awake.

He thought to himself
Remembered his old Master
Wondered if he was lonely
If he was sad that he had left

"No use for regret." he whispered
to himself

Suddenly the Princess sat up.

"Whats your name?" she asked,
"you do have one, don't you?"

"yea," he laughed. "It's Patrick.
What's yours?"

"Patricia."
She fell back asleep

Where beginnings no longer matter
Forage through
Outside
What a Place!

"Lets go."
"Now? I've Just
gotten comfortable."

"Now yes grow
yes yes"

As soon as it began, they fleed the stability of their surroundings. Checked out, packed away for a new ride. It was their original intent, after all. The urgency of their departure left no room for any sort of scheduled destination, and this idea frightened them with excitement (Hay!). "What if all history is a lie?" he would often ask. Not again. Worthless arguments like these will always end up hurting someone's feelings. *Who is able to make such claims?* "History always tells of our ancestors suffering. Only .o3% of the population was invited to Julius Caesar's Anal Adventures part 3: The Conquest for a Larger Gape. Stray nay stray okay. Teach me to sleep and I will learn to fly." She would often stop paying attention after only a few sentences. Regardless, he would carry on. Over time, her abilities in such matters (Medical Term: Zoning Out) allowed her to completely forget about nearly every aspect of her previous life. "Previous life?" "Are you thinking out loud again?" Shhzizzle. Out here with you in the wild wonders of adventure, free to somersault into a ra-vine skyline. We laugh. "Yay, we laugh for all!" See, that is exactly the error of our ways. We laugh for one, forgetting one for all. "Ha! Undoubtedly I see no reason to accept such statements as a mere assault on language to the $O^{st}$." Let it be, for we still have many roads to travel before we meet again. "Who?" My... "Say it, love." My... friends. "Yea?" Yes. I will one day see them again, on better terms. "Okay. How does unnamed excitement find fertile exclamation within such a gentle, timid, petri dish slut?"

Your eloquence attracted me until the bitter sampling of your concluding WORD WORD WORD WORD WORD WORD WORD WORD WORD WORD WORD WORD WORD WORD WORD WORD WORD WORD WORD WORD WORD WORD WORD WORD WORD WORD WORD WORD WORD WORD WORD WORD WORD WORD WORD WORD WORD WORD WORD WORD WORD WORD WORD WORD WORD WORD WORD WORD WORD WORD WORD WORD WORD WORD WORD WORD WORD WORD WORD WORD WORD WORD WORD WORD WORD WORD WORD WORD WORD WORD WORD WORD WORD WORD WORD WORD WORD WORD WORD WORD WORD WORD WORD WORD WORD WORD WORD WORD WORD WORD WORD WORD WORD WORD WORD WORD WORD WORD WORD WORD WORD WORD WORD WORD WORD WORD WORD WORD WORD WORD WORD WORD WORD WORD WORD WORD WORD WORD WORD WORD WORD WORD WORD WORD WORD WORD WORD WORD WORD WORD WORD WORD WORD WORD WORD WORD WORD WORD WORD WORD WORD WORD WORD WORD WORD WORD WORD WORD WORD WORD WORD WORD WORD WORD WORD WORD WORD WORD WORD WORD WORD WORD WORD WORD WORD WORD WORD WORD WORD WORD WORD WORD WORD WORD WORD WORD WORD WORD WORD WORD WORD WORD WORD WORD WORD WORD WORD WORD WORD WORD WORD WORD WORD WORD WORD WORD WORD WORD WORD WORD WORD

  "Well, you mean you want to go back home?" In a way, that seems to be the ultimate truth. My goodbyes were harsh, and I'm sorry to say I even betrayed my closest friends. "How?" I guess I was taking their love for granted. I let them down. Un-returned phone calls and forgotten promises.

A silence rested calmly between them for the whole of 18 hours. During this time, no eye contact was made between the Bright Princess and Patrick. She stared off into the endless distance that spanned between her and home. "I understand your feelings better than you have yet to realize. I share a similar regret in my soul." She finally looked at him again. "But look around us. You've been lost in a sorrowful gaze. During these endless thoughts, we have ventured into unfamiliar territory." Forget me if I may sound foolish, but could you please elaborate upon your remarks? "Well, while you were dreaming of home, we spent the past twelve days travelling deeper and deeper into an unknown land. We can't just simply turn around now and go home!" She grew quiet again and stared at the ground. Contemplative. Like a scientist examining The Great Question.

We shall continue on until someone can point us home. "What?!" I have begun to examine the true calling of my soul. I must return home as soon as possible. "Have you forgotten our **dreams**?" I will live 1,000 dreams after I can spend one last week in the town of my birth. "I can see your intentions already. You're doubting this whole plan! At dawn we shall maintain our current trajectory. Regardless of your sadness, I will not allow you to repeat the very act you are now attempting to resolve. You wish to return to the kingdom, seeking to mend the hurt you caused to the friends you left behind. You left. It was your own decision. And now that you've taken this step, you're scared because we are uncertain of ourselves right now. We don't know where we're headed, and at this precise moment we don't even know where the hell we are. But there's one thing I am certain of. The one truth I believe is we are on our way to something important, something real. And I won't let you betray me just like you betrayed everyone back home."

Given I don't really have any other options, I'll follow you until we reach the next town. "Fair enough. We will travel together. You can juggle your problems and select which ones to solve. Until then, my pride will overcome my worries of you. Ugly conversations we'll share." Such wasn't always the case. "Regretfully so. We'll ride this ship until the nearest docking point. When we arrive, perhaps we will be forced to part ways. In your vulnerability you have revealed your true self, which I happen to find quite unattractive." So easily you switch your taste. "It is you who has switched, you who has gone back on your WORD WORD WORD."

His accuracy slammed into her. She knew it was her fault. She had been blaming him for her own errors. With this realization she shut her mouth and fell asleep for a new day.

A sudden tension took shape amongst. Tough-willed and trustworthy, they continued their travels. Indifferent, regarding awkward and uncomfortable moments between friends, Princess and Patrick brushed off their damage and resumed the true intentions of their journey. Only, given her sudden realizations, they now had somewhat of a purpose to their tale. Untimely sorrow through an unborn lexicon, kidnapped in a complicated landfill.

Their relationship had begun on the pretense of a surprise! surprise! slip-mat. Excitement was guaranteed by their submersion into an unknown world. Along the way, settlement was accounted for and made possible by a proposition mandate passed, approved and put into action, allowing a subdivision of confinement at an affordable price.

The once comfortable silence had departed. Angry silence, Painful silence. "Let's go!" It had become a motto, a promise never fulfilled.

Princess Passing By
In The Corner of My Eye
Let it Grow in Time

In hours of search, a new attachment stirred. "Fuck this," she interjected, shattering the prolonged ~~silence~~ "Where are we going if not an unmatched brilliance could hold us back?" In nature's reply, the ground disappeared beneath their feet. After a momentary free fall, their landing was cushioned by an undistinguishable force. Descent had translated into bounce, though they were still traveling in a given direction. The darkness of the area complicated their reasoning, offering not a single resolution to identify their location.

**is it true?**
Light switch, tushy sliP
slide on down on down

how common a catch phrase
subject to change
gratis

o O o
as they SMACK the ground, O  o  O

```
Sudden stillness of despair
motionless
unfamiliar air
glance around
Hideous Stare
Hideous Stare
Hideous Stare
Offer (rejoice) Grace
Receive Hideous Stare
Beholder laughs, evil grin
Eager to return again
```

Such a situation was a far cry from the truth. "What was that?" questioned Pat. She had no reply. It had been quite some time since they were in the presence of another being. "Well, it sure didn't look very friendly." He was intrigued, or maybe it was the adrenaline. "She," Princess spoke. "Huh?" "She was a young woman." "Come on." He couldn't believe it. "That was definitely no human." "Let's follow her." It was understood that whatever they saw carried with it a promise. A promise of new life, of growth, of civilization. Is that what we've been searching for? Albeit a mere potential, they chased her like a drug.

THROUGH A CURTAIN OF BRANCHES,
MOSS MATCHES,
RED BERRY BUSHES,
GREEN CONVERT CHURCHES,
THICK PRIMAL SCRAPINGS,
SAFE SACRIFICIAL ENCASINGS,
IN A STUBBORN RAIN...

Underneath a colorful overpass, Princess and Pat encountered their first definite others. It was a man and woman sitting together and talking. "Let us not interrupt this delicate exchange. We shall pass by quietly without acknowledgement," Pat urgently whispered. They proceeded carefully and were certain to avoid all forms of contact with these beings. In passing, the conversation between the man and woman was overheard.

"Everyone forgot about me," the man confessed, barely able to convey the sorrow in his breath.  He was noticeably older than the young woman he was speaking with.  His appearance also suggested that his life had been a rotten one, all potential cast adrift upon an uncertain crowd.  "Wow," was her answer, as if her innocence envied his haggard tales.  She seemed to appreciate his sadness and, for whatever reason, found interest in a broken man's suffering.

**Keep walking ... try not to listen**

Slowly approaching, an entrance, a gate of glass suspended between a twin grasp, cast and tough in an unwilling welcome.  Oddly familiar was their presence in this strange place.

"I seem to have a memory of this land, as though I've been here before," Princess proclaimed, comforted in her knowledge.  "I know who to be and I know where to go.  It's already outlined for me."  Her guiding inspiration led the way.

Patrick was unmoved and attempted to pass through the entrance alone, to no avail.

"Goddamnit, is this locked?"

Princess slowly made her way over to the gate.

"If you would have waited for me–"

"It's locked."

"Well, of course it's locked.  What is the function of a gate if not to remain locked?"

"I'll spare you the minor exceptions."

"Had I been allowed to complete my statement, you would have known, as I now do, the requirements for us to pass through."

"What's this all about?  You have a twitch of déjà-vu and suddenly you understand all the rules of this place? Which, mind you, seem wholly irrelevant."

"First of all, I promise you I have been here before. I can sense it beyond all doubt. I possess a previously catalogued relationship to this land. I assure you, there's more to this area than either of us can comprehend. But for now, may we please pass through the gate as a pair?"

"I'm not sure I understand."

"In order for us to enter, we must pass the threshold side by side."

"Because...?"

"Because no one is allowed to enter on their own. Everyone needs a companion to share this journey with."

"Is it an issue of trust?"

"Cease your questioning! We must enter together or not at all, for we are visitors to an area that requires our entrance as a pair."

Patrick refused to believe that Princess's visions carried any validity. He continually attempted to enter the gate on his own, but was withheld each time.

"Just trust me. It's not going to work if you're alone; but together we will be effortlessly welcomed into this land."

Once he was finally able to let go of his shrugged selfishness, they passed through.

Fitting, he thought, that a place such as this would include an arrogant ideal right at the gate.

"I have a feeling you're underestimating the positive implications this journey holds for both of us." Princess, the eternal optimist and forward thinker, had persuaded yet another dull observer into becoming a passive participant.

They arrived in a territory possessing an unusual calm. The soothing quiet was new to them, yet they took refuge in its embrace.

"Welcome," a stooping troll approached, "to The Land of Forgotten Souls."

Patricia's mind became inundated with questions to ask this peculiar gatekeeper. However, before she was granted a chance to speak, the creature let out a piercing sneeze and vanished into the void.

**Odd, she thought,**
**germs lingering in the air,**
**an infected perfume.**

Kunt Klit

They spent the rest of the day aimlessly wandering the grounds, taking it all in. It was a land of contradictions, sparse abundance filled with emptiness. Patrick was sparked by unpleasant memories of his life from long ago. His mind became flooded with desperate regrets of mistaken identity. "So strange," he thought, "this place of new and unknown pleasures remains haunted by a familiar presence."

One last shred of honesty, before the induction of an era where unspoken anguish was considered an attractive quality. A land where time was captured and preserved at a precise moment of celebratory excellence. Sedated by romantic sentiments, the clock of certain concern remained stuck in a comfortable position.

"I am at once confident and unqualmed by the judgment and laughter of the educated. Obtrusive orators of self-obsessed intelligence, bred in houses of betterment." Pat shit himself in hedonistic loathing.

A bird, so unlikely a friend, rested upon Patricia's shoulder.

"I like him." She was intrigued by its gentle touch. Its soft innocence delighted her nastiest appetite.

Patrick was pleased to see independent joy in the Princess's eye.

"I imagine a caress of empathetic abandonment between me and this bird. We would share tales of a cursed life, of victimization and disappointment, only to realize that these past incidents were endured as preparation for our bond, our kinship." Patricia meandered off into a poetic daydream.

Meanwhile, the fateful bird carelessly flew off into the openness...

What's the point of trying to grasp onto what is inevitably a solitary entity? Pat wondered.

Patricia drifted about in a romantic haze, prophesying the lifetime of bliss this bird would afford her, all the while oblivious of its absence.

It wasn't the duration or the extent of their exchange that had moved her so profoundly; it was the gentle touch of skin upon skin. The physical convergence of two desperate partners shatters all innocence and doubt. She at once felt reawakened with the passionate inspiration that had eluded her in the kingdom. How wonderful it felt to believe again! And all from this simple interaction. "I shall remember him with a name. Yes. I will call him Jel," she whispered. Funny though, she thought, I figured we would become friends, piano buddies.

Suggestion: Try to remain focused. Don't fall in love with every bird that passes you by. Learn to explore further before abandoning the prospect of unlimited options in favor of restrained comfort.

Patricia and Patrick were immediately on the correct path, establishing their presence with every step they took. Soon, immediate reactions began to take place, and what they saw in no way eased their desires. The streets were lined with broken glass, a daylight reminder of the reckless night before. A gentle crunch emanated from underneath their feet, as they stepped upon shards of green, brown and clear debris. Pat and Pat carried themselves with a slow, forgetful pace, attempting to blend in with their surroundings. They adopted the town motto with ease, as it reflected a similar sentiment to their own:

*Perpetually stoned. Constantly on the verge of solving the ultimate riddle.*

"I could get used to this, yeah. I could spend a lifetime worshiping this lifestyle. I could settle myself on some property, grow profusely and call it quits. I've heard an Eastern-philosophy phrase acknowledging the importance of gardening. Something about infinite return benefits? Existence is worthwhile on the outskirts," Patrick erupted, articulating an ode to his amazement. He was possessed by the spirit of the land and was showing no signs of drifting. The area was enticing and contained a unique power, capable of convincing one to abandon their rational prospects in exchange for sensitive training and debilitation.

Patricia began to question Patrick's plea for permanent residence. "Planting seeds will guarantee that you remain a citizen instead of a traveler."

"It is the fate of every traveler to eventually arrive at a zone of rest, in order to reflect on their voyage thus far and to contemplate the remains of their journey." Pat was pleased with himself and his rapid-fire comeback. It was a well-crafted sentence he had been waiting for a ripe opportunity to deliver.

Unamused, Patricia responded, "It is the destiny of every reluctant warrior to refuse his responsibilities and deny his power."

All of a sudden, Spider Man entered the scene to deliver a stirring address. He appeared saddened and worn out.

"Let me share my tale with you," he whispered in Patrick's ear. "I have become disregarded and neglected. I am the unbeknownst. I am the spat upon and disheveled."

Spider Man did not present himself in the way I had always imagined him. He was not the hero of 1,000 youths, captivating us with his merciless accomplishments and painstaking bravado. Spider Man, are you not the purveyor of unlimited dreams? Have you left us and forgotten your audience? Have you fallen for the age-old showbiz trope of suddenly becoming victim to your own passions? You have demonstrated the mark of the unforgiven, adorned across your breast, admonishing all sorrows, as the foul beast would proclaim. Celebrity suffrage (this two word pairing sounds pleasant and comfortable, yet has been found to be unjustifiable as an explanatory phrase. I mean to suggest the useless threat of entertainers feeling ashamed of being "monkeys" that perform at a whim's notice. The shameful blue notes of celebrities do not deserve our attention, except to provide an amusing distraction. I have always been deterred by the superiority assumed by anti-TV and anti-media types. Not necessarily those who completely ignore the medium altogether, but those who wish to only view films of substance and arcane significance. Sometimes it is nice to just doze off and not be immersed in a school lecture every time I decide to gaze admirably into a glowing screen. Why do the intelligent often shun the working class? Eh, Adam Carolla's podcast is seeping into my viewpoint. I have been listening to that man's voice since my early years, yet I could never fully interpret his opening line. Does he say, "Mandate"? I think he does, though I also used to think Rancid sang, "Deport the time bomb!" Is it wrong to not like a band because you think the lead singer looks like someone who may or may not have fucked your ex-girlfriend, even though he was a close friend and confidant during the initial demise of the relationship? Anyways, all I was trying to say was not every show you watch has to be seeping with profundity. Also, my second point was to illustrate the cursed sanctity given to proper usage of the English language and the corresponding rules of grammar and definition. To demonstrate, I wish to use the phrase "celebrity suffrage" in reference to a non-voting issue. The Man Show bit on people not understanding what "women's suffrage" meant was not a highlight of their stupidity, but rather the stupidity of the English language. What is the point of succeeding in our society if we all rely on each other regardless? The purpose of language is to be able to communicate and talk to the man who is standing next to you. Why then are we being raised to praise sacred formats and gerund phrases? If we are able to speak and inform one another of our feelings and doubts, correct use of language is then only reserved for the dignified class, who cherish their own brilliance while looking down on the misinformed and uneducated. Instead of wishing to teach those who know less than us, we would rather put our energy into mocking them for showing a minute symbol of their functionality.

Let's end the parenthesis    )        There you go

Patricia followed in step.

"Spider Man, why are you such a sad bastard? I always imagined you as an unstoppable force of central positivity."

Spider Man folded his arms and attained a posture that reflected his intention was to remain in this position for a prolonged period of time.

"I have become the laughing stock of the fertile soil I once called home. Gone is the conception of the hero I used to be. I loosely conjured my way through countless moments of trifling sentiments and mournful Radio (Cuba Gooding Jr.'s greatest performance)."

He could tell both Pats were losing interest in the conversation and veered his way toward a more conclusive, reactionary tale of his experience.

"Superheroes have it tough in this century. We used to secure the fragility of our country, before the events of a day so infamous its very date is what we remember."

**Is there any other day of remembrance we recall simply by the very numerical representation it is relative tooooooooo.?**

Spiders of suggestion, what is your true intention||||||||||||?

"I have come to confess a grievance of cinematic levity. The initial film trilogy is what I desire to discuss. Spider Man I and II were welcomed with critical and <comic book enthusiast> appeal. I reveled in the glory received by both–"

```
SMASH CUT:

EXT. SWIMMING POOL - DAY

Four individuals are gathered around a
swimming pool. Two men in their late 20s are
swimming in the pool, while a boy and a girl
(teenagers) are climbing a fence to enter
the recreational splish-splash area. This
pool would come to serve as a symbolic
ground of challenge and conquest. It was
reminiscent of an earlier scene, where it
all began. Although they had already been
friends for quite some time, it was at the
pool that their relationship finally
deepened. Walking toward the water, JARED
was confident in himself. He intended to
appeal to AMY in a method she would find
convincing and trustworthy.
```

Jared and Amy had been friends for years before the day they elevated their mutual kinship into a shrine of absolute impurity. On the graduating day of the introductory year of their most precious life period, Jared and Amy followed their friend Charlie home after school. While gathered in the confines of his divorced mother's house, the freedom to explore their illegitimate and underdeveloped desperations flourished. Charlie's home provided a comfortable and relaxing environment for Jared and Amy to finally realize their common predilections. The ice was broken at the community swimming pool. Diving into inhibition and abandonment, all three were in for a treat. Wrapped in the warmth of the water, their bodies were free to flee and parade out discipline. Similarly, as a chemical reaction forms bonds of attachment, the liquid allowed for Jared and Amy to congeal their interest in each other. He took to noticing the emotional lubrication the fluid afforded them, and was introduced to the dawning of a new era, consumed with desperation and infatuation. After a gentle swim, the three individuals gathered underneath the complimentary showers to rinse off their instincts and chlorine-scented mystique. This instance provided yet another moment of mutual attraction, brought forth by the lackadaisical spirit of the moment. Would this fateful day finally complete the growing allure between the two? After all, they had known each other long before a physical outlet was needed for such connectivity. Assisted by Charlie's charms, they carried the festivities back to his mother's house. The showering continued, yet the bathing suits luckily remained fastened and perturbed. Although all three were underneath the warm rinse of the fountain, Charlie served as the ringleader, the matchmaker, meticulously fusing Jared and Amy together through a series of exciting and invigorating obstacles. The shower remained playfully innocent and unobtrusive, even though all elements suggested the situation could devolve into a no-holds-barred fuck-fest at any moment. Thankfully, all parties were new to this form of interaction and not yet slutified enough to simply pull their pants down and have their way with each other. After drying off and redressing separately, they retired into the bedroom to lie beside each other, touch nipples and lick ears. It provided a sense of fulfillment and tantalizing intoxication for all involved. The curious body exploration continued its unusual pace of semi-restrained conquest until it neared the hour when Amy's parents would arrive to pick her up and transport her back to their home, which was enduring its final year as a cohesive unit, as her parents would soon divorce, though not quite yet. Before Amy left, Charlie requested that Jared leave the room in order to discuss a private matter with her. He obliged accordingly, and after a short minute alone, all three went outside to return Amy to her parents. Soon after her exit, Charlie explained that during their private discussion, Amy revealed her strong desire to court Jared and pursue a steady relationship with him. Jared was enthralled by this notion, as he was hoping she shared his urges. This would serve as the beginning of the official relationship between Jared and Amy, selflessly assisted in part by their friend Charlie and his keen observation of their flirtations. He knew that in order to seal the deal, they must both be dipped in water; only then would she remain wet for Jared. And timely enough, throughout the course of their relationship they would gather in countless swimming pools, pushing the limits of their physicality. Perhaps it was the freedom of limb movement in the water that ushered in the inspiration of limitless potential, forcing daydreams of an entire picturesque lifetime. "You and me, girl. This is nice." Jared counted his blessings daily. She was, after all, a gymnast with innate flexibility.

AMY and JARED reached the fence separating them from the pool. Eager to go swimming after a failed game of tennis, they proceeded to climb over the locked gate.

AMY effortlessly flew over fence with grace.

                    GUY #1
         Wow!  She must be a gymnast.

JARED meanwhile was struggling to make it over, fluttering about like a fish on its final bow.  Even AMY was stunned by his lack of physique and ended up siding with the two gentlemen already in the pool, who took to mocking Jared's inability to perform at the level of a conditioned athlete, as AMY had. After an enduring struggle, JARED made it over into the pool area.

JARED and AMY decided to swim in the opposite side of the pool from the two gentlemen.  This, however, did not prevent them from exchanging some insightful observations.

```
                        GUY #2
              Are you brother and sister?

                        JARED
         No!  We are boyfriend and girlfriend.

AMY became embarrassed when confronted by
the strength and buoyancy of these
alternative men.  She doubted whether JARED
was up to her standards as a lover, and
vaguely fantasized about a violent three-way
with the two men, abandoning JARED in the
dust.

They left the pool fractured by this
exchange.
```

"How unfortunate were the circumstances concerning the conclusion of my tale, the tortured third installment forever cursed and summed up brusquely. How could anyone be so cruel as to blame their disappointments on me? <u>Spider Man III</u> is a reminder of missed expectations and boyhood vagary. Could not one audience member appreciate satire? I honestly was deeply moved by the third film.  The message of forgiveness purveyed throughout, as battles were won with enemies looking into each other's eyes and seeking to understand the man on the other side of the tracks. We conveyed ourselves with honesty and used our movie to communicate a message of brotherhood. If anyone is against such a concept, then why would they be a fan of Spider Man in the first place?"

Patricia was eager to display her virtuosity. "Fans of Spider Man want to see him kicking some ass and stopping crime with his ballerina moves, not hugging it out with a bank robber."

Spider Man knew he would never get through to Patricia. She was accustomed to her pre-established image of what Spider Man was supposed to be, and couldn't accept him behaving any other way. It was like the wasteful criticism of a music fan that is upset when a band's style evolves throughout subsequent albums.

## The Jews developed Wingdings: the tireless conspiracies we undoubtedly accept as a means to grasp our complex world. 9/11 doubters are the New Religion

*Was this town going to be worth the trouble?* For the first time, Patrick doubted his stay in the forgotten land. He felt increasingly overwhelmed by the subtle undertones of desperation, as the well-educated paraded their liaisons in front of him, like brilliant refugees of a corrupted culture. Who guaranteed a story would be told? Yet there was still hope for spiritual renewal in the possibilities of uncharted territory. He became aware that language could be manipulated and dramatized to portray any situation as either positive or negative, offering equally important and convincing perspectives.

## Example:
- A sporting event, which involves a large crowd of people cheering and screaming.
- A particular attendee becomes swept up in the excitement and joins in the cheering.
- The cynical consider this Mob Mentality
- The hopeful consider it A communal experience that illuminates the connective life force within us all

"Would you be willing to reconsider?" Patricia insinuated.
PATRICK: "Sure. I feel invigorated by my disgust."

in lowercase, the world pleaded forgiveness. Pat wondered how this location got its name, since The Land of Forgotten Souls was an altogether terribly unflattering title for such a vibrant area. Were the citizens insufferable victims **or** active purveyors of their own exile?

Maybe they wanted to be forgotten, cut loose, off-the-grid, wanderers of the New Age dynamic. They were surrounded by a cavalry of sinners, desperate to escape the terrors of their previous existence. No one here was a local; rather, they were all damaged transplants seeking another chance to shine like the angelic practitioners that long ago existed beneath their thick skin.

Luminescent luminaries of underappreciated wisdom, a casting couch for the weak and frail of mind. Handpicked guinea pigs for Gandhi's revolution lined the streets waving flags of surrender, empowered by their resistance. A visitor to such a location must decide whether they want to become fully immersed in the radical notions of this culture. If instead they wish to distance themselves from the celebration, there is always room on the sidelines for bitter eyes to judge the oncoming traffic.

**Onward through the forest they ventured,
visibly affected by their harsh introduction.**

Truth Be Told:
What really
happened to John Nelson the
night we took
his life away

Patricia knew. Patrick knew, too. It was time for them to sit down and discuss where they had come from. Their relationship existed as a mutual momentary masterpiece, yet they never delved too deep into their origins.

Patrick began. "You go first, bitch. Who is he?"

"This may take a while. We are about to hatch an egg that I have devoted my entire life to preserving, in the hopes that not a single crack would form to reveal its contents," Patricia responded.

Patrick had been methodical in his questioning, offering a vague anecdote for Patricia to reply to, in accordance with her own misgivings.

## HAPPY HOLIDAYS, YOU ARE OFFICIALLY OUT OF THE LOOP

Amy was never a fan of metal (the music genre), as she would often explain, "It stutters. The bands never let the beat ride. It's like they're afraid of letting a groove last for more than one full measure. I'm all for complexity and precision, but not at the expense of the groove."

Jared, overcome with mixed emotions, felt the need to object in favor of those who understand the genre. "I love you, girl; but you sound like a fragile hippie who couldn't handle anything heavier than a White Stripes concert."

**Patrick, being the obedient watchdog, ushered in the conversation.**

In the uncertain atmosphere of this land, I call upon you to confess your fortunes and betrayals. Share with us the legendary misfire of your youth that has since cemented itself into a permanent remembrance for all who knew you.

Buried beneath the kingdom, rests a secret often still
A delicate disturbance would ignite her frail will
Of consequence and lunacy, abandonment of doubt
Altogether untied, united once without

At once!
No longer shall you admonish defeat.

### <u>Classic</u> a correspondence among the Paiute territory
There's not a day I waste where you aren't my main thought
My main attraction
My golden cherry
Winning times they ring a bell inside
My eyes, a lucky wheel rolls by
This is heaven, my dear, this is heaven
Fairy's fortune it reads, someone is in desperate need
Little pig, little pig, how much gold did you win?
Have they granted you the kingdom yet?
It's time, stake your claim
At least give me a name,
So I have someone to use this wild magic on
Rich girl, rich girl, where did you get that snow crystal?
The money's in the bank,
It's all kept away
Tonight we can't lose,
Tonight everybody wins

**- John Nelson**

Patricia had with her a journal belonging to John Nelson. "This was written entirely by John on the hillside beneath my home. Any insight or clarity you seek regarding his condition can be learned in his writings. He made one entry a day. That is, until he committed suicide. The rest of the pages are blank."

Patrick was eager to learn more. "These writings, are they about you?"

"I didn't realize the influence I had over him. We shared a joyous relationship together, which eventually came to an end. It seemed the natural outcome of anyone's first serious romance. But he held onto that grief. I was ready for both of us to move on and grow as individuals. He was determined to preserve our bond. He would show up at my window late at night, awaking me in a sudden terror. I was afraid of him. When he wouldn't leave me alone, I was forced to banish him. He spent the last few days of his life scribbling in that notebook, while residing at the outer boundary. After they buried him, I was given the journal. Not as a condolence, but as a burden. A reminder that I played a part in his death."

<u>i.ii.iii.</u>
Why are we running?
Why are we running and
running and ruuuunning
away? Awaaaaaay!
Why are we running? Why
are we running away?

(pause a beat)

This is the science that destroys us
The evolution that creates me
The bonds that break me
Everyday we are forced with more forgiveness
On these streets that delay me
On a cold winter's night I pray out
G-d you'll save me
But to what G-d?
To the G-d that hates me
The G-d that had placed me in a world that 'as betrayed me
With lies, lies, lies, lies, lies, lies, lies
Behaving
Under a strict code/We won't break our seals
While we are made to deal
with this unwanted repeal
Force fields
Preventing our every meal

ALLOW ME TO BE TRITE AND HONEST WITH YOU
YOU ARE AMONG THOSE GREATS CLAIM, TRUE PERSONS
A FIELD OF VISIONS, NOT OVERDOSING MEATHEADS
SOUL, CLASS AND SUCH GROOVY PERCEPTION
WIDTH, DEPTH, WITH OVERWHELMING DIMENSIONS
IF YOU SHOULD SO SHOULD I SAY
A BLISSFUL BLEED HONORS MY DAYS
IN KINGDOMS OVERWROUGHT WITH FEAR
FRENCH NOBLEMEN SEARCHING PERIMETERS CLEAR

THE DAY BREAKS; A NEW MORN' HAS COME
SO STEP OUT OF THY VISAGE, SHOW US WHAT YOU'VE WON
WAS IT NOT ALWAYS THERE?
BUT FINALLY,
NOW YOU CAN SEE

END

Administration of degradation

Whereupon the quest for human intimacy forms the basis of our interactions, we must allow decency to shine through. Do not become disturbed by your own attractions.

Amy returned home from a cheerleading competition with a languid chronicle of her journey. She had been granted the opportunity to compete among her squad in an out-of-state competition, the kind that seemed significant and worthwhile. Her father, seeking to maintain a positive relationship with his only child, decided to attend his daughter's glorious moment. They boarded a plane together, a double-decker of magnificent proportions. Arriving at their destination, her father opted to reserve a room for himself only, as Amy was to be sharing the quarters with her fellow cheermates. Throughout the weekend the girls endured grueling bouts of discipline and triumph, ultimately placing seventh in a contest between thirty other teams. Being that they were staying in a heavily populated area, and in a well-deserved celebratory mood, Amy and the rest of the girls decided to explore the offerings of the hotel commons. Somewhere between the bedroom and the lobby, Amy met a man. They would eventually end up back in her room together. She positioned herself strategically on the bed, while he took a seat in the comfort of a hotel chair. He told her that he was an enlisted member of the United States Marine Corp. and would soon be shipped overseas to do away with the bad guys. Amy was clearly impressed and aroused by his masculinity and confidence. Sensing this, he displayed a maneuver of incredible honesty. "I really want to have sex with you right now," was all he said. That was all it took. She had already placed an order hours ago, and was merely anticipating his reaction from the moment they met. They went through with it, twice. She claims it was the most amazing sex of her entire life. However, up until that point, Jared was the only other person she had consummated. She was sixteen when this occurred. The Marine was twenty-two. She returned home the next day, and he went off to war.

Back at school, her naughty tale provided a beam of excitement to all those who dared to listen as she eagerly shared her achievement. Jared, of course, did not find her anecdote nearly as amusing. He was disheartened to hear that she had slept with another man, and took it upon himself to somehow find revenge. He demanded that Amy share the auspicious man's name, but she refused to tell. Luckily, the age of the Internet provided an up-to-date list of all fatalities in the armed forces. Jared spent his evenings browsing through countless pages, glancing at photos of fallen men and imagining them fucking Amy. He felt chastised by their strength and effortless brutality, taking solace in the hope that the mysterious Marine that dirtied his sweet Amy experienced a tragic death shortly after their sexual encounter.

## A dog is a peculiar animal, a woman even more so

Search deep within yourself
You'll find nothing
Emptiness occupies my soul

Beyond each man lay orchestral pastures,
the triumph and the release.

Outside his skin, an indefinite presentation
of his courage and his disease.

Upon his hands the cycle grows,
his frustrations never conquered.

Math deviates,
Bite persists,
The undying loneliness of man's soul

So if you're hungry, why don't you chew on some gum?
It's pink in color, I'm pink in abstract forms
You are the teller, she lost faith in our love
So in this weather, we are delighted only when we die
I have some thing for you to chew

*There's gum on my CD.  Who put gum on my CD?*
*Someone please set me free.  Look what she's doing to me!*

**PLEASE NOTE THAT AS OUR PERCEPTIONS CHANGE,
OPINIONS ARE BROUGHT TO THE SURFACE AND
SUBJECTED TO A RIGOROUS ASSESSMENT.**

# The willful Testimony

What a day is today,
that I would feel so nice.
Why springs ~~lead~~ me here
And a cuddling of sorts
that wonders.
"Now will never be happening;
a memory to keep in my pocket."
I will name you my best friend,
and share with you all my stories.

Somewhere, between the curious
juggler's hands and the tumbles and falls of
our modern day society, there is a lesson.
A meaning, an answer and hope, to guide us
through the blood-soaked, tear-stained
windows we use for sight. Eventually, the
common outlook (which has been cascaded with
insurmountable poise and threats) will alter
and change. Though certain regions will be
extremely tough, it is nonetheless, possible
in every aspect.

*Well, Patrick, how did you end up venturing outside your comfort zone? What was it that led you astray?*

"Escape. That was my plan. It became an impulse. I was so focused on leaving that it nearly offset my entire thought process. With each passing moment, I nestled into my decision. Soon I will be gone. Soon I will be out of here. I have no route of perfection set before me. It is only revealed after, when we are defeated."

Run! Go! Run! Go! Run! Go!

## FOR A LOST DOG, REMEMBRANCE

"Placed between the territories of loss and defeat, I decided to isolate myself, completely, from those with whom I would formerly associate. Friendship is the soul of man. Friends are always there for you. When this is proven to be false, the body slowly falls apart. It is more than a stomachache, it is a cannon ball shot to the heart, passing straight through but leaving a permanent mark."

**The all-knowing cadence of self-doubt, regression and pity prevailed. I knew this social scene was involved in a great deal of self-destructive behavior, and I was all too eager to indulge myself. I immediately befriended a man by the name of Alto Undershed, and together we discovered the true limits to our psyche's potential. I never knew such decadence. To forget trauma is to receive blessings. If anything, I would behave senselessly in order to (at least,**

**attempt) to contort my own demonic onset into
something less hideous.**

In the days
It would be
Set in stone
And forever thought true

That any sufficient amount of
Sadness
Could be overcome

With strength,
Dignity and
Heart

When ocean currents
Cease to break
Upon the beaches

And a preacher
Is deprived of
His faith

Where do we go?

When a stone you wear
Around your finger
Loses all its meaning

Do you move on and throw it away?

Or do you find way?

Alto served as their guide through the underground. Claiming to be the mayor of the forgotten land, he behaved more as an influential friend than an esteemed political representative. He was desperate to persuade Patricia and Patrick into believing that this was an exciting and necessary landscape. "We welcome the homeless here, as they embody the personification of our legacy. Wandering ascetics of unhinged wisdom." He guided the Pats to the far ends of THE LAND OF FORGOTTEN SOULS offering minimal insight into the crime and corruption that plagued the area, opting instead to highlight its progressive ideals and socially-conscious lifestyle.

Their tour took pause at the town plaza where a feminist rally was being held. Patricia watched in horror as ladies denounced the image of classic American housewives. Advertisements from the 1950s, portraying women as kitchen-dwelling masters, were viewed as oppressive and objectionable. "Why are people disgusted by the opportunity to not have to work? I would be more than willing to chill at home and relax all day if all that was asked of me in return was to cook dinner." Patricia, a proud woman herself, offered her slight opinion.

Jared became suspicious of the whole situation while eating breakfast with Charlie. "Why don't you let her park in front of your house?" he asked, between chomps of pancakes. Jared, dumbfounded, inquired as to the specifics of Charlie's accusation. "What are you talking about?" "Come on, man. You force Amy to park down the street from your house when she comes over. Why? Are you ashamed or something?" Right then and there Jared's entire concept of reality was shattered and dismantled. Does Amy confess her grievances to Charlie? What other information does she share? Are meetings held in undisclosed locations where Amy and all Jared's friends congregate to discuss their relationship? He was disheartened to learn that his time spent with Amy was neither sacred nor private. In this moment, Jared shrugged it off, yet he spent the rest of his life wondering how Charlie knew. Doubt permeated his mind. Yes, it is true that she parks around the corner when she spends the night at my house. Indeed. The door to my bedroom remains locked as well. Both are methodical strategies pursued in order to prevent an awkward encounter with my parents. "Nah man, it's just so my folks won't know when she sleeps over." Okay, you're right. I do make her park down the street, but why do you even know this uneventful factoid? A simple phone call could dissuade any assumptions and provoke meaningful discussion. However, I have decided to shadow the path of endless typing. A trillion pages, capable of consoling my sensitivities, would prevent sound. After breakfast, they both went home, respectively. Charlie watched the greatest film ever made and Jared listened to **Pet Sounds** on headphones.

Swirling serpentine, a salient being summoning surface remedies. Evidence remains suspect of curiosity, thoroughly managed and positive. Tiny + Trip shared the fracture. Tosie was a witness; played no part, but knew. Their three-way home provided an unusual anecdote of brotherly advances. Would residing in said atmosphere disrupt the already furious level of stationary statistics that Eddie knew?

REQUIRED: participation of all readers that currently attend school in a publicly funded education facility. The **following** (next) page must be torn from the binding and posted in the hallway of your translucent metamorphosis sanctuary.

**Ode to the god of Winsor Pilates:**

**I refuse to believe that anyone is** perfect
**Having been shown this quite abundantly,**
**Where will I hide, my children?**

**You, in these halls**
**The Terrible Bunch!**
**The Cold-handed Punch!**
**The Envious Ducks!**

Work is extremely crucial to life$#@!

But I am here today
Begging you to please
STOP AND LISTEN

*Take a minute out of your day*

IT IS OKAY IF YOU ARE LATE TO CLASS.  READING THIS
AND EVENTUALLY UNDERSTANDING IT WILL SHOW
YOU WHY THIS IS SO.

Please question your mere existence.
Never stop asking "Why?"

Everybody makes mistakes.
There is no reason to quit.

### *Why are we all alive?*

None of you know what is happening.  Do not take this in a
negative sense.  It is not a threat of any sort, nor an insult.  It's
merely a lesson.

How did it feel to escape for a moment?  Get to class.

## A friendly tale of similar names

In his formative years of elementary school wisdom, Jared shared a wondrous friendship with a fellow by the exact same name. The Jareds partook in many marvelous childhood adventures together, such as the awesome wonder of trading basketball cards and playing arcade games. One weekend during their 4th year of grade school, both Jared and Jared decided to pitch a tent in their neighborhood and attempt the great suburban tradition of front-lawn camping. After a day spent scaling near-vertical hills on their BMX bikes, they retreated to the cozy confines of their makeshift housing. Mickey, the community bully (the only child of a local real estate mogul), arrived in sufficient time to impress the boys with his lackluster skateboarding skills. After gaining their admiration, he introduced them to the rudiments of another troublesome hobby. He taught them how to remove the cap off a valve stem from the tires of a luxury car. This would yield a precious semi-stone amulet, a token of their victorious rebellion. Thoroughly inspired, the Jareds scoured the streets seeking merchandise, maintaining manageable loot and procuring a small fortune. While unscrewing the caps from a Porsche, the resident of the corresponding house departed angrily, with resolute accompaniment. He grabbed Jared#2 and dragged him inside. Other Jared, terrified, sheepishly followed. The homeowner called their mothers, and had them escorted out by angry maternal wardens. The amusing significance of this small tale is that the last name of the bully who inspired this delinquent behavior was Amy. Yep, his last name way Amy. Mickey Amy was the town troublemaker. Though after this instance of criminality, Jared never saw Mickey again (aside from a few Taekwondo classes), it was nonetheless peculiar that his last name foreshadowed the curse of his near future.

Oddly enough, Jared also lost touch with his counterpart, Jared. They shared the same name and countless experiences of innocent excellence, yet parted ways after elementary school. Although they ran into each other at the occasional concert/social gathering/school reunion, their friendship did not maintain its productivity after the initial split. Regardless, the moments they spent together remain an immaculate dream.

Patrick precluded, to gain further insight into the tiff between Patricia and the lonely John Nelson. She was the keeper of his concluding ventilations, the revelatory mystery of mister Nelson, sexposed. O, provider of truths, tell us of his final entry before the chronicle became an empty opportunity unfulfilled. She finally mustered the gustavo enough to speak. His final entry was written on the night of an unrelated event that rippled throughout the entire community. It would be immortalized in a song titled "Fire," written by the young man (Paul) whose own home was damaged by the flames. As the backstory goes, he announced that a luau was to be held at his house. All in attendance would come to learn that never before had a night, so properly kindled, resulted in such an unmitigated lapse of sanctity! John was at the party, profoundly enjoying himself, until Patricia arrived in the company of her diminutive wolf pack. He saw her in her natural habitat, womb swelling with delight, and ready to fuck. She laid claim on a young hound dog known as Dandy Lion, and John watched through the brush as they giggled and rubbed nerve-endings. No sooner than he smelt her mating call, John rushed over to interrupt the unavoidable sex that was to occur between them. "I fucking hate you. I never want to talk to you again." His words were harsh and off-putting enough to disengage their cautious exchange. Patricia rushed her cute, enormous, pale behind over to comfort and reassure John into believing that he was her one true love, and that her promiscuous behavior was only an outlandish reactionary attempt to express her fallen harpsichord reversal.

Her consolation prize consisted of wishing John a pleasant evening and continuing her relentless pursuit of man meat sandwiches, force-fed and stuffed into every orifice, with the capacity to expand when challenged by an enduring and devoted force.

John was escorted home from the luau by his eternal friends. Upon being released of his assurances and resolutions, he anxiously exerted a damaged scrawl into his beloved journal. This particular entry was labeled:
Purple Joy.

Later that evening, John noticed a signal rising from off in the distance. Patricia had unleashed her desperation, forfeited her exclusivity, abandoned her eagerness and settled for less. She waned herself in favor of John's homeliness. She knew he ensured an evening of untamable, unfit and unthreatening accompaniment.

While gazing toward her signal call, John concluded that Patricia's attendance at the luau did not result in the full-fledged gangbang he had imagined. She was a failed romantic as well, who yearned for his company. John responded, and arrived shortly thereafter to escort her to his residence. They quickly entered the solace of his bedroom and screwed intolerably into the night. Jared's woes of self-mutilation, brought upon from his initial state of mind and expressed in that night's journal entry, effortlessly vanished into the air, captivated by Patricia's decision to commence the thrill of his wildest plea. The advent of the in-home bathing system offered these two sexual partners the opportunity to pleasure each other while basking in the soothing descent of falling water. Make believe. She danced a solitary reprieve of idolatry.

They enjoyed each other's company for another resolute night and awoke to a sudden concern. Patricia had misplaced her keys, a requirement inextricably linked to entering her heavily-guarded stomping grounds. "Where are my keys?" she spent the sunrise wondering. "I believe they may have been unintentionally left at Paul's house, during his revolutionary luau."

John guided Patricia back to the scene of the crime, where they scoured the surrounding streets in hopes of rediscovering her mislaid keys. They soon ventured near enough toward Paul's house to learn that after most of the guests had left the party, a fire erupted and destroyed most of his home. Irreplaceable artifacts of careless beauty were lost in the blaze.  Immovable to disappearance and loss, John quickly rushed Patricia home and dissuaded his despair by mourning the unthinkable fate of Paul's sacred shrine.  After dropping her off, he returned to his bedroom.

John would end up killing himself later that week, a retributive consignment of his shaking stature.  We are still unsure whether it was because of his interaction with Patricia, or the comparative disastrous state of Paul's house and how it negated his own qualms of lovelorn luminance. John's journal offers insight that untimely expires, as Purple Joy would be his final exposition.  A single page of sustained mutiny, upheld through confidential contributions.

Well, you be the judge.

Read for thyself:

This was the end for him.

These sharp worries have rested in my head for too long. Thanks to everyone who tried to help me. I fear that it will always feel this way.

A drastic change is needed in all areas. Perhaps you are too late.

If everyone had a good time, nothing matters. Life is too short to not have fun. Unfortunately, we rarely think about the ones we effect when we get in the way. Or, forget to think clearly.

This letter does not matter.

I wanted to make this amazing, but FUCK IT.

IT DOESN'T FUCKING MATTER.

The reasons and the whys? are useless.

Just knowing that it is done is all that matters.

Birthday party, approximately, held in the year 2004, to commemorate the cycling transformative life of Charlie, age 17. He had developed a pure fascination with hockey, brought upon by either (a) a middle school science teacher offering lurid equivocations of whimsy and good-natured mischief, fancifully recounting the weekend bum-rush of broomstick hockey, offering children communicatory anticipation of adulthood exceptionalism; or (b) a desire to make up for lost time, by recreating the memories he had missed out on. It was evident that Jared and Eddie had been friends since the throwback days of level playing fields, fusing together memories and jokes of a specific, contextual understanding. Charlie, however, was a relatively newer member to the group, having undergone his initiation in middle school. But by the time of his seventeenth birthday, he had become the irreplaceable savior and master of ceremonies, slouching atop the brotherhood's untended throne. Regardless of his motive, Charlie's party was held in the frozen den of a recreational practice space. Sharpened blades, fastened from toe to heel, enabled fluid movement against the ice. The whole gang of delightful kinship scholars were invited, slightly honored by the lack of female participants, aside from Charlie's younger sister. Polar conditions of temperate suffusion permeated their surroundings, instigating a competitive atmosphere with an oriented goal (to conquer). Guided by a spotlight, the grand entrance spectacle was conducted not for Charlie, who remained engaged in the game since the glint of his arrival, but for Amy Carousel and her abrupt decision to thwart the dynamic by inserting herself into this participatory exercise. Modus operandi: calamity. To stoke the tension forming between this brigade of young men. Once a fertile girl is introduced into the scene, all promises of infallibility and trustworthy allegiance vanish in favor of getting your dick rubbed. By this point in time, Jared and Amy had shared a steady relationship for nearly two years. Naturally, in the abundant hours spent with Jared during the course of their courtship, she had befriended nearly all of his close compatriots. Seemingly tame and futile interactions elevated her status to that of a merry acquaintance capable of being innocently invited to Charlie's birthday party without anyone considering the threat she posed to their pendulous friendship. Frost upon saddles, adhering insincerely. The ice cavern hindered unborn beliefs of absolute incredulity, meticulously maintained by sanctimonious honesty. A retrospective haunting of desperate entitlement, dangling mythologies and unkempt multitudes, bowing to enlightenment. Shine. She lingered cursed mouthfuls of bare-boned vestige, providing a scale upon which to gauge our insecurities. Or, for the hopeful, a weapon of masturbatory, messianic proclamations. Jared was agitated by Amy's decision to attend this function of young men's sanctity, as she infected all promises and untethered their emotional loyalty. "Hey Amy, thanks for coming. Hope you know how to skate." Charlie politely welcomed her as any gentleman would. A sleight of hand, clever and disguised. As the evening progressed, Jared offered paled glances in her direction, useless in avoiding his attraction. She smiled and performed with admirable virtue during their endearing game, while Charlie's father took pictures and spouted memorable couplets of unintentional hilarity. It seemed fitting that both Amy and Jared were assigned opposite teams, forced to pursue defeat at the other's expense. Jared's team struggled to maintain a coherent structure in their defense, and succumbed to the strength of their temporary rivals. Jared looked on, and found himself both ashamed and surprised by Amy's nonchalant ability to interact seamlessly with his friends. Oh, how they laughed and laughed, like old pals with an insurmountable scroll of memories. He thought it odd that their teamwork maintained a balanced fluidity, and became lost in the distractions of his mind. Pitted against his one true love, Jared sought victory in sacrifice of his morality. "I will not lose to her!" With force, might and piety, he fought against his obligations and ignored the path of disciplined practice. His selfish mires placated resolute despair. Tearing through the offensive line, Jared located his once delicate Amy mingling indiscreetly with

Charlie, all the while neglecting their assigned duty of blocking the net. Jared swooped by, between friends and lovers, and flung the object of competitive reasoning directly into the goal. The puck lay nestled in the battered netting, preserved by this rare but comforting moment of fleeting protection. After hours of endless obliteration, a hockey puck is blindly rewarded with a dwindling moment of repose. Jared swung his arms into the air, hailing the esteemed achievement of his prized play. Proudly, he steered his vision toward Amy, eager to bask in the scorn and defeat in her eyes. However, in actuality, she didn't seem to notice his accomplishment. Amy and Charlie's conversation aroused their interests to the point of neglect. Jared rejoiced among his fellow teammates, and granted Charlie the principle of forgiveness, on account of it being his birthday. He could tell Amy was a reckless girl. She refused to be tamed, and would hunt her prey with mystique and sexual allure. Charlie would never do something like that, he's one of my best friends. And if there's one single truth to life, it's that men honor the decency of incomplete trust, in regard to sleeping with girls.

Aggregate reasoning shielded the terrors of knowing. Bold evidence suggests that the belief in distraction upholds insolence. A fully functioning parking garage with multilevel traction, capable of providing indefinite spacing of colleague awareness. He said, she said. Gossip fueled their thirst for skintight titillation.

A mystery was told

an internal **memo** to all, but one!

He shall never hear of this, Jared will never know

Cabinet searchers

Dwelling to succumb

All (3) parties more than willing to oblige

Concealed to resolution

Unbound by common thought

A perfect storied performance

Eternally dismayed

Condolences, remorse

Tearful phone calls on the ride home

Swathed bystanders of neglect

In the womb of entitlement

Forsaken reports of seductive balance flooded the small town. Incomprehensible documentation of a night scorned by passionate abandon, retold to succulent eardrums palpitating with delight. Limited intelligence was needed to appreciate these lurid and fanciful entreats, where mystery was sideswiped for an all-expense-paid soirée to a feeler's paradise.

Through the guise of a misdiagnosed phone call, Jared answered. "Hello?" Nothing. No conversation or accompanying ambience. "Is anyone there?" He was about to hang up when someone finally spoke. "He did things to her, man. I fucking saw it. He did some wild shit with her." –click–

We have begun to grow weary of ourselves. (Not yet! Please not now. I was hoping to hold on to the flavorless comfort of my disease for a bit longer. I've got it!) Let us perform the requisite initiation ritual, in order to succumb, wholeheartedly, as full and complete citizens of this township, with all the accompanying rights pertaining thereto. Declare, robustly and unvarnished, a vow of allegiance to The Land of Forgotten Souls. I seek solitude in hills of darkness. With storm clouds shielding the sunlight, we will fuse our bond; and in doing so, we shall forget all who reside beyond the county line. Pre-addressed and pre-stamped envelopes to my grandmother will forever remain unsent. She will check her mailbox everyday, and everyday she will be disappointed. This is the life I am choosing for myself. I have decided to hide, because I am too scared to confront the curse that sent me away. Patricia was engulfed in the refreshing breeze of nuanced pleasures, she whispered midnight in his ear.

We are all living creatures who have been granted the opportunity to view the world around us through two separate vantage points:

Cynicism and Anger VS. Appreciation and Pride

"Are we free to determine our own mindset, or are we merely subjugated to the inheritance of our parents and their own tribulations with unrequited love?" On the brink of becoming a burgeoning psychologist of Freudian stature, she retired her glistening thoughts; but not until one final assessment of her terms. "Let us critique the

**extended family of Sigmund and question the excellence of his reputation. Even that rotten nephew of his."**

# Release judgments to gain understanding

Even though Carousel had recently terminated their contract, she and Jared would still exchange sexual advances, discreetly. However, they did not immediately transition into this new course of conduct, as they had yet not acclimated to the peculiarities, nor formally proclaimed its terms. In actuality, it took quite some time for the initial wounds to heal, until they could maintain any semblance of post-relationship interaction. Their encounter at the ice cavern contained an acute significance, in that after two years of devotion, they had called it quits all but a month before the game. Charlie's chilling birthday party was their first reunion since the initial breakup.

**IF YOUR EYES ROLL BACK IN YOUR HEAD, KEEP GOING**
"This town is a warzone, Charlie. We have come to battle unprepared"
**CHOOSE WISELY, YOUR PATH TOWARD OBLIVION**
"I can't stand emo monkeys. They indulge my insecurities"
**HARK THE CRESCENT MOON SCANDAL**
"Provide for my intifada, soothing rage"
**GOLEM THE SHIPS**
"Hazards abound"
**DWINDLE**
"Spin"
^

John Nelson was desperate for a partner to the quadrennial formal, the singular social gathering to commemorate the conclusion of their preliminary life teaching. Patricia had been advocating for the preservation of her princesshood, yet vowed to augment her reputation in order to accompany John to the dance. Their LOVE had been undergoing a rough spot, a sexual lull.

This evening seemed pungent enough to reinstate their passion and invigorate the electricity within. John was certain to borrow a tuxedo from a close enough proportional relative. At the dawn of this elusive day, he was nervous. He spent the morning precariously snipping rose hedges, in hopes of attaining enough for an acceptable bouquet. While searching through his neighbor's foliage, a tired old man approached him and offered the following proposition: "I see you are of acquired health and ripe fitness. If you would be willing to deliver a message to my misled friend, I will exchange with you a plethora of gifts pertaining to mystic significance. My friend lives a half mile from here, yet in my feeble condition, it would take me nearly all day to reach him." John was eager to tend to the wishes of a kindhearted man of ultimate wisdom.

We should honor the intelligence and learned knowledge of our elders, as they have reached the pinnacle of LIFE.

John scrambled and dashed in the directions offered, carrying with him a message that read:

Dearest old pal,
Let us reignite the wonder of our friendship. Meet me tonight in the plaza, and I will dissipate your vague incantations.

Your one true friend,
Teldo I. Dee

John paid no mind to the contents of the message, and focused metaphysically on completing his given task. He left the letter with an elderly woman and rushed back home. Teldo was waiting in the exact same spot, leaning against a crooked cane. He was shocked to witness John again, in what seemed an incapable time span, given the distance. He honored his promise and rewarded John with an Outkast CD and The Wizards Handbook. They shook hands like true men in the accords of reliability.

Upon returning home, John declared the night a splendid routine of wonders and quickly enveloped himself inside the threads of his temporary suit. Sharp dressed and hair combed, he kissed his family adieu and skipped off through Grandelinoid Parkway, catching glimpses of amusement as he passed.

Patricia's attire struck a nerve, aghast in beauty's pronunciation. John nervously introduced himself to her family and was informed of an odd alteration to their plans. "Young Sir Nelson, we command this night's eternal luminance and have summoned the creation of a gifted illustration. Parlay your stature and gain comfort with our daughter, as a painting will been worm whipped in your likeness."

John and Patricia posed politely and were pleased with the flattering results. The painting was to be hung in the south chambers, after being left outside to dry for the night. John thanked Patricia's family for commissioning such a generous testament to their young and genuine romance.  Eager for the release of adult supervision, the pair forged ahead and exited the kingdom.

Confident in their coupling, rambunctious threads loomed their entrails. They goose-stepped their way toward the lightning.  Anticipatory nodes of entertainment provided a path.  The event was to be held at the local fairgrounds, in an adjacent tent.

Patricia fastened a cloth bonnet and attached a rose pendant upon her frame. Secure and landlocked, the lovers crossed thresholds of neglected sapiens and presented themselves with dissonant indomitability.  The moon fell over them with a cure-for-all left unturned.  An advantageous escort, John Nelson carried his date up the steep incline that housed the festivities, taking each step with indignant posture.  They arrived to discover countless ganders of their teenage counterparts, acclimating to the newfound social atmosphere of inadequate equalization.  Born into rigorous classifications of ordered masses, the evening of dance weltered a wondrous gathering of unaccustomed acquaintances and awkward interactions.  "Oh well, I'd prefer to seize this dwindling moment of commencement by bidding a fond and warmhearted farewell to my trusted peers. Maybe not all of us were great friends, yet we nonetheless endured together, cooperatively."  John was uncharacteristically welcoming at the ongoing verification ceremony, lending a hand to his forlorn hallway broods.

After completing the cycle of casual greetings, John and Patricia devised a peculiar seating arrangement for the night. Being that she was eager to slurp the semen out of his friends' cocks and he was literally devoid of the ability to commiserate with her group of friends, they agreed to sit separately during the evening's dining portion. This decision was not without an amenable clause that accommodated their bleak plea for togetherness, as they managed to arrange two tables side by side, directly in proportional circularity. John and Patricia would sit with their respective group of friends, their backs to one another...

This allowed for the closest physical distance between the two, while still allowing them to converse among separate social circles.

The food, long lasting and nutritious, sufficiently negated the risk of hunger for the remainder of the blank sky's descent.

Hearty, wholesome, meaty delight. When
Patricia maneuvered her musculature near the
dance floor, to synthesize the fluidity of
the feminine experience, John decided to
explore the surrounding area, thus allowing
his girlfriend to continue her plunge into
the realm of neglected instigations. He
teamed up with a fellow mate, with whom he
shared identical aspirations.

Andrew Algebra was ALIVE to the
fullest extent humanly possible. A man so
free, his existence seemed guided by the
natural tendencies of the wind. He'd
playfully seek out new and unusual
opportunities, totally spontaneous. John
anxiously soaked up the zestful radiance of
Andrew's shine. True to form, he had found
an alternative method for capturing the
purity of this night. "Let us fully know
where we are. Exactly. Follow me toward
the carnival equipment, all shutdown and
retired for the night." There was
absolutely no reason for John to miss out on
this once in a lifetime adventure.

"Let's go!"

John had completely abandoned all
concern for Patricia's wellbeing, as he and
Andrew entered the fairgrounds. This
particular amusement park was known as The
Universe, a crummy gimmick to familiarize
guests with the rides, all of which were
named after cosmological terms relating to
the sky and the stars. The boys experienced
a night of unknown enlightenment, as they
were able to stand still in this place,
preserved by the calming quiet of its

unnatural emptiness. Never before had they been in this area while not a single soul was around. They seized the moment and snuck behind every abandoned tourniquet and unguarded memorabilia display. They laughed hysterically while disrupting the cages of animals that were, by day, unwilling performers in a circus sideshow. The pinnacle of their delinquency arose when they stood in the majestic glow of the unmistakable sign that informed all surrounding neighborhoods of this area. They were staring straight into the eye of a neon sign that they had viewed from a distance their entire lives. To commemorate this lasting achievement, they placed a ladder against the letter V. A residual, left-behind remnant of their sly presence. John and Andrew were drowning in the excitement of the moment, a childhood dream fulfilled and conquered. They returned to the tent in which the dance was being hosted, only to discover disconcerting faces.

Another of John's table friends was solemnly consoling Patricia. She was visibly distraught and shaken, saddened by the disappearance of her partner. "Where did you go? What's wrong with you? Why would you leave me?" She let loose a barrage of questions, unanswerable and unnecessary. John explained that after seeing her dancing and having fun with her friends, he decided to engage in some fun of his own, with a friend of his own. Though she did not merrily accept his alibi, she did not desire to elongate the tension of this public mockery any further. "Well, now that you are finally back, can we go?" After pouring an entire glass of seltzer water on the floor, John grabbed Patricia by the elbow and rushed her out the door. She was in no mood to hear of his mischievous accomplishments. She required delicate soothing and uninterrupted attention.

JOHN: For the rest of this night, let us share the same quarters and attempt intimacy.
PATRICIA: You have barely made any effort to quell my suffering. I was, and still am, badly hurt by your selfish actions. How dare you flee the scene so carelessly, abandoning your post and violating the commitment you swore to your woman!
JOHN: I thought you wanted to be with your friends. I figured I'd go away for a while and be back in time to get some dessert with you.
PATRICIA: Well your skills in time management are sorely lacking, as you missed the crowning of the most admired patrons and the farewell toast; all tender moments I dreamt of sharing beside you.
JOHN: Goddamnit! I'm so sorry. Okay? I love you, girl. Come on, I'll make it up to you. I swear. This isn't meant to be happening. I care about you too much.

Just then, to express his boiling shame and self-anger, John grabbed a nearby stone and proceeded to violently slam it against an innocent pillar, while chanting, "I'm Sorry, Forgive Me, I'm Sorry, Forgive Me." The stone eventually crumbled in his hands. Patricia was frightened and upset by his cruel act of discontent. She began to sob like a victim of malnourishment, while John yelled his apologies into her supple face (quivering lip and all). His sanctimonious apology outlasted her own will and she eventually caved, in order to avoid any further agony.

JOHN: We shall gain residence in the nearby lodge. I hear that entire sections of the property have been reserved precisely for fellow honorees such as us. We can easily obtain a room and spend the remainder of this night embracing in swift solitude.

Patricia was unwillingly attracted to his offer and complied wholeheartedly.
A bedroom was acquired with ease and reservations were made for a romantic evening of apologetic meandering. John escorted Patricia up the stairs and they headed straight to their specific room. Along the way, they were stopped by a fellow gentleman of ample guilt, who questioned them for an offer of temporary fire. Unbeknownst to all but her, Patricia happened to be an esteemed flame forager and happily obliged the young man by creating a portable, controlled burn, able to last at least three hours of heavy usage. John was growing tireless. He desperately wanted to

conceal his woman and have her all to himself.

Finally, they entered the room.

The layout seemed ample to ignite uproarious moans of pleasure from both parties. Patricia proclaimed her preference for using the shower, and simultaneously manipulated the discreet methodology she gained, in order to shave her vagina. John tried to contain his stereophonic display of sensual embellishment. He mixed alcoholic beverages while she groomed her naughty parts. He poured two sparse concoctions of vodka, soda water and lemonade, and got comfortable on the bed. Pat exited the bathroom dressed in lingerie of a whorish stature, fit for a high-class porn star. Needless to say, John was ready to burst at any moment. Patricia slinked her way over to him and they went for it, tearing apart their fractured history together, letting go of shame, forgiving assaults on reason and pardoning betrayal. Each kiss was a stamp of approval. The lovers began to partake in the elemental progression of sultry triumph when John was struck by a thunderous intuition.

**There is another presence in this room**

"Hold on. Are you kidding me?"
He couldn't resist the pull from within, guiding his piety and tempting instability.

**They are trying to get inside, they're tearing through the walls, pigeons, attacking our intrigue and interrupting this moment of ascension, pigeons are entering from all around, flocking from within the wallpaper, an army of sufficient force, pigeons dismantling our desire and terrorizing my conquest.**

For their own protection, John urgently announced that an evacuation was in order. They were required to leave the room at once, before this swarm of viscous pigeons broke through the permeable walls of gypsum and glue.

They rushed out of the building. Patricia was a saint to comply with the insufficient reasoning that caused their mandatory exit. Although she followed his unruly orders and mental tirades of fearful retreat, she had a strong opinion to share on the matter.

"This night in my useless little life was dreamt of and anticipated for years upon years. Now I only wish to no longer maintain this languid fancy of ill-repudiation. You have shattered my vision of kindled lovers and tender romance. I will oblige your demented wisdom, though I share no relevance. I will never forget the wasted grace of this night. You ruined my princess promenade. O what spectacular spoils and toe-licking grumbles we could have shared. Instead, we are forced to sleep outside in defense of your pigeon-attack hallucination. What a pathetic turnout to what could have been a buffet of pleasures. You have laid waste to my dreams."

Gargling misfortune guided the path to righteousness
"You Threw A Book At Me" she screamed
Christ! I never meant for it to hit her
I was only trying to get her attention
A flyby textbook reminder

"Damn girl, thanks for sharing. You have kept silent for ages, keeping to yourself and offering unfulfilling conversation, but now that I posed a specific question in your direction, you have responded with an outpouring of insight. Thanks... just, thank you," Patrick stated, bereaved from the onslaught of an overpowered storytime. He continued, "You are quite a simple passenger, with a depth of tales to tell; though it requires great effort for them to be heard. You really should speak up more often."

Pat and Pat had been reminiscing for a while, a dozen mosquitoes looming above them. On quest or assignment, they veered toward finding out the governing bodies of these coordinates, beyond the congressionally astringent mayor, Alto Undershed. They were seeking answers to the great riddle, allowing the concept of higher power spirituality to crowd their insight. Three fluttering goddesses responded to their hopeless plea, counting vestibules upon sky lit backdrops. Twinkling, sun-drawn messengers pointed toward belief in premonition. 3 named HOLLY, NATALIA & MADELINE descended, telling of pleasantries that enabled agreement. Particular penetrations of confounding strength, tending **the fountain of bitter regrets**, filled with tears of failed dreamers and ashamed travelers. A local spot for mourners to grieve in the nurturing support of translucent beings floating gently above the water. The goddesses were this town's unintentionally exquisite refreshment, amidst scorches of chaotic maelstrom. A reflective, oceanic breeze of cool crimson shade paved the way, brightening the grief of saddened soldiers in life's eternal battle between discipline and desire. Three elegant maidens with the capacity to heal the wounded stood guard. Visitors would kneel beside the pond's edge and contribute their tears to the collection. Once they had shed their mental anguish and cleansed their bodies of all troublesome sorrows, the goddesses would emit a strange fog that billowed around mercilessly, encapsulating all bystanders.

Pat and Pat took interest in this unique subcultural practice, sharing their own tales of gloom and narcissism. Patricia told of her coldhearted cuckolding, the smash enhance lactation, grueling manshit mustering murderer, elated slurp of suction, disease groveling, morose treatment of her one true love, John Nelson.

The ladies would never judge or condemn a participant; rather, they appreciated the courage it took to share personal tales of painful experiences. Patrick wept for his master. In the pool of droplets, he saw an obnoxious glint of regret creeping up on him. Am I missing out on important memories? Every prolonged traveler has made the decision to abandon the life they once knew. He wept for his undying wonder of the alternate paths his life could have taken. Am I the pinnacle of who I should be? Have I tapped into all my given capabilities, or am I still searching for another function? He gloated, expelling the dementia of his subconscious whims.

Neither Pat engaged in eye contact. Instead, they gave all they could to the water, alone. Personalized pain. Unrelenting cohorts of visionary entanglement, subjected to the woeful appetites of a selfish melody. Catatonic demands of singular rejection. After contributing their tears, the Pats were privy to a whiff of the alluring flavor. Pleased and specified, they stumbled about the time zone.

Silly Goose: the movie

BLANK SCREEN - Sound of a car driving down a dimly lit, tree-lined road at approximately 50 MPH. Music playing out of the car stereo is the beginning chorus to "Shine On You Crazy Diamond" by Pink Floyd.  When the song reaches the moment where the title is sung:

Fade in.

3 young gentlemen, glossy eyed and grinning, are sitting inside the car.  One driving, one in the passenger seat and one in the back.  An homage to the beginning of Goodfellas.

A stammering, debunked rattle is heard from the rear of the car.  Concerned and confused, they decide to pull over and investigate the unprovoked noise.

The trunk is opened.  It is revealed to be full of various stimulatory paraphernalia (i.e., bongs, pipes, bubblers, etc.), an assortment of mind-altering provisions and enablement apparatuses, stockpiled by disposable income.

One of the young men reassembles the contents of the trunk, in order to prevent the irritating hum of the jangling suppositories.

Once the problem is fixed, the trunk door is slammed shut.

RAGS of assortment/devious indeed// legendary woes/END scene

"Look at us, man!  Disposable goons, consumed with individuality, only to discover that we're just bit-players in the chuckling sideshow of creation. Beasts lending screen time, meandering fortune. Praised me mighty! Pick-pocketing sleight stability, more of an irresponsible scorn. Re-creation, indestructible."

Jared and Charlie reminisced the struggle of life. None such a meeting spot, suitable of man, afforded their attitudes with greater appreciation than to perch among the track and field bleachers.

While gauging their insincerities, a resentful specimen approached, repeating decibels of nauseating sentiments. Amy herself, the behemoth queen bee of distress-signaled madness, graced the loyal friends with her debilitating presence, hovering over their boyhood sanctuary. Jared was immediately perturbed by her presence.

"Goddamnit! What is she doing here?"

An elegant beauty with the power to dismantle and shatter any bonds of decency, interrupting a friendship beyond concern. She was imperviously breaching the trenches of their fortunate qualm.

"Hey boys. Greetings and condolences. I've grown overburdened in hurtful boredom. Curdling, tree-bound messengers adhere to my will, bestowing blessings of tailored grief and curtailed appliances. I was crowned a temptress; and he, a casualty of impulse."

She planted her butt, a seedling of suspicion and unmanaged emotions, seating her stump in between two friends. Before she had received the required lull of ingrained silence, in order to assert her profuse, trampling verses of skull-fucked wisdom, Jared abruptly rose from his position and left the moment, without exchanging a single word or gregarious glance. He knew better than to await the droll allure of Amy's moistened temptations. She knew just how damned sexy and stunning she was; enough to leave an enduring mark of memory upon even a casual eye. Her beauty was unique. She carried the dark charm of damaged vulnerability. A girlhood trauma that could only be appeased by endless cocks thrusting vigorously inside her gape. All who were witness to her pleasing disposition immediately succumbed to perverted desires of asshole licking. The wet nectar dripping from her vaginal lips, and crowds of men, all too willing in their enthusiastic, volunteer poise. Jared exited the scene before the infectious thrill of a pleasure filled moment of sexual abandon clogged his judgment. Charlie was a different story.

Desperate to depart from the vicinity of Amy's fluttering flirtations, Jared scanned all nearby evacuation points. The guarding fence stretched the entirety of their school, with a single opening that transported the partaker onto a busy city street. God no, too risky. Another pathway led to an upper-level baseball field. Eh, I desire to leave, but I also must retain the ability to keep an eye on these two. We don't want things to get ugly now, do we? Let's all be mature and politely sociable with the significant others of our excellent good friends. Jared found the congruent length of the six-lane, red-sponge-terrain running track a profitable match for his burgeoning disgust (and attentive apathy). He treaded heavily upon the buoyant ground. He ran round and around, pummeling his rivals and suppressing the impending forces of anger and betrayal, a cruel sensation. While he circled the vicinity of the cradling pathway, the two offshoot cases sparred audible decencies, prompting an undercurrent of sexual foul play. Jared's laps accumulated, and the newly minted pairing began to walk together across the field. They stopped where their route perpendicularly intersected with his.

"Hey man, Amy wants to go home and watch the greatest film of all time. I'm thinking of joining her. You want to come with us?" Charlie asked, innocent of ill-thought and ulterior motivation.

"No thanks. I'm going to stay here. You guys enjoy."

Jared was friendly and accommodating, mistaking their forthright statements for honesty. He trusted Charlie unflinchingly, and was certain that although Amy was a feast of pleasures, his best friend would never enter that forbidden territory, and that to worry of jealous deeds was a waste of mental processing. They said their goodbyes and split parties for the day.

Jared, masked in unintentional, sacrilegious isolation, drifted home, impaired. Retaining an unbearable urge to eradicate his primeval impulses, he strived for a healthy catharsis. Hmmmmmm...

It was to be a long walk home from these stomping grounds. Luckily for Amy, her house was nearly around the corner. It was also exactly like this:

If you were to be walking along the main road that the campus was on, past the football field, the running track and the baseball field up top, you would make your first available left turn into a section of town where the streets were named in a manner signifying an unabashed tribute to America's altruism. I mean, there's Paul Revere Drive, Declaration Avenue and Magna Carta Road. A visit to these parts warranted reading a couple chapters in a history book before venturing any further. Not that this wasn't a respectful and dignified gesture in street naming conventions, but being within earshot of Flamingo Street (located within what was appropriately refereed to as "the Bird Streets") kinda negated any semblance of the town's overall concern with the astuteness of its citizens. So does disinvolving spellcheck, for that matter. But seriously, if you really want to find Amy's house, just after you make that first left you take the next available right turn, and then, after that, you make the next available left turn. That is all I will divulge on the matter, as I fear I have already said too much. All you really need to retain from this entire paragraph is that Amy lived really close to school, and Jared (a good-natured man) lived far away.

A whispered assurance of his subconscious wisdom pondered thoughts of intrusive fact. Jared trembled home, with a long road still ahead of him, fully aware that Charlie and Amy were already settled and comfortable. The voice in his head questioned, "Why do you always walk so fast? Where are you going?" THINK about it. Needless to say, he slowed his pace.

To confide his displacement, he stopped at a nearby store and purchased parchment and ink, the equivalent of two body-size poster boards and a hefty felt-tip. He proceeded to construct an appropriate messenger wardrobe, commonly reserved for those advertising newspaper headlines or apocalyptic warnings. Only, his was to deliver a separate implication. Both sides of the paper read:

## HONK IF YOU WANT TO KILL ME

Thankfully, none responded to his ridiculed request. Only the immature or imbalanced paid him any mind. However, a singular instance of contemporary dishonor shook him to the very core of his existence. As he recounts this experience, please take into consideration his riled state of self-revelation. "A car drove past me very quickly. I thought about how if I were to have been standing in the street when it passed, how suddenly it would have killed me. BAM! A 70

MilePerHour boulder being controlled by some loser's material-drunk mother." Fatal potentiality swishing past, bygones of the long-haul trek toward the mega; & Jared carried with him the badge of knowing that trouble was brewing behind closed doors, unknown and unseen.

Under the influence of premiere pleasantries, Patricia was free to lower her guise and allow urges-often-suppressed to seep through spontaneously. The whimsical tone of violin strings pulled her toward a hidden nook, nestled thick behind heavy brush, intrinsically burdened by being forever hard to find, a bohemian refuge, only for those willing to enter into the hidden depths of the forest. A magical force was undeniably present in these parts, and Patricia was delighted to have stumbled upon this theatre of festive, practicing grounds for celebratory passengers and eager actors; those who seek to elevate life's majesty and reflect upon its brilliance. All around her were humans brimming with excitement and lustful exuberance for their well-honed craft(s). Various workshops were being offered, ranging the full spectrum of stage presence proper. Currently being observed was "How to Properly Simulate a Physical or Weapon-Assisted Duel." Patricia sidestepped the class and headed straight for the amphitheater. A stunning outdoor playhouse, curtained by nature's own design, illuminating the imagination toward a sense of dignified privilege and an unabashed appreciation of excellence. She gasped, overwhelmed by the entire scene. The stage was tastefully decorated and a full audience stocked the seats. Seeing that a play was soon to begin, she snuck in and situated herself subtly among the accomplished luminaries. The town crier entered center stage, carrying a megaphone.

"Ladies and Gentlemen, thank you all for attending. Before the evening's main attraction, we here at Teatro Botanico are pleased to present a skit written by a local artisan who recently parted ways with his wife after finding out that she cheated on him. Please enjoy Zookeepers by Arthur Duino."

(Two actors enter, dressed as guardian contenders of a shackled lion's den. They position themselves beside one another and gaze into the calm sanctuary of a knowing silence resting gently among the trillion memories of friendship's indomitable grasp.)

**Guard 1:** A bronze night wouldn't share such a splendor.
As an unpredicted forecast would prove,
there is calm underneath clouds of darkness.
A still moment, possessed by the moon.

> **Guard 2:** Your awareness is quite remarkable,
> the preceding supports well-informed.
> Though I know the reasons why you speak,
> in my own voice, I must go on.
> I find the air is ideal in the light,
> the sun's radiant glow leading the way.
> Embrace the given potential,
> and the required assistance becomes available.

**Guard 1:** But of course a man such as yourself
would then require the leading time of day
in order to shine adequately.
I insist the present be unfulfilling to your obligations.

> **Guard 2:** Your facts are true.
> I may be in an unsuitable circumstance.
> However, I reserve my excellence
> for the moments after my tasks are accomplished.
> Only then am I able to emerge without constructs.

**Guard 1:** Your language dishonors the established order.
Unappreciative of the task, you deserve a formal release!

> **Guard 2:** Forgive my offenses,
> I cherish the enabled authority we're allowed.
> Yet still I value in a greater respect
> the understanding afforded once those boundaries are disabled.

**Guard 1:** I contain the verses of discipline,
which you have rightfully earned.

> **Guard 2:** Oh, suspend this droll reply!
> Have you confused both my statements and my efforts?

**Guard 1:** If ever a casual exchange perished as sudden,
it be inadequate in comparison.
Such is my decision, I will share my reactions elsewhere.

> (Guard 1 exits the stage in a stubborn stumble.)

> **Guard 2:** Foolish paradox,
> the undivided commitment they demand.
> A disagreement perceived as a threat worthy of dismissal!
> I have displayed my trust and proved my loyalty,
> only to be once more betrayed by a friend.

> (Guard 2 sits down and
> solemnly stares into the eyes of the beast.)

> **Guard 2:** A glimpse of nature, captured and confined.
> The attempt to tame what is wild,
> to control what is meant to be free.

> (He rises, furiously resolved.)

> **Guard 2:** Some of us aren't even given a choice!

(Guard 1 enters as both actors join hands and bow politely.)

Patricia contently clapped along with the crowd,
eventually erupting into a ceremonious applause, launching
accolades toward the stale acceptance of local theatre,

preferring communal warmth in favor of polished mastery. Her appetite had been satiated by pleas of self-admiration and cultural significance. "What a whirlwind of inspiration this land offers, an amusement park of promise. I too claim a shared distance. Outliers of the social prototype, skinned alive for our withholding of a verbal presence. Where was I when the embankment snapped? For the last ship set off to find this place and I stood ashore, waving a bruised hand, claiming bon voyage. Let me wash in your purified soils, forfeiting the right to obey, clenching the still-intact flame of belief." Her otherworldly chalice flooded decency, pampered discovery and romantic musings.

She resolved to ditch out before the main show started, frightened that she would be scolded for her intrusion onto the property. Although Patricia was enamored by this untapped reservoir of stage-bound fury, she couldn't resist wondering what other dwellings were around her, hidden from view of the casual observer, reserved for only the patient and appreciative.

During an unforgettable evening of adolescent clairvoyance, Jared and his raucous group of friends shared an eternal truth. Together, Eddie, Bernardo and Charlie joined Jared in his automobile as they cruised their home turf, on assignment to discover the inequities for all causes of doubt, trouncing negativity into clumps of steel wool. Bernardo had procured a sampling of fine tranquilities: the ground residue of gingko leaves, packaged and bagged, a consumer's delight. They risked a cruel, assigned punishment for their deed, overtly disobeying the law in exchange for personal dignity. What's the point of following rules when our intentions outweigh our actions?

Each young man in that car carried the weight of a troubled mind, in his own unique way. Burdensome woes and sidestepped memories, emotionally roughed up through fate's unfortunate circumstance. Hey! Who doesn't have a mental pathway that, when explored, only produces reassurances of battles lost and upset defeats?

Jared himself was, in this moment, disguising his grief, as Amy had provided an endless cycle of remorseful enterprises. Although she remained in contact with him, their role as mutual lovers had been temporarily halted. She endured about two and a half years with him, and was eager to explore the outer realm. Outside of Jared's jurisdiction, where she was considered a fugitive, she thrived. Armies of men lined up, ready to plow right through her, fresh and floppy, leaving their specimen atop her unstoppable beauty. Jesus, right there in her bedroom! She claimed the walls were painted the shade of autumn, a transitional color between orange and yellow. God, what a room she had! Her desk right over there, where a TV took up most of the space, her stereo, which appeared to float above it all, and of course, the photo of her with her parents. She must've been about nine in that picture. Her parents looked younger too, and slightly happier to be together. Maybe they were in love early on... Oh well, not anymore. It was always a troublesome quandary when Amy would attempt to fellate Jared within view of that photograph. It never felt proper to receive head from a girl while her dad was glaring at you through the picture frame. "Hey mister, I'll take good care of her, I swear, just as soon as she's done crouching on the floor and slurping the ever-loving cum outta me. Oh yeah, she is sucking on me like an anxious beast, wild beyond repentance. Oh man, how did you raise this girl? She's going for my balls and everything! Damn, now she's stroking it while she looks me in eye with that ferocious twinkle of nastiness. Oh god, I'm gunna cum soon. Oh shit, should I tell her? Nah, I'll just let this load jettison onto her waning face, plastering her freckles and lightly pasting her lips and mouth. I'll watch my earthen seed travel downward, dripping slowly under the ridge of her chin, leveling out among the mounting points of her breasts. Wow, what a girl!" Of course, nowadays, Jared was no longer invited to such intimate occasions. He was beginning to accept that they were now a separate unit, and he prepared to lose contact with her. On this singular night, he forever cursed her name and settled in with the brilliant strength and loving respect that flowed between his friends, unshaken and pure.

They pulled up alongside the curb right in front of Charlie's house, underneath the translucent pyramid of light created by a nearby streetlamp. Four proud and confident young men, ready for life and nothing less, parked and ready. Eddie attempted to forge a percolation chamber. Miniscule bubbles captured within a vacuum seal, to accommodate their bountiful foliage. He constructed a rather imperfect but still functional utensil, proper in form and technical specifics. An elongated pipe, chaliced and triumphant. A complete cylinder for the fog's trappings, with a murky puddle of water sloshing away at the bottom, defined. Bernardo dug through his grip, grabbed a helping of gingko and stuffed it into the chamber, fulfilling the purpose of its construction. Eddie was the first participant, holding a lighter over the verdure, incinerating a neatly rounded portion of the overall bowl. The water bubbled calmly as he inhaled. The soothing sounds of a Zen garden were (unintentionally) recreated, while a cloud formed inside. Eddie plunged through, took a large gasp and clasped his mouth shut, allowing the contents to stew in the inviting confines of his inner self. Ah, the accumulation of inebriating enchantments. He then exhaled an enormous cloud of pungent scents, delightful upon the palette. Eddie passed the apparatus to Bernardo and the whole group laughed together in joyous understanding of the innocuous blessings of their brotherhood. Heartfelt trust and blatant promises of mutual suffering.

Bernardo prepared for his chance to smolder, as Jared turned on the CD player in his car. "Brand New Colony" by the Postal Service was playing. This was an important track on an album that was, upon its initial release, a universally respected and adored piece of music. At least, if you were in high school at the time, not only was it a unique blend of digitally programmed melodies overlaid with soulful crooning, but the lyrics resonated heavily with the boundless exploration of life during this period of maturation and its accompanying tests of spiritual endurance. Jared patiently waited for his turn to smoke when the bridge kicked in and carried him away. "Everything will change." The lyrics swam in his mind, presenting future potentialities of unknown sanctity. What will enable this fortune of systematic balance? He felt inspired, interpreting the song as a message, a telling of times changing and the mental metamorphosis of progress. This too shall pass, I know it.

When Jared's turn to vaporize came, he spared no expense and took a deep breath, a toast to his newfound enlightenment. He knew that recovery was beginning. He blew the smoke out onto the dashboard and watched as it spread out evenly in all directions. He found it oddly peculiar when miniature trees began to sprout up out of the dispersing mist, forming the curved row of a tiny, tree-lined street on his dashboard. Does anyone else see this? The rest of the gang was cheerfully wrapped up in an amusing conversation and laughing heartily in turn. Jared couldn't articulate the proper verbosity. He was stunned beyond words. Time had slowed to a delicate tremble, heightening his awareness of lush details beyond significance. Suddenly, a simple glance or friendly smile carried the depth of G-d's finest moment, possessed by a monumental truth. They were offered a chance to glance at life through a time-shifted, microscopic lens, fine tuned and unrelenting.

Just when he thought all sanity had departed, a green cricket appeared, strutting down the small-scale road of trees, wearing a top hat and holding a cane. Taking center stage, he began to sing an engulfing version of "I left my heart in San Francisco." What a moving rendition! With appropriate gestures and tasteful showmanship, he was conjuring spirits of spectacular prowess. Gene Kelly, reincarnate.

Jared was staring with such intense focus and utter amazement that he appeared entranced, through the eyes of his fellow cohorts. Charlie shook him to break the spell. "Jared. Hey, you alright?" He looked over at his concerned friends.

They were happy, but worried. Jared smiled to let them know all was well. A gentle laugh solidified his state. "Yea, damn. I think I should open the doors and get some fresh air." He hopped out of the car and immediately went over to the trunk. He drove a station wagon, which created an atmosphere of singular spatial differentiation; i.e., the seating area was directly connected to the rear compartment. Once Jared opened the trunk, a plume of smoke erupted out of his car, freeing the contained substance in a glorious display. The fresh air withered all fantasies in his mind and restored the coherence of his imagination. Covalent bonds of friendship and forgiveness, alert in the raging new. Testimonial provinces plunged into a lifetime, recounting and reminiscing. This would be a balancing act toward trust falls entangled.

**Slated for a breakdown – if Bernardo knew the whole time, why didn't he tell Jared? He was fortunate to have obtained valuable and precious evidence, yet avoided all opportunities to share these facts with Jared. If anyone deserved to know this information, it was Jared himself. By god, him more than anyone else. Fucking lord! Can you just image this?**

**Hey folks, let us take pause and reflect upon the material. Yes, we all saw a loving semblance of friendship; that is, through Jared's eyes. But in fact, a rotten distaste slurped through the aura, plagued and reputable. Charlie had fucked up big time, and Bernardo knew the truth. For all the exchanges and stories told, never once was any mention made of this unfortunate tale. God loving, can we simply put words together? Can simplicity provoke? If you knew the truth, what would you have done? If you knew that Charlie fiddled and faddled with little Amy's good parts (whoa man, she's reckless), if you knew she kinked the slippery fun time good-good show, free tickets and all, let him just fuck her plain and simple (he was so young and stupid then / thanks for sharing / a tear jerk phone call to prove his innocence), if you knew the whole goddamn story, don't you think that Jared would LOVE to know that tidbit? That miniscule tale of him**

**fucking her sideways. He deserves to know! It's a tough pill to swallow, your lady love-licking and riding your own best man, getting off on his own accord, and then going to hang out.**

During a screening of Michael Moore's latest documentary classic, Jared witnessed a rather unusual tension between whispered rationalizations of angry blowhards. Huge moleculed remnants of human beings hissed and growled at the screen, whenever Rumsfeld, Cheney or the President himself appeared. The audience blurted out horned timbre calls. Hoot hoot, I dare not bow to Bush. They were sure to get their money's worth, clapping and clamoring. Bernardo was acting strange at the movie, quiet and reserved, but smirking the whole time. Charlie, instead of being amused and enthralled by the audience's reactions, panicked. He was unusually self-conscious of his behavior, and yelped to contain his guilty memory. Whoa now, are these people mad at me? Their angered hisses, aimed at the movie screen, struck Charlie as accusations. Disappointed scorn from the elders of his town. I'm sorry, I'm sorry. I was overcome with sexual desire; lust, I guess. Come on, she's hot and horny. Man, she's a slut and we all know it. No no, forgo such selfish acceptance. You done wrong! There he sat, no longer a virgin, a milestoned man, fucked his own friend's girl, and here they are, hanging out together the next day, as "the group" goes to the movies. Yeah, let's see this exciting new film, let's all go be friendly together, let's play play play. Yay PLAYTIME. Here he sits, and the whole audience is scowling, cursing, ha ha ha! I don't feel sorry for him at all, do you? Charlie is sitting in a well-worn, cushioned seat at the popcorn matinee, expecting a calm, distraction-filled, cinema experience. Oh dear! Is he hearing this? The whole theatre is screaming, blaming and shouting. Good boy, they're screaming at you, you and you only. And you want to know why? How could you own up to a single hesitation? Here's a matter of fact:

Jared was sketching in his diary,
making note of hopeful boyhood promises
*My friends are the greatest* ☺

How could he know such unsuspecting triangulation
would present itself as an auspicious means of possibility?
Nothing to worry about here, he assumed. We are all bound in
certainty and admiration. Skirmished intensity ought distract our
breath. Our daily rations of affection and commiseration, bundled
per the ghost of adherence. O me and a quarter too late, granted
luxury and refused.

An elegant beauty with nothing to lose,
Portions desired, ability to choose,
Willed to conquer,
and who is left to clean up the mess of eternal betrayal?

She spun among the roughage, clipping against thorns
and paddling her commitment. Holy matrimony, disgusted
and grave, skipping and sliding all through the day. Bright
Princess on the loose.

It was to be a miraculous occasion, a day to remember
indefinitely. Hordes of film freaks lined up and pledged honor
toward the completion of a fantastic trilogy. We had watched the
first two episodic adventures unfold before our gleaming faces.
There we sat, politely in awe, lapping up the gorgeous gleams of
light in the flickering framework. We had seen part one during a
birthday party for Charlie some years back (not to get all fussy
with b-day scat, but that's how it happened). The sequel was
attended by Jared and Amy together, a cute date for them indeed.
They had to walk to the theatre from her house, as this occurred
before either had been granted a license to operate a vehicle. Ah,
sweet memoires of simplicity, unknown were the shambles of it
all falling apart.

The release of the third film was rampant with anticipation and good ol' fashioned excitement. O how splendid it feels to be excited, no matter how mundane the source. It's all the same emotion. To properly acknowledge the siphoning conclusion, three buddies feasted before the showing. Jared met up with Charlie and Eddie at a local restaurant just down the block from the theatre. To prepare for a film that was sure to exceed three hours in length, and why not, Jared ordered a full-on steak dinner.

"I must say," he began, "I honesty am not that big a fan of these films. I feel like I'm the only one saying this, but they seem somehow incomplete, lacking. I mean, don't get me wrong, they are exquisitely made, high quality and all that shit. But something's missing. I can't quite identify the problem. Oh well, I still like going to the movies either way."

Eddie and Charlie were fans. They didn't understand. The steak arrived, and Jared was given a serrated blade to slice it with.

"If you haven't read the books and gained a prior familiarity with the storyline and the characters, I could see how it might seem overwhelming to take in on the first go-around." Eddie offered an understandable reason. "It's dense stuff. I don't blame you. I just don't get how you haven't been exposed to a more detailed description of the story, seeing as Amy is such a die hard fan of whole series."

"Ha! I can't tell if she's really into the movies or just that goddamn actor, the blonde fucker with the bow and arrow. And how is Amy's obsession with these movies supposed to affect my own personal taste? If anything, I should be trying to distance myself from any and all Amy-related material."

"You guys'll be back together soon enough, cut it out. Unless Charlie over here stakes his claim."

Jared stopped eating. Charlie looked him dead in the eye.

"What the fuck does that mean?"

"Are you kidding? You mean he didn't tell you? Oh shit. Come on Charlie, how can you go around like that? Sitting here face to face with the man and you don't let him know? Damn Jared, I though you knew this whole time."

"Can you fucking tell me what's going on?"

Charlie finally spoke.

"Man, I'm sorry Jared."

"Is the for real? Come on… No… You?"

Sigh

Shrug

"You know how Amy is in my Cisco Networking class?"

"Yeah."

"So, she's been coming over to study and look over notes and stuff. It's a grueling course, I tell ya. Real troublesome."

"I don't give a fuck about your little Cat-5 cult. Tell me what happened!"

"Well, while she was over the other day, she, uh, sorta kissed me."

Jared started to cut into his steak.

"Can you elaborate?"

"We just kissed, okay?"

He had already cut clean through the meat, but continued to carve into the plate.

"Tell me, Charlie."

"Okay… Shit, I'm sorry, this is hard. We made out. I didn't mean for it to happen."

"She did. Fucking slut never leaves a guy's house without fooling around with him."

Sudden shock coursed within Jared.

Pause. Let it settle in.

"Why you, man? What the hell is wrong with you? I'm your friend."

"It was sudden and unintended, that's all."

"What else? Fuck, I know neither of you horny bastards would quit on step one."

Eddie glanced at Charlie. Already aware of the whole tale, he knew one more detail and his presence ensured that all of it was to be confessed.

"Don't be mad, Jared, but I also felt her boob."

Silence

Stares

"And sucked on her nipples a bit."

"Okay shit, stop stop stop stop stop talking."

He had cut into the next layer of the plate. Cracked the foundation and penetrated beneath. How unbelievably unpleasant to learn of this masquerade. The day remains unaltered.

Jared received the first of several friendship confessions!

"You're a shitty friend. What else can I say to you? That's fucked up and I can't believe you would do that, when I make is so abundantly clear how much that girl means to me and how much it hurts me when we're apart."

"Look man, I really am sorry. It was a stupid, selfish act on my part. I would only hope that our friendship is more important than some girl."

Jared gave up. He was silent during the rest of their meal. They split the check and headed to the theatre. While waiting in line, Jared excused himself and retreated to his car where he listened to "God Only Knows" approximately four times. He had parked in view of the grounds and could see Charlie and Eddie standing together, probably assessing the overall situation, how it all went over better than he thought and he's so lucky I wasn't more upset. Fuckers, I'll let them hold my spot.

When the line began to move, he rushed back, entered alongside his friends and claimed a seat in the back row of the cineplex. Once the film began, Jared was completely engulfed. The conclusion demonstrated the capacity of magic, as alignment was achieved. Hearing part three of the tale gave new meaning to the previous two, and his appreciation clicked into place. Having been privy to the whole story, Jared was able to adequately understand every misstep along the way, and the boldness of their journey astounded him. When exiting the theatre, while the credits were still crawling up the screen, off into the heavens above, Jared spoke.

"Now that I have seen all three, I feel I can properly and adequately judge the work as a whole. I must say, I believe this to be the greatest film of all time."

She gasped, concerned. Where is he? My companion throughout all this. Have I been so lost in thought that I neglected to monitor my franchise? Patrick! Patrick, where are you? Oh, crumbling dilemma. A ruined empire. I wish to share my passionate excrement with a dog I call my own.

She found him huddled between hooded scoundrels, wavering guidance in accordance with recessional activations.

"What are you doing, Pat?"

In his hand was a can filled to compaction with red paint.

"Are you sketching the side walls?"

The crew stood guard of their new hood rat.

"Get out of here, lady. We don't want any trouble. Yes, what we are doing is considered wrong. Vandalism, graffiti. We are leaving our mark upon this city and your disgust will not stand in our way."

"I shall cede to your convictions. If you indeed produce these things as a means of artistic publicity, please elaborate upon the expression you seek to convey by this dull illustration."

Patrick has constructed a rough stencil of symbolic energies.

"Well listen here, missy. I carved this here drawing of a dog's face. Just a dog's face, looking straight ahead, using the least amount of detail needed to suggest a dog in the format of a spray-paint duplication. But look here, Pat. His left eye is closed and his right eye is open. What does that mean to you?"

"Uh, utter happenstance, according to the principles of shattered time travel repentance."

"Oh goodness. How desperate, how hopeless. The troubled plea of the atheist. You've heard it. They all have a quick three-sentence summation of their entire belief system, eager to erupt into their memorized outlook for all who argue against their lack of faith. My dog stencil suggests the act of winking. Don't you see it? The left eye is closed, the right eye is open. He is winking."

"Yea, that's cute. A winking dog, I get it."

"The religious implications are suggested with the surrounding words. Above the winking dog's face: I HAVE SEEN. Underneath: THE FACE OF DOG."

"You mean?"

"Uh huh, you guessed it. The face of dog, right?"

"Well, this could only entail a longwinded hog report."

"Precisely! The face of dog, written in capital letters around a winking dog's face, is a devotional plea. You see, have you ever witnessed the wink of a dog?"

"Yes. I've already explained, I have seen a dog wink several times without any revolutionary visions."

"Instead, how about you learn to think this way. Alright? Whenever a dog winks, you are seeing the literal face of G-d."

"Yea, right. G-d flipped is dog. I see the connection."

"It's not just a verbal gimmick. I am telling you there is an incredible significance to the similarities of these two words. When a dog winks, you see the face of G-d. Nature is laughing and mocking our hopeless humanity, ruling the destiny of all life forms."

"So you are spreading this image as a means of influencing spirituality? Trying to convince people that they see G-d in a winking dog? Jeez, now I've heard it all."

"Laugh if you want, but there is a commanding force being channeled behind the eyes of an animal."

"Okay, shuck shuck hoo."

"You've either never known grace or have been severely deprived of unconditional love to not see the Great Spirit in a dog's wink."

"I will hold strong to my useless opinion."

"Fine by me."

Patrick sprayed another stenciled remark upon the wall, the red paint residue smeared and spilled down the concrete slab's coarse texture.

"Hey, Patricia, now that you're here, I've been meaning to ask you a question. And, since we're delicately treading the subject of life's bane significance, I sense pertinence in you sharing a valuable insight justly obtained. Witness to devastation, a traumatic tale for all to tell. You saw the world in his shrinking light offerings. Tell me now how he died. How did his trial run expire? Was he worthy of your bumblings? Of his skid row alimony, pandering emotions?"

"Cure my whims if I didn't understand every word of that. I'll tell you the damned truth. You question me and ask my side of the story. How my treasured love took his own life and left a village to mourn in vain."

"Indeed."

"If you seek information regarding the death of John Nelson, you must begin by understanding the time, place and reason for his actions. He committed suicide right before our very eyes, in a spectacle he constructed and preplanned. God awful, I admit, his state. We were in our final year of required schooling, twelve years I believe is the number. Yes, 12, it was our last year of school and we were administered another student body celebration, the rousing of excitement to fuel spirited cheers for the upcoming football game."

"A pep rally?"

"Is that what you call it? Yes, it was an entire school-wide assembly, which only took place in accordance with a football game, instilling a sense of loyalty and pride (nationalism). We all gathered in the auditorium to applaud our local athletes and enjoy risqué cheerleading routines."

"This sounds awfully pleasant for a suicide tale."

"Well, that's just the thing. It was such a blissful, delightful time for everyone. It was unexpected, to say the least. Shocked us all. After a vigorously aerobic cheer routine— hey, did I ever tell you I was a cheerleader? Well, back in school I was. Anyways, after an intense routine, me and the rest of the squad lined up to form an entryway; a path for the football team to walk through as we introduce them name by name. Kinda like a London Bridge formation. We stood alert and peppy. So, just as the first player is to cross the threshold, John comes running through our line, out into the middle of the gymnasium, stark naked minus a top hat. The entire school erupts into hysterics. Amused beyond bewilderment, they laugh and applaud his rebellious entrance.

"You see, a year before, there had been a young man brave enough to strip down to his underwear and dash through the building, only to crash straight into a locked door, adding a cherry to the top of his already silly deed. Ha! We thought that was funny; but now here comes John, dick swinging and everything. Us teenagers couldn't handle it, this scene of blasted morals. He was to be a hero for that performance. There he stood, completely naked, in a top hat, this nerdy kid exposing himself to the entire school. I couldn't believe it myself. The quiet kid in class decides to run naked in front of the whole school during a pep rally. God, it was epic! Until he took off the hat... He had hid a pistol inside the top hat. He had a fucking gun and was waiting for the perfect moment to off himself, and here it was. The whole school was watching, all the kids he blamed for not giving a shit about him and not understanding his perspective. Cheering, excited, scared and panicked. As soon as he brandished the weapon, he placed it to his temple and pulled the trigger. Finished. Silence. Complete shock. The gunshot echoed a mark of indifference. This brat decided to dampen our lives with his selfish act. I'm still bitter and upset about it to this day. Fuck you, John Nelson."

"God, that's wonderful."

"What?! Excuse me?"

"I mean, look at this kid. He's depressed, mainly because of you, and you're only angry because you feel responsible. But for the casual observer, removed from this act and hearing this story, I must say, it is pure excellence. All of that youthful energy and unresolved anger, released so profoundly. He had been shown the curse of life and the dangers of love, and he proved his angst. He demonstrated to everyone that he refused to live in such a world; a world that would defile his tenderness and leave him shackled in terrors of betrayal. Hell, what's the difference between his sacrifice and those monks that burned themselves in Vietnam? I say bless him."

"You are unkind and insensitive to share such delight in this story."

"I have no pity for you. If I'm not mistaken, you blatantly admitted to being partially responsible for his sorrows. Forget love, beast. Go back to your theatre friends, maybe they'll let you guide the spotlight."

**A ripple formed. "You're drifting."**

Hiss hoo hoo, hollered resentments floated his way. Could Charlie contain his customs? An angry theatre loathed his very being. They stood pitted against him. Boo boo, him and his half-a-heart. Curse the day he took his first breath. Shame and spasms. Hatred.

He stood up and left the cinema immediately, once the end credits began. The rest of the group had to rush to catch up to him. On their way, they discussed their peculiarities concerning the picture. "O what a madman president."

Jared rushed over to Charlie, seeking to tend to his grief, or whatever had caused his rambunctious exit. "Hey man, are you okay?"

"I swear I would kill him if I could."

"What? Are you serious? The film got to you that much?"

"No, just that crowd in there. What was wrong with everyone?"

"Oh, come on, you know how the old liberal crowd loves to cause a scene when they're watching documentaries. They can't fully comprehend the disconnection with the man on the screen."

"I can't believe them."

"Relax, Charlie, it was just a fucking movie. Are you sure you're okay?"

"Yea, I've just never been involved in such a tense group reaction."

"Hey, suit yourself. I had fun. It's surprising how much entertainment is provided in political tragedy."

They left the theatre, separately.

**Scrawled expressions, tampered and evident.**
**Could she seduce another victim?**

A peculiar evening, a chance phone call.

"Hey, wanna go for a drive?"

"What?  A drive to where?"

"Who knows?  Just a drive into the outer realm, the unknown and the impossible."

"Spontaneity represents an exploration of potential's forgotten blink."

"We can converse and enjoy each other's company while listening to comforting music and driving around the neighborhood. I find the nighttime shade of darkness, plus the isolating loneliness and lack of humanity, really gives you an interesting view of the world."

"Let's go!  Zoom zagoo."

"I'll pick you up soon.  Wait outside your
house in 10 minutes.  And bring a CD to
listen to."

"Okay, got it."

What in G-d's enlightenment could be gained
from this date?  A friendship, a fuckship
(at least a make out session on a pool table
and an exchange of oral sex while <u>Babe</u>
flickers on the television set).

Eddie was at her house in 10 minutes and 23
seconds.  Amy was already outside, holding
Keane's first album.

"Hey, hop in."

"Hi!"

He put on the music.  "You were looking
pretty good out on the ice at Charlie's
birthday party."

"That was fun."

"You know, I thought we really worked
together pretty well.  As a team, we
cooperated properly."

"You are quite the sportsman."

"I'll admit I'm competitive, but with the
right allies we're bound to win."

"I'll play with you again."

"Let's take it slow."

They drove without any regard for direction or necessity. It was indeed a triumph of life's burgeoning wonder.

"Check this out."

Upon approaching an empty road with no streetlights, Eddie switched off his headlights and plunged the two of them into complete darkness, their only reference point being the strong force of the car pulling them forward and the warm melodies of Keane swooning in their ears. The powerful excitement of this moment was undeniable.

"Wow, that was crazy!"

"Yeah! I love doing it, when the circumstances arise."

"I can't believe what a surreal rush that provided. Do it again. Let's go another round."

And so Eddie switched off his lights once again. Amy let out a youthful yell of temporary freedom. Caution soon set in. Once Eddie turned the lights back on, both he and Amy were eerily frightened by what they saw. The freshly ignited headlights revealed a man wrapped in a dark trench coat, pacing forward along the edge of the road.  Eddie gasped.

"Did you fucking see that?"

"Ha!  Yes, that was creepy."

"There was some weirdo walking with complete conviction, middle of the night, middle of nowhere, in all black.  What the fuck?"

"That was scary."

"Yeah, fucking mystery murderer man on his way to kill a family or strangle some animals."

"Oh god."  Amy was truly enjoying herself, laughing and creating memorable moments with Eddie.

They held hands the remainder of the evening.

THE FOLLOWING DAY:

Eddie awoke and immediately called Jared.

"Hey, let's go for a drive.  I want to talk to you about something."

"Okay."

Amy had a certain fascination with the National Geographic Channel; the bizarre glimpse it provided into the natural world, of culture's boundless imagination and the animal kingdom, a breadth of brilliance. Whenever Jared came over, it was guaranteed that her television would be on when he arrived, a lion being eaten or ritualistic scarification (oddly her favorite episode) performed in a far-off land, illuminating her mind and eyeballs.

The conditions were no different the night she invited Jared over. It was to be their first private interaction, outside of school, since the inadequate departure of their conjoined pairing. "Oh girl, I'm anxious to see you again." "Will you do me a favor?" "Anything for you." "Bring me some Taco Bell." "No problem." The drive to her house conveniently included her requested dining institution as part of the route.

"I want a burrito." Wow, this girl could make anything sound sexy. I want a burrito. She sounds so innocent, with a throbbing sensuality swirling beneath.

He rushed over, including with her order one regular nachos and a large drink for both of them to share.

"So, what's up Eddie?"

"Man, you're a great friend, and I just wanna get this out of the way."

The eager excitement quickly washed from Jared's face. There was absolutely no way this cautionary disclaimer of loyalty foretold positive events. Still, he listened.

"I mean, I know how Amy took you through a perilous tirade of anticipatory actions, resulting in the miserable failure of your relationship. I know this."

"I thought you were anxious to tell me something. I don't get why you're now recounting a pointless tale. Goodness me, I've carefully dissected all routes of this legend and you're reciting the cursed abbreviation."

"Jared! I just know how sensitive you are about her, even still. You're getting upset that I'm simply mentioning her. We should be able to, as friends, discuss such matters without an uncivilized reaction."

"Go on, and I shall listen with quiet restraint."

"Imperfect as we are, there is a common understanding among the brotherhood, concerning matters of truth, both wanted and not, that any such discrepancies must certainly be discussed and brought to the surface."

"Yea? So spill yourself."

"Fuck, okay, here it goes..."

Jared was soon to arrive with the warm Mexican food and a hopeful application of desire. He was eager and able. She must have implied sex in her request for such delicacies, right? Why else would she contact me? She could easily ignore me, or at least say hello and postpone a potential physical meeting.  But no, she's practically begging for it.

"I have developed a romantic interest in Amy, and I'm pretty sure she feels the same way about me."

"Are these positive feelings?"

"Yes.  I just don't feel right taking any serious consideration in this flirtation without first consulting with you and receiving your blessing."

"Wait..."

"I want to ask her out, and I will only go through with it if I have your permission."

He approached the window.  Amy was inside.  Before knocking, Jared stared into her bedroom, watching her.  As predicted, the television was on and she lay sprawled across the bed, giggling.  Footage of elephants played on the screen, hopeful.  Look at this girl!  She is gorgeous!  She had on a black t-shirt and a pair of green and white cheer shorts, stunning.

Maybe she could hear Jared's lustful panting against the window, because Amy glanced over and was frightened by his ominous presence.  "Whoa!  You scared me, Jared."

"Sorry.  You just looked so beautiful.  I was awestruck."

"Oh, shut up.  Come on in and gimme my taco."

He tossed the bag into her room and clumsily climbed in through the open window.  "What are you watching?"

"It's this riveting documentary on elephant behavior. A married couple spent five years filming and chronicling the lives of these massive animals, studying how they interacted. The condensed results of their strenuous efforts were made into this movie. It's really quite interesting."

Jared and Amy unwrapped their food and began munching away, rabid and wild. While Amy continued watching her elephants, Jared's mind swam with dreams of romantic implications. A married couple shooting a nature documentary together. Wow! Such a passionate existence. Two lovers, out in the wilderness, alone, basking in the glory of magnificent beasts. Days of intensive study, evenings of embrace. Oh Amy, let this be us later in life.

Her focus on the television was unwavering. A group of elephants were gathering around the remains of a deceased brother of theirs. They huddled together and flung sand onto their faces, a sign of mourning, as explained by the narrator.

"You know what, Eddie?" A calm silence rested between them, while Jared processed this newly-confessed information. "I must admit, I am honored to call you my friend."

"What? Come on, man. What kind of reaction is that? You mean to tell me that you're not upset?"

"Oh, god no. I'm plenty upset. Frankly, I am horrified by the thought of you sliding your tongue upon the trembling folds of her knotted butthole. I am forlorn and defiant, blasted with rage. I am troubled by this,

with wide-eyed discomfort, believe me.  Oh,
I wish nothing more than to erase this
potentiality, I do.  But I am comforted by
your honesty.  I admire your actions.
Rather than burying this burgeoning romance,
sprouting thorns and bristled thyme, you
have made a delicate choice.  Because you
knew, Eddie.  You knew this would upset me.
You were certain of my reaction, but you
still felt that I deserved to know.  I
needed to know.  There is no doubt I would
be disgusted by this info.  Absolutely!  You
made the effort to speak with me, face to
face, and express your crimes.  You halted
all petty distractions and sat me down to
tell of your private affair, knowing that my
relationship with the girl in question would
certainly influence a poor reaction on my
part.  Thank you, Eddie.  Thank you for
treating me like a man.  Thank you for
understanding that although this news may be
painful and perhaps even shocking to hear,
you knew that I could handle it.  Thank you
for not planting secrets and hiding in the
dull promises of let's never tell him.
Thank you for not treating me like a scared
little boy who couldn't possibly handle such
tales.  I am strong."

### Trance unbroken, countless days

Studious practitioners, disciplined & diligent in their pursuit of answers, sat undisturbed, meditative.

How could they distinguish the separation between dream and memory? Both remain as frail recollections of the past, entombed in our master's eyes. We see only what he has seen, we know only what he has thought of already, only what has been conjured in his mind.

We are endlessly meandering in the confines of an afterthought, staring backwards down the tunnel.

Needless to say, Jared and Amy spent the rest of the night together, reminiscing elephant fascinations and performing patchwork maintenance on their love-dumps. Pumping, pushing, salivating and coercing their own vulgar fantasies, blank and fused. Bygone retributions of a pulsating love. Candid elements o'er thy meadows of spring. Hear me, my lady, talk to me. Lavish your etiquette and please me. My first ever hand job, I had my arm around her neck. She starts working me out. I'm so enthralled that I tighten my grip and start choking the girl. She only blew me because, down there, she's outta my reach.

## Maybe the only thing we have in common is that we're both lonely.

The summer between $10^{th}$ and $11^{th}$ grade, Jared traveled to Europe with his family. He abstained from masturbating for the entire 2-week trip. The day they returned home, Jared jerked off while sitting on the toilet. When he came, the backlog was so voluminous and pressurized, and his posture was such, that he came all over his face.

Skipping through the forest,
Patricia stopped to inspect two banana slugs.
One was alive,
the other was dead.
She was hypnotized by the sight.
The living slug was wrapped around its deceased partner.
Patricia felt an immediate, sympathetic connection to this creature.
I am the living slug,
slithering among remains.
Life shall continue for us.
What other option do we have?
We will endure the loss,
there is no escaping our grief.
But still, we must go on.

                              "My dad says you're a good kid."

    Jared, regrettably, wet the bed on a fairly regular basis, well beyond the point where such behavior was socially acceptable. Sleepovers were never much fun. Fortunately, peeing in your sleep causes you to wake up early, allowing ample time to (attempt to) clean up the mess (or at least conceal the evidence). Jared must've soaked so many blankets, couch cushions and mattresses.
    It is believed that such incidents (i.e., adolescent bedwetting) are symptomatic of a certain trauma, the physical manifestation of an unresolved inner turmoil…

Step 1: Where?
Her destination was unknown at the time.
She wasn't sure.
Onward, travel

    While driving home from Sam Ash, after having purchased a new set of guitar strings, Jared and Charlie listened to Dane Cook's latest stand-up comedy album. He did a bit about how when a man receives a blowjob he simultaneously becomes a hair stylist to the woman fellating him. The two boys laughed together. Jared understood the joke. He had lived its premise. One day you'll understand it too, Charlie.

**I knew a young man**

**He was sent to jail**

**For asking if you**

**Had some drugs for sale**

**An ill request**

**At a resolute hour**

**Offer your praise**

**And relinquish your power**

Alto Undershed was never one to confuse calamity with self-delusion.
He was destined to complete the guided tour of wonderland,
culminating in the grand entrance of the king and queen.
All mystic waterfalls and sleight-of-hand sorcery,
bereavement of magnitude, blistered and red.
They would have to face a desperate deed.
Magnificent, indelible twice over.
All illusions trampled, gone.
Punctuating poetry?
Klepping me
O my
Ic
u

girl, nibbling on your glasses  ; )

Alto would soon escort both Pats into the guardian towers, the housing structure of the parliamentary factor elite.

"Follow me."

To access the castle, a bridge crossing was required.

Amy's official cohort in crime, a young woman named Katie, was a guarantor of sure-fire weekend madness for the two young maidens. Her lustful intrigue guided Amy into the depths of indulgent abandon. Parties of severe entanglement and hallways of unmasked potential soothed their desires. Lovingly escorted throughout throes of testimonial vestige, Katie & Amy both cooed with excitement, as they were immediately swept up in the gaze of overshadowing peasants.

You see, the mating ritual of a female is an effortless gamble, a selection of choice and a buffet for the orderly. All that is required of a woman during a social gathering is the establishment of her presence. Once she enters the room, whether she stands in the corner or dances on a table, she will be noticed, noted and framed. She will emanate the quelling of men's desires, the soulful squeeze of wholeness. The stern and brave, the nervous and shy, they will all flock to her, eager and thumping. Her power is that of choice; to crown the victor in sleeveless might and pump his throb knob until he gushes the virgin sacrament upon her porous face. Needless to say, Amy was bombarded.

From the moment she entered the festive atmosphere, delicacies were flung her way. The alcoholic reservoir was conveniently positioned and poised for her arrival. A lone bartender, slinging bottles of burlesque surrender, stood at attention and awaited the desperate thirst of his customers. The queen of all nightmares approached, eager to imbibe.

"What can I get you ladies?"
blink blink giggle

"Well, give us something to get our tushies wiggling."

"I know just the thing, girls."

<u>Flaming Blue Jesus</u>
1 shot of tequila
1 shot of peach liqueur
1 shot of peppermint schnapps
a dash of blue coloring
2 shots of rum

He made two.

The gimmick of this drink is to light the alcohol on fire while serving it, creating an entrancing and enticing allure for the women. An appropriate distraction for the feverous night ahead.

The girls slurped down their beverages, fiddled their toes and escaped into the wild spirit of tonight. Katie grabbed Amy by the hand and pulled her toward the selection marquee. *I can fuck anyone here.* They glided along merrily, alcohol sifting through their veins.

Amy approached a handsome man perched atop a reclining lawn chair. He was the nightmare of every ex-boyfriend. The new man she would run to and fuck the second you 2 split. She licked her lips at the sight of him. To make matters worse, he was equipped with an acoustic guitar. Bastard. She twinkled her magnificent presence toward him, sashaying her warmth and beaming radar signals of light. She's irresistible. No one could match the beauty of this woman. Amy, you kill me. You are such an incredible force, a banshee. You know who you really are! Cut the metaphor: ~~Ashley~~ Amy, I am lucky to have known you. I forgive you, and I love you, always. You are the passionate muse of my life. My yearning. My blues.

"So, little lady, how are you feeling this fine summer eve?"

giggle

"I feel liberated, restored."

"Hey, cheers to that."

He raised a beer toward the heavens. Erection.

"I wanna hear a song." Little brat bitch, makes a man her puppet.

"This is for you. It's the song of your soul."

He positioned himself and played the opening notes of Hendrix's "Little Wing." It sounded magnificent. What can I say? I want to tell you how terribly trashy it was, simplified chords and quick strums, but no! He was spot-on perfect, vocals and all. Soothing, to say the least. He was destined to penetrate. He played the whole damn song, with graceful precision and honest emotion. She was stunned.

"Fuck, man, you got some chops. That was unbelievable."

"Hey, thanks."

"Really, that was great. Truly moving."

She was wet. No need to hide it.

"I appreciate it. Nice to meet you. I'm Nick."

"Amy. Let's get a refill."

Their bond was sealed.

He would take her home that night.

It was certain.


Meanwhile, Jared was at home, huddled against the receiver, frantically dialing Amy's cell phone, which she had conveniently abandoned for the night. Redial. Redial.. Redial...

Nick and Amy were impatient lovers, anxious to pursue the demented lust of their mutual impulses. Evil urges of man and object.

At the expense of neglecting romance, chivalry, patience and anticipation, the two drunken bastions ascended the staircase and claimed dominance of an unattended bedroom. You know the rest, no need to puncture the unspoken temperance of ragdoll-raving sex.

Redial. Fuck it, I'll leave a message this time.

"Amy, hey, it's me. Just wanted to see how you've been and if you maybe wanted to meet up this weekend. Okay... So call me back and we will be together." His pathetic pleas, transmitted straight into the passenger-side ashtray.

After fucking in a stranger's bedroom, the newly enshrined dust leaders, curiously able-bodied and hormonally driven, exited their private abode.

"I need to tell Katie that we're leaving."

"Forget it. She's long gone. Took the same route as us."

O my, quite a party!

"I don't know. I really shouldn't be driving. Let's just stay here or something."

"Girl, if you got a car, I can drive. Trust me."

She tossed him the keys.

curtsey, blush

"Nicky, let's go to your house instead."

He took the wheel of her Toyota Supra, stickshift, hooptie, the like.

She suggested they both chew bubblegum to distill the alcohol vapors in their breath. 2 pink pieces, withdrawn, pulled from the pack.

Franz Ferdinand's first album was playing on the stereo, cranking shitty songs of finger fucking faggotry. Do me in the butt tonight, baby. All the liberated sexuality of European rock stars. God, this girl has terrible taste in music.

He floored the gas and rushed home. Along the way, Amy tried to spit her gum out the window, but the wind pushed her projectile back into the car, landing on the Franz case. A sticky sprawl of pink paste would remain affixed to the CD for the remainder of its lifetime. Who cares?

"Right this way, brethren."

Conveniently positioned beside the center crevice of the bridge stood two musicians. Their gleeful tune perplexed the nervous foreboding of the passerby pair. While Pat+Pat embodied the traits of narcissistic road warriors, the song they heard spoke of another, less-worrisome stylization. Why were they here, and what had they to offer? A selfless plea of faith? An ode to optimism? An act of generosity can startle even the most hardened individuals. The delightful pulse of their melody comforted the nerves of all listeners.

Patricia gleamed with joy, as the soft-spoken hymn washed over her. She found solace in the simplicity of a musician's life, all existence contributed to an eternal song of truth. Like a soothing birdsong greeting the morning, music allowed for a certain tranquility. A pause.

"Let us continue," Alto interrupted the moment. "They are expecting our arrival."

The characters kept walking, as the laden lullaby faded off into the distance.

"Truly a beautiful song," she continued. "How welcoming and friendly, that they choose to serenade us and all other strangers."

Alto was discouraged by her appreciation of these derelicts, and attempted to convince her otherwise.

"While some are humbled by their persistent discipline, others are bothered by the lack of hard work and struggle in their lives. Don't misinterpret my notions. They certainly earn my respect, only not my sympathy. To pursue a life of mystical ease is no accomplishment."

They walked, passing over yet another bridge, until finally, they reached the grand entrance. The castle doors.

## THE RAVING SLUT LUNATIC
Maddened upon awakening
She stammered
Wholesome
Innocuous
Her mind scrambled
"Delicate musings of a semi-audible storyline struggling to transmit, through countless filters and unorganized thoughts." This entire book is a daydream distraction, with segments of honesty seeping through.

They stood at the door, motionless. Before knocking, the travelers basked in amazement at the grandiose structure before them. Patricia took a deep breath and immediately started coughing.

Here we are again, standing shoulder-bound against a locked door, anticipating the release of hours upon minutes. Timely. Beyond are unknown riddles and questions, not provided.

"You like what you see so far?" Alto beamed slightly, a coy finger wag and a mischievous grin. He continued, "You're all having fun, giggling and gallivanting about, recklessly enthusiastic. I get it. But so far you have neglected to question the means of production. Or, should I say, the reasoning behind these structures. The strings holding up the entire charade. You are beneficiaries of both the great solitude *iquietness!* and the pendulum party participants. Conduct is served (overabundance) as you tour the lands effortlessly. Miracle. My fair foreigners, the royal treatment ends once we pass through these doors. You will no longer be able to chuckle at life's inadequacies, for you will understand their necessity and their function in maintaining a balance. We call this the status quo. The stragglers and the rich, get busy or get quick, fend for your own and workworkwork. You will witness, firsthand, the elbow roughage that keeps us tree-dwellers afloat. We're all happy on the inside, after all. I beg you to ponder the quandary: at the expense of _____? Whom? What social mechanism preserves our peaceful habit? Yes, we have a place to run to, a home of goodbye nightmares, of nomadic dignity. What allows this? Long live the theatre, built by nameless craftsmen. Long live our motionless artists, drunk off ritual and exclaimed sexuality. We are always there for you. I will always be there for you in times of need, trust me. Friendships thrive in debauched locales. Who rolls the dice? Inevitably, we succeed and become the quotient-bearers of value & sophistication; or else, we risk finding out the hard way that no one gets a free ride. Question life among the shadows. Go beyond! With triumph and diligence, we'll glide through our days, barely able to identify that sad sap tugging the rest of us along." He finished, paused and bowed his head. The deep silence of learning, of mind-blown wisdom, settled among the group.

"Well, thanks for the vigorous pep talk, officer. I sure can't wait to go inside." Patrick exuded a thinly-veiled, half-honest sarcasm.

"Ha! We shall see who can truly carry the weight of privilege."

Patricia had grown bored with Alto's borderline-political, semi-threatening and forcibly-provocative rant. Her gaze shifted toward the moat that flowed against the edge of the tower. A steady, easily swimmable, unthreatening stream. Currents pushing along with ease, a babbling brook of tranquility. The moat seemed to serve a purpose that was more aesthetic than protective. At the base of the castle, where the water met the wall, a small hut had been built. Only it was more akin to a nook. The perfect home of simplicity and guidance. A small resting place for a laborious creature of caretaking nursery rhymes.

From behind the windows she could sense the creature within, mulling about on scraped knees. A rare form, indispensible and shy. Essential to the group dynamic (i.e., maintaining the castle grounds) and fastening sparse details. A keeper of homes well-furnished and spotless. This miniscule lurker! Never says a word, is polite and calm. He does his job and never bothers a soul. The invisible, the wasted. Shadow object. Look at him! Careful to never make eye contact, slides by without touch. A smile to please the talkers, and to ease confrontation, ensuring all interaction is temporary.

Old man, underneath the tower, what is your purpose?

"Shall we?"

She couldn't shake her focus. What an odd being.

"Patricia, let us enter. They have unlatched the doors."

Alto nudged her, slightly. She quickly brushed aside her anxious thoughts and marched forth, venturing into the palace of grand enlightenment.

Upon access, they passed through a corridor wherein the pathway seemed to glide beneath their feet. A scrolling sidewalk scurrying across. To walk or not to walk, that is an option. Patrick and Alto stayed put, while

CoLaToLa skipped alongside the walkway, taking in observations of her surroundings. Paintings lined the walls, flickering magnetic suggestions of sinful servitude. She took notice of one particular display, which insinuated a gathering of ten strong, bare-boned thieves, performing ritualistic disembodiment for the amusement of thousands. Not quite her taste. She continued forward, while her two compatriots stood motionless and droll on the cycling passageway.

cough

certain disgust

mark your territory

The absolute, definitive, resolute visual representation that is needed to picture her is a pink cow backpack. Precisely, for the reader's sake, a plain white JanSport with cow spots splattered throughout, with pink marker. She wore this bag during the entirety of her middle school career. The year in question, for this particular tale, of course, is seventh grade. A year in the life of a girl with a pink cow backpack. A significant, formative and damned time; not only for her, but for a young boy, as well, since the intersecting of their lives brought down the courage of both parties in question. This was when they first met. Innocent. She offered a taste of darkness, of ruthlessness. Hair nearly black, straight, matted, disheveled, unkempt, rude, some strange thing with her gums. Her front teeth were, and still are (god forgive me if I change tense midway), adorned with an oddly distributed gum line. No matter. Freckles. Squinty. Short. Red sweater. Only child. Amy Carousel. I can't recall exactly how we met, but I remember eating lunch with her in seventh grade. We would sit near the girl's locker room and eat our meals together. Included in our little lunchtime group, for frame of reference, were a varied cross-section of our friends. For, you see, the lunch period during our seventh grade year was a peculiar instance, forcing compromise and dividing friends. The school we attended taught grades six through eight. To let all the students loose for one single lunch hour would yield chaotic and crowded results. The school was forced to divide the students' designated and mandated lunchtime into two separate occurrences. Grades six and eight were evenly split, maintaining the solidarity of the freshman and senior classes. However, caught in the middle of this dilemma were the seventh graders, ripped in half, torn apart and scattered. One half of the class would eat during the sixth grade lunch period, while the other half ate with the eighth graders, the following hour. This system was efficient and orderly for maintaining a functioning environment on campus, but left bonded groups of friends suddenly cast adrift from one another, missing out on inside jokes and wondrous memories. Nonetheless, this may be the fated decision that led us together. The systematic boardroom, PTA decisions that forever shift and change lives, forever. I liked her; that much I can remember. We'd eat and I would notice the sadness within her, the underlying desperation. Try as I might, I would fight her gloominess with humor and joyful perspectives. Seize the– oh, fuck it. Somehow I was enthralled by the sensuality in her suffering. She was sexy. I remember the first physical touch we shared: she licked the inside of my ear. Erotic. Chills down my spine and around my asshole, immediately. She was captivating. One day, she revealed a frightening character trait, a dark secret. Her youthful pouting had advanced to the stage of self-harm. She was taking out her frustrations in the poorest and most unloved of ways. To prove these claims, she pulled back the sleeve of her sweater to reveal cuts across the inside of her wrist. Oh no! Small dashes of red markings, some freshly scabbed, others already scarred. Amy, what the fuck? No no no, this can't be true. You are lying. Prove it! Now, maybe I was slightly aroused by the thought of her sitting alone in a dark bedroom, sobbing, empowered, with a sharpened edge, metal or glass, a strong, structured substance, slicing through the softness of her skin with ease, gliding through the wet fat that makes us human, tearing apart our material form. The mind has taken control. I want to watch you cut. Prove your worth. Prove you're worthless. Show me how much of a disgrace you are. Demonstrate the pain of your life, the mourning ritual of the everyday mundane. She stood up without hesitation, marched to the back of the gym and found a pile of light covers that had yet to be installed. These were sheets of textured plastic that could be secured in the ceiling of a classroom, to dampen and disperse the light emitted from the overhead fluorescent beams. Amy placed her shoe on the corner of one of these covers and pulled up on the remainder of the sheet, instantly snapping the compressed section of plastic. Underneath her foot, in an instant, she had created a makeshift jagged edge, the perfect tool for body mutilation. Jared watched as she dug the shard of broken plastic into her wrist. His only thought during this moment was how fragile and helpless she was, how troubled and endangered she seemed. Jared was astonished, transfixed and tantalized by her evident self-loathing. In love, admiration! His heart fluttered as her skin slowly split apart. The maroon blood of life oozed from her veins, dripping down the pale curve of her wrist. Had she abandoned all hope? What sort of perverted devastation could cause such a tender soul to retreat into complete spiritual darkness? While Jared stood lustfully intrigued by her sacrifice, Amy herself maintained a blank stare. Stunned, paralyzed. Her eyes never wavered from the fresh wound she created. "Does it hurt?" he queried, suddenly concerned with Amy's well-being. She glanced up and locked eyes with Jared, the vulnerable longing of despair smeared across her face. "No. It's a release. It frees me from the tension of existence. It gives me power and control over my feelings, a balancing effect. When life becomes overwhelming, I have the ability to drain myself of all woes and misery." Certainly this girl is in desperate need of salvation; and I, the cheerful bedfellow, am eager to restore her sense of pride and self-worth. He was smitten, asked her to marry him and she agreed. They even arranged to have a preliminary wedding on the soccer field. They designated a specific date and treated the proceedings with truthful and legitimate intention. She even requested that Jared wear a particular pair of jeans on their special day, insisting that they "make [his] ass look good." Oh great, what a hick she turned out to be. Just like her mama, the slut that cheated on her husband. Hand jobs for everyone!

Odes of entanglement to all who share a glance, strangers dreaming ONE

Q: "What is the purpose of language?"
A: "To communicate and express ideas and feelings."

> we speak, we understand
> we write, we understand

Grammar is a useful tool and a necessary guideline, but not a religion.

To a grammophile, witnessing improper punctuation is equivalent to denouncing G-d in the presence of a devout soul. The collapse of the universe's fragile structure is felt in both cases. Something as simple as a misplaced ladder\ could disrupt the ebb and flow of day to day to day to day.

Yet, we can still intertwine. If understood, proper grammar is a useless plea.

Consider this:
A busy intersection in a heavily populated city is the scene of several automobile accidents, within a relatively short span of time. Noticing this dangerous pattern, the city council unanimously agrees to install a traffic light, in order to control and regulate the flow of vehicles. The signal is set to change lights in 40-second intervals, ensuring an even and orderly

commute for all drivers on the road.  A month passes, and the council members rejoice in the fact that not a single accident has occurred since the implementation of the light.  RED GREEN RED GREEN.  It's a simple system and it works flawlessly, as long as all drivers follow the rules.  Within the context of this intersection being busy and crowded, the traffic laws generate a balance, an equal exchange of stop and go.  The rules provide adequate regulation and a systematic procedure to ensure safety and cohesion.  Without the light, drivers would crash into each other; yet with the light, they patiently take turns.  We can immediately observe the success of the traffic light.

However,

While heading home late at night, a driver stops at the intersection, as is now required.  While waiting for the light to change, the driver recognizes that no other cars are within view. Impatient and rational, the driver proceeds to pass through the red light, ignoring all governing functions.  The car makes it through without incident.  The driver is unscathed.  The key ramification in this matter, and the significant differential variable, is the context.  If the driver had waited for the light to turn green, what would this prove?  To sit motionless on an empty street, waiting for permission, would honor the sacred power of law.  The act of waiting reveals a belief that no mater the circumstance or context, rules must be followed.  What is achieved by requiring a car to remain idle amongst nothingness?  There is no equal exchange of traffic, nor dignity, in the act of observing frivolous laws with blind obedience.  As the driver runs the red light, society does not collapse.  A rule is broken, yet no one is harmed.  Again, the importance of this example is context.  During peak traffic hours, signals and stop signs are essential in maintaining a cohesive structure.  But, in the infinite potential of night, where traffic is practically non-existent, these rules have an adverse effect on drivers, limiting their travels, rather than enhancing them.

You choose.

Who is this little gnome man?  He lives so quietly among the ruckus of an enterprise.  A company man, of sorts, he never shifts his gaze until the boss is out of reach.

First thing she notices once they enter the royal boundary is this same old man, scurrying about, hurrying his hobbled hands.

"Who is that?" Patricia asked.

"Oh, that's Bijan, the billower of prophetic retentions, acclimating our correspondence with the outside world."

Patricia was dumbfounded.

"From a distance, I view this creature as a nuisance, a disruptive troll commandeering authority and stifling productivity."

"Aha!" Alto snapped.  "That is where you are wrong, for your observations are based on misleading and ill-informed evidence, supporting a false notion of this industry.  His contributions are essential and unwavering.  Irreplaceable etiquette in the hands of a gentleman.  I urge you, Patricia, not to neglect the efforts of a disciplined worker committed to the cause.  After all, who do you think brought you here?"

"Excuse me?  I take offense to your smug assumption, as I brought myself here.  Patrick and I ventured into this town on a whim, a chance fork-in-the-road shifted our alignment."

"Yes, of course.  We all reside here by our own accord.  Yet it was an alluring puff that drew you in.  An invitation of excess."

Patricia scoffed at the notion that perhaps her intentions were influenced by an outside source.

"I refuse to accept such illegitimate claims.  My actions were independently decided by Pat and I."

"Fair enough," Alto resigned.  "No one forced your arrival, but it would be a disservice to all the forgotten souls if you were to deny that your travels were pampered by the alluring plumes of green smoke billowing from the furnace."

"No..."

"And who would you guess is tending the flames?"

Patricia felt no need to verbalize her answer, as she knew all too well that Bijan was responsible for the smoke signals.

4 journeymen traversing the mountainside. The brotherhood, once again. Armed with a joint and a hacky sack, Eddie, Bernardo, Charlie and Jared made their way toward a sentimental destination of their youth. The day was warm, with the sun gently dangling in the sky above. A mood of mutual admiration permeated the cadence of their conversation. Altogether they spoke freely and lovingly of the trust enshrined among them. Loyal until the end, blood brothers. Their friendship was music, a complimentary rhythm of understanding in which each soul shared a unique contribution, all separate pieces of a full composition. Their destination was a hillside resting spot known as Earth, a majestic territory claimed as their own, with a swooping view of the town below. After taking a brief pause to bask in the vast glory of nature's offerings (G-d is often found while gazing into the infinite emptiness of a scenic view, which contains both the full abundance of life and the sparse openness of space), the boys got into the proper formation for a casual enactment of sport. The ball was kicked around with playful ease, bouncing between feet and knees, establishing a calming moment of focused teamwork in the midst of daily chaos. Eddie, eager to elevate, produced the bundled herbs from his satchel and sparked the fire of eternal truths, inhaling fumes of mental purification. He breathed deeply and passed the conduit to his fellow comrades, officially initiating the rotation. The delightful façade of intoxication washed the blanketed trills from their faces. Nothing remained except grins of careless wonder, a dance of innocence.

The laughter lingered, but Bernardo suddenly became silent, as if he had an urgent realization that he was afraid to express. Doubt swarmed the inner confines of his mind. Numerical reasoning was glitched and obscured. He thought, 'How can we continue to play and celebrate as friends, when days before I was informed of a terrible betrayal?'

Courageous secrecy of a cowardly act, Bernardo trembled to contain his newfound knowledge. The reflective force of the sacrament shattered the calm of the unknown. Right then and there he should have blurted out all his truth, the powerful facts he promised to contain. The dull guise of knowing, yet complying in a lie. The game continued and the brotherhood played on, as Bernardo checked out to swim in his inner monologue. 'How can they so easily laugh together after mangling the unspoken trust of friendship? I am emotionally sickened by this, and still I remain completely uninvolved.' This was his golden opportunity, his chance to reveal a disgusting fact, a tale of solemn treachery. He could have blurted out the secret, screamed, and let his words echo through the valley. But no, not at all. Instead he kept his mouth shut. 'It's not my place to step in, to become involved in this manly drama. Nah, I'll just keep to myself, dwell in my uncertainty and get high daily.' Aye! Now there's a prophetic solution. Stay doped up and shut up, removed from the action but still watching it all tumble before me. Good show, boys. Three cheers for giving in to our worst possible urges. Jared laughed, blissfully ignorant. 'How could I ruin such perfection?' Whereas Bernardo had the opportunity to terminate any and all false notions, he instead chose to bury it all deeper and deeper, worsening the impact of the inevitable reveal. Why, Bernardo? Why did you choose to play along in maintaining this lie? Every day you spend with Jared is another opportunity to share this evidence, yet you continually refuse, further perpetuating a despicable secret. How fucking pathetic, to consider yourself an honest, goodhearted man when you possess knowledge that would crush Jared, pulverize his soul, and you remain silent. You'll look him straight in the eye and speak of trivial nonsense, yet the one single profound earth-shattering revelation of enlightened truth, you decide to keep to yourself. This bit of awareness is discussed behind closed doors among all casual parties except the one person who deserves to know!  The only person who would be genuinely affected is kept in the dark. And your refusal to tell, your inaction, is only worsening the crime.  You have abandoned your service as a friend.  Oh well, let's just keep getting high, since this arid sense of intoxication is the bonding glue of false personas that keeps our kinship together, as it offers the illusion that all is well and makes it easier for all of us to keep our mouths shut.

Let us now enter the royal chambers, the discussion council room of the King and Queen. As they approached, a low rumble of anger seeped out from beneath the door. The cackling dispute of broken adults. A certain tone of yelling that transports you back to your 5-year-old self, huddled beneath the covers while mommy and daddy thrash about in the next room, cursing and pleading through the night while you're praying for peace, for silence. Trying to drown out the noise with reruns of <u>The Jeffersons</u> on Nick at Nite.

"Oh boy," Alto muttered, "they're at it again."

Pat and Pat stood still, unsure how to react, confused by the prospect of conflict within a land drenched in blissful ignorance. Alto was suddenly nervous. "Eh, maybe we can just pop in to say hello and be on our way. After all, they demand a personal meeting with all new residents, regardless of their duties. I see this instance as no exception. Come friends." He anxiously placed his hand upon the doorknob and opened slowly, clearing his throat to alert them of their presence. The room plunged into quiet reserve. Speechless.

"Pardon our interruption sire, madam, but we have 2 new visitors who wish to meet you. This is Patrick and Patricia."

"It is an honor to meet you," Patricia stated, a friendly gesture of appeasement.

"..."

Still not a word from the royalty. They stared blankly at the strange guests in their doorway, the King's eyes beaming a certain interrupted terror.

Alto hesitated. "Well then, we should be–"

Suddenly, the King snarled a response, his voice booming throughout the hall. "Let them stay!" The power of his voice injected a paralyzing shockwave to all within earshot. His words carried a physical, tangible force that stunned the onlookers.

Patricia spoke up. "Your Majesty, we have no intention to distract from your business practices. We mean only to introduce ourselves and to offer our thanks for providing such a lush landscape of serenity. There is a certain comfort in this land, an atmosphere that celebrates originality and encourages outcasts to be themselves and to cherish their differences. I, for one, have never felt so spiritually relieved. My soul is healed of all sadness and regret. Sir, I thank you."

"Well, how delightful. How truly moving and resounding are your pleas," the King started. "Allow me to infer from your statements that you have obtained a certain resealed bond of shattered innocence. You are reawakened by the hedonism of this hilled terrain. Our abundance of resources offer partially glorified sentiments of power without practice, the withheld might of the masses. Yes, we are fortunate to reside among purified riches. But you see, through the eyes of the elite, this only provokes conquest and greed. Aye, I seem to be getting ahead of myself. Please excuse yourself, Alto, as you are no longer needed. I will join my new friends in a luncheon of sorts. Patrick and Patricia, perhaps once I explain to you the ramifications of our current dispute, your foreign mindset can provide a fresh perspective on the matter."

Alto hurriedly shuffled out of the room while the Pats stepped closer to the King.

"Forgive my initial outburst. Let us start anew."

"Certainly, Your Majesty."

"Surrender such markings. We will converse as friends, as equals. We have no hierarchical structure here. The crown is worn by all citizens. Address me by my proper name, in the absence of eloquence." The King reached out his hand. "I was birthed by my mother and given the name Deryk. Pleased to meet you. My wife, sobbing in the corner, is Kelly. We wish to thank you for your visit. Welcome."

"How truly kind of you, Deryk. I must admit, I was terribly frightened when we first met."

"Nah, I beg you forgive my chaotic temper. I mean no harm."

Patricia smiled.

"Well then, let us partake in the sharing of the holy sacrament and then we shall commence our business."

Deryk led them into a backroom closet adorned with tapestries and the calming ambiance of scented candles.

"Have a seat. Make yourselves comfortable."

The floor was littered with various pillows and blankets, offering a makeshift couch for visitors to recline on.

"Will Kelly be joining us?" Patricia asked.

Deryk laughed.

"No. She's an artist, spends days on end crying in the corner. She'll get up when she's ready. No use in forcing the creative process, right?"

"I guess so. Are you sure she's okay?"

"Of course. She finds inspiration in her selfish suffering. Misery is the nourishment of creation."

Confused, Patricia decided to cease any further questioning regarding the emotional state of Deryk's sorrowful wife.

The peace pipe was lit and the pungent aroma of forgiveness wafted through the air. The smoke itself was visually alluring, as it momentarily lingered, encased in beams of sunlight, dancing and swirling about in a sudden glimpse of wonder.

After several rotations and brief episodes of inane laughter, Deryk mustered the confidence to offer his stance on the pressing political matters affecting The Land of Forgotten Souls.

"As you can tell, we enjoy our lives off-the-grid from conventional society. We are a commune of outsiders, hiding from the so-called 'real world.' Well, my friends, I insist that you consider the true reality of this life, this momentary existence we are all offered, and tell me which world you prefer. We have stumbled upon a division in perspective, a mental rift between the strict confines of modern society and the peaceful freedom that nature provides. All those who congregate here, by choice or necessity, are hereby making a statement. We are denouncing government and abandoning the tired rules of tradition, which take for granted the complexities of man. We are not mindless worker bees, slaving away for the cause of greed and power. We are passionate souls, flawed and brave, with unique stories and indivisible life experiences. We have broken free from the shackles of corruption and forged our own little utopia in the depths of the forest, out of reach from the empire's grasp."

"I commend your efforts, and the corresponding mantra of this area. I have observed nothing less than a flourishing culture during my stay. It has been truly rewarding."

"I'm glad you understand. You see, to most we are viewed as a gang of careless fools, squandering all potential in favor of a life of exile. We are the wasted, giving up on life. This is absolutely not true; yet we remain unappreciated."

"But this is the enduring struggle of your life, a disagreement that will extend indefinitely. I ask you, in this particular instance, what is the recent development that has troubled you so?"

"Fair enough, my boy. I seem to have rambled. However, my only aim was to offer the proper context of our dispute.

"A strong advantage of living in harmony with the natural world, rather than seeking to dominate it, is how this lifestyle allows our resources to flourish. This area is home to the mighty Six Rivers of the North, one of G-d's finest gifts to mankind, an interconnected stream of water pulsating throughout the entire region. It offers water to drink and fish to eat, providing sustenance to us all. For decades we have enjoyed the bounty of these waters, undisturbed. That is, until recently, when our town crier reported that several gentlemen dressed in suit and tie (full enemy regalia) were seen surveying the waters. This caused great concern, as we were certain that their intentions were of ill repute."

"I don't get it," Patricia queried. "What is the significance of your water?"

Deryk scoffed at her lack of knowledge.

"Well, you mean besides being the most precious and valuable resource on the planet? Allow me to offer a brief history lesson.

"Up until the development of large city dwellings and metropolitan areas, tribes and villages would congregate and nestle themselves alongside lakes and rivers, always remaining within reach of freshwater reserves. This is how humans have lived since the dawn of time, thoughtfully navigating our lives in balance with our surroundings. It's a logical concept that, given our essential need to consume water, we should live in areas where water is bountiful and readily available. Would you agree?"

"Sure."

"A recent advent of our modern culture is the concept that we needn't reside in accordance with such limited options, as we can rely on irrigation systems of pipes and waterways to divert our water away from its natural habitat and send it through artificially-controlled canals. Eerie indeed. And herein lies the dispute. The nearby town of South Forts has taken to formulating a plan to essentially steal our water. They wish to bleed our rivers dry in order to nourish their capitalist agenda."

"So the suits that you saw recently..."

"They were plotting, man. They're plotting against us. They'll use whatever bureaucratic nonsense to get their way, pumping the life force out of this area to fund their shallow, greed-infested existence."

"How can you stop them? This is an outrage. This shouldn't be allowed!"

"My friends, all citizens are in agreement that this shall not happen. We are willing to do whatever it takes to prevent the decimation of our glorious landscape.

"We are a peaceful people (kindhearted and calm, drug addled and reticent), but when threatened by an outside force we are more than ready to take arms against our oppressors and wage war against them, for the cause of maintaining that which is sacred. By any means necessary, we will dispose of and tarnish the corrupted hearts of our enemies."

Patricia was suddenly terrified. The enemy territory he spoke of was her own hometown. Her parents, her family and her friends were seen as evil through the eyes of the King. She felt a romantic longing for the days of ease spent long ago within the realm of South Forts. After all, it was the very land in which she spent endless summers of adolescent innocence, carefree in the comfort of a nurturing family, enthralled in the eternal celebration of friendship.

Why had she left? So soon, without any chance of reconciliation, she fled. Surely any conflicts would be easier to resolve within the territory in which they arose. Disappeared, instead.

She retreated to an escapist's paradise, a seemingly neutralized area priding itself on local agriculture and close-knit communal bonds. Yet buried beneath the dense shrubbery, under the influence of tranquil seedlings, lay the cruel resolutions and harsh judgments of a sinister counterculture.

"Are you troubled, o mighty King? Your morals askew? What is the disturbance in your reasoning that has forced you to march to the front lines, swords drawn, waving a flag emblazoned with a peace sign?"

"Sweet Patricia, the tender sincerity you display only heightens your adorable persona. I hereby elect you to be the sacrificial lamb of our conquest.

"The Land of Forgotten Souls is a preservation society, a refuge camp for those fed up with the corruption and competitive struggles of this world. We have renounced our citizenship, and all we ask for in return is to be left alone. Let us live within our means, in this small patch of territory. Our battle is a defensive one; to preserve the purity we have sacrificed our lives to attain. South Forts is bringing the fight to us, and it is our obligation to protect what is rightfully ours."

Patrick arose, eager and proud.

"I will stand beside you during this trying ordeal."

"That's the spirit, pup! We shall fit you for proper armor and wardrobe once the surge grows closer. Until then, I invite you both to reside in the visitors' chambers here in the grand estate. It has been a definite pleasure becoming properly acquainted with you two, and I strongly suggest you remain in close quarters, as we can offer adequate protection from foreign influence.

"Please excuse me, as I must now meet with my fellow administrators to formulate a defensive strategy. Farwell, my new friends. Kelly will show you to the residencies once you are ready."

And with that brief conversation, the strongest semblance of a plot thus far in the story has formed.


Jared, our reluctant hero, was coping with Amy's recent departure as appropriately as any abandoned infant would, with overwhelming pathos and shame. Aside from weeping incessantly, he had developed a new hobby: while listening to songs of mourning in his room, he would repeatedly punch the display case of his stereo until the plastic cracked and his knuckles bled. It was cathartic, a release of anguish while she was out with her latest fling.

Nonetheless, he would still call her, unremittingly, just to hear her voice. But, as expected, she would never answer and he would be left listening to her voicemail greeting; which, for reasons unknown, was a recorded segment from Robin Williams's latest stand-up special. It was a convenient selection, since Jared would only call when he felt utterly alone and helpless.  Rather than reaffirming his woes by hearing Amy's gentle, quivering lips verbalizing her absence, he was instead presented with the genius ramblings of Mr. Williams.  Now, I cannot recall the exact quote; however, the significance was the revelation it offered, a reminder to Jared that all of life's chaos has the potential to be contained, and thereby transformed, into brilliance.  This is demonstrated by Robin Williams not only during his exhaustively-detailed stand-up performances, but also his substantial work as an actor, both comedic and dramatic.  I need not provide any more evidence, nor formulate a proper assumption, to conclude that Robin Williams is the great American artist.

And just as Jared was preparing to watch <u>Hook</u> for the umpteenth time, his phone rang.  After countless missed calls, Amy suddenly mustered the courtesy to return the correspondence.

"Hello?"

"Hi Jared."

Cheerful.  She must be fucking someone.

"Holy shit!  How are you?"

"I'm doing okay.  Sorry I missed your call(s)."

"Oh… yeah, don't worry about it.  So, um, how was that party the other night?  I haven't heard from you since."

"It was fun."

He was informed of Nick, the new character, during a casual, yet restrained conversation, in which she confessed to sleeping over at his house, without clarification of their having copulated.  Though it was safe to assume that they did in fact have sex, for the sake of his own sanity he assumed she was pure until proven filthy.

"So, listen, I was wondering if you could help me out with something.  My dad just gave me his old guitar and I'm almost positive it hasn't been tuned since the sixties."

"That's awesome.  Is it a nice one?"

"I guess so.  It's an acoustic guitar, that's about all I know.  Do you think you could possibly tune it for me?"

"Ha!  Yeah, I would love to help you out."

Here she comes, crawling back to me under the guise of an unnecessary excuse.

"Great. Is it cool with you if I come by?"

This is all happening so suddenly.

"Now?"

"Yea."

I am overjoyed. My persistence has finally paid off.

"Of course. See you soon, Amy."

"Bye."

That dreaded cunt. I can't wait to see her.

Lo and behold, she arrived no less than half an hour later, guitar in tow. Jared tuned it with the help of his handy electronic tuner. Even though he had been playing guitar for almost five years, he still couldn't tune by ear. Amy watched excitedly as he plucked the strings and twisted the pegs.

What is she doing here? There is still a chance for us. I know it. We've only been apart for a couple months and she's already back at my house. Are we going to fuck? Is that why she's here? It must be.

"There you go."

He handed her the guitar.

"Thanks, Jared. I know this was a quick visit, but I have to go now."

"What? You just got here."

"I know. I'm sorry, I just really needed your help with this. But I have to leave. "

"Oh well, it's okay. I'm still glad I got to see you, even if it was only for a brief moment."

She got up to leave.

"Well, I'll see you soon."

"Let me at least walk you to your car."

"Sure."

He followed behind, shrugged shoulders, hands in pockets. Knowing he probably wouldn't see Amy again for a while, he seized the opportunity to speak with her face to face.

"Can I ask you a favor?"

"Um, okay."

"This new guy you're seeing, please don't fuck him."

"What?"

"It's just that I believe we will one day be together again. But if you sleep with someone else, you'll get all stretched out and then my penis will be too small for you."

"Oh my god, you're rude! Could you be anymore of an asshole?"

"I'm serious. I know I'm not that big, and once you start sleeping with other guys, you'll never want to return to me."

"And what makes you think I haven't already slept with Nick?"

silence

"I already told you I slept over at his house."

"Yea, but that's because you were drunk, so he gave you a place to sleep it off."

"Are you serious? I'm not 12 years old, Jared. Yes we had sex. What did you think I meant?"

Jared reacted the only way he knew how. Suitable for the situation, he punched himself in the face, repeatedly. A full-blown, one-man fistfight. He wailed away, battling against his own suppressed emotions. How could Amy deliver this heartbreaking information with such playful ease? She certainly neglected the significance of her statement. Every impact of fist against face transported him beyond words, into the realm of physical sensations and mind-quieting pain.

"What the fuck are you doing? Stop!"

Amy grabbed his arms, restraining any further inflictions. "Stop it! You are crazy."

"Amy, I need you!"

"Oh god, I need to leave. This was a bad idea. Maybe we shouldn't hang out together anymore."

She got in her car. Luckily for Jared, the window was rolled down.

"You can't do this to me, Amy. This isn't fair. I still love you and you're hurting me."

"Fuck you! Fuck you! You think you're mortally suffering? Really? You think there's such an overwhelming abundance of sadness in your life?  Well, consider this: once we're done here with this bitter, anger-fueled conversation, you at least get to go back inside to your happy little family, where everyone's cheery and in love.  But for me, instead, for my rotten home life, I am blessed with a coke-addicted father and a mom who cheats on him by fucking some other guy in the bushes while he's at work.  I have to lock myself in my room, listening to him scream at her and call her a bitch.  And you want me to pity you?  To apologize?  Fuck you, Jared.  Stop telling me you're suffering."

She drove off.  He wasn't about to try and stop her.  He went inside and had dinner with his parents and his younger sister.  Grilled chicken, Caesar salad, watermelon and steamed rice, with iced tea to drink and an ice cream sandwich for dessert.  It was delicious.

## The friendship disguise
A wavering, transitory dance,
playing hopscotch against the soul.
Fools conspiring to conceal a secret,
rather,
a suppression of their guilt.
The hidden truth, known to all.
Sneaky scumbag actions,
and promises withheld.
Time will overturn all lies,
revealing the universal cadence of who we are.
The inevitable manifestation is imminent.


Patrick and Patricia were thrust into the desolate caverns of the palatial estate, dungeonesque and bleak.

"Here you shall rest, as the eve of battle approaches," a guard called out.

Patrick unleashed an empowered howl.  He was ecstatic, completely riled up and eager to fight.  The war hound within had awakened, unchained and dangerous.

"I can't believe you're buying into this," Patricia said quietly, adrift in contemplation. "Just yesterday you and I were enthralled with the gentle mantra of this land and it's commitment to practicing peaceful resistance. All of a sudden you're gung ho, ready to go. Fight! Fight! Fight! It's pathetic."

"Don't you get it? This dispute is in defense of everything The Land of Forgotten Souls stands for. If we remain passive and idle, we are destined to vanish. Our actions are that of resistance. We have been shoved, so now we shall push back."

"Listen to you, Patrick, speaking as an honorary member, using *our* and *we* to discuss such matters. I can't comprehend your flailing logic. How easily you fall for the agreed-upon notions of the majority."

"Did you not hear what the King told us? Why else would those inspectors be testing the waters, huddled beside the river like the thieving bastards they are? They're only looking out for themselves. That's how these people operate. They pursue only that which offers immediate, material benefits."

"I think you're wrong. I think the entire concept of this strife is a direct contradiction of everything this land represents. So what if they take the water? Can't we share our resources with those who reside in a drier, less-nourished climate? I mean, it's not like these men are using the water just for themselves. It's for the entire region. Why aren't we cooperating with them? I would be more than pleased to provide them with essential resources. Why do we deserve what they don't have?"

A steel gate slammed shut, imprisoning the Pats in the dank corridor. Patricia became worried, while Patrick sat, unfazed. She peered through the rigid beams.

"Excuse me? Hello!"

A stoic guard appeared, adorned in knighthood regalia.

"We were told to keep an eye on you."

He relayed his assigned objective and vanished into the mazelike halls of the castle.

"Can you believe this?" she asked Pat.

"I can't believe what a dreadful bore you've become. Consider your judgmental words and mind our location. You're voice is reverberating down the hall as you preach in favor of the enemy. Aside from the material distribution that this battle is being fought for, we are also upholding a principle."

"And what moral code is that? The admittance that The Land of Forgotten Souls is rooted in anger and passive hostility?"

"The belief that within a nation conceived and sustained by corruption and greed, a miniscule town of pure-hearted love and cultural advancement deserves to proliferate, undisturbed by the very swindlers that we moved here to avoid."

"But we are not an island removed from such policies. This is a town contained within that very nation you speak of. Yes, we are hidden behind curtains and buried in a dense fog; however, we still exist as part of the greater whole. To deny these people a valuable resource is criminal. They are still our fellow citizens. Look around. Six Rivers is an abundant quantity of water for our small population. Elsewhere, people are thirsty and parched. To fight against this notion is to deny their right to exist. It is a denial of the soul of man. So go ahead, chant 'Glory!' on your homemade rickshaws and trample the hearts of your neighbors. I, for one, stand against you."

An uneasy tension lingered long after Patrick and Patricia finished speaking. The argument ceased to continue, as both parties were favoring opposable viewpoints with no middle ground whatsoever. The unlikely partnership had reached an impenetrable stalemate. Only the divisive power of political debate could disrupt their mutual bond of shared experience. Their once empathetic conversations had denigrated to the level of a sharp-tongued sparring match. With no escape route, they remained trapped in the undercurrent until further notice.

This was certain to be a transformative summer. The winds of change were approaching with sudden urgency. Jared and Amy had parted ways, at least temporarily, and the horizon appeared cleansed with renewal. That is, until Amy decided to intervene once again. She was clever with excuses, always reuniting the two for a specific task. Whether she was hungry or just desperate, she always had a reason to see Jared again. Her newly-obtained guitar was no exception.

In the interim period since their bitter exchange, Jared had taken to reorganizing his life, adorning his days against a backdrop of all things Amy. He had succumbed to the role of a predatory stalker, seeking to maintain a sense of close contact at any cost. One night in particular, he thought it wise to neglect all implications of ignored telecommunications and approach her in person. The layout of her parents' house (only now it was simply deemed her mother's house, as her father had since moved into an apartment on the opposite side of town) was situated in such a way that Amy's bedroom window could be accessed without disrupting the other occupants, which at this point in time included:

-Amy's mother, who radiated an overjoyed sense of relief after the divorce. The kind of happiness attained only when one is no longer carrying the weight of secrets untold. It is, after all, quite difficult to maintain a lie for an extended period of time. In a way, the divorce cleared her conscience of all guilt and hushed concealments. She was gracefully entering a new chapter in her life. Way to go mama!

-Maestro Mitchell, the body snatcher, the new houseguest, and soon to be elected as Amy's new stepfather. The shameless homewrecker himself who single handedly tore the family apart by plunging away at

Amy's mother in the backyard while daddy was at work. He moved in immediately after her father left, literally a day or two after he was gone. Clearly there was no time to waste in rebuilding the perfect family. Jared had met the guy on several occasions already. He was good humored, without a hint of remorse, and uncomfortably funny, given the circumstance. Whenever Jared would visit, Mitch would greet him at the door, arm extended, pointed hand, the invitation for a handshake. Not wanting to impose any negative feelings, Jared would politely comply and reach out, seeking to complete the gesture. EVERY SINGLE TIME, without fail, Mitch would retract his arm at the very last moment and instead slick back his hair, giggling mischievously, leaving Jared's hand dangling, empty between them. Goddamnit. Was this supposed to be a symbol of male camaraderie? The jovial bond of practical jokes and man-on-man embarrassment? Perhaps it was to ease the enmity he himself helped to create, preserving the laughter by ignoring the heartache. Through Jared's eyes, through my eyes too, it was a defining trait of the evil this man harnessed, as he found it necessary to make a fool out of me whenever I was in his presence, displacing the power dynamic as soon as I walked in the door. Mitch, you sonovabitch, I knew you'd eventually weasel your way into this story.

-Grandpa, a dusty old man, quiet and unresponsive. He's enduring the last throes of life, and his need for supervised care afforded him the luxury of moving into the home of his daughter and granddaughter. He could be found either in front of the television set or in the guest room he occupied directly adjacent to Amy's bedroom. His dwindling health allowed him to be present during the tumultuous transition that resulted from the divorce.

Luckily, Amy's bedroom window was positioned toward the front lawn, allowing Jared to clamber through during the evening hours without having to maneuver throughout the entire house. There was a certain charm of adolescent romance in climbing through her window late at night, equipped with condoms and weed, the proper ingredients for creating a timeless memory.

O how fondly I recall such a time,
that years later
amidst an open world of endless opportunity,
I instead find myself reminiscing,
yearning for the innocence in her breath
that has long since perished.
But still I dream of what remains out of reach.
Today I settle for the next best thing.
To recreate that cherished time,
through endless verse
and irregular rhyme.
So long as her memory stirs in my heart,
the story shall continue;
until,
in writing,
I have flushed out every minute we ever spent together.

And all because of the sweet, serene thought
of approaching her window.

Yet at this point in the retelling, during a brief hiatus of their relationship in which Amy was pursuing a boy named Nick, Jared, after failing to establish contact, decided one night to show up at her house unannounced, without warning or approval. He gently tapped on the window, startling Amy.

"Jared, go the fuck away. Are you crazy? Leave me alone. You scared me."

It didn't go over well. But if Amy refused to answer her phone, Jared had no other option than to become an intrusive pest.

A certain disease infects the mind of a young man when he finds himself cast aside in favor of a more distinguished and appealing taste. It is a peculiar rage, unmatched in a computational sense, with no rationale or systematic thought process involved; rather, it is of pure emotional malaise, the brutal and the raw. Caught between his desperate hope of reconciliation and a destructive desire to eliminate all potential threats, Jared weighed his options and assumed the role of a predatory chancellor. To preserve his relationship with Amy would require eliminating all deflectors, which consisted of the army of men marching toward her door, cock gripped and ready, a trail of cum mapping their progression. Snails to her lust.

The primary enemy was Nick, her newest penetrator. If any progress was to be made, Jared needed to set up an encampment within the vicinity of Amy's house and wait for their arrival. A sneak attack. It was the perfect plan, pathetic and obtrusive in every aspect. Jared sat crouched in a nearby garden, anticipating their return. Any minute now...

For the next several hours, he patiently perched in her mother's meticulously trimmed and maintained garden. Waiting, with no clue as to what action would be taken upon their arrival. Nevertheless, it seemed appropriate. This was Jared's Kennedy assassination, and he was the illustrious Oswald, grinning eagerly in the foreboding hope of catching a glimpse of his dear leader. Time slowed to an endless crawl as he anxiously monitored the approaching headlights of every car that wasn't hers. Beacons of doubt on the horizon.

Sadly, this proved to be a wasted evening. For all the hours he spent hiding in the bushes, she never came home and he decided to abandon the scheme. This was for the best anyways, as he hadn't anticipated what to do once he saw them; and surely seeing Amy wrapped in the arms of a new gentleman would only rip his heart apart, beyond its already fragile state.

The proper alternative (more precisely, a preferable and exceedingly beneficial plan, which Jared neglected to implement until all hope was vanquished) was to call upon the compassionate charms of his friends. The brotherhood was

summoned and the remainder of the night was spent casting
healing spells of intoxicating elegance in the good company of a
few trustworthy buddies.

Patrick laughed, not an amused lackluster chuckle of
casual joy, but a hearty, full-bodied growl rumbling outward
from the bottomless depths of his gut. There was no sudden
motive or cause for his ebullition, as during the past twenty
or so minutes, neither a single word nor even a glance was
exchanged; nothing but the cold, uncomfortable silence that
hesitates between two stubborn beings heavily involved in
the solitary restraints of mental processing.
"It takes a great deal of effort to laugh. In fact, I'm
nearly certain that you must be forcing it. A naturally
occurring laugh would have been more subdued."
"Believe me, there are plenty of amusing factors
regarding our situation."
"Is that so? Then please share your giggle-inducing
anecdotes with me."
"Well, I've been thinking about our initial meeting
and the mutating status of our partnership. When our
paths first crossed, you were the runaway princess, a girl
blessed with all the comforts and privileges one could ever
dream of. Yet you abandoned that life of ease in favor of a
more meaningful struggle. To say the least, it was an
admirable feat. Forsaking a sheltered and coddled
existence, and truly roughing it, calling out to G-d for truth.
There is a peculiar irony in seeing you here now, locked in
the dungeon of a kingdom similar to your own. It's worth
laughing about, my dear."

A leisurely stroll quickly descends into the maddening
urgency of a hunt. Jared left his house with the intention of
enjoying the calm, introspective guidance of a solo hike. He
strapped on a pair of trail boots and loaded his backpack with
water, granola bars, an apple and a hushed pinch of his precious
ganja (with the appropriate accessories, of course), and proceeded

to rush out the door. He scaled the hillsides that surrounded his neighborhood, digging his feet into the muddy swamps and scouring the bristled landscape, which offered an alternative perspective of rugged imperfection against the manmade elegance of suburbia. With a song in his mind, "Pictures of You" by The Cure, he continued across the skeptical terrain, careless and kind, as the gentle balance of the wind carried him onward.

He approached a stone fastened high atop the mountain and decided to take rest, situating his posture in alignment with the slight incline of the rock, to ensure a comfortable relaxation spot, while also obtaining a gorgeous view of the open-air wilderness around him. He crossed his legs, Indian style, and removed the pipe from his satchel. After several generous puffs and the calming chill from the onset of effect that arrives soon thereafter, he let his mind wander about the curious happenings of a particular moment in the life of a particular individual. Himself, included.

He gazed off into the surrounding expanse and wondered if the entire universe was contained within the surrounding bubble of the valley's perimeter edge, a cutoff point for all known exploratory land. At least, that's how he saw it; for Jared wasn't the least bit concerned with anything but the immediate drama and interwoven love triangles of his hometown. The rest of the world might as well cease to exist, as it offered neither comfort nor comprehension for the chaotic confusion that Jared festered with daily. He remained entrenched in the common plight of every teenage boy: selfish suffering of the ego and unresolved woes. He took a deep breath to let his troubled thoughts settle.

In the distance he noticed a jumble of white feathers aimlessly fluttering about, and quickly discerned that a chicken must have escaped from a nearby coup. Without offering much consideration or empathy for the poor beast's misfortune, Jared watched, amused. This lowly chicken radiated a confusion of direction and lack of purpose. Separated from his farmhand's grasp and the camaraderie of fellow chicks, his identity was forgotten. A strength that reaches beyond the individual. The power of a team is achieved when each member is playing a separate role for the cause of a greater triumph. There was absolutely no denying that Jared was guilty of sharing a similar weakness. In the company of his friends, he was fearless and loud; yet once alone, he quickly retreated into his shell, quiet. He was only brave with his friends nearby, synonymous to the bond of Puff and young Jackie Paper.

The ballad "Puff the Magic Dragon" is arguably one of the most devastatingly honest songs in the Western canon concerning the loss of childhood innocence. Particularly, the observation of Puff's loss of courage and his subsequent decision to retire his powerful roar directly demonstrates the sadness of growing old, of abandoning your supportive friends, and in turn, the powers they provided. The countless adventures they shared (frolicking and traveling) were nothing short of magical, a prime example of the intuitive creativity that spurs from two misshapen minds joining together.

A partnership provides the necessary collaboration of pushing, provoking and urging each other to be great, fueling the fire that burns within. Never settle for anything less than absolute brilliance, regardless of the difficulty. It is the struggle of hard work, performed outside of one's comfort zone, that yields a fulfilling payoff.

Let us consider the alternative. The solitary life, lived quietly alone. This is an easily obtainable lifestyle. In modern Babylon we can effortlessly sit back and let the world dance for us, soaking up the joyous existence of being a permanent spectator. Reading books and watching theatre, a continual input of art and culture, vacuuming up all the sacred creations of the world, with nothing to offer or contribute in return. Sure, we can be judgmental and critical, spewing lofty opinions of self-satisfied rage; but this is nothing more than a response, a reaction instead of a creation. This isolated, cynical lifestyle is the direct personality mutation that results from forgotten partnerships. One cannot survive purely on their own virtue, as it is the positive influence and helpful suggestions of others that truly shape our character.

In Puff's peculiar case, his partner in crime, Jackie Paper, is responsible for the demise of their relationship. Puff did not succumb to any selfish temptations, he was merely abandoned and unable to carry on by himself. We, the listener, are left to assume that Jackie Paper was unable to maintain such a bond, and neglected the significance of their pairing. This course of events also correlates to the plight of Peter Pan, as evidenced by Robin Williams's grim portrayal of the shattered dreamer in <u>Hook</u>. Rather than celebrating the playful adventures of the traditionally-referenced story, we are presented with a harrowing alternative: the Peter Pan that turned his back on his friends and forgot his own ethical mantra. He is the musician that forgot how to play his instrument, the out-of-shape athlete, the stiff-limbed dancer, or the forlorn friend who stays home on the weekends, once considered the life of the party, now an introverted recluse. So uncertain is the effect of time.

Whereas "Puff the Magic Dragon" chronicles the crumbling disintegration of imagination and merriment, <u>Hook</u> presents a startling rejuvenation of the human spirit. With the Lost Boys and their compassionate assistance, Peter Pan rediscovers himself and his triumphant abilities. The prospect that his peers believed in him instilled the confidence and courage he needed to soar once again. Peter resumed his position as the guiding light for Neverland. He can fly, he can fly, you can fly.

So what can we conclude from these observations? What meaningful life lesson, adaptable to all individuals, can we discern through over-analyzation? If I never finish this story, if I'm killed on my drive home today and a proper ending is never written, allow me to leave you, the reader, with this: "Puff the Magic Dragon" and Spielberg's <u>Hook</u> share what I believe to be the single greatest human truth. The fucking meaning of life, if there is one, is revealed in both stories. The power of friendship! I know, I know, maybe it sounds too basic. Maybe you've heard it all before. But believe me, it is a truth of immovable certainty. Friends will make you stronger. They will force you to reach your full potential.

However, throughout our lifetime, our relationships are often challenged and damaged. More often than not, a girl is involved. A cock-sharing whore who decides it's a reasonable idea to sleep with your best friend. Yea, that'll sure tarnish a close brotherly connection. Yet we all possess the ability to forgive, to grant empathetic understanding of our eternally flawed nature. Mistake after mistake, backstabbing insults and heartbreaking betrayals will test the strength of our bonds. To forgive is to reaffirm the importance of friendship and the meaningful significance of the connection. So there you have it: Friendship and Forgiveness, the themes I believe.

We seem to have meandered, ever so suddenly, off the beaten path. The irony of the entire situation didn't fail to amuse Jared, as he was well aware of the humility and desperation underpinning his thought process. His vow of self-sufficient independence had gone haywire, fragmenting into a status of self-serving ineptitude. The smoking, previously a cherished group ritual, was now being habitually practiced as a lonesome means to an end. If plans were cancelled for any given day, Jared could simply engulf himself in a blaze of glory and allow the residual confusion to whisk away his boredom. Today was no exception, as he meditated on the sheer vastness of his surrounding world, eventually narrowing his perceptions with pinpoint precision, surrendering excellence and gratitude, and instead setting his sights on a runaway chicken. This wasn't a sacrifice or a loss of will; rather, it was the right thing to do at the perfect moment in time. Symbolically, Jared saw all his faults and weaknesses represented in this aimless bird. He could never survive on his own, never be his own man. He was always relying on the opinions and suggestions of others. The freedom to follow his heart, to carve his own path through life, always ended in vomit and bloodshed. To console his desperate inklings, Jared reasoned that all animals exist as social beings, and our need for connection, our desire to belong to a group, is inherently natural. No sense in feeling shame or weakness over a bunch of primal instincts. Yet somehow, seeing this chicken prance around without any semblance of determination or goal-oriented pursuits, this pathetic sight, poked straight through his comforted reasoning and tore a fucking hole in Jared's sad-man acceptance. This godforsaken clucker reflected all the inadequacies he tried to avoid. Yes, we are communal creatures with a need for social outreach, yes we gain strength from group collaboration, yes there is not a single I in team; but given this consequence, all individuals must cultivate a unique and differential strength. What do you bring to the table? What is your contribution to the group dynamic? This is the determination of value in a species, the rare combination of differences that congeal into a unified whole. He was fed up, exhausted by the emphasis on victimization that predominated his trail of thought. To erase such notions, and to purify his narcissistic self-loathing, Jared concluded that the only feasible option was to destroy that which reminded him of his own inadequacies. To remove his own shattered sense of self, he must ravage the foul beast that mocked his worth. He stood up, arose, and rushed toward the insolent chicken. His feet carried the rage of a challenger, violent and misused. Jared charged. The bird, sensing a dangerous oncoming presence, attempted to flee the scene.

Unsuccessful.

Jared viciously grabbed the runaway bird by the legs, secured a firm grip and carried it home. The return journey was a slow, contemplative stroll, his mind calm and certain while he struggled to contain the chicken's buckling panic. His fingers trembled with firm restraint as he smirked ever so subtly. Maniac! Upon arriving home, Jared entered through the side garage door. His father's workbench was cleared of all tools and paraphernalia except for two scrupulously positioned clamps and a freshly sharpened handsaw. The layout was beckoning to Jared. A use most unnatural, a practice beyond repentance. The light from an overhead lamp illuminated the table in a descending triangular beam. Jared unhinged the clamps and forcefully fastened the chicken's legs into place. He reached for the saw, and, in preparing to desecrate the beast, mere moments before tearing it apart, he paused and stared deep into the eyes of the poor, helpless animal, suddenly realizing the dwindling fate of all G-d's creatures. We are all forced to endure the same untimely repose of death's ultimate sleep, the infinite dream-state that borders our biological life. Be it the mangled machinery of a car crash, the infectious diseases of old age, or the pathological incisions of adolescent angst, skewed into violent outbursts, we all shall face our own demise. Hopefully (to instill a sense of hope in our otherwise hopeless understanding of death), once the finish line is crossed, as the reaper's scythe pierces our chest, we can endure the ritual free of regret, without a need for last minute confessions of things left unsaid. Allow us to practice life with raw honesty, as the fluttering pages of an open book, without the need for concealment or lies. The true mark of friendship is not one who can keep a secret, but rather one who recognizes the weakness of character in requesting that a secret be kept in the first place. For there is absolutely no honor in perpetuating a lie.

And then, in the midst of his prophetic proclamations, Jared killed his prey. The first stab invoked a shrill scream, accompanied by a miniature geyser of blood, which sprayed across Jared's face and the surrounding walls. Eager to finish the job, he initiated the motion of repeatedly plunging the blade into the chicken's body, rendering it unrecognizable, until all that was left was a red, pulpy corpse resting beside a disheveled young man. MURDERER. Jared stood over the remains, staring contently with uninterrupted focus at his masterpiece of abstract, expressionist performance art. A certain fulfillment coursed through him. Not the pride or the accomplished triumph of having created something; instead his heart resonated with the impending doom that illuminates the mind of a destroyer, the eraser of existence. He had killed a living, breathing creature and felt not a tinge of guilt. In fact, he was elated by his actions. Powerful. Jared's heightened emotional state eventually overwhelmed his system and he suddenly collapsed atop the carcass, unintentionally bathing in his fresh sacrifice. Jared's body lay draped across the table, his face buried in the thick, chunky stew of chicken remains. The deep red hue of blood coated his face, like the smeared war paint of a tribal combatant basking in a sacrificial offering of warm flesh. His breathing pattern created an odd bubbling sound, as he repeatedly exhaled and inhaled (his mouth only partially submerged) into a small puddle. Percolation. It was in this tranquil state that Jared would rest for the next hour, victorious and exhausted. He had competed a task of self-effacement, performing the procedural murder of his spirit animal. Likewise, as our hero lay unconscious in a poultry bloodbath, his romantic interest, the never disappointing, always horny, heartbreak mistress, Amy Carousel, was on her back receiving a load from the faceless stranger who called himself Nick. Both estranged lovers were afforded the luxury of an evening spent bathing in bodily fluids, graciously provided by foreign entities.

I would like to take this opportunity to make the obligatory cock joke.

## Report filed: South Forts Registrar, 1804

Findings herein stated are conclusive to the remembrance practices performed upon John Nelson, an individual. Subject appears to have suffered a severe case of first love syndrome, a common disorder among adolescents. While most of the afflicted are readily capable of enduring this disease by means of "moving on" or "getting over it," John appears to be a wild exception. Rather than passing through the developmental stages of self-betterment that allow for the infection to run it's course and ultimately become expelled from the body, John appeared to be trapped in the anguish of betrayal and abandonment. In his failure to seek medical, spiritual or emotional assistance, John saw no way out of his predicament and succumbed to the refuge of a self-inflicted gunshot.

First love syndrome can be detrimental to one's health, as it alters the brain's framework by introducing a new emotion into the system. Similar to the reaction of a sober individual drinking alcohol for the first time, the body becomes aware of a brand new mindset. An unknown pleasure is revealed. The danger that results from discovering the ability to alter our basic perspective is the instinctive desire to repeatedly pursue such a heightened state of being. To deny the wisdom of "everything in moderation" is to entrench oneself in a state of permanent want. When the relationship is terminated, as is the case with all first love patients, the body and mind are left craving and yearning for a re-acquaintance with the satisfactory pleasure that the emotion provided. An effect of withdrawal is imminent, absolute and imperative.

To relate this scenario for those who are not recovering drug addicts, I shall offer an alternate metaphor. Imagine your entire existence is spent gaining sustenance and nutrition from life affirming, health-beneficial foods. Your diet consists primarily of raw fruits and vegetables, whole grains, probiotics, and most importantly, no dairy. You are a skinny, pristine motherfucker with a smooth moving digestive tract. The absence of cheese and other dairy products from your diet subsequently eliminates any and all obstructions from the colon, allowing you to fart directly into your girlfriend's mouth, on cue. And that dumb bitch loves it. She brags about inhaling your essence. However, your healthy lifestyle is not based on restraint and willpower, as you are altogether unaware that junk food exists. There are no moments of inner struggle at the supermarket. Rather, you have never been introduced to any food types beyond the required, essential dishes of pomegranate, beets and oats. You are the unwanted lovechild of Plato and Jenny Craig, raised in a cave of health foods, free of all temptation and outside stimuli. Your sheltered upbringing has yielded the perfect individual. Now, consider that approximately seventeen years into your purified life, a friendly, generous neighbor approaches you. A girl, slightly older than you, but close enough in age to call her a peer. She descends into your cave carrying a sealed porcelain jar. Your curiosity gets the best of you and you inquire as to the contents of the mysterious container. She lifts the lid, reaches her arm inside and pulls out a freshly baked chocolate chip cookie. A warm (but not so warm that it burns your tongue), dripping, crumb-tumbling cookie. You grasp the cookie, take a bite, and suddenly your entire worldview shatters. Imagine the ecstasy, the overwhelming sensations of pleasure and joy. The shock to the body's homeostatic state could prove traumatic. It would alter all foundations regarding what you understood to be true and definite about food. Suddenly, you realize the universe has more to offer and you are left craving another. The simple act of biting into a cookie has reinvigorated your excitement for life. Never before had you eaten anything so sweet and delicious, so incredibly tasty. You look forward to moments spent eating more sweet treats. Unfortunately, she vanishes. The girl with the cookie jar disappears, never to return to your fortress of hunger. The tragedy of all this is that you know she is out in the world, somewhere else, sharing her delicious cookies with anyone willing to take a bite. And all you're left with is a pining in your stomach to once again taste the perfect dessert.

In conclusion, it appears that John was unable to move on and mend the wounds left by Patricia's departure. His death is to be ruled a suicide by a self-inflicted gunshot to the head. The only consolation of this disgraceful act is my hope that he was able to find the sense of calm tranquility that he deemed unobtainable in his waking life. It's quite pathetic, really. Death is not an appropriate method of making amends, as true strength is born in overcoming hardships and conquering the mini-battles of everyday life. In my professional opinion, I find John Nelson to be a reprehensible, weak little boy, a whining bitch unable to cope with the common discrepancies of life. Frankly, I'm glad this emotional goofball is dead. Close.


It had evolved into somewhat of a tradition, a time of father-son bonding followed by the romantic endurance of young lovers. The two events were not mutually exclusive, they just happened to occur in immediate succession. During the 11th year of school (junior year, as it was called) the district implemented a modified schedule in which students would be released early on Wednesdays and would subsequently begin the day later on Thursday mornings, 8:30 a.m. instead of the usual 7:40. Being a young lad with a driver's permit, Jared, along with his dad, would take advantage of the extra Thursday hour and drive around town, getting acquainted with the power and responsibility that operating a vehicle instills upon a young man on the brink of freedom. The streets were fairly empty this time of day, so Jared was afforded a certain parameter of leeway to learn from his mistakes. Hands at 10 and 2, check your blind spots, turn signal, all the fun new rules. Jared's dad was the perfect driving instructor, calm and assured, confident in his son's abilities, never yelling or panicking when a misstep occurred. This was a cherished time for both men, a milestone of adolescence, just father, son and the open road of endless potential, tossing talk and lessons of a learned life. The driving practice would always come to a close at the same spot: directly in front of Amy's house. This was always intentional. Jared would park in the driveway of her mother's house, exit the vehicle and allow his father to maneuver into the driver's seat. "Have a good day, son." Wait, he never called me son. We aren't that wholesome. "Bye, Jared." "See ya, dad. Have a good day at work." The agreed-upon schedule stated that Jared would knock on Amy's door, she would answer and the two kids would walk to school together. At least, that is what Jared told his dad; but he must have known better than to believe such innocence. For one thing, they usually arrived at Amy's house well-before school began, and she lived no more than a five-minute stroll away from campus. Also, the driveway would always be suspiciously vacant, implying that Amy's mother had already left for work, providing an empty house for the two horny teenagers. It must be assumed that his father knew perfectly well what his son was up to. Maybe he even felt a sense of pride. 'Atta-boy! Sow those wild oats. Go get yourself laid. Fuck to your heart's content.' Whatever his reasoning, he and Jared would exchange a knowing grin while approaching the home of the Carousel family. A grin of approval, of support and admiration. I'm positive he must've known what happened inside once he drove off. For a while, Jared would either knock on the front door or simply climb through her bedroom window. She would always be dressed in her comfortable bedtime garments, still half asleep. They would cuddle, spoon in spoon, amongst the autumn walls of her bedroom, gently napping, which eventually led to kissing, which eventually led to all the rest. Thursday morning provided a false maturity, an empty house, a fantasy glimpse of independence. This is what it'll be like every morning after we graduate and move in together for real. Until that day, Thursday morning provided a marvelous practice. Two lovers in bed, happy. Eventually, Amy gave Jared his own key to the house. He now had the ability to enter unannounced and climb into bed with her while she slept, surprising and delighting her, waking her with an eager embrace and neck kisses. These moments were tranquil, and writing this makes me wish to return to such joyous simplicity. But she's gone now and all I'm left with is an entire novel of memories. Oh well, let us soldier on... They would always make love on Thursday morning, sometimes more than once. Afterwards they would shower together with the radio on. It was during one of these shower sessions that Jared first heard "Don't Worry Baby" by The Beach Boys, a song of pure, innocent love, with a creeping sense of madness. Hearing that gorgeous melody while the love of his life stood naked in front of him under a downpour of warm water nearly stopped his heart. In that moment, he knew that love was real and he and Amy were in the midst of the precious pinnacle of human existence. Sometimes they would end up making love in the shower (occasionally neglecting to use a condom, as they were caught up in the excitement and passion of the moment). Sometimes they would make love in different rooms of the house. They would lie together in the den, in the guest room, even in the pool shed out back. Sometimes they used her mother's shower, as it was spacious and had stronger water pressure. Sometimes they would watch a few scenes of 10<sup>th</sup> Kingdom (her favorite movie) and sometimes they would drink beer and watch the live Paul McCartney DVD. Sometimes she would wear this incredibly sexy red satin shirt, which only heightened Jared's arousal. After all was said and done, the two children would get dressed, strap on their backpacks and walk to school, hand in hand. It was their Thursday morning ritual. A time of purity, of young love in its rawest form. A pristine, crystallized moment upon which I look back longingly, as my heart still swells when I remember her. Asleep. On a Thursday morning.

"Kiss her. She wants you to kiss her. She's just waiting for you to make a move."
"She told you this?"
"Yes. She wants you to show some affection."
"And why is she talking to you about this?"
"I guess she was getting worried. I mean, you guys have been together for about 2 months now and you still haven't made out with her. What are you waiting for?"
"Charlie, I appreciate your concern. I truly do. I understand that you're looking out for the best interests of my relationship, but why is she coming to you to discuss such personal matters?"
"I don't know. Don't be jealous, man. Your hookup status is hardly a personal matter. She's probably just confused and eager for some loving. My take on the situation is that she's starting to suspect you might be a fag."
"Delightful."
"Just quit being so goddamned shy and polite. She's ready to go, Jared. You just have to make the first move. She won't resist. Trust me."
"Are you her fucking therapist now? She comes to you with all her complaints and worries?"
"Not at all! Jeez, ya paranoid bastard. We were IMing and she told me she wants you to kiss her is all."
"Alright, alright."
"..."
"..."
"Well, why the fuck haven't you?"
"I'm not sure. It just hasn't happened yet. We're building up to it. You wouldn't understand. It's a gradual process."
"You sure?"
"Charlie, honestly I am sorta weirded out that she confides in you about this. Just stay out of our business."
"Whoa! No need to get so upset. We've both been friends with Amy for a while; but suddenly, because now she has the title of

being your 'girlfriend' you feel this entitled sense of ownership over her, and like, no one else is allowed to talk to her. You need to relax, Jared. You don't control her. You are barely her boyfriend. You haven't even kissed her yet."

It's worth noting, or rather, reestablishing, at this point in the story, Charlie's significant status as the kindler to the embers of the rise and fall relationship that is:

**J+A**

Bold initials etched eternally in a neighborhood tree, carved into the spruce, a wooden inlay of lasting commitment. Quite an odd tradition practiced by young lovers, the initials in the tree, a sort of romantic graffiti, an obstruction of nature dedicated to pubescent hormonal synchronicity, at least temporarily. Surely the tree's lifespan, granted it isn't chopped down or potentially rotting from the inside during the time of the engraving, is destined to outlast the duration of the relationship. When the lovers inevitably separate, parting prior to death, the initials will serve as a reminder, a tombstone to their love, long ago lost to the allures of new things and other people. Odd too, still, that a girl with a troublesome history of self-scarification would graciously condone an act that is certain to recall complicated memories.

Nevertheless, the relationship itself was properly instigated and maintained by Jared's right hand man, the effervescent, always present, Charles. The good man served as a matchmaker, a liaison between the two waning lovers, reigniting their spark when it threatened to dwindle, as was often the case in the early months of their courtship.

Recall, once again, the fateful afterschool special; you know, the day that truly elevated Jared and Amy's love fest. The instance at Charlie's mother's house on the last day of 9th grade. It would soon become apparent that the final day of the school year would always be a time of shape-shifting transformation in Jared's life, of renewal and rejuvenation. The final day of the school year carried with it the weight of a needed celebration. A full-body flush, master cleanse catharsis. A chance to drain the pressures and responsibilities of the previous year and let loose.

To honor the successful completion of a hard earned report card with relatively decent grades; well, good enough. It was with this mindset that Jared, Amy and Charlie embarked on the configuration of an urgent reaction. With Charlie's mom scheduled to be at work for at least a few more hours, the trio had the house to themselves. As a youngster, having the parents out of the house, even if only momentarily, is an empowering, free spirit ramble, offering all the amenities and perks of adulthood without the soul-sucking job and burdened liabilities.

This brief tale has already been told in a previous incarnation; however, a seminal detail was neglected. It appears the teller of the story, the voice of the author, failed to recognize the flat-line importance and burgeoning connotations of an overlooked circumstance that occurred on the final day of grade nine.

That evening, Charlie had invited Eddie over to join in the festivities. This happened after the poolside cuddling and the bedtime nipple rubs. Besides Jared, Eddie was also known to harbor an attraction to the supple flirt, double squirt, cute cake that was Amy Carousel. Hell in a handkerchief, nearly everyone in their circle of friends with slowly descending testicles and voices dropping an octave (occasionally cracking high pitched and strained, hahaha! never gets old) had a crush on Amy. She was irresistible, a goddess of teenage wonderings.

If we're to view the evolutionary struggle of males competing for a mate through the concise and orderly format of a tournament bracket, it would appear that on this day, the final championship round was relegated as Jared v. Eddie, the ultimate matchup. Both young lads shared an equal chance at capturing the heart of an unrestrained girl on the brink of sexual deviancy. We, the readers, observing this whole story from afar, uninvolved, already know the outcome. Yes, Jared will win. "Yes!" she declares. Sorry Eddie, but you'll get your chance eventually, she'll get passed around the brotherhood like a burning joint on a summer weekend.

Anywho, the grand reveal, the anticipated moment in which Amy chooses the winner, unfolds in a befuddling, psychological game show methodology. First, Amy and Charlie (the mediator) disappear into his bedroom, soundproofed, sealed and locked. The agreement is as follows: She will confess, to Charlie, the name of the boy she admires, the victor. Once he has obtained this vital intelligence, he will then sit separately, one at a time, first with Eddie and then with Jared, revealing the answer in private. As for Amy, she will go home and let Charlie reveal her answer, after she has vacated the premises. The reason for this decision being she wishes to avoid any uncomfortable confusion or conflict.

The door opens. Charlie motions for the first contestant, and Eddie nervously enters. After several minutes of uncertain silence pass, it is Jared's turn. He enters.

"Well, as you know, I spoke with Amy earlier and she told me that she likes…"

dramatic pause
cue the lights
drumroll please
"Eddie."

Wait, what? The unanticipated answer hit Jared's ears with the decaying disappointment of a record player slowing down to a full and complete stop during an otherwise exciting, slow-build jam.

"She told you she likes Eddie?"

"Yep. He wins."

Jared is silent for a moment, letting the news sink in, saddened.

"Huh. Well, good for him. It's her life. It's her choice. I was kinda hoping for the opposite selection, but that's that. Oh well, I guess."

To say the least, Jared was disappointed. To say the most, he was distraught, pissed off, fucking furious and defeated. He had a severe crush on Amy ever since he first laid eyes on her in 7th grade. She was the perfect woman, a thrilling combination of sexy nerdiness. And finally, on the brink of a breakthrough, she denies him.

The whole day was spent in a flirtatious dance of entanglement. He thought Amy shared his same attraction, that the romantic interest was mutual, but no. After swimming, showering and groping, she selects the other boy, the mysterious and hard to reach boy. Of course she wants Eddie. She's intrigued by his unpredictability, how he doesn't overtly display his arousal toward her. Goddamnit. Jared had been too obvious, too available, while Eddie was off to the side, unamused and calm, a restrained cool that apparently left her wanting more. Of course she preferred Eddie. He's leaving more to the imagination. He's not throwing himself at her like an eager puppy dog. Of course she chose Eddie. Jared seethed with jealousy.

It wasn't until about an hour later, after Eddie had left without congratulation, that Charlie confessed his true experimental mindset.

"She picked you, Jared. You are the man she wants."

"Umm…"

"I told both you and Eddie that she had selected the other, just to gauge your reactions. I told you she picked Eddie and I told Eddie she picked you." Charlie grinned with the eager pride of a mastermind revealing the complex solutions of a puzzle.

"Are you fucking with me?"

"Absolutely not. She chose you. She's liked you for a while. And you know, and I know, and she knows that you like her too."

"Why would you trick me?"

"I wanted to see how you would handle the information. You were respectful, but I could clearly tell that you were upset. It was cute."

Jared suddenly blossomed with excitement and unfiltered joy. His dream was coming true.

"So how did Eddie react when you told him?"

"He said he knew all along that it would be you, like, you and Amy are a couple that's destined to be together. He wasn't surprised. He expected it. We all did. Congratulations Jared, you win."

Their shadows appeared to overlay each others in a crisscross pattern, a striking silhouetted X on the stone floor. Something about the light trickling in through the windows, illuminating the dungeon and stuff...

The Pats has been locked inside the holding cell for the past 3 days, being fed from trays of food that were routinely tossed underneath the steel bars, gliding against the grain. A daily diet of peanuts, broccoli, vegan cookies and pasta. Scrumptious and clean, healthy as can be. Brittle bones of an organic fish farmer. Spare us the delicacies of life, disavow our indulgence. Here, in confinement, I shall reevaluate my choices made, thus far. Admirable suffering of withheld willpower, no more dairy no more meat no more sugars, fat fat fatty eat eat eat.

"So, why exactly are we still here? I don't believe that we pose a single threat to anyone; at least, not me. You're the rebel rouser."

"Am I? Am I a bad person? Was this entire journey a terrible mistake? I deserve this. I have rightfully earned my lock-boxed heart. I fleed the scene, Patrick. I fleed the scene."

"Am I missing something?"

"Context! It's all in the context of our situation. I ran away from the life I spent an entire lifetime building. I had a gang of compassionate friends and a family that supported me in all my irrational decision-making. I took for granted the privileges and opportunities offered to me, opting instead to abandon all that was familiar and cozy; which, some could argue is admirable, right? A rich, white girl turning her back on a sheltered existence and breaking free from perfection. Getting her hair dirty, for once. I wanted to experience the trials and woes of the every man, the working class, roughing it day after day. I wanted to relate and converse with poor folk."

"Allow me to interject, as you are sounding dumber and less-than-enlightened the more your ramble progresses. A bona fide spoiled brat. Here's my whole take on the situation. You are skewing your sources and misinterpreting your motives. You didn't run away to escape the ease of your hometown, the anti-struggle of suburban living. You ran away from the pain and heartache you went through. Yea sure, you had the reigning social status of a debutante, but let's not forget that your boyfriend fucking killed himself. Am I overlooking something? Am I reading too much into this? Yes, your life was privileged and you inspired all your friends, they looked up to you. However, some serious shit went down in your life. You aren't protected from reality, no matter how rich your family may be. I mean, that's gotta mess with someone's head, dealing with the suicide of someone you're close to."

Patricia was suddenly stunned by this harrowing revelation. A truth she attempted to avoid. She didn't want to talk about it anymore.

"I... I've come to terms with it."

"Really? So that explains why you still carry his journal."

Ouch.

Patrick resorted to enabling his Scorpio instinct, pulling out a dagger of harsh truths. Every scorpion life form has on reserve a collection of cruel comments capable of disabling any nearby predator; or, in this particular case, a friend in need of hearing an honest suggestion.

"Listen, I'm not blaming you or trying to make you feel guilty, but it's okay to be upset about it. It's okay to be sad. You don't have to deliver some elaborate speech about the plight of the workingman and how rich people don't know pain, because you clearly know a thing or two about pain."

A lingering silence allowed for the processing and interpretation of Pat's insight. It was clear that his words resonated strongly with Patricia. The expression on her face suggested that great mental knots were becoming undone. The clarity astounded and frightened her. Untapped reservoirs of her brain, too long ignored and silenced, were once again on high alert, full function.

"Thank you, Patrick. I needed to hear that."

He shook his head, upset with her ease of influence. "It's not that easy."

She let a tear descend, to emphasize the revelatory transformation she was experiencing.

"You're on the right path. I'm happy for you and all, it's just, realizing your apparent weakness (or weaknesses, as not all of us are fortunate enough to possess one and one only. Most chipped souls are burdened with an entire manuscript of faults, shattered memories and buried laments) and, more importantly, a certain underlying tragedy of adolescence and how this particular moment, a regrettable moment indeed, comes to affect and ultimately dismantle every seemingly rational decision of your adult life, is a process. It's a whole ordeal. A long, drawn out quest with plenty of opportunities to turn back and resort to old, childish ways of thinking. And trust me, turning back and running home to the cradle of cooked meals and the complete absence of responsibility will only further diminish your strength. But if you're true to yourself, and honestly want to improve your situation, then I believe you will get better. So good for you, you managed to take the very first, miniscule step toward self-betterment. You're starting to realize your motivations (as we like to say in the queerest sense of the word, during private meetings of storytellers and dream menders). Just don't think shedding a tear is all that is required."

Patrick let loose a college-level lecture concerning the psychological effects of childhood trauma and the resulting implications; mainly, poor decision-making and issues of confused identity in later years. His lone audience member was stunned and defeated. Yet, rather than unleashing the overbearing and powerful qualities that her normally defensive self was all-too-well-equipped to dispense, she seemed miraculously humbled and contemplative.

"I'm grateful I met you, Patrick. You are a wise soul and have a way of cutting to the core of my reservations. Talking to you is akin to glancing into a mirror that reveals the ugliness I attempt to hide from on a daily basis."

"Well, it doesn't matter. I mean, I'm glad you can find some consolation in my ramblings, but that doesn't change the fact that we're currently locked in a fucking cage."

Patricia felt suddenly dashed with wit and awareness.

"That's only because the writer is having a hard time with us."

*Too self-referential for my taste. Let us attempt to honor the Vonnegut misfires I so despised in Breakfast of Champions. Or, rather, let's see what they have to say about me. Speak for yourselves, my darlings. Be free. Hold nothing back. I can no longer be considered your creator. You have taken the reins from my fingertips and charged forward on your own.*

"Quite right. Whenever our storyline is making any sort of progress, we end up stuck somewhere. Often a small, enclosed room. My theory is that our jumbled and incoherent transgressions are faulted by the fact that we are merely made-up characters, whereas those other foolish teenagers are direct representations of the writer, his past lover and all his friends and family."

"I wouldn't be so sure of that. We clearly share some of his qualities, maybe just less literally at moments. Nevertheless, everyone in this tale is either an extension of the writer himself or a direct observation made by him."

"Fair enough. Still, I would love a climactic moment of my own. I'm tired of being treated as a secondhand interruption of the woebegone languishes for his precious ex-girlfriend."

"I agree. It is truly a grotesque disservice to the reader, as we are such compelling and interesting characters. Like, come on, you're a talking dog. That is so quirky and fun!"

"Okay, now you're just being rude. The condescending backlash to your epiphany of guilt ridden sadness."

Patrick slumped backward against the wall, a schlub on a rub. He exerted a sigh of great frustration, condensing all his stress and resentment into a single breath. Poor Patrick thinks he is nothing special.

Meanwhile, just outside the castle walls, word had begun to spread all across the land of the great battle. Pamphlets commissioned by 'The Council of Peacetime Maintenance' (an organization created to ensure that no outside forces threaten to disrupt the sanctity and serenity of the local pastures and green-thumb initiatives of The Land of Forgotten Souls. Their primary objectives thus far have involved arranging protests to block large-scale industries from setting up shop on sacred grounds and circulating petitions to be sent to the federal government regarding the environmental impact of coal mining. Waging an all out war was definitely their most ambitious project yet) were being distributed to all taxpaying residents and freeloading drifters alike.

With incredible convenience, just as Patrick was beginning to doubt his purpose in this tale, one of the pamphlets fluttered in through the window of their holding cell. A call to arms of the disenfranchised minority. A Rosie the Riveter for the well-intentioned, yet painfully ignorant and idealistic, hippie generation. The flyer was printed and distributed with the intention of riling up the spirits of even the most passive of souls, lighting a fire in the belly of the lethargic and droopy-eyed.

ATTENTION: All residents

As I'm sure you are well aware, The Land of Forgotten Souls is a territory that prides itself on localized ass kissing and progressive political ideals. We are an enlightened population, determined to offset the widespread corruption and greed that is commonly misconstrued as being the American Dream. By living here, you are making a statement to the rest of the country that you refuse to be another faceless pawn, spinning the gears of the war machine. We are unique and freethinking souls. We aren't obsessed with money. The only green we're concerned with is nature. We are aware and therefore ashamed of US history, which is why every October 12th, instead of perpetuating the hero worship and indoctrinated admiration of a mass murderer, we celebrate the annual Great Weep. All residents are encouraged to gather in the town plaza, join hands in a massive circle (symbolizing the geometry of the earth and our well-'rounded' perspective of cultural cooperation) and cry together. We cry for the Native Americans, and we cry hard.

Sidenote: Last year's turnout was slightly less populated than usual, which is why during the next Great Weep, for the first time ever, we will be allowing children under the age of 10 to attend, free of charge (of course). Also, the Six Rivers Pub & Grill will be serving locally brewed beer. Hope to see you there.

Now, I know as well as anyone else that we are a self-loving community unlike any the world has ever seen. There is an inherent sense of pride in living here, and nothing will ever change that. We all share a deep admiration and a spiritual respect for the natural wonders this area has to offer. From our sprawling forests to our expansive beaches, The Land of Forgotten Souls is a haven of nature's beauty. Just think back to your first visit here... Most of you were probably living in the overcrowded and fast-paced scramble of city life, rushing back and forth between your dingy apartment and your stuffy office. Now take a deep breath and remember the refreshing relief you experienced when you first set foot here. Suddenly, all the tension and stress of your life seemed to drift away. The cool ocean breeze, the mighty charge of the riverbanks and the mystic refuge of the forest all seemed to sweep away the pain in your life. It's no wonder our community is so sophisticated and cheery. It is simply impossible to be upset in such a gorgeous environment.

I know what you're thinking, and I'm sure you've heard this all before. Why are we writing and distributing a letter to all residents just to be self-congratulatory? While that wouldn't be completely below our standards, there is an important issue at hand. So, before you continue reading, please sit down in a comfortable position and, time permitting, perform some of your favorite stretches before going any further.

All right, deep breath.

It is with great sorrow and difficulty that I write to you today, as I was recently informed of a debilitating threat to our habitat. It appears that during recent months, the town of South Forts has been sending over environmental engineers, irrigation specialists and (worst of all) lawyers to examine our river system. They concluded that we have an unfair abundance of freshwater rivers, meaning our ratio of citizens to resources is improperly balanced.

According to the leader of South Forts, they plan on diverting a significant portion of our water flow to help meet their growing demand for hydration and nourishment. Apparently, their rich, bourgeois lifestyle of waste and excess could not be sustained by their limited supply of available resources, as they have now resorted to pillaging our land in order to maintain their soul-sucking life of greed and shame.

As per a statement issued by the South Forts Planning Commission, portions of the rivers will be dammed and aqueducts will be constructed to carry the water the required distance south to the bustling metropolis of South Forts. This process is certain to destroy and forever tarnish the lush, beautiful landscape we love here in The Land of Forgotten Souls.

Try as we might, there is not a single legitimate method of blocking or resisting their advances. We have pleaded to the high court, yet received only snickers and smiles. They simply have no sympathy or compassion for a reclusive town such as our own. All legislative bodies are in favor of the impending encroachment. Outside forces seem to feel owed, or, more so, obliged, to reap what is rightfully ours. We are being forced to concede with their demands. The ultimate surrender, giving up our sacred body for the profit of self-serving goons.

My friends, we have no other options left. We shall not remain idle while they destroy our mother. When they arrive on our soil with tools of ungracious and unforgiving power, it will be viewed as an act of aggression. Our only choice in this situation is to defend ourselves and protect the hollowed ground we cherish so dearly. If you define this as war, then so be it, this document is hereby a thorough and true declaration of war. As they trespass upon our territory, we will uphold the vow of sanctity and preservation. Fight along side me, my brothers and sisters, fight for all that has been forgotten.

Within a weeks time, the contractors, construction workers, demolition teams and other mindless henchmen shall descend upon our land. I hope, with urgent sincerity, that you will join arms against these tyrants. They shall never blemish our natural masterpiece.

!Fight for what you believe in!

!Fight to save The Land of Forgotten Souls!

As always, I shall sign off with my beloved and accustomed valediction, though in this instance it seems rather foolish and banal.

Love, Peace and Happiness,

King Deryk


Pat rapaciously crumbled the letter.

"Grant me a sword and I shall do battle," he sneered.

Excellence is only maintained through the vigor of sacrifice. It is never satisfied by half-hearted accomplishments or the inevitable kickback.

Earn only what is deserved, no more.

Divorce seemed to be a common misfortune among Jared's group of friends (the actual legal procedure and painstaking mumbo-jumbo of partitioning resources endured by the parents notwithstanding, but more so the brutal emotional toll inflicted upon their children), a sort of 'rite-of-passage' for all youngsters on the verge of becoming so-called grownups. Whether this happened during the precious childhood years or the precious puberty years, divorce, the sad announcement and the comforting aftermath, became a main staple of life for all no-longer-innocent incumbents, a heavy dose of learn-to-deal-with-unexpected-struggles reality check.

It's basic Conflict Resolution 101. Two parties are heavily feuding and bickering for an extended period of time, and the mutual decision to separate, to divide assets, is met, agreed upon and put into action. No more screams of scotch-tinged hostility, no more sneaking out and allowing secrets to fester and propagate. Divorce is a conscience clearer, a romantic degauss. Children. Let's not forget about the children, the true victims of this mediated agreement, the innocent bystanders of love's withdrawal. Amidst all the heartbreak, sorrow and broken-home downtrodden blues in E minor, a valuable lesson is learned, directly, hands-on experienced. First and foremost, the illusion of happily-ever-after, fairy tale 'love is eternal' nonsense is shattered forthright, and frankly, for the best. Being taught this early on will toughen you up and prepare you for the road of life and the plethora of unavoidable disappointments you will inevitably encounter. Secondly, divorce reinforces the notion that change is a constant availability in every circumstance. Settling is never a requirement. To divorce is not a cowardly act of running and hiding; rather, it is to walk away slowly, with pride and dignity remaining intact, while your home (now broken) burns in the background. Dramatic, yet boring.

Before the inevitable split, torn-to-shreds, deconstruction of the Carousel family, Jared was gifted with one special moment of mommy and daddy togetherness, a single outing of intact, seemingly healthy and stable, domestic tranquility. It was to be his very first meeting with Amy's parents, and they were determined to arrange an entire carnival celebration to honor the occasion. The game plan, structured and concise, laid the groundwork for a promising excursion. Activities abound to ensure group laughter, family bonding and memorable moments, captured and remembered.

Papa Carousel was a man of grit and determination, a toughened road warrior of the upper echelon. A steel beam soldier, maligned minotaur. He was unquestionably, without the darkened, diminishing shadows of looming doubt, an honest, hardworking man. He championed the seminal sort of good-ol'-boy attitude presidential candidates attempt to convey when they're giving speeches in rural, working-class sections of this great nation. The whole bootstraps, factory man mentality. Born and bred in the pulsating artery of the American heartland. The canoe digging, show me yours and I'll show you mine, fur trading state of Missouri. He authorized his citizenship by insisting upon the correct pronunciation, enlightening the uninformed that it's called Missour-ah and not Missour-e. A blatant show of some bullshit hick pride still bellowing in the shallow depths of his memory; although a proper California suntan has the acute ability of darkening the shade of many a Midwestern neck.

Career wise, and as an adult one's career is their defining characteristic, the daily grind of self-worth and sacrifice, while hobbies of adolescent angst and childhood grace deteriorate into the occasional release of a weekend-retreat's backseat patronage, Papa Carousel was a professional set designer for television shows aimed primarily at teenage girls. The type of show that always seemed to be centered, locale wise, on the bedroom of a young woman; and we, the privileged audience, are allowed the perverted fantasy of watching (from afar) this actress and the character she portrays, blossom into a sexual deviant, coming of age, accepting and eventually loving her blemished cheeks and limited aspirations. The televised empowerment of sluggish American teens. Hot Disney sluts just waiting to get pinned against a wall or smothered by a detergent-scented bedspread. His claim to fame was a stint on <u>Clarissa Explains it All</u>, spackling drywall or god knows what. He kept himself busy and was valued within his specified field. He would construct flats, paint walls and fundamentally decorate illusions, conveying a sense of sound-stage reality. It seemed a silly job for such a man. A rough and tumble construction-worker type caught up in the soft-skinned, faggy femininity of the entertainment industry. It's a delicate balance, the grunt work that allows for the prance.

Jared was scared as shit to meet her family. Utterly terrified. Already a shy and antisocial young man, the pre-anxiety of meeting his girlfriend's parents proved to be a grueling challenge, far greater than the preshow jitters of standing in front of a half-asleep classroom and delivering an uninspired oral presentation. The anticipatory suspense was burgeoning beyond the level of terrified excitement.

Activity time soon to commence. The scene was instigated by a phone call.

"Hello?"

wet breath

"Hey Jared! Are you busy this weekend?"

gleeful exhale, the warm comfort of her voice, in that hushed, near-whisper tone

"Even if I was, if I had a dense calendar of important events, I would just as easily clear my entire schedule for you, Amy."

giggle

"Aww, you're such a sweetie"

"What do you have in mind? We could catch a movie or something…"

"Actually, my intentions are slightly broader than your clichéd request. I am calling, on behalf of the Weekend Fun-Time Patrol, with a commitment to instilling life-to-the-fullest grandeur in the hearts of those young and spunky enough to receive such blessings. We shall not waste away in a darkened auditorium, slurping syrupy soda and gobbling buttered popcorn. Cinema = mindless distractions with the occasional chuckle, or, if you try hard enough, a measly tear shed. I wanna get to know you, Jared. I wanna talk to you and learn how it is you're coping with this blessed curse of life. I wanna hear you speak for yourself, sharing experiences of excellence and sorrow, rejoicing in our own miracles, our very own adventures, and definitely not through the guise of relating our identities to those assholes on the big screen. I couldn't care less if you feel a desperate connection to some schmuck in a film. I wanna feel you dripping your own sweat, pouring out your own essence, homegrown and unique. No no no! Not a fucking movie. We have idealistic plans, naïve and stupidly optimistic."

deep breath, Amy, deeeeeeeeeeeep breath, inhale, exhale, carry on

"Don't get me wrong, I'm a fan of slouching in front of a monitor and gazing idly. I frequent the tube. Do not misinterpret my ramble. And if I didn't have a superior alternate option, I could see us surrendering all senses to the glow of celebrity and excess, allowing shadow puppets to dictate our morality, inscribe the dividing line between right and wrong, learning valuable lessons for us. But not this weekend, buddy. No escapism for us. You see, in all actuality, my dad was thinking of taking the boat out on Saturday, and I wanted to invite you to come along."

"Whoa, Amy! I must say, not only does that sound awesome, but that was quite the pep talk. Damn, girl. Let's go right now. Carpe diem and all that fluffy shit."

"I'm not trying to sound condescending or derogatory toward the film industry. In all honesty, I devote plenty of wasted hours to watching, watching, endlessly watching. I've grown accustomed to flicking on the idiot box whenever I am bored or even quietly still for more than several seconds. It has become my instinctual reaction to any and all silent moments. Quick, drown it out! But you see, now that we have some weekend plans that involve outdoor adventure and the thrilling rush of hydro-mechanical motion, I must say, I am thoroughly pumped. I can't fucking wait! I am absolutely enlivened and liberated by the promise this day holds. It'll be great. We usually drive over to Lake Castaic bright and early, cast off, and spend the day doing some amateur wakeboarding."

"I've never been. That's like the snowboarding equivalent of waterskiing?"

"Correctamundo.  We also have an inner tube for when the strain and disappointment of too many failed attempts at remaining afloat becomes overwhelming, and a full-speed surface drag is needed."

"Well, goddamn, I'd love to go.  I've been hankering for some nautical shenanigans."

"Great!  So the plan is to leave super fucking early on Saturday morning, meaning you are much better off sleeping over than stumbling here at sunrise."

O boy… Sleepover?

"Um, yea, yea definitely sleeping over sounds like a safe bet.  Early to bed, early to rise, right?"

giggle

"Don't be nervous.  This is gunna be fun.  And you'll get to meet my parents."

gulp

"Of course, of course.  I can't wait."


The first meeting of the parentals: endurance round

It's safe to assume that at this early, formative stage in their relationship, Jared and Amy had logged a total of approximately 1-2 months together, duration wise.  Given the limited accumulation of romantic memories (thus far), this was an opportune time to breach the advancing/soon-to-be levels of 'getting to know each other,' cohesively.  Simply put, it was time to get cracking on the formation of the greatest love story Western civilization has ever known.  At least, that's the lingering sentiment consistently throbbing in the ribcage of all teenage boys as they enter the throes of vaginal pursuits.  There exists no convincing validity or logical proof whatsoever to such claims; rather, it's purely an emotionally-charged reaction.

Now, to understand Jared's descent into the world of debauched psychosis that is otherwise referred to as 'young love,' we must introduce and offer honorable mention to the shimmering influence of Griselda.  A mighty force, propagating maturity.  The raindrop that forces a full bloom.  During his preteen and early-childhood years, Griselda was the babysitter

Jared's parents would hire to keep an eye on him while they went out for a pleasant dinner or a weekend getaway. Rather than hiring a young, wholesome teenager with freckles and pigtails to watch over their son, his parents opted for the upper-class suburban route of hiring a middle-aged Guatemalan woman. Whereas the teenage girl-next-door will spend the night chatting on the landline telephone and fleeing at the first sign of actual responsibility, immigrants from Central America, on the other hand, are tougher than steel. Truly hardened. They are perhaps the most disciplined, committed and strong-willed individuals on the planet.

Griselda was, to put it lightly, a ferocious woman, a true warrior of the night, always coming over equipped with a warm pizza and a rented horror movie. Needless to say, these were fun, happy-go-lucky times, as Jared was kept comfortably entertained with recreational fright while his parents were gone. It was during these late night sessions, in the comfort of Griselda's genuine presence, that Jared was introduced to some of the finest, most god-awfully terrifying films of American lore. The two pinnacle, paradigm-shifting titles being: The Shining and Sleepaway Camp, as both of these films contain a seminal scene of horrifying delight. Singular instances that embrace the unforgiving spirit of surprise. The Shining, for all its many sequences of creepy unease and mental instability, transmits its most pitch-perfect moment of torment in what has become known as 'the bathtub scene.' A classic clip in which Jack Nicholson approaches what he observes to be a gorgeous, nude woman, only to be confronted by a grotesque, decaying, shivering corpse. The perceptual transformation occurs while Jack is going in for an embrace, reaching for her soggy ass. It's fucking horrifying beyond repentance. Similarly, the closing moment of Sleepaway Camp rattles the same unexpected emotion of crippling fear. During the final scene, the film's protagonist stands up, naked, and reveals an unexpected physical character trait. The last shot of the movie, in which these sensitive details are brought to light, is then freeze-framed and kept on the screen for the entire duration of the end credits, offering not a moment's peace from this unexpected climactic declaration. It's worth noting that not only are these the 2 films that stuck in Jared's mind after countless weekends of horror flicks (a.k.a. the Griselda Mind-Fuck Film Festival), yet also, within these 2 movies, the scenes that remain ingrained in his memory occur when our (the casual, moronic audience members) preconceived notions are proven false. When our comprehension of the enveloping world is suddenly flipped, confessing our true underlying nature. The zombie transvestite within us all.

Which reminds me, both scenes also involve nude women. This seems an appropriate instance to share another Griselda memory. When Jared was beginning to show signs of maturity (in the form of prepubescent horniness), she would ease his urges with the gift of pornographic magazines. The Gideon Bible for teens in the pre-internet porn explosion era. My goodness, what a gift! Griselda was the designated provider of sex and violence during these formative years, instilling a sense of self-worth and identity, slightly tinged with a disturbed moral outlook. Horror films and dirty magazines are the seminal ingredients needed to soothe the preliminary flush of testosterone that disrupts the counterweighted chemistry of a young man's changing body. Thank you, Griselda, for providing relief from the inevitable.

As time progressed (as it always does, no matter how arduously we attempt to maintain its precious singularity), Jared became less and less inclined to require a babysitter, or rather, adult supervision.

Which brings us to the task at hand: the sleepover at Amy's house. The weekend during which this bonding adventure was to occur inconveniently coincided with Jared's parents going away on a brief vacation. This was inconvenient only because at the age of fourteen, Jared lacked a sufficient means of transportation to get where he needed to go. However, this did allow for an amusing phone call when Jared's mother called to check in on him and make sure the house was still standing and all the animals were being adequately nourished.

"Yes ma, everything's fine."

Doesn't she understand that I know how to take care of myself? Why does she always assume that I am an invalid, incapable of self-reliance?

"Have any plans for the weekend?"

"Actually, as a matter of fact, I do. Amy invited me to go waterskiing with her and her parents."

"Oh wow! That sounds fun," she replied, with the enthusiastic, surprised shock of a mother anticipating the usual answer of 'ho-hum, my friends are coming over and we are gunna play Mario for SNES until we have every single level memorized well enough to play blindfolded.'

"Yea. Her dad has a boat, so I guess they go every summer."

"How exciting!"

"I'm sorta nervous, cause I've never been before."

"I'm sure they'll teach you the proper posture and all the other miniscule details that constitute a decent rider. So when are you going?"

"Actually, we are going to leave early Saturday morning, so she suggested I sleep over at their place on Friday night."

You could just feel his mother's peppy excitement instantly fade into concern and worry.

"I see… A sleepover… And her parents know about this?"

"Of course. Who do you think suggested it? They drew up the whole game plan."

"Hmm, well, do you intend to sleep in the same room?"

"Jeez ma, I don't know. In all honesty, I highly doubt they would condone such behavior. I'll probably sleep on the couch or in their guest room or something."

"Well, whatever you do, be careful."

"Sure."

"You do know what I mean, right?"

"Um…"

"Be careful."

"Yes ma, I get it. I understand. However, I think you're a little premature on the cautionary words of wisdom. Don't get me wrong, I appreciate you looking out for me, but there is no cause for concern. Mine and Amy's relationship is still in the very early stages of development."

"Well, it better remain that way."

"It will, trust me. At least for now. Have fun in Vegas and tell dad I say hi."

"Thanks, I will. Have a great weekend. Bye Jared."

"Bye bye."

The next easily conquerable dilemma was arranging conveyance to Amy's house on Friday evening. The solution to this uncertainty was none other than the ever-helping hand of Griselda. Although she no longer took care of Jared, as had been the case for the past few years now that Jared's parents figured he was grown up enough to hold down the fort without legitimate adult management, she remained a quick phone call away at all times. Griselda had established a respectable reputation within the community and was frequently babysitting children in nearby proximity. Whenever Jared was in trouble, or wanted to get into trouble, Griselda would be there for him. He'd send out the distress call and she'd indulge his solicitations. She was like the Batman of juvenile delinquency; maybe more so the Joker with Batman's communication setup. And so it was incredibly appropriate that none other than Griselda would chauffer Jared across town for his very first sleepover at a girl's house. A true milestone indeed. As the story goes, she dropped him off on that landmark occasion, a moment in which fates seemed to align symmetrically, destiny and divine intervention, what have you, in the brilliant luminescence of knowing a decision is right. Perfection. The universe hath provided a messenger for us, to console the weak of heart, to assist the ready and the brave, embarking on a quest along the new, uncharted terrain of life's scroll. While she drove away she shook her head, wordlessly communicating the 'crazy kids' sentiment, quietly laughing to herself.

He approached the doorway, carrying a backpack that contained a clean t-shirt, a toothbrush, a bathing suit and most importantly, a towel. Before knocking, he paused, slowed his breathing and mentally prepared himself for the adventure that beckoned before him. Not only would this be his first time meeting the full cast of the Carousel family, but this was his first time setting foot in Amy's house, seeing her bedroom, her makeshift oasis.

This is it, he thought, and knocked gently against the door, the gateway to his dreams. Immediately, as his knuckle tapped the wood, a cacophony of chirps, squawks and tweets rang out from inside the house.

Here we go.

Aside from the oft-imitated and traditional trademark catchphrases of 'hello' and 'I love you,' the Carousel family birds, or at least one of them, had developed the habit of replicating the sound of a telephone ringing. This gimmick was pleasant and amusing in a sort of lackadaisical, unthreatening way, similar to the shoved instigation and conversational fodder in which casual acquaintances discuss traffic or the weather, as it effortlessly quells the anxiety of silence between strangers. And since the bird sanctuary that littered their home was the first distinguishable facet of non-expected décor and unusual home practices, it was the preliminary point of reference for all newcomers and visitors, which in this particular case was the dimwitted and nervous Jared. He was greeted in the entryway by both of Amy's parents, with firm handshakes and forced smiles, plus a onceover look from her father, scaling down to size the boy his daughter may potentially screw vigorously in the near future.

There had to be at least ten different bird varieties held hostage in the Carousel household: cockatoos, macaws, budgies and the like. The living room had ever so gradually been converted into a miniature zoo. In every square foot of habitable space stood one of those off-white, thin-wired cages, adorned with newspaper flooring (for obvious reasons) and those odd, dangling seed clusters. It was a noisy, disruptive and colorful spectacle that provided a reliable distraction to Jared's flustered psyche as he struggled to maintain his projected sense of collected tranquility.

"It's a true pleasure to meet you, Jared. Amy has been gushing about you for weeks now. It's been absolutely adorable and, in all honesty, a comforting refreshment to see her so giddy and excited."

"Oh, well, she's a great girl. You definitely raised her right."

Flattered laughter.

"Put 'er there, young man. It's good to finally meet you."

"Likewise, Mr. Carousel. I must say, I am greatly excited for tomorrow's festivities. There's nothing like the rush of a speedboat's menacing fury against the buoyant currents. I've been thirsting for some adrenalized recreation. Thank you so much for inviting me to come along."

"Don't mention it. We'll have some fun out there. That much I'm sure of."

Smile.

Smile is returned.

Silence slowly beckons. Amy has yet to make an appearance.

"Wow, this is quite an animal kingdom you've got here."

Mommy and Daddy both turn toward the bird habitat.

"Sure is. Do you have any pets?"

"Well, I've got three dogs, two cats and a varying assortment of fish at home. But my grandma has a lovebird."

"Aww."

"Yea. She always puts a towel on the cage at night to get it to shut up. Haha?" Jared nervously intones, saying whatever comes to mind, regardless of its significance or whether the receiving parties of this anecdote care at all about his grandmother's bird-related practices. But hey, it's semi-relevant to the whole bird issue. Although it does run the risk of seeming unsympathetic or overtly-aggressive in regard to caring for birds, especially in the noisy Carousel climate.

"I tell ya, sometimes I'd like to throw a towel over these suckers. But aside from being loving pets, they dually function as an alarm clock. Our own suburban roosters, calling out the sunrise."

"There you go." Anything to agree.

Finally, Amy entered the room, as immaculately gorgeous as ever. It is literally impossible for this girl to not be sexy. She is just naturally beautiful, regardless. Based on her outfit, which consisted of a pair of delightfully short cheer shorts and a loose-fitting, well-worn-in t-shirt, and the fact that she was rubbing her eyes as she crossed the threshold, she must've just awoke from a nap.

"Hey," she mumbled, so utterly casual and nonchalant. Her slightly bewildered state only heightened Jared's arousal, as her careless grace was one of the many attractive qualities she harnessed. Like, she could have been nervously pacing in her bedroom, basking in the pre-date jitters, wondering what to wear, how to style her hair, the extent to which makeup should be applied—for the record, Amy (or rather, ~~Ashley~~, the real life girl that the false idol known as 'Amy' represents) never wore a single speck of makeup. None. She was a natural, blessed-from-above belle—but no, she just hops out of bed and stumbles down the hall to where Jared and her parents are making awkward small talk and mutters a cavalier *Hey*. This is what I (Jared) love about this girl. She is so casually magnificent. A forsaken angel forced to exist among mere mortals.

The goddamn star of the show has finally arrived.

"There she is."

"Hey Amy."

Jared had a shy, quiet-man voice. He often felt insecure about his subdued and unexcitable aura, as though his lack of enthusiasm instantly brought down the energy level of whichever room he happened to enter, much to the dismay of partygoers everywhere. But you, Amy, you understood me. You weren't upset that I didn't scream out in ecstasy. You and I were on the same wavelength. We were the sum of love's definition. But now you're gone and I'm left writing this god-awful story about how awesome you were. Amy was always in tune with Jared's contemplative and calm sense of self. And even though he didn't physically jump for joy at her presence, she still knew he was excited beyond belief that she was there, in the flesh, emblazoned before him.

"Hi Jared."

She approached and proceeded to hug him, smack dab right in front of her parents, transmitting the message of hey mom, hey dad, this is the man I am into, and I don't care how you feel about it. No apologies, no surrender.

The rules were as follows:

1. As expected, Jared was to sleep on the couch in the living room. Under no circumstance was he to fall asleep in Amy's bedroom. Repeat: Under no circumstance was he to sleep in Amy's bedroom. A violation of this rule would result in a complete and total cancellation of the events and activities planned for tomorrow.

2. Both Amy and Jared were to be asleep in their separate quarters no later than midnight, 12:00 a.m., 0000 hours.

3. Departure time the following morning is 6:00 a.m. It is strongly suggested to awake no later than 5:30 a.m.

4. No drugs, no alcohol, no sex.

It seemed simple enough. Be in bed by a certain hour, and no sexy time. Easy. Amy and Jared retreated into her bedroom for the remainder of their designated time together. As background entertainment, Amy put on a compilation video of episodes from the My Little Pony television series. Her selection of visual media was heartwarmingly innocent, the sort of early-years innocence of future freaks. Amy's decision was akin to presenting a degenerate porn star with the tattered remains of her childhood stuffed animal, as to suggest, 'Look at how fucking depraved you have become.' How could rainbow horses intrigue such a raunch-fest of a woman?

Sensing that he was a gentlemanly soul, Amy took advantage of the eclectic intimacy of the evening and confided in Jared while the credits rolled, as they laid together in her bed, in a near-cuddle, but not quite. His left hand and her right hand were entangled in a maelstrom of flirtatious cuteness. Flicking and rubbing against each other, not quite holding hands, more like a massage of palms, exchanging the brilliance of touch.

"You're so amazing, Amy."

Scrumptious befuddlement. Content and cozy in the rapture of love's conquest, acquired. Amy and Jared floated together. The close, intimate confines of her room provided an encapsulation for their blossoming romance.

Jared's hand slowly traveled past her fingers, toward her smooth wrists. She shivered, slightly.

"I feel safe with you. I always have. You unleash a peaceful comfort within my otherwise troubled soul. When we used to eat lunch together in seventh grade, I just knew we were kindred spirits. There was an unabashed, uniquely special connection between us. I was able to open up to you about my darkest, most reserved and sheltered secrets. When I confessed to you about my remorseful habit, you know?" Her already quiet voice sunk another level down. "Hurting myself. You actually listened to me. Your empathetic amusement of my tale allowed me to finally feel comfortable enough to express myself, albeit within a much healthier methodology. But you seemed genuinely interested. I could tell you truly cared about me."

"I just wanted to make sure you were okay. I mean, at the very least you deserve to be happy, Amy. You're much too beautiful to become stuck in the woeful pity of so many unloved castaways."

She moved in for the close embrace. Jared never realized the extent to which he would benefit from those long ago acts of propriety and undivided attention. As she lay engulfed in his flimsy arms, not a sole disturbance was possible. They emitted a type of infinite joy that is normally only reserved for the lazy lifestyle of household pets. A cat sprawled out in a beam of sunlight's summery resonance. Enlightened quietude. In that serene moment, only two humans existed in the entire universe, eternally suspended in the clasp of a knowing connection. Silent, restful breathing and fulfilled sighs.

Soon enough it was time to get some sleep, as tomorrow held an immeasurable plethora of goody-good fun times. A steadfast and strict schedule had already been devised, and an extended slumber would surely disrupt the arrangement. Dedicated to ensuring their daughter remain a virgin, Amy's parents had already set up a pillow and blanket on the living room couch. Jared slowly and reluctantly made his way over to his designated resting spot, but not before getting some nipple action from the more-than-vulnerable Amy.

"Goodnight."

The sunrise was welcomed with a rousing and painfully startling call of the wild, as the entire cavalry of birds sang out in unison the moment the first sliver of sunlight breached the eastern horizon. Jared was conveniently positioned smack-dab in the epicenter of the bird reservoir, the recipient of a surround sound alarm clock, a live performance of "Wake the Fuck Up!" by The Carousel Bird Collective. He immediately lunged into an upright sitting position, just as is portrayed in films when a character suddenly awakes from a terrifying nightmare. Amy's mother was already in the adjacent kitchen, brewing a necessary pot of coffee. Papa Carousel was out front latching the boat trailer to the truck hitch of his 4-door GMC Sierra. Amy was in the bathroom releasing a gentle stream of girl pee. The Zen-inducing pitter-patter of a trickling fountain current. A delicacy reserved for only the most fortunate among us. To hear the dirty splash of a female urinating into a shallow toilet bowl is one of life's simple pleasures. Several factors are necessary to be granted such an honorable tribute, a relative alignment of possibilities. First and foremost, the bathroom door will undeniably muffle the silvery-sweet tone, to a varying extent, considering the thickness of the door, the density of the wood used, and whether or not there exists the blessed half-inch gap between the bottom of the door and the floor, a clearance. The potentially intentional gift of a carpenter keen on the importance of relatively poor sound-insulation in a daughter's bathroom. Another important and conceivably disruptive facet of bathroom intonation is the dreaded air conditioner, especially the dual, automatic single-switch for both lights and AC. At least when two separate switches are required, there still exists a 50/50 chance that maybe you (the pervert with his ear against the door) luck out and she neglects to flick on the booming, enveloping roar of the fans. Because once that AC turns on, fucking forget it, might as well kiss your sick fetish goodbye. You could hold a stethoscope up to the door and still not be able to hear the dreamy dribble. The differing factors that normally prevent us from discerning such a pleasant sound are conceivably what equate to the victorious delight that is experienced when all obstacles are avoided and the secretion resonates. It is, by all definitions, a miracle. A spiritual offering of karmic retribution. Rise and shine, indeed.

Papa Carousel rushed inside, clapping his hands together with rigid intent. "Let's go, let's go." He simultaneously conveyed the regimented accuracy of a drill instructor and the promising, friendly allure of a camp counselor. In compliance, Jared grabbed his backpack, and soon enough we were all piled into the truck, eager for enterprise.

First stop: IHOP. It has become common knowledge, accepted fact and a brain-drilled belief that breakfast is the most important meal of the day. Regardless of the legitimacy of such claims, it is irrefutably the most delicious meal of the day, especially if you are lucky enough to be eating at an IHOP, where sugary-sweet syrup flows like water.

The party of four was escorted to a vacant table, a booth of faux red-leather seating positioned against a window that overlooked the freeway below. If, or when, the conversation turned stale or unnervingly tense, Jared could simply glance outside and observe the river-rush of cars barreling down the I-5 freeway, its manmade pulse a direct reflection of nature. And so anyways, after a brief glance at the menu, a mumbled discussion concerning desired items and approval ratings of suggestions, they proceeded to order a genuine stockpile of pancakes, hash browns, sausage and the substantial, yet often ignored, complimentary toast. Oh, and orange juice. Don't forget your vitamins.

Not many miraculous happenings occurred during breakfast, save for an apprehensive moment in which, after the meal was graciously consumed and beverages imbibed until the cup's bottom insignia was revealed, both Amy and her father excused themselves to use the restroom at the exact same time. Not that they went together, I truly do not wish to suggest any incestual behavior. For precision's sake, Papa Carousel stated, "Excuse me, I must use the restroom." To which Amy replied, "I have to go, too." Harmless and coincidental. The point being, this left Jared and Mrs. Carousel (prefix soon to alter) alone at the empty-plated table. Had some food remained after their vigorous gorge, they could simply chew through the awkwardness. But no, both their mouths were hollow and uninhabited.

Somehow, during their meal, Jared had gathered trivial data that Amy's mother adored horses and would occasionally ride. Cowgirl! After a quick mental sweep through the depths of his memory, Jared recalled an image of his mother as a child sitting atop a pony.

"My mom is really into horses, as well."

"Oh?"

Shit. He was hoping to prompt an elaborate response. An entire monologue about their majestic beauty, the thrill of riding, the sound, the smell and so forth.

"Yeah, she really appreciates them."

Okay, note to self: no further mention of my family and our interactions with animals.

"That's great."

She seemed unsure how to respond to such unspecific and irrelevant statements. Luckily for both of them, Papa soon returned, flushed and clean, followed shortly thereafter by Amy.

"Everyone ready?"

"Yep."

"Thank you so much, Mr. Carousel. That was a great meal. I'm stuffed," Jared uttered, with the scripted delivery of a trained actor starring in Politeness: The Movie.

"Let's hit the road. The watering hole awaits our arrival."

For the remainder of the drive to Lake Castaic, entertainment was provided via the Howard Stern radio show. I am 95% sure this was Papa's idea. Of serendipitous occurrence, during the day of this family outing, it just so happened that John Entwistle, the bass player for The Who, had passed away and Howard was discussing his contribution, or lack thereof, to their catalogue. "Who pays attention to the bass, anyway?" He defended his seemingly cruel and unsympathetic statements by arguing the fact that bassists, and therefore the bass lines they perform, are the least influential and most commonly overlooked, or altogether ignored, aspects of all popular music. Several of his staff members defended the late Entwistle by playing clips of songs in which the bass playing was a definite highlight, such as "My Generation" and "Summertime Blues." Howard continued, "Yea, I guess. I still don't see what the big deal is. No one notices that part of the song. Especially with The Who. When I mention The Who, you immediately imagine Pete Townshend windmill-strumming his guitar, Roger Daltrey throwing his mic in the air and Keith Moon flailing around like a madman on his drums. That's it. Oh yeah, and there's some guy playing the bass along with them. Could be anybody. There's no persona. No charisma. No one cares about the bass player."

Lake Castaic is the final boundary of the California Aqueduct's Western Branch. Originating in the comparatively dense humidness of the northern wetlands, through a series of concrete channels, subterranean pipelines and imperatively positioned dual-phase pumping stations, the aqueduct transports water to the drier southern climate. Lake Castaic is a 390,000,000 $m^3$ dammed reservoir which provides fresh water hydration to the inhabitants of the greater Los Angeles basin.

For recreation, the Lake contains two separate launch ramps for the purpose of docking and/or loading boats: the Lagoon and Main Reservoir. Wakeboarding and waterskiing are permitted in designated areas only. Maximum speed of motorized watercraft is 35 mph. Motorized watercraft are to travel in a counter-clockwise motion at all times.

Now get out there and have some fun!

Based upon Jared's candid observation of the involved process required to get a boat into the water, he determined that Papa Carousel was a routinely experienced boater, a man of the sea. A situation that could easily prompt frustration and irritability was performed with relative ease and admirable prowess. The vessel seemed to slip into the water with the lubed fluidity of wet anti-friction, not unlike a bowel movement that results from a fiber-rich diet. It carelessly plopped into the water and bobbed gently as the family members climbed aboard.

"Ahoy, mateys!" he proclaimed. Apparently the sensation of being on a boat and gazing starboard brings our inner-seafaring scalawag to the surface.

"Greetings, captain." Jared played along with embarrassed enthusiasm.

"Before setting sail, I must request that we all become fitted with the proper attire: the stylistically repugnant, yet functionally essential, floatation vest."

The mark of merit for any reasonably minded mariner: safety first. Jared and Amy were also given the directive to put on wetsuits, another necessary requirement for those about to endure the whip-thrash of being dragged across the water's surface. Amy slipped into her suit with unbridled ease, while Jared was less-than-thrilled to don an outfit that suspiciously highlighted the shape and size of his nether region. The skintight fit of the wetsuit scrunched his dick and balls together, and allowed for the maximum view of his slight bulge. Was Mrs. Carousel going to gauge my heft? Make sure her daughter is getting her money's worth? No use lamenting the size my miniscule penis, for I have my whole life ahead of me to sulk in such self-conscious woes.

Once everyone was strapped and secure, Papa fired up the engine and coasted out, skimming graciously along the lakeshore dance floor. Top speed zoom and rush, the directional wind and misty updraft washing over their eager faces. Smiles, absolute. The all-American grin, the result of speeding aimlessly, directions obsolete, for no other reason than the pure joy of acceleration, whirling will-o'-the-wisp hair and an idle hand dangling off the edge. Summertime, defined. The free-time celebration of a weekend. Dashing over the water conjured the sensation of losing track of all time and space, however fleeting this feeling may be. Nevertheless, nothing in this life can compare to the miracle of getting captured by the majesty of the moment. Gazing out into the surrounding wilderness and simply allowing uninhibited euphoria to wash over you is a soul-cleansing triumph, a doubtless rebirth of the spirit.

After cruising around for an influential, epiphany-generating joyride of immeasurable duration, it was time to get wet. Papa slowed the boat to a rollicking sway, allowing a brief moment's pause before attaching the tow-cable to a sturdy, stainless steel section of the canopy's frame; the metal perimeter of the polyester, UV resistant cloth that provides shade to the boat's passengers. He gave a few tugs to ensure the rope's tension was adequate.

"Alright. Who's up?"

Jared, being new to the procedure of wakeboarding, was selected as the first rider. He leapt into the water, enduring the initial chill with a combination of strained reactionary discomfort accompanied by an overlay of forced gusto, and was tossed the board.

"Now just slip your feet into the bindings and let the nose of the board poke slightly out of the water."

Jared complied. He was goofy footed (for those of you who wish to recreate an accurate image of this situation in your mind). Amy and her mother watched from the comfort of the boat as he nervously prepared.

"When you're ready, yell out 'Hit it' as loud as you can, and I will respond with vigor. Just scream it when you're ready."

Oh great. It's already enough of a struggle for me to maintain a customary conversation. It takes great effort to pass selected syllables through my timid lips. And now I have to shout a tubular statement at the top of my lungs.

"Got it." He obliged with apprehensive hesitation.

"Oh, and for a visual signal, how about you also throw me a thumbs up."

Well aren't I just a regular James Dean, a naturally born pretty boy with a rough edge. An attractive air of mystery eludes me, yet still I will saunter on. Oh boy, let's see, we got Papa at the ship's helm, while Amy and her mom sit patiently, waiting for me to prove my worth.

"You ready?"

Jared nodded.

Papa tossed the terminus end of the tow cable toward him. A polyethylene low-stretch rope, the handle resembling a clothes hanger with a squishy foam-lined grip, splashed into the water, directly in front of our boy. He assumed the position and prepared for the worst. After a deep inhale, he gave the thumbs up, followed by an impressively powerful and manly "Hit it!"

Papa grinned and floored the engine. The tension in the rope immediately pulled Jared out of the water, lifted him entirely. The sudden boost startled his balance to such an extent that he barely managed to articulate a proper surf before tumbling back into the lake, sending the rope skyward. Amy's mother promptly lifted the red flag to alert all surrounding watercraft of a downed rider, and Papa performed a swift U-turn.

"It takes a few tries to get used to the initial force of the boat pulling you."

"Yea."

Smile wide. He could tell Amy was giggling sheepishly.

"Give it another go."

After countless attempts, Jared's form failed to improve, even slightly. Once he gained the preliminary lift, he instantly quit and fell back, every time. This was repeated over and over until Papa finally concluded that Jared would never manage to submit to the fortunes of beginner's luck and that continually 'try[ing] again' was not paying off. Practice makes perfect, but we only have so many hours to spend out here today.

"I just can't get the hang of it."

"Hey, no worries, you gave it your all."

He climbed back onto the boat and exchanged duties with Amy, the more experienced of the two. She jumped in and proved to be a highly skilled and worthwhile rider. At least, compared to Jared. She was averaging at least a good ten seconds, minimum, per run, sailing atop the surface with indelible grace. Her face, whenever she caught momentum, signified stern athletic concentration and determined perseverance without neglecting the importance of recreational fun as the reigning purpose of the entire experience, never regressing into the overt seriousness and detrimental self-loathing that often accompanies the failed collapse of striving toward physically oriented, and ultimately finite, goals. Her #1 rule involved some motivational jargon about always having a good time.

"Whew!"

After Amy's successful, skilled skim and the supportive accolades bestowed from Jared and her parents, it seemed an appropriate and well-earned progression from the hardened strain and intense exertion required to wakeboard properly to now inflate the two-passenger inner tube and enjoy a more passive form of whirly, high-speed adrenaline. The tube owned by the Carousel family resembled the number eight; or, more appropriately, given the direction in which it is used, the infinity symbol. A side-by-side seat for each passenger, allowing maximum togetherness. J&A nestled themselves into the complimentary, fitted holes and attained a measure of comfortable anticipation. Their seating arrangement conveyed the romantic allure of a bicycle built for two, with the sort of glee and energized rush that precedes a rollercoaster's plunge. Once you're strapped into place, all that's required is that you enjoy the ride. Nothing more is asked of you. Amy called out, "Hit it!"

Anyone who has gone tubing, whether single or double passenger, knows the glorious leisure it provides. The air-filled tube cushions the constant bounce of the waves created by the boat's pull, and the speed-demon thrill is equivalent to a steep canyon motorcycle ride without the risk of a debilitating, life threatening injury. The two teenage lovers aboard the rubber vessel were howling like wild beasts in the midst of a natural fury, with enough earned wisdom and life-dangling serenity to make Al Ginsberg blush.

An odd sensation crept into Jared's emotionally-riddled psyche as he glanced over and saw Amy smiling beyond stars. He couldn't quite believe the wonder of this moment. Such a precious segment of life. He looked at Amy and felt smitten by the limitless potential of their relationship. How truly fortunate he was to be with her. Suddenly, he understood the lyrics to every love song ever composed. He knew the feeling. He could relate to the sense of completeness these songs often spoke of. The triumph in obtaining life's great reward. At once, he comprehended the purpose of the human heart and the endless art created under its captivating influence. In particular, he though of "Crash into me" by Dave Matthews Band and the line "in a boy's dream." This was the absolute summation of his swelling heart's standing ovation. Such purity of thought. I get it now. He knew right then that Amy was his one true love and they were destined to spend forever together.

His unprovoked, theoretical realization was further supported by evidence of the precise moment being shared by the newly minted love-of-my-life sweethearts. Let us proceed by isolating the two competing situations: the adrenaline-junkie rush and the lover's eye twinkle. (1) The act of being towed by a boat while on an inner tube is fun, no matter what. It is a fun activity. If I were alone, being tugged by a robotically-controlled boat, it would provide an equal level of fun in the sun. The mere physicality of the event yields pleasure and enjoyment. (2) By his side during this aquatic gallop, is a girl. A girl he had been admiring and masturbating to for years. A girl who has finally reciprocated his infatuation. Now, here they are together, sharing not only a physically pleasing and exciting experience, but also an emotional connection, a meeting of the body and the mind. Eternal. Jared dreamt of their future together, and the glorious promises that beckoned on the horizon.

'She makes everything better. By her side, I'd feel content anywhere. Her presence infinitely increases the meaningful magic of any given moment. And knowing that she feels the same way about me is delightfully unfathomable, yet somehow true. She is my blessed guardian angel, incarnate and real. Loving, and offering the touch of consolation. Together we shall remain for the rest of our lives, forever perpetuating the lingering devotion we share.'

Jared was intoxicated by the sudden surge of new and unknown feelings. The emotion of love had been successfully uploaded to his mental registry. He stumbled through the rest of the afternoon in a daylight slumber, all giddy and resolute. It would have been impossible to wipe the smile from his face. As they packed up to leave the lake, Jared hovered carelessly above the needless weight of all the uninspiring and detrimental facets of life where love was not at the ultimate forefront of all action and thought. He simply couldn't be bothered otherwise. The precision required to load the boat onto the trailer did not resonate within his 'love, and love only' mindset. He was therefore wholly useless in his assistance with this effort.

His only resonant memory of the remainder of this day was a brief stop made on the drive home. For a late-lunch/early-dinner, depending on your dietary schedule, Papa decided to stop at a McDonalds to pick up some grub. Not wanting to drag a boat trailer through the drive-thru and cause unnecessary congestion for the swarm of hungry, vehicle-ridden customers, he and Mrs. Carousel went inside to obtain an assortment of burgers, fries, sodas and nugs, leaving Amy and Jared alone for the first time since igniting their newfound adolescent passion.

Jared, presented with a perfect opportunity for either an adorable first kiss or even an innocent session of hand holding, instead opted for nervously rubbing his fingers across Amy's face. Like, he was literally gliding his hand over Amy's lips and cheeks, completely unromantic and altogether irritating and intrusive. She was confused and bothered. Jared simply did not know how to express his burgeoning love. He wanted desperately to establish a close, physical connection within the confines of knowing her parents would return any moment, not to mention that Mr. and Mrs. Carousel could potentially be observing this entire interaction, as car windows don't provide much in the realm of privacy.

"What are you doing?" she asked, in a tiresome tone.

"I…" He immediately quit his awkward hand rubbing technique, clearly a failure. Prodding at a woman's face does not result in mutual arousal.

"Are you hungry?" She desperately wanted to talk about something, anything.

"Yea, you bet," he replied, doomed.

Amy felt that given their location, it was an appropriate time to offer an amusing Carousel family anecdote.

"My parents actually have a strong, meaningful connection to the McDonalds franchise."

"Oh, really? How so?"

"Well, after their wedding, which was more like a hitching ceremony, only close friends and family, a small, intimate affair, anyways, after they got married, they went to McDonalds for their honeymoon. Not for their post-wedding meal, but their legit honeymoon was spent at a McDonalds. No weekend in the Bahamas, no European cultural jaunt, not even a day at Disneyland or a fucking Indian casino. McDonalds."

Jared somehow found this story adorable.

"I love that. I mean, if your love is true, it doesn't matter where you are as long as you're together. In true love's grasp, a McDonalds can be just as seminal and tender as a tropical island getaway. I would suggest that the less flashy the honeymoon, the more assured the love. Confidence needs not the bouquet of a grandiose declaration."

"You know, I never quite thought of it that way. To me, it always seemed to suggest a lack of commitment. Like, somehow making a big to-do about their vows would tarnish the ease and simplicity of their relationship. They never put any effort into their relationship before, so why start now? Almost as though their love wasn't worthy of such eloquence. You know?"

"Hey, there's nothing wrong with keeping things low key. As I already said, regardless of their physical location, they knew that the value of true love was obtained and nurtured in a mental plane, not an aero plane."

"Ha! Good one."

Through the window, Jared saw her parents exit the restaurant holding 2 large paper bags and 4 cups, all products adorned with the trademark M symbol, a subtle vestige of the renowned Gateway Arch. As they approached the car, a laugh was shared, the knowing laugh of an inside joke shared between lovers, well deserved and wrought with time.

In a sad irony, or for the technically precise and conceptually gifted: an unfortunate outcome, Amy's parents filed for divorce a month after the getaway to Lake Castaic. As it turned out, the fun-in-the-sun splish-splash weekend was not just another casual summer day for the Carousels, it was, in fact, a last ditch effort to rekindle their suffocating marriage; which, as was later revealed, turned out to be a complete failure. Such a strange weight tugged at their chances, ultimately drowning the foolish parents. The plight of the American love story, tragic and unresolved. Amy's BREAKING NEWS about the divorce lifted a veil of joy about the boat trip, to reveal, in hindsight, an underlying desperation. They were trying to make it right, clipping jumper cables to their dying romance. O what an intersection of fates and chapters turned. Jared discovers the throbbing beat of love in the company of a tattered, war-torn couple on the brink of divorce. A simultaneous rise and fall. Just as one airplane's takeoff cleared the runway, another descended for landing. Picture this.

How could Jared console her in this time of need? Sure, he could pat her on the back and tell her how everything will be okay, but he possessed not a single shred of life experience that would qualify him as a provider of legitimate sympathy in this situation. He had not undergone the adequate devastations needed to soothe her catastrophic woes. Sure, he could provide a shoulder to cry on, but absent was the emotional resonance of a heart to match. "I'm sorry to hear about that" can only provide a limited amount of comfort to a sobbing daughter untimely forced to endure the grim realization that love is not always forever.

Charlie, along with the better half of Jared's childhood friends (the bruised and roughed-up half), had already undergone the heart wrenching despair of climbing through the shards of a collapsed nest, alone, or with the uncompromising aide of an equally fraught sibling. Apparently, judging from his eager (bordering on forced and aggressive) attitude and pure-of-heart desire to comfort the blithering mess that was Amy in the immediate wake of learning the grisly details of her parents' shattered fairytale, Charlie felt that he was a qualified spokesman for how to cope with divorce in a 21$^{st}$ century landscape. Granted, Charlie was, without question, a more credible source on the matter, having worn the badge of visitation rights and duplicate holiday celebrations, going on nearly three years now. Boy o boy, how time slips away. As a natural action of recourse, Charlie took it upon himself to capitalize on her suffering. Duly noting that she was a pristine and private only child, he assumed the role of the wise, guiding-light savior. The older brother who whispers "we'll get through this, together," with a scruff of the hair and a friendly punch on the shoulder. In this particular case, Charlie composed a note. A handwritten, folded sheet of notebook paper, schoolboy note. The contents of this interface were never shared with Jared, as he simply didn't understand the severity of the situation and lived too sheltered and smiley a life to offer any relevant support. So instead, as the class sessions let out during the summer school interval between 9$^{th}$ and 10$^{th}$ grade, in which Jared was enrolled in European History/World Studies and Amy retook Spanish I, Jared was subjected to his first of many emotional surges of jealousy and suspicion while watching Charlie slip Amy a tri-folded sheet of paper.

It was a sudden and unhealthy transgression, Jared's shift in attitude. He began harboring resentment toward his own friends. His best friends, who repeatedly pulled him aside in a drastic attempt to slap him out of his weakling trance, having observed that ever since he began dating Amy he was no longer the same. Often this discussion would arise among the camaraderie of the Physical Education locker room, a space of man-on-man gruff (brutal honesty and testicular compulsions often flourished here). Like, listen here: there was this boy, a poor boy. Literally poor in financial terms. Empty-walleted and downtrodden. Get this: he lived in an apartment. A fucking apartment! Seriously? How badly did your parents fuck up to end up as middle-aged apartment dwellers? Context. Ah, precisely. This indeed demands thorough context. Where Jared grew up, everyone he knew lived in a sturdy and extravagant house. Full on homes. The house was a symbol of completeness, of a faceted dream's attainment. Apartments in prosperous suburban communities were, in comparison, barracks, shantytowns, refugee camps. Not some high-rise, swanky New York apartments; rather, they were backstreet shame huts. Unfulfilled and broken-down settlements (appropriate verbiage, as leasing an apartment is the literal synthesis of settling, giving up), the rotting remains of abandoned ambition. Yet in terms of mating calls and attractive personality quirks, the sad lives of the poor kids elicited much more desire and admirable dignity compared to the 'I'm never sad, life is FUN FUN FUN everyday, PLAY PLAY everyday, never ever work unless it's exciting' mentality of the rich faggots. The financially disenfranchised often held the upper hand of respectability and distinguished renaissance-man aptitude among the affluent and privileged, where most of the boys and girls had rich families. Their demure stature held great weight in social circles. It was safe to assume that po' boys carried an attractive, victimesque allure. A downtrodden sadness that girls found irresistible, as they were smitten by a sudden eagerness to heal these dopey-eyed hobos. After all, rich kids often live meaningless lives of unappreciative excess. They take their privilege for granted, and as such, their joy becomes a blank joy. A happiness without meaning, without struggle. A reward without winning. Sure, they were always smiling and comfortable, but their wealth was misunderstood and unearned. Hence, it is not at all difficult, in fact it's rather easy, to grasp the attractive charm of the dirty-clothed, scraggly poor kid. And it's especially straightforward and uncomplicated to comprehend Amy's fascination with one particular apartment dweller by the name of Adam, a young rapscallion with hands of feeble vulnerability. Adam was a dignified savant in contrast to Jared. For instance, a fight once erupted between Amy and Jared concerning the proper method of popping pimples. Amy preferred the traditional method of leaning in close to a bathroom mirror and letting your fingers do the work; i.e., locating a glistening zit and squeezing it until the pressure builds and the thin outer membrane splits and a sudden splooge of puss launches onto the reflective glass. Now, Jared's method consisted of getting his mommy to drive him to the dermatologist for a proper facial cleanse, complete with tantric music, candles and all that bullshit. Amy scoffed at his suggestion and declared that he was a spoiled brat for his participation in such ridiculous practices, reserved for the rich. His response to her assertion was a raised arm, finger pointed skyward, like Travolta's famous pose, and a sternly shouted "Get out!" The guy literally kicked her out of his house for calling him spoiled. She wasn't even being accusatory. She was merely making an observation. Amy bitterly obliged his request and headed for the door. A long, disheartened walk home. Left foot right foot, begrudgingly. So, point being, of course Amy respected this Adam kid, of course she dug his vibe, he was a gentleman, a humble dude. When Amy was spotted chatting with him during an uninspired hour of P.E., which consisted of walking around and around in endless laps, Jared steamed. Fifty clicks away he could see the two casually conversing, and this was absolutely not allowed in the Dating Jared Rulebook. He immediately stormed over to them and aggressively, almost rape-worthy, kissed Amy on the lips, right in front of this awkward Adam kid. Jared was marking his territory, like a cat pissing on a select sofa. This forceful kiss suggested, 'Hey man, you can look but you can't touch. She's mine, all mine!' I almost feel bad for the guy. A cute high school girl is talking to him out of the kindness of her heart, and up comes her hostile boyfriend and he just starts making out with her right in front of his face. Like, his one glimmer of hope, of butterfly happiness, is squandered by this asshole that demands to have it all for himself. It was unpleasant, to say the least. An ugliness crept into Jared's otherwise generous and cheery persona.

   With the coming of Amy Carousel began the part of my life you could call my life of possessive insecurities. Somehow, now that Amy was officially branded as being his girlfriend, his one and only, everyone else became an immediate threat to their precious and wholesome relationship. Evil insurgents determined to steal her away through the luring tactics of laughter and hugs. Any outside influence was deemed unacceptable and dangerous. The unexpected shift in Jared's outlook was greeted with disdain and absolute bewilderment. You see, Amy had been a member of their friendship coalition years before they (J+A) began dating. She was the object of attraction not only to Jared, but practically all of his male friends shared a mutual, boner-forming infatuation with her. Amy was hot property. She was fucking sexy. There's no denying she was and still is a beautiful specimen, not only physically, but in her nerd-slut demeanor as well. It was like, 'How do we have this super cool chick in our group? How did we convince her to hang out with us?' The brotherhood was, at the time, the official Amy Carousel Fan Club. She was absolutely gorgeous and we often bonded over the shared, unequivocal love we had for her, which was an enduring constant among our circle.

Now, I'll be the first to admit, and I'm sure I'm not the only one with this specific secret to share, that Amy Carousel was the first girl I ever masturbated to, repeatedly. Obsessively. She was my dream girl, the target of my desire ever since my initial pangs of adolescent horniness. I fantasized about her nonstop. I'd be lying in bed, tugging away feverishly, while images of potential scenarios between her and I filled my imagination. I soon developed a strange habit of putting on headphones and listening to "Red Sweater" by The Aquabats while jerking off to her, as I found the adorable sense of innocent romance conveyed by that tune coincided perfectly with my own heart's outlook on love. The excitement and overjoyed enthusiasm toward a particular girl. Hell, I even went so far as to referring to her as my happy thought, my spirit animal, whose mental image alone was enough to inspire and delight me. I recall writing a poem in 7$^{th}$ grade titled "The Box." I don't remember it word for word, though it was basically about how no matter the troubles in one's life, we all posses a metaphorical box that we can look into and/or reach into when times get tough and we'll instantly feel rejuvenated and happy to be alive. For some, the box is video games, music, a family photo, a puppy, or a vigorous workout. Whatever cheers you up. For me it was just the thought of Amy, of knowing I would always see her again soon. She made me excited to go to school everyday. I wrote this poem during drama class (a class Amy was also in. Coincidence? Fate?), and the teacher enjoyed my little foible so much that she ended up tacking the thing to the wall. Bless her heart.

The point of this whole meandering tirade is to illuminate the simple fact that Amy was a woman adored by all, and by either dumb luck or sheer perseverance, Jared ended up with her. He won the grand prize. The sought after seductress was now his. However, his victory brought about a change in the overall group dynamic. No longer could the guys joke about having the hots for good ol' Amy. Suddenly any sign of affection or playful camaraderie toward her was a personal assault on Jared. At least that's how he saw it. As soon as it became official that J+A were together, a cease and desist letter was sent to all his friends, outlining the new protocol for how Amy was to be treated. Jared became a psychotic asshole, dictating and monitoring Amy's social life. He would flip his shit if he ever saw her hugging someone else. G-d forbid she ever became engulfed in another man's arms. Once, he spotted Amy far off in the distance receiving a hug from a lad and he screamed out across the vast expanse between them, demanding the 2 huggers immediately separate. Ain't no Johnny-come-lately gunna snatch my girl away from me. He was making a fool of himself and Amy felt embarrassed enough for both of them.

Through the cluttered pathways of Jared's abstract reasoning, he positively believed that once their relationship was firmly established, consummated and publicly broadcast to the entire student body, a mutual commitment of monogamous social interaction was justifiably enacted. But she, the fluttering flirt, could not be tamed. And why would she? Thus far she had grown accustomed to reveling in the gross attention her titillating sexiness afforded her. Men (boys) simply flocked to her. Magnetic pull. Prior to their coupling, Jared had been one of many clamoring fools. Though he had always felt a special connection to her, a privileged position amongst the scramble. He is not at fault for feeling jealous, even if directed at his own friends; yet he neglected to consider the fact that he and Amy dating would not diminish or cancel out the mass attraction toward her. Sure, his friends could suppress their lustful summoning, but the fantasy would remain indefinitely. Had not everyone reveled in the teenage masturbatory intermingling of Amy and __[insert your name here]__ ? Consider this: Eddie, Bernardo and Charlie were not introduced to Amy as Jared's girlfriend. Had that been the case, they would have been given ample time to dim their yearnings, shunt all notions of Amy as a sexually desirable mate, and engage the ethical code of honor among men, eloquently decreed as 'bros before hoes.' But with Amy, it was a contest. Who would be granted the dignified pleasure of courting, and eventually deflowering, young Amy?

Jared, in his younger and more vulnerable years, had developed a strict fascination with televised game shows. His introduction to the genre being the easily accessible constants of Jeopardy, Wheel of Fortune and Family Feud. These shows provided the bread and butter foundation of a young man's descent into the dramatic, suspenseful spectacle of reciting obscure trivia in front of a live studio audience.

Game shows signified a quest for ultimate knowledge, the race to be the smartest man in the room. When taught of a peculiar or insignificant factoid, the promise of appearing on a game show and being asked to recite said datum validated our being required to possess intelligence beyond practical functionality in the first place. The war cry of the lazy student: "Why do I need to know this? When will I ever implement this wisdom?" In a culture in which smarts are shunned and being a worldly, well-versed individual with a scope of understanding beyond your daily needs and comforts is viewed as counter-productive, the dangling ribbons of cash prizes, new cars and all-expense-paid trips to Hawaii gave practical reasons for striving toward any glint of mental betterment. "Why learn formulas when we have calculators?" Why bother? Human beings should constantly be hungry for knowledge, I would hope. We should always be seeking to expand the shallow confines of our mind, without the need for material incentives to reward us.

Along with the skewed praise of intelligence that game shows celebrated, there also existed a sense of havoc, of competition, a brain battle where only the smartest survive. Physical advantages will no longer benefit the warrior, as natural predatory functions are surrendered to the quiet synapses of mental ingenuity. Darwin would've shit himself if he ever saw an episode of The Price is Right, where every morning, fat wobbly tubs of white trash and brittle-boned grandmas repeatedly defeat decorated soldiers fresh out of combat. But this is not a new revelation. Ever since the advent of weaponized warfare, combatant bloodbaths are won by the smartest rather than the strongest of men. The barbaric battle methods of hand-on-hand fisticuffs and physical dominance have faded into the past, replaced with the innovations of chemical rain, distinguished engineering breakthroughs and the all-powerful atomic bomb (encoded by the great mastermind of science and imagination). In game shows there are rarely any physical elements of endurance-based competition implemented into the festivities. The war is fought purely with wisdom and wits, and a properly enunciable speaking voice. Talk it out, comrades. May he who has read the most books leave as the unscathed victor.

In all of the major syndicated game shows, Jared saw rare glimpses of the great human spirit, beamed through the glowing orb of television. Each individual show celebrated a particular triumph of mankind's greatest ambition, endlessly striving toward excellence. Jeopardy, clearly the most distinguished and challenging of all game shows, measures the financial worth of the contestants by gauging their knowledge and understanding of the grand gamut of known and established human fact. It encourages the attainment and recollection of encyclopedic volumes of fine point historical indexes. Questions range from vast expanses of literary and artistic developments to modern scientific discoveries, geographic confines and even mundane pop culture references. No subject is off limits, as contestants are just as likely to be quizzed on details concerning the development of ballet during the Italian Renaissance, as the discography of Bruce Springsteen.

"What is 'Thunder Road'?"

"Who is Domenico da Piacenza?"

As if the content of the questions asked wasn't difficult or mentally stimulating enough, the show incorporated clever wordplay schemes in transmitting the already mind-bending clues. Portmanteaus abound!

Jeopardy existed on a higher echelon than most other game shows. The competitors were borderline geniuses, there was no goofy ra-ra celebration for the winners and aside from a rare chuckle, laughter, induced by a highbrow reference occurring in between questions, was few and far between. However, a brief a moment of rare personality existed after the first of three required commercial breaks in which the master of ceremonies, the perpetually well-dressed and pleasant Alex Trebek, would interview the three warriors. Aside from sharing their job titles, they were also prodded into sharing interesting anecdotes from their lives, proving to the audience that there was a complexity to their existence, beyond coffee-drenched library lounging. Contestants would often reminisce about vacations to remote locations, further highlighting their worldly, scholarly personas. These interviews were often brief and rushed, just a quick glance at your humanity and then it was back to the game.

The whole format of the show was aristocratic and formal. Even the buzzers sounded warm and inviting, a soothing tone that cuddles up closely to your eardrum. Watching Jeopardy was like spending a quiet day at your grandparents' house, diligently reading through their vast library of books concerning various subjects and listening to reposeful classical music, after a week of rambunctious youth-oriented bombast; i.e., punk concerts and shitty movies. A tranquil palate cleanser.

The lower-tier game shows, which had also become accustomed staples of American television, were much more upbeat and exciting in comparison to the straight-laced academia channeled by Jeopardy. Wheel of Fortune, another Merv Griffin creation, was a game of words, a tournament of parsing out phrases or titles, one letter at a time. There was no element of question and answer; rather, gameplay was a slow moving peek-a-boo reveal. A rich man's version of hangman, the fear of death induced by the gallows replaced with loss of money. BANKRUPT! Wheel of Fortune was an altogether pleasant and unthreatening game, simplified for the at-home audience. It transmitted a bright, visually stimulating look with the rainbow whirl of the wheel and the seaweed green of the puzzle board, not to mention the sexually-arousing objectification of women that was the mute and (since the digital overhaul of '97) useless co-host, Vanna White. Every correct guess of a letter was rewarded with the glamorous strut of Ms. White, who is rumored to have never worn the same outfit twice; which is quite a feat in itself considering that Wheel of Fortune is the longest running syndicated game show in televised history.

It's a cute show, almost silly, with an overhanging dread. The format of the game itself, a bastardization of hangman, conjures up thoughts of murder, execution, possibly even suicide (we will elaborate further once Family Feud is called into question), ritualized methods of government approved and publicly exhibited killings. A sickeningly gruesome reassurance of justice. The dangling corpse of a criminal, wiped away and eliminated for his wrong-doings, as an audience views with full attention. The wheel itself also carries deadly overtones. The quick spin of a revolver's cylinder, the careless gamble of roulette, where a flick of the wrist can yield either rewards and riches or poverty and termination. Wheel of Fortune is the modern incarnation of an afternoon in an old western town, a man being dragged to the noose while a spectator spins the cylinder of his gun, a single bullet in the six-capacity chamber, the prospective threat of eternal rest looming restlessly in every breach of the moment.

The show also forces us to ponder the English language in written form; specifically, the significance of letter frequency. This is made most apparent during the bonus round, in which the player with the highest earnings is summoned to perform a solo puzzle. What is peculiar about this particular segment is that a predetermined group of letters are revealed (if they so happen to exist within the word or phrase). Any casual viewer of the show can recall that the letters are, consistently, R S T L N & E. It's a seemingly obscure jumble of consonants with a single, sympathetic vowel. Displaying these letters, if they were indeed included in the hidden words, offered support to the struggling contestants, a clue or hint, encouraging a correct guess toward solving the puzzle. However, this begs the question, why are these letters specifically designated as the helper letters? Clearly any printing-press enthusiast specializing in Linotype keyboard assisted hot metal typesetting will be quick to point out the mythological term ETAOIN SHRDLU, which is, inarguably, the assemblage of the most commonly used letters in the English language, in descending frequency. Unlike modern QWERTY keyboards, Linotype machines arranged letters according to the rate of repeated use. So, out of pure strategy, a <u>Wheel of Fortune</u> contestant, when asked to guess three consonants and a vowel, in addition to the charitable RSTLNE, ought to guess H D C and A (just some advice for any readers who intend to appear on the show). The familiar QWERTY arrangement was designed to alleviate gear jams in the metal-armed typewriters of the mid-1800s. The QWERTY configuration alleviated this issue by separating letters that would otherwise be typed in sequence, and thus cause the gears to jam. This unique distribution of letters, for implementation in a typewriter, was designed by Christopher Latham Sholes and Carlos S. Glidden, in what came to be known, appropriately, as the Sholes & Glidden Typewriter, the first functional and successful consumer typewriter.

Okay, so this is a slightly amusing and barely interesting history lesson, and maybe I'm only concerned about it in the first place because I'm writing this pitiful page-turner, doused in schizophrenic font shifts, and I sit in front of a QWERTY keyboard everyday and I finally wondered, 'Why are the letters in this distinct and mysterious order?' But behold, there is significance to my telling of the development of the modern keyboard. You see, the Sholes & Glidden design was eventually acquired and distributed by E. Remington and Sons, a popular gun manufacturer during the Civil War, and both WWI and WWII. This gives an entirely new meaning to the phrase 'the pen is mightier than the sword,' as apparently E. Remington and Sons had the foresight to realize that the pen would soon give way to the typewriter and the sword would evolve into the gun. All of this, though, further instills the eerie aura of murder and death that pervades the set of <u>Wheel of Fortune</u>.

A quandary of suggestion regarding the use of past or present tense when discussing television shows. Admittedly, at the time of this tangential ramble these shows are currently still being aired, but let us remember the tried and true maxim of 'nothing lasts forever.' Therefore, what if? In a future landscape these words may be looked upon without the gentle flicker of <u>Jeopardy</u> in the background, a constant comfort. So please forgive my scrambled tense, as I am subconsciously scribing for the now as well as the later. A down the line time when such shows are looked upon as ancient relics of a simpler past.

Moving on, let's see. If <u>Wheel of Fortune</u> represents man's fear of death, the prizes given out to the potential victor signify all the modern amenities that can successfully distract us from mortality. Well, not necessarily distractions, that's a bit harsh; instead, I'd like to view the prizes as tools for living life to the fullest. When properly utilized, the prizes are merely providers of experiences. Like the oft-coveted new car, which the recipient can either park in their driveway and admire, washing and waxing, or they can get inside, fire up the engine and go out into the world. Explore the surrounding terrain, get lost, get swept up in an adventure. Go! The prize of a tropical vacation getaway is self-explanatory, as no physical object is won; rather, an experience is arranged and provided, all expenses paid. Fortunate one, fortunate one, spin the wheel of chance and tell us what you've won.

If we're to consider Merv Griffin as the reigning supreme sultan of syndicated game shows, then let Mark Goodson be remembered as his snide, snotty younger brother. The shit-shifting younger sibling struggling to prove his worth beside a landmark contribution of genuine greatness. I'll show them, yea. I know what it takes to spearhead a turnbuckle of trivial swamp meat. I can assemble roundabout know-it-alls and dump suggestions of an inquisitive nature their way. I know how to muster the anticipation of one solitary, gleaming moment of brainpower. What is the entertainment industry if not a dumpster dive sacrament of languished brain cells and useless knowledge? Behold my creation: <u>Family Feud</u>! A true anomaly of the unified one-mind theory, uniquely suggestive and lambast worthy.

Fundamentally, <u>Family Feud</u> selects what is perhaps the most divisive, tangled and conflict-ridden units of civilian life: the American family. Corralling the disparate and anxious members together in one bright-lit, orange-wallpapered studio and forcing them to consider the similarities and likeminded nature of human opinion. For instance, the average team consists of an uptight, working-stiff father, a happy-as-a-bunny-rabbit mommy, a drug-addled twenty-something son, the overachiever, smarty-pants sister, and one additional member, be it a bored grandparent or an eager, nothing-better-to-do, unemployed uncle, all standing together behind the horizontally-exaggerated podium as one singular group, united. Their differing viewpoints and values are combined, strengthening the vast multitude of what could constitute a suitable response to the forthcoming questions.

<u>Family Feud</u>, potentially, depending on the level of romanticism one exerts upon their perspective, represents the strength (or weakness) of family (or any sort of team), as the inherent differences that often separate us and commonly lead to arguments at the dinner table, are combined and appreciated as unique points of view. As such, the method of inquisition practiced on the show concerns the use of polls, or surveys, in which a singular question is asked to a group of one hundred people. The members of the two competing families then guess the top answers. For example, the first question asked in the premiere episode of <u>Family Feud</u> was "Name a famous George." It's more of a request than a question. Regardless, each family member is granted the opportunity to offer his or her (or

transgendered) own distinct answer. And thus, you have a game. Play ball. Correct responses are gauged in the all-powerful, mass-market strategic measurement of the beloved survey. One hundred individuals are asked for a response to an unthreatening, simplistic question. Top five answers are on the board.

The key to winning at <u>Family Feud</u> is the ability to think in a majority mindset. Neglect the oddball curvature of the poets and the unique brilliance of the physicists connecting wires and dissecting frogs. After all, they're too busy to waste time on some meaningless survey. Dumb down your sparkled mind, approach the game from the perspective of a below-average, semi-educated specimen of American mediocrity. Simplification is crucial, as the intention of any poll, whether concerning politics or consumer habits, is to paraphrase the variety of opinions into a synthesis of easily discernible factoids. Eliminate the acid-eaters attempting to skew the stats, and focus only on the big picture. The enormous overhang of groupthink. Play your cards right, and you'll be on your way to receiving a fat check from a prodigious television studio.

The host of the show, the master of ceremonies, was a flirtatious man (often kissing the female contestants) by the name of Richard Dawson. Richard would saunter around the set with unabashed grace. He was born to host The Feud. Although the show has gone through several hosts (still, to this day, they keep changing. I can name at least five off the top of my head), Richard fit the part better than any of them. He carried himself with a certain, undeniable charm. However, and this is a strong however, <u>Family Feud</u> does indeed have quite the tale of a particular host who took over in the interim period between Dawson's dual reign. You see, when CBS took ownership of the Feud franchise, a spry lad by the name of Ray Combs was fastened to the driver's seat. Ray held tight to his position and hosted the show for nearly seven years, until he was given the metaphorical boot, axed, laid off, in order to make room for Dawson's return. Ray Combs bid farewell to <u>Family Feud</u> in 1994 and went on to become immortalized in what is perhaps the most disturbing and sadly pathetic legends of game show lore.

Two years after his dishonorable discharge, Ray Combs committed suicide by hanging himself in the closet of his room at a psychiatric ward, with a noose made of knotted bed sheets. His death brought to light the dark undercurrent of the smiley-faced game show hosts. The provider of riches and vanity, a perpetual giver, never being rewarded himself. Although Family Feud marched on gallantly, Ray certainly left a dark stain of eternal woe in the eyes of every anxious audience member peering into their television screens in search of an escape from the harms of mortal drudgery, only to be greeted by Ray's plastic smile in the reruns. The pretend happiness of a dead man, beamed into our homes.

Lest we forget, it would be a definite disservice to neglect to mention The Price is Right as a reflective mantle of American consumerism. This is a show where contestants are rewarded for reciting educated guesses with regard to the monetary value of various household products. It championed an appreciation for the engulfment of free market capitalism into our nimble thought processes. The ability to discern value in financial terms became a respectable skill, and prizes were given out accordingly.

While all of the aforementioned shows aired during the evening hours, The Price is Right remained steadily as a daytime show. Some would even consider it a morning show. School-aged students would often wax lyrical about watching the show when they were ill and therefore made to remain home instead of attending class, in order to rest off their sickness. Obviously, the spontaneous audience of sick schoolchildren was not a viable enough market to keep the ratings afloat. So, who else could be relied upon to tune in? We are left with the retired, the unemployed and the non-employed. In other words, old people, slackers and stay-at-home parents. The working-class, toughened day laborers and stressed out stockbrokers had no time for petty games. They were already preoccupied with busting their sweaty asses day after day, literally paying no mind to the trivialities of pondering dollar values and the sad glory that followed a correct guess. However, this game is ripe for the idle, available minds of the homebodies. While one family member is at work earning money, the other is at home devising methods for spending said money. Not necessarily in a wasteful or superfluous manner, but for practical and essential purchases. Sustenance. Supermarket dwellers, price checkers and cart-pushing card-swipers are the prime demographic for such a show, as they revel in the world of endless purchasing.

The Price is Right is basically just a commercial transformed into an interactive game. A tiresome gamut of yearning for the solace and stability that material possessions lend to the empty hands of a potential purchaser. Albeit, the show is fun. It's exciting and playfully entertaining. So if you happen to find yourself blessed with the chance to view an episode, I suggest you watch. Oh, and I almost forgot, don't forget to have your pets spayed or neutered.

A harmless victim of the excitement and suspense induced by game shows, a deeply enraptured viewer, was none other than our own Jared. He soon discovered the escape provided by zoning out to the TV and relying on his mental capacities, firing off answers in surefire anticipation.

Everyone, at least every television fan, has their own niche of preferred content. Some enjoy high-concept drama, some adore talk shows, while many are partial to sports. For Jared, it was game shows. He loved the brainy game play, the kitsch sets, the charming hosts and the genuine joy displayed on the faces of the victors. Game show contestants could be anyone, glowing highlights of the enduring quality of the human spirit. For instance, athletes are highly trained warriors, brutish and tough. Talk show guests are well-established celebrity flaunters. All are specialized, walking success stories. The contestants on game shows are average folks plucked off the morose streets of life. Savages. Primal beings struggling to exorcise the demons of the everyday charge. Although Jeopardy has a certain elitist, Ivy League, no-idiots-allowed mindset. For the most part, the people that appear on game shows come from all walks of life. Spotless sweater pride-hounds and trailer park bumpkins all share the same stage. All are equal in the illuminated studios. Jared was enthralled with the prospect of sudden wealth dropped in the hands of any random passerby with at least a couple functioning brain cells. He became a game show aficionado, entering a trance in front of the TV and merrily playing along, like ol' Guy Montag's wife with her soaps. He surrendered himself to the power of the game. It's also worth noting that during the incline of his amusement, Who Wants to be a Millionaire? seemed to capture the desires and imaginations of an entire nation. Millennial game shows were emerging alongside the tried and true syndicated shows, adjusting, for inflation, the excesses and heightened insatiability of the modern man. The stakes had been raised.

Observing their son's growing interest in game shows, Jared's parents decided to encourage his peculiar passion, as they figured it was at best a mentally-stimulating hobby, or at worst a harmless joy. Now, just as a baby boomer will throw on a Beatles record once their kid displays a fascination with music, to introduce them to the songs of their youth, which in the ear of the beholder is always better music ("Oh, you seem to really be enjoying that new Green Day album. Take it from me, you should really listen to Abbey Road instead."), Jared's folks were compelled to show him the game shows of their generation. Not only do the relics of yesteryear provide sentimental value to the initial, first edition audience, they also reveal the inspiration that is later adopted by the youth of the following decade. Some refer to this process as artistic evolution. To illustrate this point, let us further consider the American musical trio known as Green Day. Now, when discussing Green Day, music enthusiasts are inclined to mention prior acts such as The Ramones, The Clash and Operation Ivy. These bands can be cited as a direct influence on the sound that rewarded Green Day their success. Point being, to truly understand and appreciate the art of the modern era, one must be well-versed in the historical implications of the past.

Conveniently, for a nominal fee added to the cable bill, a family dwelling could tune in to a television channel know as the Game Show Network, a twenty-four hour non-stop broadcast of vintage game shows. Alas, Jared was consumed. He had entered the game show hermitage. All day long he was greeted with the drug-addled shows of yesteryear. The classics! Shows like The Gong Show, Card Sharks, Match Game and Password. These were the legends of retrograde entertainment. Yes, there were plenty more shows worthy of mention (the entire black and white era, for one), however these are the four that stand out in my memory, the four that truly shaped my childhood.

We could go on and on listing game shows, but the moral of the story would be neglected. There is one, though. One more show that begs reference. The Dating Game. The Dating Game, in a warped way, mirrors the jangled yearnings of Jared and his buddies. In brief summation, The Dating Game consisted of three bachelors competing to accompany one gorgeous woman on a date. After responding to a series of questions asked by the bachelorette, the most charming of the three gentleman would be granted the opportunity to court her. It was up to the woman to decide the winner. Maybe she wanted the funny guy, or maybe she wanted the meanie. Either way, it was entirely her decision.

In reviewing the preliminary years of Jared and his friends all lusting for Amy, and only one eventually being awarded the title of 'Amy's boyfriend,' it was not all that different from a pubescent, three-year long episode of The Dating Game. In the aftermath, Jared was the winner. The champion du jour, conqueror. The star-spangled hero of the playground rumble. Every man entered the gamut with equal potential and only one would exit as the victor. Hooray Jared, you won.

Congratulations. Collect your prize and enjoy. You've certainly earned it. After intensive sessions of deliberation and self-reflective contemplation, Amy has decided that you are the one she wants. She has a gang of men at her feet, readily available and sworn to protect and console her vulnerabilities. She has unlimited options. And through the murky cesspool of man buckets, you are the chosen one. You are the young boy displaying the most promise. You'll treat her right. You'll engage her first non-self-inflicted orgasm. Jared, accept this vow as my promise to always love you. We are meant to be together. Can't you just feel it? I believe in us. Jared and Amy. O brother. G-d help us all, as they discover the flailing fault of young love.

Through the musky pathways of a trembling kingdom, Deryk paced, slowly, his body a great stooping silhouette. A once brilliant and exuberant man, rattled with uncertainty. All confidence drained. It's nearly impossible to gauge the leadership skills of a man who is never challenged. Thus far, his reign has consisted of maintaining order in an already peaceful, isolated nook, hidden amongst the forest walls. Not once had he been taken to task, at least, until now. Destiny had determined that it was finally time to prove his worth, to spread his shriveled wings. Mighty warrior, remind us of your power. Cast a glance of fearsome wisdom toward us, your feeble followers.

He approached the holding cell that housed the Pats. His presence caused a stir of bitterness in Patricia's internal barometer.

"You bastard! How could you keep us trapped in such miserable conditions? I was fooled into believing that you valued our presence. But instead, your hospitable invitation has proved to be a lockdown. We are not deserving of this treatment. Let us out! I demand to be regarded with at least the bare minimum of human decency."

She paused to catch her breath. Deryk, meanwhile, stood in a casual recline against the steel bar barrier.

"Well, thanks for the warm welcome. You done?" Condescending beyond measure.

She inhaled deeply, presumably in preparation for unleashing her follow-up tirade. Patrick immediately seized this brief pause of potential energy and leapt up, preemptively interrupting any speech that Patricia was about to transmit.

"Majesty, Your Highness, o dear King," he began, "allow me to speak on behalf of us both when I declare that we are at your service. You need not explain your intentions for placing us in this less-than-luxurious accommodation, for it has provided us many-a-moment of deep contemplation, of soul-searching solitude. And within these precious moments of togetherness, we have come to the conclusion that we are eager to fulfill your every command. Let us vanquish the greedy, noxious, self-righteous inhabitants of South Forts. They deserve eternal damnation, hellfire."

"Thank you, Patrick. I knew I could count on you the moment we first met. Thank you for reiterating your stance on the matter. In fact, we are currently devising strategic battle plans to infiltrate the coming raid. The mindless drones that occupy South Forts have no right to our territory, and they shall be sent away in a cavalcade of misery. Now, Patricia, I have recently been informed that you feel slightly different with regard to this matter. The general consensus around here is that you harbor a certain loyalty toward the enemy. Can you confirm my suspicions?"

Patricia held her ground, firm and resolute. She detested the irrational, close-minded thinking that was being propagated throughout the kingdom, under the veil of 'inalienable rights guaranteed in sovereign statehood.' She outlined her rationale, emphasizing the fact that the forgotten souls were not being deprived of their necessary water supply. They would instead be sharing their excess resources, while still preserving their own portion. Everyone gets a fair share of the loot.

Unfortunately, formal logic and compassion are not looked upon kindly in these parts. The folks here are busting at the seams with pride. This is the determining factor in the whole water scuffle. It's an issue of pride. To them, it's not about the water, it's a matter of maintaining their dignity. Well, that and the strong belief in preserving nature. The whole 'Save the trees! Think about the salmon!' sentiment. And hey, I get it. I can sympathize with the environmental sustainability movement. It's a noble cause and all, but what about humanity? Doesn't every human being deserve an equal chance at achieving his/her full potential in the 21st century hyper-tech age of now-now-zoom instant gratification? I feel that the living conditions of human beings should supersede those of animals.  Yea, sure, fish are precious and all, but I'm sorry if I support human rights over animal rights.  It's just like that part in <u>Of Mice and Men</u> when Slim drowns the puppies instead of burdening himself with raising them in an unfit habitat.  Not only to help himself, but their lives would have been miserable, too.  If my thoughts be cruel, I blame Steinbeck.  Honestly, that passage in his book completely changed my understanding of this world.  Humans too often take on unnecessary responsibilities and end up forging their lives around tending to and nurturing these meaningless distractions.  Dog owners being the primary example.  They shape their lives around caring for these stupid fucking dogs.  Just kill the damn beast and move on with your life.  Anyways, point being, we need not weep for the fish, just share your goddamned water with South Forts.  Patricia simply did not approve of the self-righteous pride that the forgotten souls demonstrated.

In regard to her pledging allegiance to South Forts, well, to be honest, Patricia wanted to keep these details to herself.  Sure, Patrick knew all about her decision to run away from a life of ease, but this tale needn't be shared with King Deryk, certainly not now.  Perhaps he suspects she has friends who reside there, or maybe he even thinks that she herself is a resident; but the truth is dangerous, and there is no legitimate reason for her to reveal herself as being the actual daughter of South Forts' monarchy.  Such information could prompt drastic measures of brutal ransom, a hostage situation, without a doubt.  This vital factoid would provide a weapon for the forgotten souls.

'Fuck,' she thought.  'What am I doing here?  These people are pathetic.'

"Listen sweetie," Deryk was not the least bit impressed with her impassioned plea, "I honestly appreciate your concern for the health and wellbeing of the dregs from South Forts.  It's cute.  But the decision has already been made.  Anyone who steps foot in our habitat, with ill intent, will be murdered. There's no changing my mind. And frankly, it's quite disheartening to hear about how much you despise fish. We cherish them sons-of-bitches here. So, will you be joining the fight? Or should we just take care of you right now and move on with our lives? Silly me, to believe that after a week of confinement you'd eventually see the light and change your ways. I was under the impression that your little friend here would be able to persuade you. After all, he's rabid and rearing to go. I was hoping to avoid this, but I'll give you two options. Either you join our fight, or we eliminate you. It's that simple. Well?"

Patricia swallowed. Reluctance. The threat of murder, of non-existence, always manages to dim the ethical absolution of virtue. Because who is genuinely willing to die for their beliefs? A true life-on-the-line ordeal of steadfast moral certainty is seldom verified, as survival displaces all high-minded ethics. Verbally expressed principles are rarely put to the test, as we are never forced to endure a proper, sacrificial, flesh and blood demonstration of all that is held to be essential within our own personal sense of nobility. Words are simple and expendable. Anyone can spout out a tirade of altruism, a desperate yearning for respect and positive attention. Hey! Look at me! I'm such a wonderful human being! Statements such as these can instill a sense of deep admiration, yet it is falsely earned. How often are we confronted with a singular, seminal moment of proving our worth? Of enacting the physical justification of our beliefs? Rarely. Some go an entire lifetime speaking, speaking and speaking some more. Never challenged. Comfortable in their words. Safe in their thoughts. Undisturbed. So what if Patricia swallowed? It's a human flaw. I can't blame her for abandoning her integrity, especially if the alternative is death. There's the rub to end all rubs. It's one thing to uphold your internal doctrine of right and wrong; however, it's a whole 'nother game when eternal rest is the penalty for noncompliance. Needless to say, she obeyed.

"I will serve the territory by any means necessary."

Deryk was more than pleased. When he smiled it was pure evil.

"Atta girl. Let's get you two out of here and onto the training ground. Get you both in adequate physical shape. Can't have a couple of pudgy fatties out there on the battlefield. Let's get the blood flowing, the fat burning and the muscles growing."

A guard appeared, literally emerging out of thin air, with a set of keys attached to an enormous ring, all jingling and jangling together.

"Let 'em out. She finally realized."

"Yes sir," the guard replied, with regimented respect and submissive honor. He unlocked the latch and freed the peaceful prisoners.

Well, they weren't technically free in the sense of American, prideful, endless-terrain liberty, but they were at least out of the cage. The next stop on their unnecessary tour of imprisonment was an abandoned field currently being used as a training ground. A regimented boot camp was underway. Every citizen of The Land of Forgotten Souls was presently enduring a brutal disciplinary quantification of their physical capacity. The strongest of the citizens would be sent to the county border, the offensive line, battling the onslaught swarm of mercenaries sent from South Forts. That's the spirit! Don't even let them get close to their desired encampment. Those bastards don't stand a chance! The remaining souls would patrol the banks of the river, a procession of chubby, stinky bodyguards. Barricade the property! Infiltrate the threat! Extinguish all those who willingly oppose our sanctity! Oorah!

# The Rocky Whore

She likes to dress up
a chance to get fucked
or at least touched
by the eyes of the boys
with shame in her name
and parental pain
brings no chance of solace or comfort
only pound the ground
pound a frown
into a wedding gown
become a clown
but here, that's okay
here we welcome it
it's natural
you're actually quite
tame by the
measurement of man
the strong openings in our hands
made perfect
made sane
why such overwhelming pain?
Kill the name
            Ha!
Kill the name
            Ha!
Kill the name
            Ha!
Kill it
make it dead
make it gone
extinguished
calm down
relax
it isn't that bad
it's just that she's the
only pussy you've ever had
you loved her, I know
but she doesn't see
she's busy
but who fucking cares about that bitch?

Midnight screenings of <u>The Rocky Horror Picture Show</u> provide an excellent excuse for young ladies to exhibit their inner sluts. A supportive gathering where they can flaunt their scarlet tendencies and embrace the throbbing impulse of sexual deviancy that surges within all of us. Abandon the prude, puritanical attitudes of long ago, and give in to your body's true nature. We are creatures built for fucking. Rocky Horror allows boys and girls to strive for depravity. The filthier the better. It's a recipe for a delicious disaster. Ingredients for a proper screening include: one theatre full of horny, scantily clad youngsters and a raunchy film that glorifies bisexual, hedonistic, orgy-fuelled, uninhibited pleasures of wild and unrestrained excellence, to be shown during the wee hours of night, when the freaks emerge from their dwellings. The film also incorporates a commendable level of audience participation. It is not at all a passive theatre-going experience. Oh no, you must play along. There is a certain interaction that takes place between the audience and the film. To begin with, all first time guests are labeled 'virgins' and imprinted with a red smear of lipstick on their forehead in the shape of the letter V. During the film, audience members recite lines that coincide with the dialogue in the movie, creating a faux conversation where the spectators are interacting with the film. Props are also an important part of the experience. At various pre-determined moments, rice is thrown and toilet paper is hurled in the air. It's truly a gorgeous happening. Perhaps most important to this event is the song and dance. The film is, after all, a musical, so there are plenty of wonderful songs and choreographed dance scenes. And you better believe the audience joins in on the jamboree. Especially during "Time Warp," where the dance moves are taught within the film itself. So there you have it. Sexy outfits, group camaraderie and dancing. The perfect prescription for getting anyone hot and bothered enough for a night of psychotic, untamed coitus. Sinful servants to the sensation of touch.

It comes as no surprise that Amy Carousel would eventually develop a deep fascination and troubled respect for such gatherings, as all dedicated pleasure seekers sooner or later find themselves in the midst of a Rocky showing, either out of sheer, inescapable curiosity or calculated intent. Worthless whore devastation. Gathering of the harlots, the queers and the masochistic misogynists. Who cares? Everyone's getting laid.

Soon after her initial virgin sacrifice, Amy became a frequent attendee of the midnight menageries. She was a consistent presence, eager to get swept up in the party and divulge the whims of her hormonally-dominated labia lips. It's not like she was dressing up as specific characters (although she does share certain physical traits with Columbia – a Groupie) from the film. There's no semblance of loyal fandom, she just wanted to get slutted out (high heels, fishnet stockings, leather, full-on glam) without feeling ashamed. It's quite similar to Halloween, in that it's an excuse for young women to dress provocatively, naughty for a night, abandon your inhibitions and emerge as the trollop you were born to be. Don't let society shackle your dreams. Instead, become your dreams, your esteemed vision of self. There rests a potential within us all, waiting for the great reveal. This supreme status must be cultivated and encouraged, as we are not simply born great; but we all can become great. And if your definition of human excellence is slippery sex and various taboo practices, well then you'll fit right in with the degenerates that flock to the theatre when The Rocky Horror Picture Show is scheduled to erupt. O the excitement and the anticipation, the kinky decadence. Naturally, Amy was an active participant in such events, hooting and hollering at the screen like a sexually depraved banshee. She was regal in her perversion.

Seizing the fire from the underground, a midnight screening was arranged at a distinguished venue in Los Angeles, the great Hollywood Bowl. Just imagine the glory that is contained in the sight of eighteen thousand transvestites viewing the film in an outdoor amphitheater. The permeation of attained desires is slightly unsettling. There was no question, not a sparkling moment's hesitation, that Amy would, of course, attend this grand spectacle. As a date, she convinced her recent victim, the enigmatic Nick, to escort her, garter belt and all. Her new boy toy was surely in for quite a treat.

Meanwhile, the mope-laden homebody, our pitiful protagonist, Jared, was imprisoned in his bedroom, clutching his telephone in the hopes that it would soon ring. For, you see, Amy had informed Jared of her plan for the evening. He was less-than-enthused, but supportive of her newfound independence. Well, not really. What the fuck am I saying? He was not at all supportive of her new boyfriend, but he was comforted in knowing that Amy was always a simple phone call away. And she checked in frequently. It always felt good to hear her voice. To be completely accurate, it's worth stating that he cherished any attention Amy granted him. Any charitable payment of mind was, to him, a generous offering, a secretion from a goddess. Amy, on the other hand, wanted Jared to leave her alone; but she also wanted the solace that came from knowing he wasn't miserable without her. As long as she chimed in with the occasional phone call, a quick hello, he was somehow calm. Basically, she despised the sickening notion, the heavy, burdensome load to carry, of knowing that she broke his heart. Of being a villain. She at least had the decency to feel a sense of remorse, of self-condemnation. How could she possibly enjoy herself tonight, if in the back of her mind she knew that Jared was at home composing break-up songs? Real pathetic, weepy shit.

"What's the plan for tonight?"

"Going to Rocky."

"Of course. Shoulda known. Doesn't it ever get boring? Same fucking movie. And not even that great of a flick, mind you. I can't stand that campy shit."

"The movie itself is only half the experience. And this time it's special. They're playing it at the bowl."

"As in the Hollywood Bowl?"

"Yep. It's gunna be massive."

"Sounds fun."

Jared could teach a master class in feigning interest.

"I'm excited."

"Dare I ask who you're going with?"

"I'm going with Nick, of course. He's picking me up at around 10:30."

"Fun."

The subdued, half-dead shrug of a bystander, the uninvited.

"Jared, come on."

"Well, can you at least call me when you get home? Ya know, to confirm if it was in fact fun."

"Eh, I'll most likely be getting home pretty late. We plan on stopping at Denny's after the show, to catch an early breakfast."

"That's fine. I just want to make sure everything is safe and proper."

Jared had assumed the role of the overbearing mother, demanding phone calls no matter the hour. In truth, he wanted to become an obstruction, a burden, anything that would prevent Nick from fucking her that night. A sort of telephonic hurdle to hinder their plans. Yes! A quick ring to her ex-boyfriend will certainly spoil any and all romantic momentum. Kill the beast at the source. Cut off the head and eat the heart. Oh, but she'll just as easily sleep with him anyway. There's no preventing their copulation. That asshole, he gets to slam her while she's looking so goddamned sexy. He gets to gnaw away at her when she's at maximum-level whore status. I admit defeat. I am beyond jealous. He is going to fuck her past G-d's designated threshold for human awareness. Oh no! If she ever were to take it up the ass, it would be tonight. Just slide it right in. No resistance. So dirty, so foul. A real primal session. Such a lucky bastard. They will both see the light, the highly sought after post-Rocky relations. O boy.

"Sure. I'll talk to you later."

"Bye."

Shall we take bets on whether or not she called that night? Anyone? Care to speculate a legitimate wager? Like, what are the odds she'll actually call? 23:1 seems reasonable, though highly improbable. Still, it wouldn't stop Jared from confidently plunging headfirst into the belief that he'd be rewarded by the great temptress of fortune. He's all in, chips on the table. She'll call. I know she'll call because she said she would, and she always holds true to her word, always. Jared's fearless determination was merely the result of his mismanaged denial. His powerless delusion of reality. Of course she isn't going to call. Why on earth would she interrupt a date to call her dopey ex-darling? But still, he waited. Stayed up until four in the morning. Any minute now, any minute now...

There is not enough space in the human mind for both rational and emotional thought processes. You're either one or the other. We can view the world one of two ways: through the lens of our brain (think) or our heart (feel). Hell, even using the heart as a symbol of love & despair, of sorrow & empathy, coincides directly with the emotional mindset. The heart does not regulate feelings. It's all in the brain, baby. But the sappy, poetic summation of life really goes over well with the 'feelers.' It makes their stupid little hearts swell with wonder. Logical reasoning, careful consideration of the pros and cons of a given situation, can easily be neglected when a flood of emotion breaches the restraints of philosophical deduction. Could this very predicament be the fatal flaw of man? The dividing line between science and faith. One asks *how* while another asks *why*. And thus, a conflict arises. Some prefer technical precision while others opt for the abstract blur of personal interpretation. The carefully arranged, theoretically-balanced piece of classical music vs. the spur of the moment guitar solo. The painting that mirrors reality vs. splattered chaos. It goes without saying, but I'll say it anyway, that Jared belongs to the emotional tribe, practicing the immediate, unthinking response method. All feel, indefinite and complex. It's worth considering, contemplating, gripping reality and eventually admitting that this particular mindset is a fragile, flawed and fundamentally weak outlook on life. Sooner or later, you'll get crushed, either by your own delusions, or your lack of conviction. Defeat is guaranteed.

Amy and Nick enjoyed an unlimited supply of pancakes and coffee at approximately three o'clock in the morning, reflecting on the evening's many memorable moments. Their outfits were worthy of stirring up uncomfortable confusion and leering glances from fellow diners. Yet, given the location, none of this was strange. The begrudgingly-late-evening/unbelievably-early-morning hours at an all-night eatery are destined to attract an odd crew. The swamp monsters tend to emerge from their shelter once the straight-laced, clean-cut drones are asleep, cozy in their beds, paid for by their soul-destroying jobs. The sort of folks that follow the rules a little too perfectly, obedient to the point of dangerous self-deprecation. No sense of danger or lunacy, just tradition followers, carrying the torch of their ancestors. The same, again. A repeated lifetime. No risk, no out-of-bounds treachery, no leap of faith. Precaution, shelter. An existence spent fastening the reins of a safety net without ever relishing in the perilous plunge that it's protecting you from in the first place. The timid trapeze artist too scared to climb the ladder, shunning the fancy talkers that always seem to have a clever response to everything. A plagued mind full of thoughts like:

> *"O, I hate that guy. He seems so secure and comfortable in his own skin, emanating not a shard of self-doubt. So fucking witty and smart. I bet he doesn't even know any dumb people. He just cuts them out of his life. YOU MUST READ THIS MANY BOOKS A YEAR TO BE MY FRIEND. Like, just the other day, I was asking this guy about his tattoos, because he had these weird designs all over his arm and I was curious about what they meant. I figured every tattoo tells a story, so this would be a perfect conversation starter. I ask him, 'What do they mean?' And he gives me this bullshit joke answer. It's a lie. He's not trying to hide it. He just wants me to inhale the self-righteous fumes of his pouting asshole and admire the lingering intelligence. Why do you refuse to tell me the intention of your*

*tatt?   Was the reason you got such a vague design permanently inscribed on your skin really just so you could waste time with these bullshit stories?   I am not amused.   If you refuse to be real with me, and instead prefer to be a silly faggot, then let's just forget I ever asked. I'm sorry I was interested in you. You seemed complex and intriguing.   I though I could get to know you by discussing your ink, but that has proven to be too much to ask for.   Forgive me. Like, honestly, I think you're a really cool guy.  I respect you.  But right now I just feel stupid and inadequate talking to you.  Sorry for making you feel the need to dumb down your brilliance for a simpleton such as I. '*

These are not the type of people you'll find huddled around a table at Denny's at three in the morning, pontificating life's great dilemma and clutching the handle of a coffee mug with decisive despair. Oh no, the insecure and out of touch are always asleep at a reasonable hour. This phenomenon creates a midnight playground where the rambunctious and naughty can dance away the burdens that bury the rest of us. Which is why Amy and Nick were all smiles during their early breakfast, free and alive. She also had the foresight to leave her phone at home, no need for modern distractions. I wanna live in the moment, without the threat of spontaneous interruption. Just me and Nick, my new cock. A real man with a nice, heavy set of balls on him. Meaty danglers. She had been wet the entire night.

They left the restaurant as the sun was beginning to rise. Good morning to the rest of civilization. Off into the sunrise they drove, far out of view from us, the observers. Let your mind fill in the blanks.

Jared didn't actually give up waiting for the call; rather, he fell asleep next to the telephone while musing about the potentialities of their primeval lovemaking. He has never had a wet dream, but often wakes up with a sturdy erection. Just thought you should know. Amy ended up calling him late the next afternoon, offering the usual lackadaisical apology. Jared was desperate to maintain a comfortable, healthy relationship with her. This meant no anger, no confrontational accusations. Just polite, nice guy speak.

"That's okay. I'm glad you had fun. And I'm relieved to know you're safe."

"Huh? I was never in danger. It's not like Nick is some stranger I went out with. I know him quite well and I feel comfortable around him."

Perfect. That's exactly what I wanted to hear. She's comfortable with him. What does that even mean? Like, his dick fits comfortably in her pussy? It's comfortable when they spoon in bed together? No overlap? No excess appendages? Comfortable how? Does she talk to him about deep personal issues? She's comfortable enough to discuss traumatic events from her past? Does he know about the cutting? Does he respond like a gentleman? Is he considerate of her needs? Does he treat her like the beautiful woman she is? She deserves the best. I am glad to know she's happy, but what was wrong with me that I couldn't give her that? What does he have that I don't? Is it really all about penis size? If so, I'm worthless. I never stood a chance. But there must be more. There must be something about him that makes her feel so very comfortable.

"I know. But the whole crowd that goes to that movie, it's a bunch of weird, perverted jerks."

And that's her cue to wrap up this conversation. Amy had just returned from a splendid night full of celebration, togetherness and song. It was wholly positive, and Jared's immediate reaction was to criticize those in attendance as being rotten people. Maybe this is why Amy broke up with you, Jared. You're a drag sometimes. No fun. It's no wonder she desires someone else. She wants to get away from your negativity.

You're a bummer to be around. You really think a small penis is your only flaw?

"Okay, well I just wanted to check in and say hi. So I guess I'll talk to ya later."

Quick, she's prepping her exit. This conversation, though delicately brief and cordial, is a soul-soothing triumph and I mustn't let her slip away again so easily. Who knows how long it'll be until I hear from her again, as she is officially in charge of regulating our relationship. Don't disappear, Amy.

"Um, are you busy at all today?"

He's relentless. Never mind the fact that she's probably still leaking out semen from last night. Jared's loyalty is unwavering. Sad puppy dog syndrome.

"Yes, Jared. I'm actually quite busy and I shall be going now."

"Well, hold on a minute. What's on your schedule for today?"

"Like, specifically? Gimme a break. I told you I'm busy so let's just leave it at that."

Keep your distance, buddy. Don't scare her away.

"Fair enough. It was great talking with you."

"I'll call you later. Bye."

After she hung up, Jared continued speaking into the receiver, positing his true, unfiltered feelings.

"I love you, Amy. I still truly love you. Nothing can change that. No matter how much you hurt me, I will always love you. Even though you have this new boyfriend, it does nothing to diminish the devotion I feel. I worship you, Amy. I fucking worship you."

A boy and his first love. Such a silly, pathetic disease.

Meanwhile, and this is quite a hefty meanwhile, at the CoLaToLa palace . . .

Patricia's parents were, and had been, reasonably distraught. Immediately after their daughter's disappearance, a search party had been summoned and soon all of South Forts was on the lookout for young Patricia. An entire town assigned the role of vigilant watchmen. Sentinel security for the runaway princess. Had she been kidnapped? Captured in the middle of the night? After several unsuccessful months of search, the worst had been assumed. At least, it had been safe to assume the worst; but a parent does not simply give up hope when their only begotten child disappears into the night. Especially when the family in question has a limitless supply of resources. Such was the case with the CoLaToLa estate. Patricia's image was painted on milk cartons and flyers that decorated the city. All residents were urged to 'Be on the lookout. Search high and low. Please help us find our daughter.'

Mr: I never felt like I pressured her too much. We were reasonable parents. Sure, I wanted her to get good grades, but not at the expense of providing her with a loving and nurturing home environment. I never hit her; well, aside from some toddler spankings. Nothing too abrasive, just some good ol' fashioned discipline. Why would she do this to us? We gave her everything she ever wanted. We spoiled the girl. All I asked for in return was that she did well in school. Keep your grades up, and we'll give you the world. Whatever you want.

Mrs: I suspect foul play.

Mr: Can it, Marjorie. You always assume the worst, regardless of the situation. Our daughter's escape was an act of her own free will. There's no need for you to project your own uncertainties in order to shield yourself from responsibility in this matter.

Mrs: Okay, your majesty, your brilliancy. Let's break this down, slightly. The only legitimate, fact-based evidence we have to go off of is her absence. No one saw her ride away into the great unknown, handcuffed to a chariot. Conversely, she didn't leave a note explaining her intentions. Not a single window was left open, with the shades fluttering dramatically in the wind. We have no clues or logical inklings on which to base such claims, just our own internal doubts and predilections. Quite frankly, your argument sounds like a feeble attempt to absolve yourself of guilt. Let's examine the conflict from a closer proximity. We have two plausible explanations for Patricia's disappearance: the kidnapping scenario or the free will escape.

Mr: Affirmative.

Mrs: And here you are, questioning her intent. Asking 'Why oh why would my sweetie pie leave us? We were so good to her. We provided her with unlimited material and financial support. How could she possibly refuse such plentiful offerings?' Well, Wilbur, if this is in fact the explanation we are accepting for her leaving, we need to dig deeper. Could it be, now bear with me, that our overbearing display of affectionate, nurturing TLC was a bit too much for her to handle?

Mr: Preposterous! Are you seriously lamenting the anguish of a child that was loved too much? The poor baby was anything but poor.

Mrs: Wilbur, consider her situation in an emotional context. Sure, we provided for her, bought her goods-of-plenty and funded her desired services. Even the most short-lived, impulsive hobbies she embarked on, no matter how temporary, were encouraged and subsidized by us. But still, there was a distance. An emotional void. Don't you get it? She wanted to experience the joys in life that money can't buy. A strong bond of demonstrative care. Love that is exchanged in caring words and knowing glances, not dollar-bill handshakes and stale affection.

Mr: Bah! The plight of the rich. I have absolutely no sympathy for such vapid, empty pain.

Mrs: She was sheltered. Staring out her bedroom window and dreaming of more. The wild and untamed world of the outside. She was hungry for spontaneous excitement. Unregulated madness. Staying up all night and stumbling through town, careless and happy.

Mr: So give her a rambunctious night, and then she'll come home. Except, she never returned.

Mrs: Well, she had accumulated a whole lifetime of pent-up urges.

Mr: She wasn't locked up or encaged. She was allowed to go outside. Hell, she always seemed to be running around with that Nelson fellow; that is, until he blew his head off.

Mrs: How sensitive of you, to bring that up so lightly.

Mr: Give it a rest, darling. I'm only attempting to demonstrate a rather obvious point. She had all the freedoms and amenities of any typical American girl. Fireworks and brimstone. But still, she abandoned us. Surely her capture would have prompted hostage bargaining and a hefty ransom.

Mrs: I can only pray for her safety, draining myself of tears. Indefinite sadness has swept the kingdom, cursing all triumphs and clouding all praise. Our child, the product of a carefully-earned heritage, has opted to seek refuge among the dirt and mud of the commoners. She feels a spiritual connection to the dull and the poor, as they carry a certain humanity, an enduring struggle that is absent in the lives of the wealthy. Albeit, for us, we don't harbor any admiration for the lower class, as we were born in such slums. We are not lucky birthright recipients of our success. Quite the opposite. We worked hard and struggled, day after day. You and I can appreciate the luxury of mansions and sweeping hillside palaces, horseback rides through the canyon and fine wine with dinner, because we rightfully earned these comforts. But Patricia, sweet Patricia, she was born without that internal ambition, the desire for more. Sure, we can tell her all about our rough upbringing, but those are only stories. She has to feel it. The silver spoon shields her appreciation. It dims the fire that burns in her belly. She's a rich girl yearning for the passionate life that befalls the starving artist, the homeless mystic. Oh dear, I hope she is safe. She'll come to her senses soon enough. There's a dark undercurrent to the bohemian lull; and once she discovers this, she'll come running back.

Wilbur was quiet for a moment. The words his wife spoke had struck a central nerve. It was true, in fact, that both he and Marjorie had been born into lower-class families. Poor folk. They were not blessed from birth with the legacy of an important last name. They were commoners, raised by commoners. Through sheer determination, sacrifice and perseverance they were able to climb the ranks of the class structure. The life of Wilbur CoLaToLa, in particular, is a great success story. The American Dream in action. He was born into a struggling family. Hungry and sad, always. Immigrants, even. *This is fiction, after all.* A fresh start in a new country. No privileges or nepotism to assist them, just their own self-discipline. They literally started life at the bottom of the totem pole, the pyramid of hierarchical status, and managed to climb to the top. A victory that would appease their ancestors, generations and generations ago. And the CoLaToLa's lived happily forever onward, right? Not quite. Because this tale, in turn, produces a strange, shifting dynamic in familial relations. A back and forth of rags to riches. Surely this isn't always the case, but it happens often enough to establish itself as a justifiable citation. And so the story goes: A poor boy, growing up in a depressing, lower-class home, eager to escape his familiar misery, works his ass off to gain the pleasantries of financial abundance. When he finally becomes affluent, after years and years of diligence, he retains his humility by way of countless, woeful childhood memories, and is therefore able to appreciate his wealth, knowing the sacrifices it required. Now, this same man (or woman, or womyn) has a child of his very own, and decides, 'My kids shall never be forced to endure the sorrows of my own upbringing. Since I am able to provide for them, they will have the childhood I never knew.' Sounds admirable enough. Who could blame him? After all, what's the point of becoming successful if you can't share the wealth, especially with your own family? So the kids grow up spoiled and happy, never knowing hunger, never knowing economic hardships of any kind. The only drawback to this joyous ignorance is the children are, in turn, over-nurtured to such an extent that they become indulgent, unappreciative, sheltered little brats, never knowing the common struggles of daily life. They lack the ambition of their parents' generation. These kids breeze through their early years, pampered and perfect, and grow up with fairytale dreams of becoming something as useless as an artist (or any career path that is super fun and never requires any real work, in the sense of breaking sweat and getting dirty). How wide can one man grin? They are raised believing they are superior, entitled beings. Mama says I'm special. I want a jovial job where I get to giggle and smile all day. I refuse to waste my time performing menial tasks like some boring day-laborer. Lo and behold, this doesn't always end in a 'wishes do come true' triumph. Rather, this kid will likely end up becoming a professional dreamer. One day, man, one day I'll be a star (or in Patricia's case, homeless). Regardless, both paths dwell in the temple of self-worship. Inflation of ego beyond the grasp of the simpletons is the pinnacle to which they strive. Attention whores and mirror gazers. When this self-induced starving artist has kids of his own, they'll be raised in a broken-down sad house, thus starting the cycle over again. And around it goes. One generation values hard work, while the next takes it all for granted. Poor parents give birth to rich kids, and rich parents give birth to poor kids. The endless loop of wanting to be different from mommy and daddy, and the monetary predicaments that necessitate such desires. Also, nothing instills a lack of gratitude quite like an inheritance. Unearned and underserved cash extinguishes the morale of an otherwise decent human. For instance, gauge the attractiveness level of 2 individuals: one is a self-made millionaire, while the other was left a large sum of money in the will of a dead relative. Both have obtained a similar fortune, yet only one truly earned it.

A wave of doubt swept over Wilbur's entire mental mainframe. Had he neglected to teach his daughter the importance of hard work and determination? All too often he was ensuring her happiness, forgetting the valuable character traits that are formed during bouts of boredom and sadness. Her disappearance was a statement. She needed to 'rough it' for a while, as they say. Abandon all her privileges and embark on a quest of self-discovery. Kids these days, with their identity crises. This is rugged individualism run amok.

Mr: Certainly the thrill will wear off and she'll return soon enough, blossoming with apology, claiming naïveté and modest curiosity.

Mrs: I do indeed hope so. This endless weeping has left me dehydrated. I'm thirsty.

      The dreaded first puff. The puff that initiates a decadent, infantile rebellious streak in the life of an otherwise pleasant teenage boy. The first inhale, signifying a false maturity. The deep chest draw, and the coughing fit that follows. Plumes of smoke dispersing chaotically amidst the frantic lung contractions of a body desperate to eliminate a foreign vapor. The burning sensation in the rear of the throat, and an overall lack of breath. The lightheaded thrill, a sort of dizzy joy. Smoking is a silly habit, as smoke is the waste product of a recently destroyed plant. Therefore, to smoke is to intentionally inhale death. Suck it straight down. Swallow the escaped soul of nature. When Jared and Eddie first smoked together, they must've been only twelve or thirteen. It's funny, to recollect such thoughts. Memories of dumb behavior. They were both over at Charlie's house, messing around, video games, shits and giggles, the lot, when Charlie was forced to excuse himself for an hour or so, as his tutor had arrived. All fun came to a screeching halt when the academic trainer entered the house, textbook in hand, pencil on ear and calculator in pocket. Charlie and his tutor, the purveyor of boredom, set up shop at the desk in his room and hit the books. The session began. No use going home, Jared and Eddie thought, they'll be done soon enough. The two soon-to-be-delinquents made their way downstairs where they saw Charlie's little sister disposing of a pack of cigarettes by holding them under a running faucet and ripping them in half. "I hate it when my mom smokes," she muttered, or something to that effect. She tossed the wet, torn cigarettes in the waste bin and stormed off in a huff of disappointment. Intrigued, Jared and Eddie rifled through the cigarette cemetery and procured a few not-totally-destroyed, still semi-flammable smokes. Never before in their young lives had they been so close, within reach, to the dreaded cancer sticks. It's quite unclear why the two boys had a sudden desire to smoke. Perhaps it was the whole repressed-maternal-relationship breastfeeding replacement theory, a primal need to suck on something dirty and socially abhorrent. Or maybe they watched too many films that glorified the act of smoking. Nick Cage's performance in <u>Matchstick Men</u> comes to mind. God does that movie makes me wanna smoke! Maybe, and this seems to be the most plausible explanation, they just wanted to see what all the fuss was about. After all, since about fifth grade onward they had been repeatedly drilled about the dangers of smoking. School-sponsored programs that highlighted the hazards of drugs, drinking and smoking were a consistent part of the lesson plan. Year after year, they were told, over and over again, how terribly unhealthy such behaviors were. These lectures bordered on the absurd. They were so unnecessarily over-the-top and laughable in their attempts to keep children from experimenting with the forbidden substances that they aroused a certain defiant curiosity in the students. This anti-smoking, anti-drug crusade is not only a case of relentless fear mongering, it also indirectly instills a sense of mistrust in authority. You see, the child will, inevitably, experiment with these naughty delicacies. He or she will puff a joint, drink a beer, smoke a cigarette, and will most likely be pleased and satisfied with the effects. They will enjoy a temporary euphoria and then begin to wonder, 'Why was this seemingly harmless and overall pleasant activity so shunned and lambasted by my elders?' Doubt soon sets in. 'Were we being lied to?' Eventually, the child abandons all warning signs and sets out on a path of self-realization, adopting a new mantra as a replacement for "Just say no," or, simply "Don't do drugs." The new, liberated outlook becomes "Focus on the lesson, not the pain," and thereby "Make your own pain, learn your own lesson." The advice of others can be considered and appreciated, but people must learn for themselves, from the value of individual experience, in order to discover the true potential of their nature. The dividing line between right and wrong. We're all wired differently, and to live a life based solely on following the guidance and recommendations of others will result in an unfulfilled existence. Figure things out for yourself. The counsel of others, even the pristine wisdom that emanates from hardened veterans of life's misery, does not carry the same weight, or consequence, as flesh and blood participation in the pleasures and pangs of creation. Make mistakes, they are beneficial tools for learning. Take risks. Be original. But I digress. I've abandoned the sequence of events. Let us continue… Regardless of their intention, the two rebels rushed outside with their puny butts, grabbed a lighter off the barbeque and went for a leisurely stroll. Their destination was an area that was private and secluded, yet with a reasonable draft, suitable for ventilating their pollution. They squatted conspicuously and lit their cigarettes. Mischievous little devils, on a quest for self-sacrifice, commencing a long-lasting, detrimental, unhealthy habit, as they pass through the gateway, establishing themselves as insubordinate, disgruntled youths. And thus, the first puff. Eddie and Jared quite enjoyed the nicotine high and the false maturity it afforded them, but the damp, torn Virginia Slims were a mere tease. They instantly craved more; at least, a full cigarette. Their mission for the remainder of the day was to scan the town for a complete smoke. They dug through ashtrays, unsuccessfully, occasionally succumbing to desperation and puffing on the remainder of a nearly-spent butt. Dusk was approaching. The boys had decided to give up on their pathetic search and begin the walk back to Charlie's place when the heavens seemed to smile down upon them, as lying in a nearby drainage ditch was a gently crumbled pack of cigarettes. Its contents: 2 full, undamaged cigs. Oh joy! The community golf course, a nearby enclave, was now empty, as night had fallen, and Eddie and Jared, comfortable, smoked together among the great green expanse of a well-manicured fairway. They sat, contemplative, puffing away. This provided a temporary satisfaction, but it was only a matter of time until Jared would get his dirty paws on a full, fresh pack. Plastic-sealed and everything. By chance (although fate is a valid consideration), Griselda called Jared only a couple weeks after he gained this newfound hobby. She was inquiring as to the status of several pornographic magazines that she had lent him in years prior. "Of course I still got 'em," he responded. Well, she wanted them back; though not for herself. You see, she was cycling porn, generationally, and it was time to appease the libido of yet another sheltered teenage boy.

"Can I swing by later today and pick them up? This kid's gunna bust."

"Yea, sure. Come on over."

"Thanks. I'll see you–"

"Hey, actually, do you think you could maybe pick me up a pack of smokes?"

She paused briefly and contemplated the consequences.

"What's your brand?"

"Um, I'm not sure. I guess Camel."

"Okay, I'll be there in a bit."

Griselda delivered not just one, but three whole packs of Camel cigarettes. Jared was overjoyed. He felt like a man. An official smoker. He immediately called Eddie and they arranged for a meeting at their old elementary school, which in recent years had evolved, during their transcendence from kids to teens, into a sacred location. Not the entirety of the campus, though it too provided a certain reminiscent nostalgia and sentimental yearning for simplicity, but a specific, remote area that only Eddie and Jared knew about. Atop the roof, beside the industrial HVAC system, was a special spot reserved only for the best of friends, where intimate conversations would take place, private and peaceful. This particular spot had a name, and for the life of me I cannot bring myself to mention it here. Somehow, for all of the many personal anecdotes and tales I am now sharing, the name of my and Eddie's spot is too dear to divulge. Our bond wouldn't shatter, but revealing such a special tidbit would surely fracture it. To state the name would be a violation of trust, a desecration of the sanctity of our mutual, brotherly love. I can, at least, offer a hint. On that elementary school rooftop, where Eddie and I would smoke cigarettes, gaze at the stars, dream of absurd, elaborate futures and take for granted the countless tomorrows of our itty-bitty lives, Weezer's blue album was in heavy rotation, and oh how we loved that last song.

Sidewalk stroll
During wee night hours
Deliberate
Cynical
Sad

Suddenly, a car approaches
Headlights fade
Blank
Darkness overshadows
Sound indicates motion
As car cuts through current

Steel-framed structure
2 lovers inside
Passing the time
On a midnight drive
A thrill of chaos
Deprivation of sight
Laughter and excitement
The thrill of being bad

At the final moment
The lights engage
Just in time to catch
A stranger's eye

There has been little mention upon these pages, mostly sparse fragments and casual asides, of Jared's father; his stoic, brooding presence a dramatic influence worthy of further assessment. As is the case in all healthy father-son relationships, Jared feared his dad. A proper fear, rooted in respect and admiration. Jared looked up to his dad as his one true role model. His father wasn't one of those silly 'I wanna be best friends with my kids' type of dads; nor was he a neglectful, deadbeat sort. Jared's father was the harmonious golden ratio, perfect balance of strict-disciplinarian and cheerful-captain-of-joyful-retreats. He would curse Jared if he did poorly in school, unleashing the wrath of Angry Dad, a rage that would scare the shit out of Jared and his sister. He was never physically abusive, he just knew how to lay down the law and ensure obedience in his children, as all guardians should. If you're not afraid of your parents, especially daddy, they're doing a bad job of raising you. However, on the other side of the spectrum, if Jared was performing well in school, were the fun pleasantries of vacation and recreation. Report cards served as a measurement, a prophecy, of your future success rate; whether you'll make a worthwhile adult, or end up some sad-eyed birthday clown. Anyways, when grades were good the family often went on weekend adventures, and Jared himself was rewarded with guitar lessons, having earned his extravagances. His father exemplified the concept of 'work hard, play hard' in his own career, and he desperately tried to teach the merits of this particular lifestyle to his privileged, screwball children.

He was a lawyer; and a well-established, successful one at that. The managing partner of a firm that employed nearly 100 people. Name on the building, corner office, a true power-player in the field. He had won the game of life. Victorious. Now, to Jared, as a young boy, this didn't mean much. All he knew was that daddy would leave home early in the morning wearing a suit and tie, and would return around 6 o'clock in a slightly crankier mood, feeling somewhat bitter and unappreciated. Lucky kid, born into the comforts of wealth, with all the sacrifice and struggle of reaching such a prestigious position having already been endured before his birth. All that was asked of him was to bask in the glow of his entitlement and not fall too far behind of the head start he was granted in life.

The law firm, being the workplace of a great many people, would often arrange yearly, outside-of-the-office get-togethers for all the employees, allowing everyone to enjoy each other's company in a less uptight, emotionally-restrictive environment. Mostly, these were adults-only affairs. Dinner, dancing and heavy drinking. Elegant nights out. However, being that many employees had kids of their own, every once in a while the firm would host a company picnic. A very family-friendly affair, with water balloons and three-legged races, real summertime day-camp activities, at a local ranch that rented out sections of property for parties and corporate events.

As fate would have it, the summer that Jared and Amy began dating was the summer when one of these picnics was scheduled to occur. Both Jared and his sister were encouraged to 'bring a friend.' Jared unflinchingly telephoned Amy, and luckily, she obliged.

"It'll be fun."

This was to be Jared's incarnation of the wake-boarding excursion. Outdoor adventures with the whole family. It was indeed a wholesome summer, as both Jared and Amy exerted great effort toward building cordial relationships with each other's parents, really stepping out of their comfort zones to befriend the relatives. She must've been nervous, as not only was she to meet Jared's immediate family, but also an entire workforce of legal professionals eager to gawk at the boss's son's love interest.

"I'm comfortable with you. Why should I be scared?"

Everyone piled into the car, one of those gargantuan seven-seater SUVs. Mommy and daddy up front, sister and her pal in the middle row, Jared and Amy in the backseat. The drive was pleasant and unthreatening. A sacred calm lingered. This would not last.

Hand in hand, Jared and Amy approached the sanctioned turf of the company picnic, a wide expanse of land designated for the shindig. It was quite a crowd. The normally buttoned-down stiffs had emerged from the courtroom wearing shorts, Hawaiian shirts, sunglasses and sandals. A small army of children equipped with water guns had assembled, and they intended to rain liquid terror on all who crossed their path. A barbeque was fired up, cooking chicken, hotdogs and corn. The coleslaw and beans were off to the side. Oh, and those enormous popsicles, with the swirl of red and yellow, were in full effect.

It was a lovely scene. Jared gazed delightedly upon the crowd and felt a weird tinge of pride. 'Wow! Everyone looks so happy. Families are playing in the sun, laughing together. And my father is responsible for all of this. For providing them with a career in which they're able to provide a life of simple joy to these kids. He started the business as a one-man operation and now it has grown into an elite force of content, secure, successful individuals.' There was a tugging at his hand. Amy could tell he was in some sort of deep, introspective daze. Not wanting to interrupt his thoughts, she smiled at him, suggesting an unspoken understanding. Such a peaceful scene, parents and their children running around, and Amy by my side. Everyone seemed so happy. Masters of life's promise.

Upon entering the premises, Jared's family immediately dispersed. His parents were quickly swept up in a frenzy of mature mingling with fellow co-workers and their significant others. It was an enormous social gathering and J+A were quick to bypass the entire scene. They took to walking the grounds, exploring the entirety of the ranch property. It was a great setting, lovely and quaint. Old school and rustic like some ancient fairytale, complete with streams, meadows and gallivanting horses. With the company picnic safely out of sight, Jared and Amy were completely alone in the vast wilderness, hand still in hand. A leisurely young lovers' stroll. Resplendent multitudes and the glimmering cadence of mutual admiration. They soon located a suitable tree and sat beside its gorging trunk, protected by the canopying shade of the branches overhead.

All was quiet, all was calm. The two sweethearts had reinterpreted the picnic, intended for an entire business, as a romantic, intimate outing for 2. The suits and their spoiled kids ceased to exist. Just me and Amy, in the shadow of an aged tree.

Jared reached over and pulled his darling sweetheart nearer to him, snugglin' up all close. Aside from the occasional horse-drawn hayride full of sedentary passengers passing by in the distance, they were completely alone. A private slice of natural wonder. Romantic fulfillment. During their cuddle session, the two lovebirds fantasized about the glorious potentialities of a lifetime alliance. Forecasting their adult years, a togetherness timeline.

*We are destined for eternity.*

"When we're married, I wanna live by the beach."

"Oh yes! A house upon the shore, I've never wanted anything more."

"We can wake up every morning to the ultimate, awe-inspiring sight: the great sea and the sunrise. And we'd be in bed, gazing out the window, excited for the day ahead."

They discussed matters of great commitment with sparkling ease. No big deal. It was accepted as common knowledge that their love was sealed, permanent. Always. It required no great stretch of the imagination to consider the terms of their prospective living situation. Only fourteen years old, and they're already arranging the axioms of co-habitational permanence. And on no small scale either, as beachfront property is terribly expensive. A hefty payment indeed.

"We must also consider the coastline."

"How do you mean?"

"Well, think about it. If we settle on the west coast, we bear witness to the sun setting on the Pacific horizon. However, and this option sounds more appealing to me, on the east coast we get the early morning sunrise, the glowing beams of our closest star, peering over the Atlantic. Either way we are afforded, daily, a majestic sight, the sun and the sea, crossing paths. One greets the day, while the other seals it. Would you prefer to see the sun rise or set?"

Tenderness of questioning, the decisions of true love.

"Honestly, Amy, wherever we are, I'll be happy."

"Well, we need a backup plan, just in case the beach doesn't work out. At least, temporarily."

It took Jared only a brief moment to offer a specific response. Surely he must've considered this before. His answer was too quick to be spontaneous.

"We can move to Las Vegas, get a cheap apartment off the strip, in the outskirts, and I'll get a job as a taxi driver."

She scoffed at the suggestion.

"That sounds glamorous." Her sarcasm was apparent.

"Well, it's an alternative choice, not the ultimate goal."

She smiled and brought her face right up against his, noses nearly touching.

"I know. And anyways, as long as we're together, our location is but a secondary concern."

The two lovers had only recently begun kissing, their momentous first smooch having occurred approximately two weeks prior to this moment. It was still a relatively new act for both parties, and they were eager to practice. It wasn't long before a series of quick pecks and gentle kisses transformed into a full-blown make out session.

Aggressive and passionate.

Propelled by the heat of the moment, Jared climbed on top of Amy, assumed the missionary position and began dry-humping her. She moaned. He kissed her neck. They forcibly rubbed their genitals together in a rollicking motion, simulating sexual intercourse. A tease. Their bodies remained fully clothed, providing a barrier. A preventative measure. Nevertheless, both Amy and Jared entered into a state of mutual bliss. Heavy breathing and gasps of delight.

She whispered in his ear, "Oh Jared, you're making me want to have sex with you."

Enticing, to say the least.

Motivated by her inviting compliment, he continued humping away at her jean-covered pussy.

For whatever reason (maybe it started to hurt, or maybe the short-lived thrill had begun to dissipate), Amy's panting and coos subsided. Her boiling fervor was reduced to a simmer, and she seemed detached from the moment.

"Jared."

"Yea?"

"Let's switch positions."

Currently, he was lying on top of her, nestled in between her spread-eagled legs.

"You wanna be on top?"

"Precisely."

"Alright."

It was an odd request, but he went along with it. He was in no rush to disrupt the festivities, and would, at this point, do anything to maintain the moment.

Jared laid on his back and Amy climbed aboard. Rather than straddling his pelvic region, à la the cowgirl formation, she slipped in between his legs, forcing them apart. Her request to switch positions was remarkably literal. Once the tongue-heavy make out session resumed, she began grinding her hips against his, thrusting and humping. They had seemingly switched gender roles. Jared became the docile recipient, lying on his back, still, while Amy was the carnivorous demon, seeking to implant her seed by any means necessary. The in-and-out humping motion was accompanied by a pressurized rub, as she maintained genital contact and proceeded to slide up and down, sensual. Jared was hard, erect, bona fide. He had been so for the past half hour. It's safe to assume, although no definite proof was obtained that day, that Amy was equally aroused, dripping wet, moist.

At first, Jared didn't know how to react. He felt strangely uncomfortable and emasculated, getting rammed by his girlfriend. To his relief, Amy giggled, easing the sudden, unspoken tension.

"You like that?" she asked, with mock bravado.

"Oh yea, baby." He played along, grateful.

"It's kinda weird, isn't it? Slightly intrusive, yet strangely erotic."

"Yea, I was definitely—"

"Let's hold off on the sexual advances, for now. I'm perfectly satisfied with the kisses, no need to careen through the gamut."

"Of course, Amy. I was just overly excited and got caught up in the moment. I guess I temporarily lost control of my senses, succumbing to the arousing pleasures of the flesh."

"Me too! I was ready to fuck you, right here and now. But let's take it easy. We've got an exemplary trajectory going and I don't want to up the ante prematurely."

He smiled.

"Oh Amy, you're a doll."

They kissed a quick-lipped kiss.

"How so?"

"Well, I mean that I appreciate you being honest with me and sharing your feelings right away. I'm in no hurry to sleep together. We'll consummate our love when the time is right. I enjoy simply being with you, whether sexually or friendly, romantic or silly. Hell, it took me long enough to kiss you for the first time. I am quite patient, as you know."

In a wordless affirmation of his statement, she tightly grasped Jared and kissed him with the eager passion of a civilian wife being finally reunited with her deployed-soldier husband, after a year overseas. Expressing the brilliant balance of two minds in mutual agreement, a knowing affection, unaffected by time, distance or danger.

They continued making out for another 15 minutes or so (no need to fluff it up, time was irrelevant, I'm merely stating the facts) until Amy suggested they return to the picnic.

"I guess so. Let's go back and mingle, like normal people."

They brushed the dirt and leaves off their clothes and headed toward the campgrounds. Their quaint, quiet, tranquil walk through the woods was abruptly extinguished as soon as they returned. They re-entered the fray at the far western corner of the lawn, and Jared's sister, upon witnessing their arrival, immediately ran toward them, frantic and chaotic. Her demeanor indicated that she had been crying. Her face also revealed all the telltale remnants of tears strewn: smeared makeup, bloodshot eyes, drooping frown.

"What the fuck is wrong with you?" she screamed. To say she was fuming would be an understatement. Her hostility was startling.

"Excuse me?" Jared replied, defending his honor.

The arrival of the two antisocial lovers signaled and initiated a mad scramble. The remaining members of Jared's family ran over to join his sobbing sister.

"Do you know how worried we've been?" she continued. "Sick, worried sick."

The prevailing mood of warmth and elation suddenly descended and shifted, instead, into an unforgiving dissonance.

"Is something wrong?" Jared was flabbergasted by the frenzied nature of the scene. His mother came stomping over.

"Young man, where the hell were you?"

Young man? She rarely ever referred to me as 'young man.' This must be serious. She also placed a harsh emphasis on 'hell.' Mom's angry.

Having just moments before been encased in the comforting coalescence of the womb, J+A, secure in their embrace, were untimely ripped, sent screaming and crying into a ruthless world of hostile accusations.

"Could someone please explain what's going on? What happened?"

His mother enacted a strange ballet twirl, throwing her arms up in the air, turning around and walking away a few steps, before completing her 360-degree rotation and resuming her position in the face-to-face confrontation.

"You had us worried sick!"

Jared's sister began to weep. Her repose had faltered. She hugged Jared.

"We thought something had happened to you. Something terrible," she spoke, while crying into his shoulder.

"You guys, relax. We're fine. We just went for a short hike is all, wanted to explore the area."

"You were gone for almost two hours. We assumed the worst."

Jared, still not comprehending the severity of the situation, attempted to make light of their overly-fatalistic concerns.

"What, like a bear ate us?"

His mother replied, after a brief scowl, "Don't you dare speak to me in that sarcastic tone. I really can't stand it, especially now. If you care to know, there has been a string of kidnappings in the area recently. Four in the past month, to be exact. We were already on high alert, and suddenly the two of you vanish from the premises without a word of warning. I turned around, and you were gone."

She paused, briefly, a murky puddle of tears welling up in her eyes. The terrifying potentiality (which, only moments ago had been an accepted reality, certain and resolute) that her first-born child was kidnapped, along with his less-than-gracious girlfriend, weighed heavy in her subconscious, in the region of a mother's mind that remains permanently engaged in a state of constant worry. The abysmal thought, still unresolved, and presently being refreshed by her telling, hindered her emotions and brought forth a physical manifestation of sadness, as represented by her puffy eyes and low-hanging lips. Her story, carefully articulated, factually informative and stern in tone, imparted a perspective that Jared took to heart. He knew that he had done wrong, on his own, and had mistakenly, without prior intent, designated Amy as an unknowing accomplice.

Guilt set in.

"Oh fuck," Jared sighed. "I'm sorry, you guys."

Then fear.

He had been under the assumption, however brief, that his father was too busy mingling with fellow employees and boosting company morale to express the same level of angered concern and guilt-ridden discipline that his mother and sister were conveying. His assumption was proven false when he observed his dad engaged in a private conversation with a police officer, or maybe it was a park ranger. Either way, the fella was some sort of authoritative figure, adorned with a badge and uniform. The sight terrified Jared.

"Um, does anyone want to explain to me why dad is talking to a cop?" he asked.

After looking over her shoulder to confirm Jared's observation, his mother replied, "Well, you'll love this. He is currently in the process of cancelling the directives for the search party."

"You mean...?"

"Oh yes. During our panic a search party was summoned to locate the two of you."

"Oh god! Really?"

"Yes, really. The grim prospect that you two had been kidnapped, and were either being brutally sodomized or dangling from a dirty meat hook in some backwoods psycho-lair, was not something we could easily brush aside and ignore. Our feeble attempt to locate you, coupled with your father's obligation to commiserate with his employees, forced us to seek assistance elsewhere; and thus, the search party. A well-equipped militia was sent scouring the area in search of two lovers entwined."

"Well, I sure feel miserable now. I'm so fucking sorry, really."

She put her hands on her hips, elbows extending outward, a common disciplinary stance.

"As you should be. Lucky for you, my relief that you're okay supersedes my anger. Now, if you'll excuse me, I had no intention of drinking today; but alas, you've swayed my decision."

She turned and exited the scene, which left only the guilty parties and Jared's sister, still scowling.

"Don't fucking do that again."

She too exited in a huff. Only Jared and Amy remained.

"Well, that was fun."

"I'm so sorry."

"Don't be. It's completely my fault. I should've anticipated their reaction, and in doing so, taken the time to inform them of our departure. Although it was a spontaneous, unplanned event, and the fact that we, after leaving, lost track of time, is no defense for the emotional turmoil our actions inflicted upon everyone here. Uh, my actions."

She sighed, only half-believing Jared's plea.

"Do you think your parents hate me?"

"Absolutely not. I assume full responsibility for what happened today and, as such, I will fight to defuse any accusations directed at you. This was all my doing. You're less an accomplice, more a bystander to my actions."

"They hate me."

The tense ride home provided an opportunity for Jared's father to share his reflections on the incident.

"I offer you this one indictment. No, I'm not mad, I'm not distraught; hell, I'm nearly pleased in some strange sort of vicarious longing for those adolescent-pangs-of-young-love that have since been extinguished. However, I maintain strict concern regarding one particular issue. Hear me out. Now, I have no problem with the two of you running off into the wilderness to go fondle each other for hours on end. Go to it. I actually encourage such behavior. Ask any man over fifty and you'll be quick to discover the trembling jealousy we harbor toward teenagers. Little fuck machines, engaged in the eternal pursuit of quelling their endless desires. We can do nothing but observe you from afar, off in the distance, buried deep in the imminent decline of passion known as aging, growing old. We crumble internally while watching the youthful and horny, saying to ourselves, 'Ah yes, I too recall such days of selfishness, when a wet dick was all that mattered.'"

Jared wasn't the only one hearing this tirade. There was a full audience in the car, all blushing. His mother, noticing that daddy's reprimand was transforming into a nostalgic remembrance of his perverted yesteryears, nudged him, knocking him out of his retrospective trance. He regained his composure and continued.

"What I mean to say is that I understand. Trust me. I don't blame you for doing what you did. I have but one qualm about the way things played out today, one overarching grievance. Let us consider the location where it all occurred. The setting, the specific event, the reason we all came out here in the first place. Question #1: What was the event?"

No response.

"Question #1: What was the event that we just left?"

"Um, the company picnic."

"Good. Okay, now tell me, what was the purpose of this event?"

"Purpose? Um, for everyone to have fun."

"Well, yes, that could be considered an incredibly generalized reason why we arranged such an event, but dig deeper. Get philosophical with it."

"Okay. You threw this party to allow all your employees to escape the decorum of the workplace environment. To provide a loose-lipped day of fun, free from the issues that normally clout your interactions. In essence, team building and morale boosting. Company bonding."

"Is that your final answer?"

"Yea."

"Erh!" He mimicked a buzzer. "Sorry. Thanks for playing. You put in a good effort, but you are nonetheless incorrect. There is an inherent fallacy in the concept of these 'trust building exercises,' as you described them. You overlooked the fact that I see these people practically everyday. Every single fucking day I'm in the office with them. The last thing we need is to go through a series of bonding rituals. In actuality, I know them too well, almost excessively. If anything, I'd like a de-bonding exercise, where we can forget things about each other, like all their annoying habits and personality quirks. Suffice it to say, a group of people that spend eight hours a day together know each other pretty well. Now, I offer you another question: Besides the setting, what made this different from the average day at work?"

"Um, instead of reading casebooks, you're eating barbeque and throwing water balloons."

"What about any additional participants? There sure seemed to be a lot more people at the picnic than are normally at the office."

"Well yea, because everyone brought their families along."

"Ding ding ding! That's it. That's the substantial purpose of today."

"To meet everyone's wife and/or husband, and kids?"

"Absolutely. We've already established that all the fellow employees are familiar with one another. However, the family is a whole different animal. The family gives a perspective, a validation, to the work we do. When I see all these kids running around having a blast, and spouses seeming happy and carefree, everyone confident in their livelihood, it makes it all worth it. In seeing everyone with their families in tow, I am able to understand the far-reaching joy that our enterprise enables.

"A happy family is a symbol of success, life's ultimate goal. It's one thing to make yourself happy, but to provide for an entire family, and to do it well, not just merely scraping by, but being able to offer abundance and riches, that is true success. It puts an entire life of hard work and struggle into a sharp focus of meaningful perspective.

"I'm proud of you, Jared. I'm proud of all of you. And goddamnit, all I ask for in return is that I get to show you off every once and a while. I'm not asking you to do tricks for anyone, just a quick hello and some surface level conversation. Honestly. I'm not mad that you ran off without telling us, that's another story for another day. But I must say, I am incredibly upset that you didn't talk anybody before you decided to vanish. Like I said, I'm proud of you and I wanted everyone to bear witness to the bright, young man you've become. It was the entire purpose of today. This whole upset could have been avoided if you would have at least shook a few hands before disappearing into the bushes, presumably for some deep lovin'. That's all. I've stated my case and shared my feelings."

Jared reached over, put his hand on his father's shoulder, and in perhaps the single sincere and saccharine moment to occur thus far in the story, proclaimed, "I'm sorry, dad."

He realized that as a result of his temporary abandonment, he had greatly wronged his father. It was, after all, his special day. A time of families intermingling and laughing, all in celebration of one man's decision to take a risk many years ago. A risk that ultimately proved to be greatly beneficial. A triumph of American Dream proportions.

The drive home continued, all disputes resolved.

Since Jared and Amy had missed out on the offerings of the barbeque, a brief detour was made at McDonalds before returning home. The two troublesome lovers enjoyed their nuggets and then retired to Jared's bedroom, where they spent the remainder of the day cuddling in bed, once again hidden in the delicate sanctuary of their love.

Reciprocal.  Secure in the womb.

History repeats. The human experience is cyclical, repetitive, of a limited variety. Growth and decay, ingress and egress, ebb and flow, all in all, one in the same. The spinning cycle of life maintains its transgressions without the restraint of friction, blemished by memories and battles anew, yet continually revolving, ever in motion. History is absorbed into the present tense, the ghost of influence.

It's a peculiar moment, when an otherwise peace-loving and conflict-avoiding people become suddenly enamored with the bravado of battle. A swift darkness, long left dormant and subdued, begins its slow ascent, exposed. It should come as no surprise to anyone, although it often does, that even the most gentle and warm of individuals are shielding a ravenous undercurrent, a brimming cauldron of hatred buried deep within their placid, whispering persona, ready to singe the fibers of all onlookers, when sufficiently subjected to worthy provocation. 'I never knew...He was such a nice boy...Always polite to all the neighbors,' a common crime scene afterthought. As it turns out, The Land of Forgotten Souls is populated entirely by such easily susceptible sociopaths.

The challenge of whipping a group of lazy, unmotivated, drug-addled sloths into fighting shape is a near-insurmountable challenge; but nevertheless, it's possible. Difficult, yet possible. Patricia participated, reluctantly; while Patrick, already excited and accustomed to obedient training procedures, was a willing volunteer.

The proper method of beginning a workout involves nothing more than a jog, a simple exercise to initiate the circulation of blood among the tepid pulse of an otherwise sedentary body. To those who flourish under the numbing effects (or artificially-stimulating influence) of sacred substances, discipline, hard work and sacrifice does not come easy; it is, in fact, avoided at all costs. Pleasure seekers tend to avoid any activities that require extended physical or mental exertion for no reward other than the promise of delayed gratification.

Yet even the most heavily lulled expanse of doldrums, drudging along plainly (a scathing, worthless puddle of insipid banality, a wasted existence of selfish hedonism, drooling, slobbering, sickened, scum filled, blanket-laced tourniquets of evermore, a slopped mess of unearned pleasantries, recipients of bequeathed riches, good people gone hiding), has within itself, buried deep beneath layers of self upon self, the potential to spring into action at a moment's notice. The thunderous importance of necessity begets discipline, instigating the adrenaline rush of obligation. Here, within the confines of urgent NOW NOW NOW action, arises the seminally significant role of a captain, a whip-cracking ringleader, a commander of the dull. Such an influence can ignite the requisite spark in an immobile mind.

The Land of Forgotten Souls was already well-accustomed to instances of communal assemblage, as concerts, farmers markets and the annual Potential Energy Pushcart Challenge frequently brought all likeminded residents together, united under the guise of a common pretext. This time was different. Now, the gathering was neither the cause nor the effect of a joyous celebration; it was, indeed, a somber affair.

Alto Undershed, the master of ceremonies, initiated a relentless tirade, denoting the occasion's commencement. The army was awakening, exposing their latent life force, suddenly enthralled by unusual prospects.

Consider the philosophy of the drunkard. His vice offers a unique perspective, almost radical. Yet the same substance that propels his imagination simultaneously dampens his drive. He is confronted by the ultimate political dilemma, the dual options of activism: energetic and vigorous, though complacent and satisfied with the status quo **or** righteous but immobile, engulfed in dank clouds of mental confinement, perpetuating grand delusions that wilt as suddenly as the smoke that inspired them. That is, until their lifestyle (or mantra) is threatened.

There was no cogent threat to the bubbled existence of dewdrop surprises that flourished throughout The Land of Forgotten Souls; the enemy, rather, was their own indignation toward South Forts. It's worth suggesting that this entire conflict, and the reluctance on the part of the forgotten souls, was not a fight for resources or environmental preservation, as there was plenty of water worthy of a friendly share. Oh no, this was a matter of principle and pride. An idea often purported, transmitted, discussed and generally agreed upon, is that unity requires a common enemy, for an enemy gives the union an objective.

Any small, secluded, off-the-grid, deep woods town harbors an inherent disdain for any sort of thriving, big city metropolis. Something about seeking refuge and escaping, yet ultimately living in the shadow of Babylon, instills a sense of hostility toward those without cause to run. Within such a mindset, it's sensible to conclude that the forgotten souls looked upon South Forts as their common enemy.

Now, when riparian representatives enter your property and discuss a plan to divert the water supply for their own (arguably) selfish needs, it's cause for concern. Apparently, for the inhabitants of The Land of Forgotten Souls, this behavior signified such a deplorable injustice that it warranted a full-scale battle to defeat it.

Alto Undershed, the newly-christened pseudo drill sergeant, attempted to state, with eloquence, their mission statement:

Brothers and sisters,
    recipients of nature's bounty,
let us all acknowledge,
    with full realization,
that our livelihood is in danger.

Our peaceful existence,
full of fortune and wonder,
community, loyalty and fellowship,
is a source of intimidation
to the corporate shills of South Forts.
They see us living together in lockstep harmony,
unencumbered by the restraints of modernity,
free at last!
And they seek to disrupt the very treasures we
have struggled so tirelessly to achieve.
Brothers and sisters,
today we will silence their conquest.
We will not submit,
we will resist.
When they cross the boundary line,
dressed in suits and armed with smiles,
we will forgo their expectations
of submission or civil disobedience.
No brothers,
no sisters,
we will meet them with a grotesque display of arms.
Offensive resistance is the only method worthy of
competition against a government that has grown
accustomed to dominance.
Today marks the occasion
when we put our foot down
and tell them: "No!"


Quite an uncomfortable, enduring moment commences
when your best friend begins dating your ex-girlfriend. However,
Jared was in no position to wage a legitimate complaint, as he had
formally authorized the existence of the relationship between
Eddie and Amy. Poor fool, he even admired the guy for asking
permission. That's not to say there wasn't any animosity between
them during that time, just, it was, more or less, approved of; i.e.,
Eddie wasn't breaking any rules.

The Amy-Eddie courtship, bizarre as it was, lasted only a couple months. Little is known of exactly what occurred during that time, though sparse evidential fragments remain.

Jared's first sighting of Eddie and Amy as a full-fledged couple occurred at school, on any given weekday, when he saw the two walking hand-in-hand. Eye contact was made, and a telling glance was exchanged that conveyed a tome's worth of lamentations; yet no words were spoken. Both parties (Jared and the Amy-Eddie combo) continued on their prescribed trajectories, and the day proceeded to envelop their destinies.

Jared was subsequently given precious intel from a fellow friendly confidant (a credible source) regarding the happenings between the two. For instance, the first kiss that was shared between Eddie and Amy occurred at a ramshackle party of some sort. A rollicking weekend high school kickback at a classmate's house, operating under the presumption that this poor sap's parents were out of town, while a gaggle of horny teenagers filled the corridors. Anyways, at this gathering, Amy and Eddie shared their first kiss. Oh gosh! They kissed, which turned into a wholly divine, eager and enthusiastic make-out session. And, in plural contribution to the romantic zeal of the occasion, all of this took place on a pool table. Yes, this house, home to out-of-town citizens of presumed affluence, currently occupied by a cavalcade of adolescent ne'er-do-wells, bumbling about. In particular, a pool table, within said house, where perhaps insightful, meaningful discussions took place, heated debates of global significance,[1] had undergone a drastic conversion, as it was now hosting the romantic consummation of Eddie and Amy's teenage infatuation. The green felt cushioning their fertile loins, absorbing the shock of lustful, energetic yearnings. Good for you, Eddie. Tussle her hair and let her feel important. I

---

[1] Recreational activities and games of this sort provide an adequate backdrop for masculine discourse, as man requires a preoccupation, a disinterested focal point of concentration, in order to truly evoke honesty and fair dealing when conversing with another man of equal stoicism. The shield of heavily-guarded emotion vanishes, magnificently, when diverted through the guise of gameplay and sport.

sometimes wonder who made the first move, the initial forward lunge.

A first kiss is a cruel and nerve-wracking experience. It is based entirely upon unspoken gestures and body language. There exist but few moments of subtle tranquility, wherein a kiss is appropriately invited. A momentary pause, hands held and eyes locked, when both parties' inner thoughts become well-received exterior actions.[2] Taking that inaugural first kiss leap-of-faith is itself a risk. It operates under the assumption that he/she feels the same way. It requires confidence in the conjecture that he/she wants it and enough bravery to act upon passion's uncertain surmise, as rejection awaits a foolish guess. Luckily for Eddie and Amy, both were ready for a lip-locked exchange of schmaltz; each ready to accept the kiss, to participate in love's introductory passage. A first kiss, then, functions as an affirmation of both parties' intentions. This is beyond mere friendship and cordial pandering, this is love, sweetie; or, at least, the beginnings of what may eventually evolve into love. Regardless, Eddie (or Amy, it was most likely Amy, she's always the instigator) took the first step and it was met with mutual assent, an affectionate meeting of the minds, implied in fact.

The timeline continues…

Eddie had recently acquired a copy of <u>Babe</u>, the pig movie, and he invited Amy over to his house after school for a nonchalant, desultory viewing. Of course, she accepted. <u>Babe</u> exists within a narrow corridor of films that are universally adored by all shades of spectator, ranging from arrogant film aficionados to casual escapists. The appeal of <u>Babe</u> is boundless. Man and child can weep together, unashamed, during a screening. That little pig managed to capture the hearts of an entire nation, as witnessing such loyal naiveté cripples the vulnerabilities of all humans worthy of their own pulse. Yet for all its cinematic majesty, the film failed to provide a sufficient distraction for Amy and Eddie's hormonal surges. As the opening credits to <u>Babe</u> flickered on the television set in Eddie's bedroom, he and Amy

---

[2] Granted neither party possesses the finesse of Alvy Singer.

got cozy on his bed, engulfed in a cuddle of precious proportions.[3] About ¼ of the way into the film, Amy turned away from the screen and faced Eddie directly, twirling within his grasp. She lunged, and he received her fat, sloppy lips. Once again, they went at it. She twisted her entire body and their spoon transformed into a complete frontal embrace. Lucky man, Eddie. Be gentle with her. Maybe it was because of the privacy his bedroom afforded them, or maybe it was the sentiment of the film, but their sexual persistence did not cease at the make out phase. All that remains of this tale is that Eddie ended up eating her out that day. That's right! He buried his face in her pussy. He tasted my Amy, in her special spot. What she did to him that day remains a mystery, yet it's safe to assume she was equal in her generosity.

It's worthy of mention that during the interim period of the Eddie-Amy courtship, Jared was not suffering in silence. Oh no, he had found a replacement lover, a feminine veil, shrouding his loneliness. Her name was Tea Leaf and she remains, to this day, perhaps one of the sparse, lingering fragments (the scant, limited few) of any sort of truly genuine, good-hearted women that Jared has ever befriended; romantically, that is. What's interesting about this arrangement, though, was its commencement. Since, of course, after Amy, how could he ever love again?

With the dissolution of his relationship with Amy, Jared, naturally, began a dim attempt at expanding his horizons, as Amy was, regretfully, no longer the official apple of his eye. However, this is easier said than done, since the introductory phase of a relationship is fraught with awkward, uncomfortable moments. An endearing process of trial and error, where both individuals selfishly ensure that they are putting their best foot forward at all times. First impressions and reputations are decorated and altered by exaggerated overtones and representative appearances, the ultimate deceit.

---

[3] The aptly titled 'spoon' position.

Amy was Jared's one and only true love. She had acquired soulmate status, and he was incapable of loving another. When Amy left, Jared's worldview crumbled. He seriously loved her, and was certain, in his worrisome heart, that she was irreplaceable. The termination of their relationship was not an important life lesson, an adolescent milestone, just another part of growing up; no, the end was a betrayal of their prescribed destiny. She'll return, she must, she has to. We are meant to be together. A boy in love cannot simply transition from one relationship to the next, just as one doesn't obtain a new puppy immediately after the death of the prior dog. A mourning period is necessary. A catharsis of grief must take place. Luckily for all of us, life is a constant surprise. Certainty is incessantly unreliable, predictability a boundless waste.

Beneath all his emotional appurtenance and woebegone defeat, it didn't take long for Jared to develop a crush on a fellow schoolgirl, the aforementioned Tea Leaf. She, a treasure trove of excellence, managed to capture the desolate heart of poor Jared. Simply put, she thrilled him. For all the inadequacy and nervousness of love's innocent beginnings, there is a sudden excitement, as butterflies of desire fill the belly and life gains an immediate significance. Each day is a joyous and welcome occasion.

Tea Leaf was a girl at school that Jared admired from afar, never expecting to actually accomplish anything tangible with her, just another typecast star of his masturbatory daydreams. He'd espouse loving lamentations to all his friends about how darn cute she was and how she was just o so great, while the prospect of actually communicating any such desires to her directly remained staunchly unforeseeable. Jared had grown accustomed to the notion that his fantasy would never translate into reality. He became infected with the tragic ailment that cripples many American boys: an acceptance, a forced contentment with their current position in life. No ambitious, risky maneuvers toward betterment motivating their maturation; nope, they're just a-okay with loneliness.[4]

Jared nestled deep into his comfort zone. Unthreatened, yet unfulfilled. That is, until Eddie took charge of the situation, providing a wealth of collegial urgings and unwieldy provocation. "Ask her out. Come on, man. What are you waiting for?" That sort of thing. At the time, Eddie's playful goading seemed like the generous, selfless act of a loving friend, ever looking out for his buddy's best interests. Having his back, yea? Eddie seemed determined to ensure the fruition of Jared's schoolboy crush. Gosh Eddie, you were exuding such benevolence, ventilating your full arsenal of altruistic tendencies. Jared's crippling timidity was hindering him from pursing (or even attempting to pursue) a meaningful relationship with Tea Leaf.

One day, after school, at his behest, Eddie accompanied Jared to the supermarket for a kindly shopping excursion. They were going to purchase a bouquet of flowers and Jared was to personally deliver them to Tea Leaf, a symbolic invitation to their romantic prospects. Again, this was all Eddie's highfalutin master plan. Sheer brilliance. He was adamant, and Jared was happy. After all, he needed the assertiveness of a fellow companion in order to shatter his introversion. The boys selected a blossoming bundle of roses and Eddie chauffeured Jared to the Tea Leaf dwelling.

"Man, I can't do this."

"Jared! Are you kidding? Listen, if you don't ask her, you will regret it. Trust me. Maybe not today, but one day you

---

[4] The Allegory of the Apple: A single man searching for love is synonymous with an empty-bellied man gazing upon an apple tree, the variety of potential mates represented by its array of fruit. The objective, the goal, the meaning of life is to take a big, juicy, wet bite. If a man wishes to taste a specific apple, he has two options, only one of which will be successful. He can either (a) approach the tree and pick an apple, or (b) stand beneath his desired apple, extend his hand and wait for it to fall. If he selects option b, he will either never receive the apple, because someone else will pick it in the meantime, or, if the apple does eventually fall into his hand, it will, by then, be rotten, and worse, worm infested. Jared, on the other hand, appears to have taken an entirely different approach. He convinced himself that he wasn't even hungry.

will look back on this and you will fucking weep. I'm telling you, the sense of grief and regret from all of these missed opportunities will overwhelm you. It will fucking crush you. I swear. You will be just another sad old man who never realized his full potential, who never disregarded caution, who never reached out and grabbed the life he wanted. Content with mediocrity. A stale, uninspired life. Man, do you get it? You have to make the life you want. It doesn't happen, you create it. If you have a goal, a wish, a desire, a dream, well, fucking go after it! Don't be the guy who remains idle until it's too late, Jared. You're not that guy."

"I... I'm scared. What else can I tell you? I'm too nervous. I can't help it. She sorta intimidates me."

"Okay, think of it this way. Do your parents ever tell you stories about when they were younger? Tales of the glory days, of a prior era that seems unimaginable to you?"

"Uh, yea."

"Well, perfect. When they're telling you those stories, they are just that. Words and ideas, reflections and memories. One day, this moment, this time, right now, will be a story you tell. Or maybe not. It might be more than that. It could potentially be, best-case scenario, the story you'll tell your kids when discussing how mommy and daddy met."

"Ha! That's a stretch."

"Just hear me out, okay? That's the best-case scenario, fairytale outcome. But, like, what's the worst that can happen? Say she turns you down, and you're standing there with flowers and a broken heart."

"That's exactly what I'm afraid of."

"Right. So if that's the case, naturally you'll be upset and a little embarrassed; but for how long? I mean, don't forget, even though you're a shy, scared, little wimp, you're still a man. Buried beneath layers of self-loathing and insecurity, there exists a man."

"What's that supposed to mean?"

"I'm saying you'll get over it!  You'll move on with your life.  And then, one day, this will be just another one of those boring stories that you tell your kids while they're half listening."

"Yea, I get it.  But I can't change how I feel right now.  Sure, maybe when I'm 50 I'll look back on today and have a hearty laugh about it all; but I can't just all of a sudden alter my nerves based on some concept of the theoretical potential of hindsight."

"Goddamnit, Jared.  I'm just trying to motivate you.  I realize you're scared and nervous, and I don't expect that to change.  All I'm saying is that the emotions you're experiencing right now should not be limitations to your desired goals.  They shouldn't prevent you, they should fuel you.  I'm just trying to give you some perspective, that's all."

By the time they reached Tea Leaf's house, it made perfect sense.  Eddie parked the car.  Jared grabbed the flowers and stepped outside.

"Good luck, buddy."

Knock knock

Her mother answered the door.  She was confused, yet somewhat delighted.  The flowers certainly eased any hostility.

"Can I help you?"

"Hi ma'am.  My name is Jared.  I go to school with Tea Leaf.  I was curious if she was home."

She smiled, chivalry restored.

"Yes, of course.  One moment."

The door closed, gently.

Jared waited for approximately one minute, his heart racing, feet shifting, eyes darting.  That single minute of isolated tranquility provided a much needed chance for self-reflection.  Some deep-rooted, purification-ritual, lifetime-traversing, soul-searching thought.  Well, that and the whole angst-ridden preparatory phase, a mental prediction of the lingering event.  He practiced his lines.  Inhale.  Exhale.  The clicking sound of the doorknob signaled the inevitable.  Here we go.  Deep breath.

Tea Leaf opened the door.  She appeared happy to see him, in her own sweet way.

"Hi Jared." Her voice was quiet, gentle, unsure.

"Tea Leaf... I... Hey, these are for you." He thrust the flowers upon her.

"Aww, thanks." She was genial, appreciative, accepting. "You didn't need to do that." Flattered, yet confused.

Here goes nothing.

"Well, actually, consider these flowers an offering, a promise. Well, a gift too, but a meaningful gift." Breathe. Slow down. "Tea Leaf, I think you're a great gal, truly, and I've wanted to ask you something for a while now. You see, you're special to me, and the more time we spend together, the more I like you. I can't help it. It's an ever-increasing infatuation. You're so lovely, Tea Leaf." Another breath. "Anyhow, so I came here today, with these flowers, because I wanted to ask if you'd go out with me. Like, on a date."

There it was. He said it. Sure, it lacked the poetic romanticism he'd anticipated, but he still managed to get his point across. He told her how he felt and awaited a response.

She was quiet for a beat. Then she looked away and did that slightly embarrassed, dual laugh/sigh thing, her eyes pointing in a diagonal line toward the floor.

"Oh, Jared, that's so sweet of you."

Fuck.

That's it. She's going to say no. What a fucking waste. I am the eternal fool. If she needs to preface her answer, it's assuredly a no.

"I am truly grateful for the flowers, the kind words, the whole gesture, really. Thank you so much. It's really nice of you to say all that, but I just can't. I'm sorry. You're a great guy and a great friend, but I have to say no. I'm really sorry."

I knew it. At least she let him down gently. You could tell by the look in her eyes that she felt terrible about declining the offer. Regardless, she meant it. She wasn't the type of woman to grant a sympathy date. Furthermore, Jared wasn't the type of man to put up a fight, to beg, to plead his case; rather, he gave up immediately.

"Well… hey, that's cool… I totally understand and everything… I just–"

Her mother again entered the scene, approaching from the background interior. She spoke, apparently oblivious of the exchange, functioning under the assumption that all had gone according to plan.

"Tea Leaf, are you going to make the boy stand out there the whole time? For Christ's sake, invite him in."

Jared responded, in a desperate attempt to diffuse any ensuing awkwardness.

"Oh, that's okay. I was actually going to depart soon, so it's fine, really."

"Nonsense. Come on inside."

She wouldn't take no for an answer.

Tea Leaf peeped up, reluctantly. "Would you like to come in, Jared?"

"Uh, yea, sure, thanks." Jared played along.

He entered. Tea Leaf's mother took the flowers and headed into the kitchen to assemble the floral display in an appropriate vase. Tea Leaf walked toward a couch in the adjoining living room. She nestled her butt atop the crease of two cushions connecting.

"Would you like to sit down?" She was going through the motions of a polite hostess.

"Okay."

Jared sat and gazed about the room, taking in the décor, a random assemblage of family photos and unthreatening paintings. Not knowing what to say, Jared nodded.

"Can I get you two anything?" her mother called out from the other room.

"No."

"Oh, no, thank you."

Tea Leaf's mother exuded more enthusiasm than both of them combined. She reappeared and proceeded to place the bouquet on the coffee table directly in front of them, a shrine to Jared's unrequited attraction. She must've sensed that for a pair of newly-minted lovebirds, both Jared and Tea Leaf appeared terribly unexcited, almost sad. Her innocent ignorance of the situation prompted an assortment of inquiries.

"Did you walk or ride your bike here, Jared?" Mama Leaf was doing her best to make their timid guest feel welcome.

"Actually, my friend Eddie gave me a ride."

"I see. Does he live nearby?"

"Not really. As a matter of fact, he's waiting outside in the car right now."

"What? Are you kidding me? He's out there by himself?"

"Well, yea."

"That's ridiculous. Tell him he can come in."

"Yes, ma'am. I'll go get him."

Jared arose and went outside. Tea Leaf's mother laughed as he exited. She said something along the lines of, 'You kids are too darn polite. It's pathetic, making your friend hide in the car.'

Once the door was securely closed, he ran. Hurried and quick. As Jared approached Eddie's car, he caught a glimpse of his buddy's eyes in the rearview mirror. Eddie looked so excited. Such a good guy, genuinely happy for a friend, eager to hear the results. Jared stood beside the driver's side door and Eddie lowered the window.

"Well?"

"So here's the deal: her mom wants you to come inside. She thinks it's silly that you're waiting out here in the car."

"Tell me, man, what did she say?"

"Can you just…?"

"Yea, yea, alright."

Eddie opened the door and exited the vehicle. The two best buds began their march back toward the Tea Leaf residence.

"Jared, let's hear it."

"It's not… she… she said no."

"What?" Eddie was clearly stunned.

"I guess she just wasn't into it. I don't know. She said no. That's all there is to it."

"That's absurd."

"I know, man. I knew this was a stupid idea."

"Did she like the flowers?"

"Yeah. Of course she liked the flowers. She loved the fucking flowers."

"I don't get it. I thought this was foolproof. I thought she dug you."

"Apparently not."

"How did you ask her? Like, what exactly did you say? How did you phrase it?"

"I don't remember. I just gave her the flowers and told her how great she was and that I wanted to take her out sometime. The routine spiel. Whatever I said, it didn't work."

"Well, that's terrible and all, this sounds like a complete disaster; but, tell me Jared, why the fuck are we going back?"

"I don't know, man. We just have to. Okay?"

"So, let me get this straight. You just asked out a girl, she declined, and now what? We're going to sip champagne with her mother?"

"More or less."

"You confuse me, Jared."

"It just doesn't feel complete yet. We came all this way, you got me all hyped up, and it was all over much too quickly."

"Hey, I commend your spirit, I just don't quite understand your reasoning."

Once they reached the door, Eddie abruptly grabbed the handle and flung it open. When they entered, something was different. Something had changed. My guess is that while Jared was outside, Tea Leaf had explained the situation to her mother, and she must have disapproved of her daughter's response. 'Now Tea Leaf, when a boy goes through all the trouble of picking up a bundle of flowers and shows up at your house to ask you out on a date, the least you can do is say yes and accept. It's common courtesy. How will you know for sure that you don't like him if you never give him a chance? A first date is a trial run, a test of compatibility. Even if you already know the guy from school, a date gives your interaction a completely different context. So give it a try. If you don't have fun with him when it's just the two of you alone, then you can say no with confidence; but at least give the poor boy a shot. He's so feeble and helpless. He ain't gunna hurt you. Trust me.'

And so, Tea Leaf begrudgingly informed Jared that she had changed her mind. Her rationale was that she was stunned and caught off guard, and that she didn't mean what she had said earlier. Jared, reduced to a charity case, was relieved.

"Well, alright then," Eddie began. "Shall we? There's no time to waste. Let's go, you two. First date. Right now. I'm driving."

Tea Leaf laughed. Jared was uncomfortable.

"Where to?" she asked, suddenly feeling excited and spontaneous.

"Why, Krispy Kreme, of course." Eddie, the king of romantic mediation.

"I love it." Tea Leaf, apparently in a playful mood now, was either aroused by the idea or desperately anxious to get the date out of the way.[5]

"Perfect. Jared, you ready?"

"Yea, sure." He shook his head in disbelief.

"Right this way, you two." Eddie gestured toward the door.

"I need to grab a jacket. I'll meet you guys out front."

Tea Leaf went to her room. The boys went outside.

All the while, her mother stood by the banister, watching longingly as her daughter embarked on the preliminary stages of an adolescent courtship, destined to fail.


"You are a fucking nut."

"Ahh, come on, man. This is going to be great. Trust me. You'll thank me later."


As Jared opened the passenger side door, he was met with immediate resistance.

"No, no, no. You're sitting in the backseat."

He slammed the door shut.

---

[5] Or she just really wanted a donut.

And then, almost as if it was choreographed by the creator himself/herself/itself/nothing, while Jared took the single step necessary to relocate from the front door to the back door, his cellphone sounded its urgent ring. He pulled the phone from his pocket and noticed that the familiar number of the incoming call belonged to the one and only, Amy Carousel. He felt a shiver, and answered immediately.

"Hello?"

"Jared…"

She sounded terrible, in the thick of a cry session.

"Hey Amy. Is everything okay?"

"I'm really sorry, but I slept with someone else."

The words entered his soul, transforming him into emptiness. A crumbled styrofoam cup. A corpse. His heart was nonexistent. His dreams suddenly shattered. Her purity was demolished. Up until that moment, neither Jared nor Amy had ever been with another. She was a stranger now. She was better than him. Jared's entire being burst into flames and melted. The earth swallowed him whole. Unforgiving.

Appropriately, at that moment, Tea Leaf came rushing out in her precious jacket, all smiley and free. Noticing that Jared was on his phone, she politely didn't interrupt him, and instead entered the vehicle.[6]

"What the fuck, Amy! Who was it?"

"I'm so sorry."

"Who the fuck was it? That Zak kid? That little fucking goomba."

"No. No one from school."

"Amy, who? I need to know."

"You don't know him. I met him at my competition this weekend."

"Oh great. You decided to fuck some random stranger? You're a fucking whore, Amy."

"Stop! Don't call me that! I told you I'm sorry. I had to tell you. It didn't feel right."

---

[6] Backseat

Eddie rolled the window down and, with an unsubtle hint of impatience in his voice, asked, "Hey man, you almost done?"

Jared held up a finger, as if to say 'one moment.'

Eddie knew that whatever conversation was taking place, it was going to be a while.

"We're just going to cruise around. We'll be right back."

Off they went, the ringmaster and the damsel in distress. Jared's future prospect couldn't wait any longer. She grew impatient and left, while he continued dwelling on the past. Stuck and hindered.

"Who was this guy?"

"I already told you. I met him at the cheer competition."

"Well fuck, Amy. Congratulations. Good for you."

Her crying grew in intensity. It now consisted of heaves and powerful sobs.

"I don't know what to say."

"Did you at least use protection?"

"No... It just happened. Neither of us expected it. We got lost in the moment."

Jared suddenly switched from angry to concerned.

"Amy, did he rape you?"

"No, Jared. It was consensual, just unplanned is all."

"Christ, Amy. This is absolutely delightful. You're probably disease-ridden and pregnant."

"I'm not pregnant, Jared. He pulled out."[7]

"What a gentleman."

"Jared, it was a mistake. I'm really sorry."

"Amy, what the fuck! How old was this guy?"

"22."

---

[7] When a man pulls out, he still has to cum somewhere. There are three options to choose from: object, body or mouth. Object consists of anything from a towel, a napkin, the bed sheets, etc. Body consists of anything from the stomach, chest, feet, face, etc. However, some would consider the face to exist in its own, separate, fourth category. Finally, with regard to option three, the only variant of cumming in a mouth is whether the recipient swallows or expels the load.

It's worth mentioning that Jared and Amy were both 16 at the time. The thought of Amy getting fucked by a 22-year-old man was a horrifying source of contemplation. He probably annihilated her. He probably knows techniques Jared had never even considered before. He probably made her scream with pleasure.

"Fuck you, Amy. This is seriously the worst fucking thing I've ever heard in my entire life. I have to go. I can't fucking believe you. Goodbye."

He hung up and waited for Eddie and Tea Leaf to return, as he had a date to attend. They drove up shortly thereafter. Eddie could immediately tell something was amiss when Jared entered the car.

"You alright?"

"Yeah. I just can't believe her. I don't understand why she told me that," Jared responded, quietly, in a hushed mumble.

Eddie, desperate to diffuse any tension, had to think fast. He knew the 'she' that Jared was referring to. Who else could it be? She is the cause of all Jared's frustration, sadness and despair. Even in the midst of a new beginning with the darling Tea Leaf, she manages to infect the moment. Curse you, Amy.

"Well, alright then. Ya'll ready for some donuts?"

"Yea!"

Tea Leaf, bless her soul, maintained her dignified poise and her carpe diem sense of anticipation for life's simple pleasures.

"There we go. Jared?"

"Sure thing."

He couldn't shake the mental image of Amy getting pummeled by a grown man. He envisioned his throbbing cock sliding into her, tearing apart the vaginal walls that Jared's puny penis was unable to breach. He could see Amy's eyes bulging as the sensation overtook her, her only response being to sound an impassioned moan while furiously gripping the mystery man's back. This fucking asshole, 22 years old, writhing on top of my dear Amy, thrusting and sweating, ferociously. It was an unbearable thought.

Eddie drove to the nearby Albertson's market, a designated vendor of Krispy Kreme donuts. It wasn't the authentic experience of going to an actual establishment and seeing the tasty creations passing by on a conveyor belt, but the end result was the same.[8] Eddie parked the car and stepped outside.

"I shall return bearing donuts, the fruit of indulgence."

While alone in the car with Tea Leaf, Jared realized that she was, in a way, the absolute antithesis of Amy. She was sweet, generous, innocent and pure.[9] In talking with her during that brief moment, Jared felt a renewed sense of joy and optimism. He felt cleansed of his sorrow, his pity, his unnecessary self-victimization. He had been dwelling endlessly on the unrequited love between himself and Amy, his incomplete true love.[10] Tea Leaf, on the other hand, reciprocated his desires. She was genuine, graceful and interested. *No use wasting my time pursuing someone who is currently unavailable, when right before me is a woman, willing, able and true.* Suddenly, Jared understood that his sorrows were all but a fog, a trap, a handicap, preventing him from achieving true realization. Tea Leaf was a blessing, his guardian angel.[11] She provided a dose of clarity, a reward for his suffering, a consolation prize for the tragic disaster known as Amy.

Eddie returned with a half dozen donuts. They ate them together, deservingly.

**Gluttony** – (n) The pursuit of self

Tea Leaf was escorted home. She hugged Jared goodbye, thanked Eddie and scampered off into the darkness.

Once she was outta sight, the post-date recap began.

---

[8] An air-fluffed ring of lard and sugar.

[9] As opposed to a soul-destroying slut.

[10] Her recent escapade notwithstanding, which only further compounded his misery.

[11] Jared had been blindly infatuated for so long with a single apple. He failed to recognize that the entire tree was bearing benevolent fruit.

"I must say, Eddie, that turned out all right."

"Not bad, huh?"

Jared glanced out the window, smirking and carefree, a dog in the wind.

"Not bad at all," he said, more to himself than to Eddie.

"I don't know how you do it," Jared continued. "When it was just me, alone, all she could say was, 'No thank you. I'm so sorry. No means no.' And then as soon as you entered the scene, suddenly she's rearing to go. She was gung-ho for those donuts. I couldn't believe the shift in her attitude. You sure do have a way with the ladies."

"Come on, that was all you. She said it herself, she just needed time to process everything. It's not everyday that a handsome, young gentleman such as yourself shows up at her doorstep. She was taken aback."

"Well, regardless, thank you, Eddie. Truly, thank you for pushing me, man. I literally couldn't, nor wouldn't, have done it without you. Like, I've had a crush on this girl for a little while, but I made myself think that I was content in my loneliness. I settled. I gave up on her before I even took a chance. I was a fool. That's no way to approach life, forever dreaming. No sir."

"You did it though."

"I did, yeah. But I needed a push, some provocation."

"What are friends for, eh?"

"I mean it, Eddie. You healed my soul. When Tea Leaf and I were alone in the car, everything made sense. My worldview expanded. Something clicked into place. I was visited by a spirit, or something. I was sent a message from above. It was enlightening."

"I totally get it. So you're saying she blew you and fingered your asshole at the same time? Lucky boy."

"Ha! Yea right. Seriously, it was special. I can't explain it. It was pure redemption."

"Listen, before you further espouse the many virtues of heavenly apparitions transmitted via ethereal goo, I must ask, what the fuck was going on with your little private phone call earlier?"

"Oh god. She's relentless."

"Why would you even answer?"

"I don't know. It was a mistake, I can tell ya that."

"What'd she have to say this time?"

"It was nothing."

"Um, nothing?"

"Yea… just… more Amy drama. The usual."

"I don't know about that. You seemed quite perturbed, more so than the customary boyish gloom that ever pervades your psyche whenever she's the subject of discussion."

"It's nothing, really."

"Jared, what the fuck? You can't share your feelings with a friend? You were obviously upset and I'm asking you, as a concerned citizen, what is wrong. Don't keep that shit bottled up. This is how friendships work. You're supposed to air your grievances and express yourself. Then I offer an insightful perspective and we have an honest to goodness heart-to-heart. We'll engage in a deep, reflective discussion and then conclude it all with a joke, for some much needed comic relief. Or you can just sit there stewing, saying how everything's fine and dandy."

"Alright, damn. So, she felt the need to call me and let me know that while she was away at a cheerleading competition this weekend, she fucked some 22-year-old faggot, mother fuck, piece of shit."

"Holy shit! That is fucking raunchy. What a slut."

"Yea, that's what I told her."

"Wow."

"Can you fucking imagine this guy? 22 years old, a legitimate adult, hanging out with a 16-year-old little girl, a kid. He's seriously a fucking creep, loser, scumbag, rapist, fucking pedophile."

"That's definitely quite an age disparity, and pretty creepy, but Amy is hardly a kid."

"I know. She probably loved every minute of it. Bathing in big boy cum, singing in the fucking rain."

"Charming."

Eddie and Amy would be dating in a matter of weeks. His selfless acts, his eager, matchmaker insistence, were all effectuated in pursuit of an ulterior motive. Eddie knew that the only way to obtain Jared's approval of his desired courtship with Amy would be to fill the void, to provide a distraction, a replacement lover. Thankfully, Tea Leaf proved to be much more than a gap filler. She is a divine woman.

Jared's relationship with Tea Leaf was the epitome of blissful, innocent, schoolyard love. It was absolutely adorable. For instance, one stoned night at Bernardo's house, Tea Leaf accompanied Jared to the kitchen, the purpose of their quest being to obtain and consume some crackers and cheese. Together, alone in the darkened kitchen, while the rest of the gang gallivanted about upstairs, their laughter and camaraderie faintly emanating through the floorboards, Jared and Tea Leaf shared their first kiss. It was one of those nights, eternal and glistening, suspended in time. The reason why adults always say how the high school years are some of the greatest of your life. Now, that statement, when told to an adolescent in the grips of hormonal turmoil, makes no sense. To teenage ears, it is completely senseless and insane. However, that's the beauty of it. The pulsating, unhinged emotions that seem to overwhelm your every waking moment are really a recognition of life's vibrant energy. That enduring feeling, the so-called 'glory days' sentiment, preserves its validity on certain nights, such as the one described here, where everyone was carefree, alive and happy. Death was impossible. There was an unexplainable unity, a cohesion. Everything was simply right, peaceful. Laughter of lasting friendships and kisses of blooming love. And Jared, caught in the middle, drifting gracefully, guided by a destiny he had yet to acknowledge.

Another romantic outing involved driving to PetCo and purchasing a saltwater fish, the kind they scoop out of a tank with a little net and put in a clear, plastic bag, sealed with a rubber band.  Jared and Tea Leaf drove to the beach, walked out onto a mist-cloaked dock and set the little fish free.

The paths collided, total divergence.  Jared and Tea Leaf were lying on Jared's bed.  He was on his back, while she was nestled up against his right side.  They intermittently transitioned between making out and resting calmly together, enjoying each other's warmth.  Solace attained.  The Smashing Pumpkins provided the soundtrack.

Tea Leaf whispered, "I'm comfortable.  I feel safe with you."

They remained still, tranquil, and listened to the album's conclusion.

Yes it's true the earth is spinning, and we all live on a rock hurtling through outer space.  The universe is vast, we are all going to die one day, and sooner or later we will all be forgotten.  But somehow, a pretty girl and the perfect album make it all seem irrelevant.  Let's not get carried away, though, because in the midst of this moment, the phone rang.[12]  With great reluctance, Jared reached for his phone.  It was Eddie.

"Hello?"

"I have a question for you."

Eddie was apparently in an extremely good mood.  He sounded happier than I have ever heard him.

"Yes?"

"Feel free to decline, I'll understand.  But, can Amy and I possibly come over?"

"Uh, sure… I guess so."

Although Jared deeply admired Tea Leaf, for some reason the thought of Amy returning to his bedroom, where they'd spent countless nights together, excited him beyond reason.

"Oh perfect.  Thanks.  We'll be over soon."

Tea Leaf, I don't know what I was thinking.  I should've told both of them to go fuck themselves.  I should have been offended that he would even ask me.  That boy was pressing his

---

[12] Note to self: Stop answering the phone!

luck, and I caved. That moment was a test of whether I still cared about Amy, and I failed miserably. I'm sorry, Tea Leaf.

"Who was that?"

"Eddie. He's on his way over with Amy."

I could tell she was offended, or at least made uncomfortable by the idea. She was so polite and well behaved. She tried to play along; but once they arrived, she couldn't anymore.

Jared and Tea Leaf went into the garage to steal a bottle of wine from his parents' cellar. After briefly making out, she informed him that she would have to be leaving.

"What? Stay with us. I don't want you to go."

"You'll be fine. Bye Jared."

And so, she left. That night, Jared and Amy got high together for the first time. Eddie didn't feel like smoking. As a result, the two ex-lovers enjoyed a splendid puff alone, together in the backyard. It had been a while since they shared a laugh. Sure, it was chemically induced, but it felt healthy. From that moment on, his relationship with Tea Leaf was doomed.

After going back inside, the trio decided that it would be appropriate to watch Half-Baked. Amy and Eddie got on the bed. Jared sat on the floor. I remember Amy kept laughing during the scene where the horse overeats and the guy can't remember its name.[13] We didn't make it all the way through the movie. Everyone fell asleep in his or her respective location. Jared had become relegated to a ghostly spirit watching over a world too busy rejoicing in his absence to lend him any memorial concern. He felt subtracted from the situation, eliminated. And what remained was a cuddled mass. Love's smiling globule, blissed out and stupid. Can't complain though, I submitted my approval to this whole ordeal. A dwindling charade of teenage lust. Still, granting your blessing for a proposed relationship is entirely different from witnessing the two of them sleeping together; in my own bed, no less. Seeing it presented before my very eyes, in such a literal sensory display, I didn't feel nearly as understanding

---

[13] Buttercup

as I originally had.  But what about Tea Leaf?  Wasn't she supposed to be the angelic remedy to my betrayal?  The cure to my woes?  Why am I still upset?  Is it a case of first love syndrome?  Further reflection leads me to conclude that I failed to properly appreciate her.  I was too distracted by the lure of dark forces.

Jared was the first to wake up, while Eddie and Amy remained wrapped in a warm embrace.  Rather than disturbing them, he put on a pair of headphones and let The Beatles soothe his spirit.  In particular, he listened to "For No One" on repeat for a good half-hour.  When they finally arose from their slumber, everyone was very mature and polite.  Exquisite behavior was observed by all parties, as 'good mornings' and 'goodbyes' were exchanged.  Jared escorted them to the door and wished them a fond farewell.  Split, divergent paths, toward a new day.  Amy and Eddie would get breakfast, and Jared would call Tea Leaf, apologetic and remorseful; she had, after all, been constructively evicted from the festivities.

*Well, I guess this is the state of the union.*

And so it went...  The musical chairs of romantic pairings had shifted into place.  Jared and Tea Leaf resumed their romance, while Eddie and Amy embarked on the construction of their kissy-faced monument.

A troubling thought, unshakeable from his mind, was how happy they seemed together.  A perfect little pair, exquisite.  Something in their dynamic was absent from Jared's prior attempt, and it sickened him.  A friendly camaraderie, almost familial.  Jared recalled a conversation he shared with Eddie approximately one year ago, during what could reasonably be regarded as the peak of the J+A relationship.  While discussing Amy, Eddie had commented, "I always figured the two of you made out all the time because you had nothing to talk about.  Do you really have that much in common?"  Now, when Eddie first delivered this playful colloquialism, Jared's initial reaction was abrupt and defensive. "How dare you cast aspersions at my deep, soul-wrenching connection with Amy. We are in love, you fool! How rude a suggestion." Suddenly, it made sense. Eddie and Amy shared a unique bond. As much as it pained Jared to admit it, they were perfect together.

The lingering question, then, is why did it end? On all fronts it appeared that their relationship was blooming, on a steady ascent toward true love. So why the abrupt termination?

Just as it began, it ended with a phone call between Eddie and Jared.

"Hello?"

"Hey Jared."

"Greetings Eddie. How goes it?"

"Well, I'm alright, ya know? I'm good, I feel good, yea."

"Um, that's great. So, what's going down?"

"I want to talk about Amy."

"O boy. How's that going for ya?"

"Well, man, I, I actually decided to end it."

"Really?"

"Heh, yea. We actually broke up earlier today."

Jared felt a simultaneous emotional surge of concern and elation. After performing an internal victory dance, he inquired as to the circumstances.

"And what brought this about?"

"Alright, well, I actually thought about it for quite a while. As a matter of fact, I was up almost all night thinking about it. I had to make sure I was making the right decision, you know? It was really messing with my head. I sought certainty. This was not decided on a whim, believe me. So, last night, after hours of silent contemplation, I called Bernardo to get an outside perspective, because I didn't know if I was being selfish or not. Maybe not selfish, no, that's not the right word. More like irrational, or fucking dumb. I had to make sure I wasn't being an impulsive dumbass. Anyways, Bernardo and I got to talking, and I decided to go smoke a bowl. I was so conflicted that I had to get high while he was on the phone with me just to be able to have this conversation."

"Okay… Well, what did you decide? How did you navigate through the dense morass that is The Mind of Eddie to eventually arrive at the bold conclusion that it was time to let her go?"

"Alright, so my reasoning rests upon the unwavering fact that you, yes you, Jared, you have had sex with Amy probably 1,000 times."

"Um, what? That's a gross exaggeration in more ways than one. But nevertheless, wasn't this something you considered prior to commencing a relationship with her? Wasn't this already a well-known, near-legendary fact? Yes, we have slept together many, many, many times. We have shared the pinnacle of maturity, to the point of exhaustion. The fusion of skin and soul, and the fastidious pump of a human heart, desperate for fulfillment. Insistence. Lover, I barely knew ye, unrecognizable. A thousand nights was not enough."

The recollection flooded Jared's emotional barometer. He began floating.

"Honestly, I just couldn't get over the fact that you've been inside her pussy countless times. You probably know every little wrinkle, every curve, every hidden pocket. You've got the whole thing memorized. I'd wager that you could draw a 100% accurate replica without any visual cues. Colorized and everything. It's burned into your brain, mentally ingrained. Fucking splatter paint it. A life-size clay molding, textured. Her fluids are probably infused in your bloodstream. Distinct taste buds can recall the flavor. You are partial to her pussy. You are the reincarnation of that girl's pussy. It has formed to the shape of your cock, a penile trilobite."

"Wow, Eddie."

"I felt as though I was encroaching on your territory. Does that make sense? I don't mean to suggest that she is your property or anything offensive like that, but being with her made me feel like I was violating something sacred."

Jared couldn't help but laugh.

"Yea, that sounds about right. That is the perfect summation of how it feels to fuck Amy."

"That's not what I mean. Pardon my brevity, I'm having trouble explaining myself."

"No, I get it. It's weird, but I get it."

"Well, there you go. Thought you'd want to know. So yea, Amy and I are done. I felt as though our relationship was unoriginal. I was an imposter retracing your heavily worn-out steps, hopelessly attempting to find love in the darkness of your permanent shadow. It was no use. I could only imitate what had already been done, nothing new. Who am I to disrupt your creation? Oh well, it's all over now, and that's that. I knew you would find this interesting or significant in some way. You're a good guy, Jared. It means a lot to me that you were okay with this from the start."

"Thanks, Eddie. I appreciate you telling me."

Eddie let out a liberated sigh.

"Alright then, I'll talk to you later. Bye for now."

"Bye bye."

Jared hung up the phone and chuckled slightly, relieved. Suddenly, a terrifying thought pierced his mind, shattering all momentary triumph: Eddie and Amy had sex. No! He immediately called back.

"Hello?"

"I just need to know one last thing. Did you have sex with her?"

"What?! No, of course not. Do you really think I'm that much of an asshole?"

"No... I... I just had to make sure."

"Fuck, man. Come on. You must be painting quite a disgusting picture of me in your head if you needed my assurance on that."

"I knew you didn't, honestly. Only, the way you were describing everything made it sound like you did."

"Jared, you need to relax.  Trust me, I wouldn't fucking do that to you."

"I know, I know."

"Alright then."

And so, it was official: Amy was available.

"My dad got us tickets to see Jimmy Eat World."

"Are you serious?"

"Yea!  Will you come with me tomorrow to pick up the tickets from his office?"

Tea Leaf's father was a high-profile executive of some sort[14] at KROQ (the local alternative-rock-themed radio station), and access to concert tickets was one of the many perks of his job. Jared was confronted with the ultimate teenage conundrum of whether to break up with Tea Leaf before or after the concert.  He had already decided to end the relationship, it was only a matter of time.  Upon learning that Amy was once again a single woman, a free market commodity, he was ready to have her again.  It was time to fuck.  Tea Leaf was an adorable, sweet girl, and Jared was gentle with her, almost too gentle.  She was a virgin at the start of their relationship and remained a virgin at its close.  He was apprehensive about taking their romantic connection to the next level, as though it would tarnish her of all virtue.  Destroy her purity, her innocence.  Amy, on the other hand, was a wild fuck beast, always hungry for another pump.  Any remnants of her innocence had long been abandoned in the cum-drenched celebrations of yesterday.  The memory of their sexual perversions titillated his appetite.  He wanted her again.  The prospect of raucous sexual fantasies dictated his decision-making, ill rationale.

"Absolutely!"

Jared broke up with Tea Leaf in the worst way possible. He accompanied her to daddy's office, to obtain the tickets.  After

---

[14] Program Director

completing their fortunate mission (two tickets in hand), they drove to the beach, where, surprisingly, unbeknownst to both parties, a skateboard competition was underway. 'Oh, how delightful. Wasn't expecting this.' It was the thrill of not having any plans, just going somewhere, out, and suddenly something miraculous happens, something unexpected. Those moments where spontaneity coalesces into excitement and joy, rather than an aimless avoidance of boredom. Do *you* know that feeling? I have no insight into that feeling, I am merely acknowledging it. Which reminds me, what is the purpose of art? Is it enough to simply notice and describe a feeling? Or is there more to it? An additional requirement of communicating a conclusion, an answer, a cohesive thought, with a beginning, middle and end. For instance, can a story be told where the storyteller has yet to experience an ending worthy of imparting an applicable message? Or does art provide the message? Must an artist speak from experience? This notion reaches beyond authenticity. It is broader, of more. Example: my dog died, I am sad. Can I express my sadness, my feelings of loss, and have that be enough? Or must I have lived beyond my sorrow, into tomorrow, through change and realization, where I understand that life is short and we must enjoy the limited time we have? Hence, the lesson. Must there be a resolution? It's not that simple. Not only a lesson that can be concocted in the mind of the teller, but a lesson learned and lived by the teller. I adhere to the theory that the act of telling reveals the lesson. By visiting the misty realm of memory, the lesson emerges. At least, I hope.

After languishing in the fun of the day for several hours, Tea Leaf drove Jared back to his car, which was parked in a predetermined meeting spot. It was time to say goodbye. Goodbye and see you tomorrow. Only, Jared knew otherwise. He knew, yet he wasn't ready. He struggled. He expressed his confused desperation by wrapping the seatbelt around his neck. He'd rather choke, suffocate and die than go through with this. Tea Leaf was uncomfortable. It had to happen. He'd already decided.

"What are you doing?  Is everything okay?  Stop that!
Jared, stop.  What are you doing?"

"I can't go tomorrow."

This is one of Jared's worst character attributes; and by
Jared, I mean myself.  Rather than telling Tea Leaf how he felt
right when the feeling first appeared, he instead followed her
around all day, got the tickets, played in the sun, shared kisses
and laughter, and then, at the last minute, he finally told her how
he felt.  He was inept at confrontation, indefinitely postponing the
inevitable.  Tea Leaf was so damn polite about it, too.  Quiet,
downtrodden and nice, a victim of her own manners.

"Well, alright.  But why?"

"I… I think… Tea Leaf… I think… Well… Um… It's
just… I…"

This rambling mess of unexpressed, vacant thought
endured for the next several minutes.  Jared spoke, fidgeting with
the seatbelt.  Tea Leaf looked on, confused.

"It's time we… It'd be better… I know… We… We need
to… It's…"

Finally, he delivered the glistening crescendo of true
love's untimely demise, shattering the continuity of expectation.
Forever was abandoned, time cut short.  She took it rather well.
At least, her external, car-caged reaction showed no signs of
wrathful indignation, no performance of the 'How could you do
this to me?' charade.

Instead, she quietly uttered, "Okay."  And in her
trembling whisper, a gentle sadness lingered, escaping only for a
brief second, latched on to the perfunctory emanation of her
words.

"I'm sorry, Tea Leaf."

He felt guilty, but relieved.  The hardest part was
complete.  After all, the woebegone doldrums of despair that
accompany most breakups are a relative reflection of the
relationship's duration.  The longer the partnership, the sadder its
end.  Estimations for Jared and Tea Leaf average out to around
five months; not a quick romp, but not a long-term, death defying,
I-gave-you-my-soul kind of love either.

They parted ways, even hugged goodbye in that awkward, sitting in the car, leaning over the center console, heavily angular, primarily shoulder-based way.

Tea Leaf invited her friend Stephanie to attend the concert with her, as a replacement for Jared. During the show, while the band performed "Cautioners," she got high for the first time. A bittersweet euphoria engulfed her senses.

He called Amy that night,
invited her over,
and fingered her.

It was hardly a struggle, barely an effort, vaguely an accomplishment, getting her to come over. No false pretense of missions, game plans or disguised objectives was need. A robust proclamation, requesting her presence, provided a necessary and proper invitation. She neither hesitated nor inquired into the occasion. It was as if the event were inevitable. She did not accept his offer; rather, she surrendered to fate.

Once she arrived, it only took about 45 minutes until they were engaged in their familiar kiss-kiss entanglement. It wasn't at all difficult to slip back into the usual routine.

During the interim period since their last encounter, both Jared and Amy had endured the conception and demise of a leisurely, short-term relationship. They had tried and failed to broaden their romantic horizons, to try someone new, to test the temperate waters of another. And yet, only a short while later, here they were, together again, reunited. It proved unbearable to remain apart. A pulsating beam compelled their union. His sexual yearning was rumbling with latent energy, and she was eager to receive him. There was no need for reconciliation or a probing discussion of life and all its oddities. Instead, they were simply happy to be together, drifting amid an unspoken gratitude. Their mutually afflicted and oft-troubled love was so ingrained into their very being that any principled stance toward reason was baseless and moot, gratuitous and extra. The physical embodiment of Jared and Amy had already undergone a religious and scientific fusion, of soul and biology, spirit and skin. They had attained the pinnacle of human connection, where eye contact transmits data beyond the capability of words. Some magnetic force, the lure of fate and G-d's desire, had once again drawn them together. A force beyond computation. And, to acknowledge their destiny, they kissed, their first kiss in a great while. It contained a quenching strength, replenishing their draught-stricken hearts, breathing life into their withered blood vessels. The momentum of their weighted kiss carried them forward, hurriedly, through the sexual spectrum, cycling through repressed urges with divine passion, pure and inspired.

Once they were both de-clothed, Jared left the bed to obtain a condom[15] from a drawer on the other side of his room. It was time to complete the sequence, to enter her once again and thrust vigorously, inciting the great moan of woman. He grasped the condom with potent enthusiasm and turned toward Amy, on the bed, naked and seemingly yearning for his cock. However, while he was making his return approach, she panicked. For some reason, seeing him naked[16] seemed to startle her. She franticly leapt from the bed in a fit of urgency, got dressed with maddening intensity and left out of sheer necessity. No explanation was offered as to why she was leaving. Gone. Something of crucial significance possessed her, immediately, as though she were abruptly reminded of a thought so tragic and morbidly engrossing that she had no other option but to exit, to flee from the memory. She was gone before Jared could mentally process the very happening of the event. It was all so sudden and unexpected. She departed during the impending zenith of sensual abandon, heated and wet. He stood naked by the edge of his bed, dumbfounded, the window shades on the door still swinging back-and-forth, rollicking from the fury of her abrupt exit. His penis slowly deflated.

---

[15] Love's sacred accouterment.

[16] His miniscule penis hardened and upright, pivoting with his bodily movements. His fingers clutching a condom. His face masked with boyhood excitement.

After an awkward moment of confused loneliness, Jared convinced himself that he deserved it. He deserved every painful second of that frightening confrontation with himself, without any ear licking pleasure to divert his attention or distractions of touch to quiet his thoughts. He was alone, left to endure the self-reflective torture of solitude. Amy's exit was a punishment for his selfish behavior, his desire to have it all, to jump right back into the routine. The interaction of two casual fuck buddies, humping through the vacant night. He reasoned that his haste was unwelcome and rude. There was no mourning, no proper goodbye for Tea Leaf. She was worthy of an adequate farewell; at the very least a lonesome night in her honor.

Jared dissected the entire scene, reliving it over and over, and concluded that Amy's departure was a symbolic gesture, a divine prophesy chastising his self-absorbed, uncaring, hedonistic nature. Some spiritual force was delivering a profound message, and he was the villain. He loathed himself, brutal and certain. He was a jerk, plain and simple. Not once in Jared's somber justification did he ever consider that perhaps Amy fled from his room due to a moral dilemma of her own. That perhaps she was harboring some horrendous secret, drowning in renewed multitudes of guilt and shame. No, of course not. She was perfect, flawless, incapable of doing any wrong. It was all entirely his fault.

The siphoning of sustenance, an abrupt and unwarranted diversion
a hostile reconfiguration of G-d's natural plan
hijacking the landscape
conforming it to one's own needs
without the consent or rightful allowance of the true owner
a simultaneous domination of man and environment
To conquer, or compromise?

Remember:
We are the defenders!
They are hostile!
We are protection
They, destruction

Battle plan:
a wall of humanity, human blockade, chain-linked arms
Prevention
Surround the riverbanks
We will deny them entry
Prohibit their conquest
Our violence, a reactive afterthought

It was on a Tuesday morning when the first suit-adorned, neck-tied and brief-cased, legally authorized, yet blatantly immoral, relentless and rude **taker** arrived. As predicted, he was joyous and cordial. The kind of conniving façade that accompanies all scoundrels engaged in their life's pursuit of subjugating and consuming the vulnerable and weak. An enduring quest of displacement. He was stunningly clean and carried himself with an air of dignified, political significance. Civil and polite, an inauthentic charm. Surprisingly, he wasn't immediately beheaded upon entry into enemy territory, as all able-bodied residents were currently undergoing the rigors of physical education exercises, distracted by their union of hatred. His uninterrupted presence suggested that perhaps a peaceful negotiation was still possible. He introduced himself to the gatekeeper as "Just call me Nathaniel" and requested a private discussion with King Deryk.

During school, geometry class to be precise, Jared's mind began to wander, as it often did. He thought about Amy, as he often did, too. He thought about life without her, whether he'd be able to make it through his remaining days without his affectionate companion, his significant life partner. He still loved her and missed her dearly. He was unfamiliar with ends, terminations or death. Until Amy, nearly everything in his life had been constant. That is, except for the deterioration of the relationship with his similarly-named friend and the occasional loss of a family dog. Sad, yet replaceable ornaments of a life striving toward goodness. Shedding unnecessary attachments, a cleansing process. Amy's departure was different. They had plans, arrangements and reservations for a future together. The unobtainable aspirations of beach-dwelling romantics. It was supposed to last forever; an idea he still believed in, still subscribed to, faithfully. Defeated and downtrodden, he sighed, his latest hobby, an exhale of angst and sorrow.

On a piece of notebook paper, meant for class notes and homework, he scrawled pathetic prose. The vigorous ferocity of his whirling wrist, slashing pencil against paper, gave his teacher the false impression that he was thoroughly engaged in the subject matter, frantically scribbling, refusing to let a single node of intellect go undocumented. Preserved in a student's notebook, seemingly permanent, captured and transcribed. Amy was out there, somewhere, living still.

If I could say the right thing
If I could make you happy
If I could understand you
I would
But I don't understand you
I don't even understand myself

After all, it was her decision to end their romance. She wanted this. It was a calculated choice. He wondered: what is the worth of writing all this down? It won't bring her back. Does poetry have the power to hypnotize, to charm, to lure her back to me? I am compelled beyond purpose. These words are necessary.

Sleep silently
Dream peacefully
Cry for an audience
Pretend this is all you ever wanted
But never needed

The act of writing was a lonely experience. He stared at his creation, feeling empty and disconnected. Mr. Teacher drawled on about the practical influence of geometry in our daily lives. Its profound, hidden significance. The sound of his teacher's voice reminded Jared that Amy and, moreover, writing about Amy, were both distractions from the true objective of the moment. He was supposed to be learning about triangles and the precise brilliance of a right angle. Instead, he wrote. He would rather write than learn, or live.

A written document, be it a massive book or a paltry article, is a testament to the abandoned experiences of the author. A souvenir of sadness. A refusal to live in the sacred pleasure of the moment. Rather, the writer reminisces, ever looking back, reflecting, lost in contemplation. Jared knew all this. He felt it. He was unshakably aware, yet he couldn't resist. He had to write it all down. An unknown force compelled him.

Turn your back on humanity
On the meaningless constructs we fall into
Follow Follow Follow
Mismanaged and Dull
Rocking and Rolling
Sulking and Moaning
Your mind, your Mind
Is not just inside
But part of a large, abrupt tide
It is only suspended temporarily
When the curtain falls

Tune in
again
Slender being of unfortunate circumstance
Culture on the verge of collapse
Into a time of newly discovered maps
Absent escape hatch traps
The entire world is a stage
With one BIG spotlight
always on
all of us
together
Living theatrical masterpieces
Unaware of our influence
Strong and Great
With learned respect
Silly me
To feel foolish
Embarrassed
Cuz what?  She didn't see me
They were wearing the same clothes
damn
BACK INTO THIS WORLD AGAIN

Pursuant to the classroom seating chart, Jared sat in the middle of a 3-person column, with Bernardo behind him and a mysterious cutie pie in front of him.  The class was divided into 2 sections, each facing the other, like two parallel rectangles, with the teacher conducting the lecture in between both.

How does one make it out of such a situation?  It is a struggle.  We must find another.  Who?  Who is the other person, and where is she?  Could it be this girl with the green shirt sitting in front of me?  Her long, dark hair strung out across my desk.  Could it be her?  All that is lacking is the primary connection.  If only she would turn around.  "Hi!  What are you doing after class?  Wanna go to my room?"  Yes, yes, yes!  I would die for her.  Yet in reality, I am an unknown to her.  I am a stranger.  I will never begin the sequence. Too afraid. Unbrave. Oh, how unfortunate!

Jared glanced up. The lecture had proceeded without him, bygone and refined. Mr. Teacher was speaking passionately of $\pi$, but he had not been paying attention. Absent. Jared looked around the room, at his fellow classmates, all listening intently, learning crucial information, decoding nature's hidden formulas.

He wanted to care. He wanted to find it interesting. He wanted to be amazed by the concept. But he couldn't. The fresh memory of Amy Carousel polluted his mind, as present and inescapable as a wound. What does the radius of a circle have to do with Amy? She remained the focal point of his intellectual capabilities, demanding his full attention.

But, then…

It began subtly, barely noticeable. Jared gazed at a student on the other side of the room. A punky, young rapscallion, deep inside Euclid's playground. Without warning or reason, the student's head began to lift, a gentle float. It slowly rose above his body, unattached. A clean, weightless decapitation. Once his head had completely separated from his body, a tiny string was revealed, dangling from beneath his knot-tied neck. His head continued its upward trajectory, pulling the thin, white string along with it. One by one, every student's head began to float up and lift above their bodies. Balloon heads. Jared was stunned, frightened and bewildered by the sight. Balloon heads, all of them. Fear overtook his senses. He was stuck in a panicked daze. Once each of the separate balloon heads reached a height of approximately 4 feet above its respective body, any sudden prediction of the strings' potential attachment to some sorted assortment of debased innards was vanquished and proven wrong, as the flimsy, frayed tails of the delicate strings emerged from the vacuous caverns of the gaping neck wounds, fluttering in the cool, air-conditioned, publicly-funded winds of a climate-controlled bungalow, which had since been converted into a classroom, to accommodate the ever-expanding student population. A distinguished school within a highly reputable school district, fighting to disprove rumors of rampant drug abuse, kept the temperature continually low and chilly. (As a student, I was quite fond of my biology teacher. She told me that maintaining a cold atmosphere ensured that students would stay awake and attentive.) Soon, the balloons began to reach the ceiling. Would they pop? Jared trembled with anticipation, awaiting the inevitable. Luckily, the durability of human skin was able to withstand the textured ceiling. The balloons pressed up, determinedly fighting against an indestructible friction, scraping against the rough terrain, continually lifting, in an attempt to overcome the flat stoppage. It was useless. The ceiling posed too great a barrier. Instead, they just bobbed, rollicked and slid upon the solid mass, occasionally colliding with one another, while the dangling strings swayed softly in the open gap between balloon and body.

Jared sat, still, watching. He felt blessed, lucky, significant. The only living soul afforded the delight of witnessing this marvelous spectacle. He, the lone audience member, the sole observer, lured by the mystery, was given a sneak peak into the spirit realm, the inter-dimensional machinery forever functioning on a plane beyond human perception. On occasion, those who are brave, foolish and curious enough, seek out a glimpse, eager and willing. A fraction is often revealed. A momentary mishap occurs as they force their way in, disobeying nature. A spiritual trespass. The uninvited, violently cast back into humanity, damaged and dulled by the experience. Yet for some, it is delivered without a request or desire to know. For these individuals, it is the spirits who seek them, reaching in from out. He was amazed by the gift, grateful to be alive.

While Jared remained immersed in his hallucination, class continued. He was a lost cause anyway, no need to interrupt his manic trance.


Presently, a bumbling bee buzzed about the room. It finally came to rest by perching on Jared's right shoulder blade region. The buzz subsided, as the impertinent intruder halted its aimless operation, discontinuing its vortices and planting its itty-bitty bee feet on the static allure of Jared's t-shirt. Bernardo observed the bee, crawling and exploring, mischievously navigating the wrinkly cotton terrain, plotting its attack. He noted, mentally, to himself, that it was bigger than most bees he had ever seen. It was a large bee, a huge bee, an enormous bee, a massive bee, a gigantic bee, a humungous bee, a gargantuan bee. It was, simply put: Big. However, rather than alerting his friend of the present and imminent danger that currently threatened him, Bernardo, instead, sat and watched. No reaction, no warning sign, no friendly disclosure of terrifying truths. Nothing. Silence. He watched the bee as it crawled around on Jared's back, its sharp stinger glistening in the reflective glare of fluorescent lighting. He watched and said nothing, hoping the bee would eventually fly away, eradicating any need to forewarn Jared of the potential for great harm. Consider a likely scenario: If the bee were to eventually fly away, leaving Jared unscathed, what would have been the purpose of telling him? To impose undue worry and fear? No, thought Bernardo, he's better off not knowing. Perhaps he'll never need to know. Why upset the boy?

The bee soon stung Jared. The sharp, piercing stab interrupted his daydream. The harsh, physical sensation of pain catapulted him back to reality. It hurt tremendously. He excused himself, ran to the restroom and removed the stinger, while the bee's carcass lay sprawled upon Bernardo's desk, right beside his meticulously detailed notes.

Inside the royal chambers, Nathaniel sat, poised, professional, perfunctory, genteel and polite, perfecting a straightened spine and conveying a snickered smile. King Deryk had granted his requested meeting. He remained casual, incapable of submitting to persuasion, humoring his fancy-clothed guest. A mere formality.

"Alright," he began. "Let's hear it. Show me the paperwork and sing for me."

"Your Majesty, I shall begin by thanking you for this absolute privilege. Honestly, I greatly appreciate your allowing me to speak with you directly on this matter. You and I are both aware of the vague inequities of written correspondence, and I myself ascribe to the notion that for all the benefits of the written word, there is no method of interaction better than personal, face-to-face communication. So much is lost. Nuance and tone, emotion. Now, I understand that the water issue has aroused quite a reaction among your inhabitants, yourself being a staunch provocateur of the commotion. I also realize that you have adopted the position that we, the people of South Forts, are committing an act of unprovoked robbery and environmental degradation to the natural tranquility of your land. And, judging by the reaction of the proletariat, you are quite the rabblerousing cheerleader for your cause. They're furious. They're bloodthirsty. Frankly, it's frightening. You've got a legitimate army being trained out there. And here we've always thought of you as a peaceful bunch; that is, if we thought of you at all. Your Majesty, I regret to inform you, but we have exclusive, appropriative rights to the beneficial and necessary use of your rivers. On second thought, I feel no regret in uttering that statement. It's a fair exchange, equal in all respects. We have the legal authority to divert a portion of your water supply, construct a channel and manipulate its flow toward South Forts. I'm certain you are aware that our water supply is dangerously scarce, and it's becoming more so with every passing minute. Our ancestors foolishly settled in an arid climate, not expecting the exponential rate of population growth that we are seeing today. Babies are pouring out of bedrooms in South Forts. It's a sexy time to be alive. Sure, maybe our parched landscape was sustainable for the nomadic tribes of yesteryear, but this is the nineteenth century and we've got a town to hydrate. As I will soon explain, it's really quite a simple process. If you stop and consider the essential qualities of riparian ownership, there's really no argument to be made against our actions. Your Majesty, there is no doubt that you own the land beneath your feet, the soil and the dirt, the grass and the trees. They are static, triumphantly certain, unmoving and firm. And if you were to stand in the center of a great, vast field, gazing upon your empire, appreciating your sprawling pastures of ownership, you would feel a slight breeze. A gentle wind passing by your body, curling against your skin. Now, you wouldn't be so opportunistic as to claim ownership over the passing breeze. Such declarations would be symptomatic of a certain mania. Delusions of grandeur! The wind passes by all Earth's inhabitants. All are given a complimentary taste, a cool refreshment. The wind is owned by none and, therefore, by all. None can assert a proprietary right over the wind. The rivers you're attempting to claim ownership over are but as temporary as the wind. They rush by, desperate to depart. Water travels on. It moves. It is as fleeting as the air above. Yes, you own the land; there is no doubting that. But the wind and water are passersby, travelers, en route to somewhere else. The natural design of a river itself begs to be shared. Forgive me for collapsing your feeble beliefs, but your act of wishing to contain and preserve these rivers, six in all, is an act in defiance of G-d's plan. Water wishes to be shared, and we have a right to our fair portion."

Nathaniel reached for his briefcase, opened it and removed a piece of paper, covered in fine print.

"Your Majesty, according to this permit, we are entitled to the reasonable and beneficial use of the rivers that flow through The Land of Forgotten Souls."

He handed to paper to King Deryk, sat, and waited for a response. King Deryk did not so much as glance at the permit. He spoke.

"Listen, Nathaniel, I commend your efforts, truly. I'm sure you and the rest of South Forts went through loads of trouble in ensuring that this whole procedure was executed properly. Good job. Except, you have no authority here. We refuse to recognize any rights that you so boldly claim to hold. Go ahead and flaunt your paperwork. It means nothing here. This dispute is not about legal rights.

It's about principles. It's about taking a stand against acts of tyrannical intrusion. Your power only exists within your own boundaries. This permit? We have no obligation to endorse the validity of this. It is only parchment and ink. Without the authority of law, and the firm reach of courts to uphold the law, it's only a concept. I'm sure the South Forts populous readily bow to you and salute your dominant, everlasting presence. All hail the chief! He who hath bestowed upon this sinful nation the blessings of virtue and an enhanced sense of self. A renowned community, sheltered within borders and boundary lines. But those boundaries measure the precise limit of your reach. The endpoint of your power."

"You are mistaken," Nathaniel started. "You have neglected to acknowledge the significance of the union. We are all one within the greater sphere of the government. The law touches us all. None are invisible."

"Ah, but the first principle of government is the requirement of consensual submission by the governed. For government to function, all must comply. All must bow their heads and surrender a portion of their liberty."

"Yes, but government is able to accommodate dissenters by penalty. Accept and submit, or suffer the consequences."

He had stated his case, and rested.

It was at this moment when the story began to reach for something beyond its grasp. The author had abandoned the simple concepts of love and loyalty, and instead offered a broad critique of the necessity of government. Well, attempted to, at least. Suggestion: It's worth ceasing your attention whenever someone uses the word "society" in a conversation. Trust me. When you hear the word "society," just stop listening. This is the anthem of the disenfranchised. It's all the fault of society, not the individual. It is the theme song of the victims. Of the have-nots and the wanters. Those who believe they deserve to reap plentifully without the effort of having sowed. To receive without having earned. Listen up! Revolution is no longer necessary. The

United States of America is in a state of perpetual revolution. It is ever-changing, constantly refining itself.

Don't hate him, he isn't all that bad. This was Amy's selfless plea for Nick. She urged Jared to adopt a neutral stance on the matter. To surrender all animosity and implement a truce, effective immediately. She knew such a suggestion was futile. Why bother? Why even mention his potential for good? There would be no compromise. Nonetheless, her mouth opened and she transmitted this harsh utterance, sanctifying a ruthless admonition that Jared ought to admire the guy.

Every year, when Valentine's Day began peeking its head above the wintry horizon, the local high school would conduct a survey of all currently enrolled students, titled: The Matchmaker. It was cleverly disguised as a playful questionnaire, in which students would answer a variety of inquiries concerning their hobbies, personality traits, ambitions, hopes and dreams. In actuality, however, it was a method for the school district to keep tabs on underage drug use, sex and most other unflattering adolescent activities, all in a disheartening, age-old attempt to determine the cause of the lack of interest among America's youth in anything that does not provide immediate, sensual bliss. At any expense, teenagers just want to be tickled. They seek pleasure and excitement with an urgency that suggests each sensation is necessary.

Jared was curious to participate in the survey, yet reluctant to share his name. Thus, he assumed an alias. Inspired by a recent lecture in his biology class, Jared listed his name on the survey as Anton Van Leeuwenhoek. Although he cheekily used a false name, he completed the survey with the utmost, soul-bearing honesty; at least, as much as the survey allowed. He answered each question after careful contemplation of its consequences. How will my response to this question represent me as an individual? All else being equal, what would I prefer? The questions were playful and innocuous, but Jared took them very seriously.

6. What is your ideal Friday night outing?

    (a) Going to a crowded party and dancing the night away. Weeee!

        (i) During the course of such an evening, do you engage in any of the following activities? (please circle)

            1. Drinking alcohol:
            YES   NO
            2. Smoking marijuana:
            YES   NO
            3. Sexual behavior:
            YES   NO

    (b) Watching a film with a few close friends. Afterwards, you and your friends will go to a coffee shop and discuss the film. There, you will drink espressos, pontificate about the film's true meaning and overanalyze its symbolism, all whilst improperly using terms such as mise-en-scéne.

        (i) On a scale of 0-10, how high are you during this? (please circle)

            0  1  2  3  4  5  6  7  8  9  10

    (c) Reading a book beside a gently roaring fire. Sober and alone.

        (i) Before going to sleep, what do you use to inspire your masturbation? (please circle)

            1. Tangible pornography; i.e., magazines, photographs
            2. Quasi-tangible pornography; i.e., VHS, DVD
            3. Intangible pornography; i.e., the wretched Internet
            4. Your own perverted imagination

    (d) Sitting beneath the night sky, gazing at the stars and contemplating the brilliant significance of a single human life amongst the cacophony of creation. Realizing that each and every human being, including (most importantly) yourself, is blessed with existence. Thinking about how infinitesimally rare it is to be alive, for your entire ancestral heritage to have survived and to have conceived a new generation. Pondering how great this gift of life truly is. Confidently calling it a miracle. And then, in the midst of your euphoric epiphany, you become enraged at the cynicism that has eroded the morality of your peers. You begin to wish that for once, they too could find the ability to gaze upward and wonder. To accept the glorious gift of life! To experience this sense of optimism and hope. But you are angry, for they all deny the eternal force peering out at them from beyond the darkness of the cosmos. Your so-called friends would rather suck any last lingering remnants of cum trapped in Christopher Hitchens's balls and call themselves the enlightened ones. They'd rather drown in their own self-satisfied pleasure than swim in the glory of awe, comforted by faith in an ultimate truth. You gulp and swallow the frustration bellowing inside you.

> (i) Whatever you do, please do not speak of G-d. Any mention of the "G" word and their avoidance mechanisms kick in. All attention is instantly vanquished. Good luck.

He submitted his survey and awaited the results. In a school of approximately 1,700 students, this would (using an unrealistically finite sample size) purportedly allow the young, hormonal, high school saplings to find their one true love. The school would then match up and compare all the results, and based on the amount of similarities and/or differences between your respective responses, would provide the following information:

> -Soulmate (the person of the opposite sex with whom you have the most in common, by virtue of giving similar responses in the survey)
>
> -Arch Nemesis (the person, irrespective of gender, with whom you have the least in common, by virtue of giving opposite responses in the survey)
>
> -Best Friend Forever (the person of the same sex with whom you have the most in common; or, if you're homosexual, your Soulmate)

Oddly, the school charged $10 in order to receive a printout of your Matchmaker results. 'Fuck it,' Jared thought. 'It's not worth my money.' He shrugged it off. 'Oh well, it's bullshit anyways.' Amy, however, was not only eager to find out her results, she was willing to expend funds in order to do so. Her Arch Nemesis? Anton Van Leeuwenhoek.

"Any persuasive sway that your argument may carry is without force in law. You are failing to realize that we have the authority to do this, and we will. Very soon. Good luck trying to resist that which is inevitable. You are of a dying breed, Your Majesty. The painfully idealistic. Your beliefs are rooted in nonsensical fantasia. You think you know what is right, not only for yourself, but for everyone, as though you have attained some sort of ultimate understanding of humanity's unexposed frailties. You bask in the notion that you are tuned in to a hidden truth. Ah, how refreshing! Eons of mankind, brilliant minds and courageous leaders, struggling endlessly to craft perfection. Tirelessly attempting, anew and anew. Every generation chipping away at the monument, inspired by the promise of tomorrow. They (the future generations) will reap the benefits of my sacrifice, not I. Oh, but such efforts were all for naught. If only they knew, all that was necessary was your magnificent insight. How profound! You are the wise sage of the ages, the messiah politique. I must say, I am honored to bask in the presence of such an intuitive and thoughtful mind. I shall bow to you. Your mind functions on the notion that you are brilliant; and, most dangerously of all, you sincerely hold this belief, with no inclinations of humility. However, your thoughts have developed in seclusion, far from the challenge of alternate perspectives and counter-arguments. Your mind is delicate. Your thoughts are formed and solidified without any resistance. Your nascent ideas and self-satisfied realizations are further compelled by this illusion of enlightenment. But you are neglecting to realize that there are rules in this world. Rules by which we all must all obey. For without rules, the whole system crumbles. It is rules that give order to chaos. Do you enjoy sports, Your Majesty? Soccer, perhaps? Consider a game of soccer played without rules, without order. Instead, each player is given the opportunity to play according to the whims of his conscience. How then would the ball traverse the field until ultimately arriving in the net? In this scenario, each man would presumably have a better idea as to how the game should be played. The result is chaos. Need I belabor the point any further? You are in desperate need of a visit from Socrates, a figure I'm sure you are quite fond of. Surely you honor the writings of Plato. You breathe shit upon each page. Yet the very man whose philosophy you espouse, whose very being is idolized, whose image adorns the bedrooms of your most empty-headed of citizens, would crumble your collective brains were he resurrected. Surrender, Your Majesty. This is your final opportunity to peaceably resolve this matter. Your arguments are as persuasive as the fluttering corpse of a deceased moth."

A long pause resonated. Its stale void filling the room, encumbering the atmosphere.

"We will resist."

Nathaniel sighed heavily.

"This is the very danger that arises from thinking the way you do. You see, your brain consists of synapses that are interconnected and rerouted on the basis of a false assumption. You are a bumbling idiot who has convinced himself that he is a genius. It would take an arduous, grueling effort to rebuild you, to expose you to the truth and to teach you the virtues of structure and guidelines. Still I pray one day you might understand. A certain calm emerges when a man is commanded to conform and obey. Suddenly, all are united."

"Bah!"

King Deryk began convulsing, as though his body was rejecting the concept.

"Look at you, fool! Relax your mind and listen. I am aware of what is happening within you. Forgive me for using such offensive language, as I'm sure it is received as an immediate physiological trigger, wherein your body initiates its reactionary processes, but please afford me an additional moment. This territory (i.e., The Land of Forgotten Souls) is overrun with scoundrels who further compound such thoughts. Everyone here feels the same. All are in unanimous agreement. It's quite a shame, really. And you, their leader, are perpetrating a mental fraud by allowing such thinking to flourish. As it happens, you are the worst offender. You hold these beliefs stronger than most anyone here. It's tragic."

King Deryk laughed, heartily, in a mocking tone. The kind of laughter that functions as a defense mechanism, as though the laugher were saying 'You moronic imbecile. How utterly false!' A strong, harsh laugh, cold and unfriendly.

Deryk spoke.

"I cannot believe you! You have been trained by THEM. You are a robotic shill of a man. You are the government's golden boy, blindly pledging allegiance to the national code. It's a saddening sight. Shameful."

It had become evident that neither man would understand the other's perspective. It was a centuries old argument that would continue for countless centuries more. Anarchy vs. Government, which of the two better serves man? Or, rather, which of the two is man better served by? (This is supposed to be a love story)

To Jared it had become quite apparent, from an early age (and this initial predilection had since progressed from mere hypothesis to established fact, by virtue of his inability to shake the feeling), that the pinnacle of life, the essence of all existence, was an evening spent with Amy. Not only nestling into her succulent twat, but also the warm and resulting peace of just being with her. This, he knew, was life. To spend time in the presence of Amy was to know G-d. It was a connection unknown by all, except 2: Her and I.

In her absence, Jared longed for the days that had since passed and faded into vaguery. *Ah yes, that silly girl.* Often at unexpected hours, Jared would remember and the feeling would engulf him, conquering all potential for satisfaction. *Oh no! She hath gone away. Bye bye, Amy.* Suddenly, all sense of accomplishment, growth and advancement would vanish, as Jared realized that no matter what he achieved in life, no matter how pampered his existence may become, he would not be the one. Someone else. No matter the progress, it would not be him kissing her lips, feeling her breath and hearing her voice. Someone else would be plunging her shithole. Someone else's sweat would be forming complex drip patterns on her rounded, bulbous, Thompson butt. This has become vulgar. I wish to convey intimacy, not raunch; yet the feeling overtakes me. I must destroy my image of her. I must make her filthy in order to rest easy. But I know this to be false. She is lovely. I will never again hear the gentle tone of her voice. I will never again feel the warmth of her nude body beside mine. I will never taste her. But someone else will. Someone else will have her all to himself. Someone else. Jared sighed. All in life seemed a dull replacement. No matter what I accomplish, someone else will be fucking her. No matter what I do, someone else. Someone else. Someone else.

After 30 minutes of what can best be described as a fascinating combination of rage and desolation, this feeling would come to rest as a delicate despair, gently persisting throughout Jared's day. For the most part, he could shoulder it. But every so often, the flood would hit and drown him completely. This would be his life, from here on out. Always aware. The memory, permanently etched.


"There's a cheerleading competition happening 2 weeks from today, in San Diego. I would be absolutely delighted if you'd join me."

And with the immediate, gentle quiver of her voice, the plan was set and solidified in gummy goodness. Her lips, into the telephone, traversing through utilities and ending their electronic journey in the ear of a boy. He was in agreement before the invitation had been fully transmitted. How could he deny such a grand request? How could he deny anything she ever asked of him? It would always be yes, no matter the circumstance.

"Of course, Amy! I would love to witness you twirling about, marvelously. Up until this very moment, I have been living with an internal, unspoken desire to attend one of these events. While I love your detailed accounts (after the fact), it would be a true honor to sit in the audience and experience, firsthand, my baby doing her thing. To observe her, lost in the passion of her choosing."

"Some call it a mere hobby, a means of killing time in between the working hours."

"And I pity such an existence, to live in the emptiness of the modern grind. I know the truth, Amy. This is beyond a simple pleasure. It is your pulse given form. Embrace the excitement of life! Follow your heart, girl."

From an outside perspective, I can safely say that I disagree with the sentiment Jared is conveying. This is a purely adolescent way of thinking. Unfortunately, some never emerge from this school of thought. Some remain forever entrenched in the hollow fallacies of the "dreamer" ideology. Let us consider a phrase that is often uttered by multitudes of dim-witted twenty-somethings (at least, in Los Angeles. But somehow I feel this is not a geographically-limited phenomenon): "Live your dreams." This is utter nonsense. Youngsters spout this vapid arrangement of words as though it contains dabs-o-plenty profound, ancient wisdom, elicited from a mountain-dwelling prophet. Ah yes, how did I not realize this all along!?!? It's so simple! I am supposed to live my dreams! The problem is that the dreams of the young can easily be reduced to one thing: Pleasure. The ambition of the young is to receive the Queen's blowjob. This mindset creates an entire nation of artists. And nothing could be more terrifying. Musicians, writers and actors in every direction. All pursuing theirs "dreams." Amateurs. Refusing to suffer, to sacrifice. And not in the trite "suffer for your art" shit talk. I mean honest American misery; i.e., working an office job, working a job you despise, getting up day after day after fucking day. That is suffering. That fuels inspiration. Instead, people would rather remain idle than take an honest job, just because it is not within the realm of their "dream." Hey mister, I am living my dream. Being bored and unhappy is not within the vision of my dream. I weep for us all. There is nothing more useless in all of creation than art.

"Fabulous!"

The competition was scheduled to take place a distance of 120 miles from where Jared and Amy resided, necessitating a drive of approximately 2.5 hours. As arranged, Jared would arrive at Amy's house in the early morning hours. Mama Carousel and Mitch decided to forgo the sleepover, perhaps due to the nipple play that occurred during the erstwhile outing. Although, how could they have known of the titillating enterprise between the two fiddlers? Maybe mama saw. Or maybe, down the hallway, she heard the gentle giggles of two teenagers, wracked in nerves and sweat, forecasting. Mitch wasn't around then; we needn't consider his view of the scene. He must've been a languid leap away, smacking his cock to the thought of Heidi (Amy's mom), all the while knowing one day he'd have her. One day he'd fuck that rotten corpse of a woman while Mr. Carousel was at work, slopping paint onto a slab of wood. Earning for his family. Mitch had no regard for such trite matters. He had a dick and two knuckling balls, dangling and swaying, with the grace of a swan. Think of a man. Throughout his day, regardless of his routine, his balls are always at work. At any given moment, his balls are chugging along, processing the next eruption of cum. Where will it land? Right on Heidi's face – smiling with glee – loving this moment – embracing how nasty it feels; right on Heidi's chest – succulent and bright – like a blossoming sunflower; right on Heidi's gaping asshole – still trembling from the ecstatic friction of anal sex – pulsating with the throb of an extraterrestrial orb caught in the vacuous unknown of the universe [stuck in the expanse]; right inside Heidi's C-U-N-T. This is the mind of Mitch. The all-American man. Blasting new holes in Heidi. Launching her across the room with the velocity of his ejaculate. This man. This perverted son of a bitch. This man enters the picture and instills a sense of discipline. "No sleepovers with boys. I won't allow it." This isn't even your fucking house, Mitch. Heidi's divorce lawyer scored a nice win for her. You had nothing to do with the acquisition, other than tearing this family apart, all because you needed to empty your balls and Heidi was a willing receptacle. Flood her with your fluid, as thunderous moans fill the air, extinguishing the silence of the night. I too once dreamt of love, knowing it to be false. Yet that didn't stop me from pursuing her. I don't blame you, Mitch. We're all hungry for pussy. Especially in the Carousel home. You take Heidi, I'll take Amy. Except, you still got her. Amy is long gone.

As luck would have it, Mitch decided not to attend the cheerleading competition. Rather, it would be Heidi, Amy and Jared, with no fatherly influence cramping their ascending vibe of coastal pleasantries. No testosterone-ridden biped, thumping 'neath the moon, as his balls churn on, into oblivion. No! It was just two ragged cunts (oozing) and one polite boy, with his tiny testicles, ever shrinking. Had puberty stalled? His growth and development never seemed fully realized. His transition into manhood was cut short. The Carousel women were well equipped for the long drive. Mama had her 6-CD changer loaded with Chicago and George Harrison. As I recall, there had been a recent re-issue of an acclaimed album by the late Beatle. At the time, these CDs seemed so vague and mundane to me. Each song was an interchangeable bore, infused with the dry, dull, tiresome 'classic rock' sound. Oh well, this shall be the soundtrack to our day. Heidi seemed to love it. And after all, she was the driver. A viking woman, in charge of the strident beast, galloping down the I-405. She who controls the trajectory controls the sound. Amy and Jared sat in the backseat, while mama played the part of the reluctant chauffer. Today, looking back on things, I have come to the realization that Heidi never really liked me all that much. I was too weak and passive for her little girl. Too gentle and well mannered. She deserved a real man. Not lil' J. She needed a rugged, rambunctious ruffian, slamming her head against the wall whenever she misbehaved. Heidi must've known this all along. She glanced in the rearview mirror, subtly scorning at the sight of the two (temporary) lovers, destined to fail; the entire time holding in a heavy sigh for the wasted time she saw her daughter engaged in. Some find love because they know what they want right from the start, others find love via process of elimination.

Amy had brought with her an entire box full of Juicy Fruit gum. Not a single pack, but the whole fucking wholesale box. The quantity was more than any three people could chew in the course of a day. Although, at the risk of overdoing the overt misogyny of this book, I must mention that the Carousel women are accustomed to chomping on cock for hours on end. Lapping up dick sweat like a starved artist desperate for praise. Are my efforts all for naught? Not at all. She's working for that thirst-quenching climax. Can I absorb your talent? Can you fuck it into me? All of this gum (or, at least a portion thereof) had a particular use. It was to keep them entertained and occupied during the drive. The plan was to make an angular, zigzagged chain. Each yellow, outer wrapper constituted another link. It was to be built using an origami-esque methodology of precision folds. Interwoven little papers accumulating. Amy taught Jared how it was done. Instructive. Her little fingers creasing the paper. Her cute, innocent voice explaining the directions. And Jared, listening patiently, following along with every step. Once Jared and Amy officially began the process, they were immediately swept up in a mechanical trance. Within the span of 30 minutes, they had created a meandering manacle. After an hour, an entire infrastructure was born, fastened to the interior. The coupling of gum wrappers, each piece providing another node of strength, caused a great expansion to form in the backseat. 'Twas the birth and growth spurt of a great snake, slithering betwixt their legs. Arts & Crafts be damned! One by one we are growing closer together, our love ever expanding. I love you, Amy. In the simplicity of this moment, I know you are my soulmate. You are the love of my life. I cherish this memory. And now, today, as I write this passage, while "The Warmth of the Sun" twinkles in the background, I fondly recall all these cute, little instances of semi-purity. It makes me wish this tale were a G-rated kissy dredge. Beneath all the obscenity is true love. Your endearing presence in my mind is eternal. If I could, I would build a gum chain with you for the rest of my life. Together we would engulf the world in Juicy Fruit wrappers, thrice over. But you have wandered off the reservation. I envisioned us forever! That was the plan, Amy! Conversely, you had a separate objective. Oh well, back to the gum. If I was a decent writer, I could draft an entire 5-page scrawl about the gum wrappers, in which I would explain the intricate method of folding the paper, and underlying all of this would be the symbolism of the strengthening of their love with each addition to the chain. Get it?

gum/gum/gum/gum/gum/gum/gum/gum/gum/gum/gum/gum/gum

However, building a gum wrapper chain can only provide so much amusement. Eventually, a stronger stimulant is required to ease the endless monotony of the freeway. An effortless cadence of concrete, passing by underneath. A still conduit, pointed toward their destination, only time separating them. Were they actively advancing a measurable distance along the earth's crust? Or, were they merely remaining still, allowing the planet to spin underneath them, creating the illusion of movement? Jared recalled multitudes of family road trips and the games that were played during long hours in the car, confined with his kin. 20 Questions was a favorite. But he didn't want to recycle his tried and true traditions with Amy. Instead, they would create their own game. A secret, intra-relational pastime. Yet, as one would guess, creating a game out of thin air is an arduous task. Jared tried. He thought.

Ever since he was a little boy, Jared loved customized license plates. They were miniature riddles, stretching the limits of the English language, inviting all observers to guess the word or phrase being conveyed in a coded form of communication. To

Jared, customized license plates always seemed to contain the essence of language: communication, without strict formalities. The driver's challenge, to all of humanity, was to impart a message, free from the strictures of convention. If a customized license plate could be understood, it confirmed Jared's hypothesis (i.e., that the communicative method of exchanging words – whether written or spoken – is capable of interpretation, absent authoritarian adherence to form), an idea that caused his English teachers to weep with the excruciating sorrow of knowing that your precious student not only failed to grasp the subject you devoted your life to mastering, he didn't even believe in the concept. Fuck it. If I can understand a customized license plate, your premise is flawed. We, the human race, can communicate without rules. Forget it. Forget spelling, sound it out. Forget grammar, let it happen. Jared suggested they create a game based on these charming witticisms. The problem, alas, was that part of the delight of these license plates was their scarcity. Like a rare bird, they only appeared in intermittent flourishes.

"That's not so much a game as it is a background activity. I mean, if you happen to see one, by all means let's decipher it and uncover its underlying meaning; but that will not provide the same sense of reliable continuity and focused attention as the gum wrapper chain."

"Understood. Then it's decided. We shall continue constructing our chain, whilst subtly and subconsciously perusing the license plates of our fellow motorists."

"Darling, that'll never work. Don't you see? If we are expending energy searching for the quintessential vehicular communiqué, our focus will be diverted from the dominant task. We will be sacrificing our main priority. And for what? For the hope that maybe, eventually, we will be graced by a driver droll enough to request that the DMV forgo the usual number-letter-letter-letter-number-number-number combo and instead permanently emblazon a sad excuse for English on a slab of aluminum and then dangle it from their rear bumper? As a result, you weaken the chain. You weaken the chain, Jared, because you're gazing out the window, looking for something else. And what is the end result?  We sacrifice both.  Rather than a single masterpiece, we'll arrive at our destination with two lackluster achievements."

Jared held back a deep sigh.  He hung his head, diverting his gaze from the vast expanse of the open road before him (its wide and infinite potential enveloping his mind, calling out and screaming: Be wild and free!  This is the life for which your ancestors sacrificed, gravely.  Don't merely accept your circumstance.  Make it greater than they could've ever imagined.  Listen Jared, I know your grandma is a sweet lady, but she wants you to get some slob on your knob.  She knows the pleasures of youth all too well.  She knows, because it's gone from her grasp, and she is left longing for the recklessness of yesterday.  Don't let her down) and redirecting his focus to the bevy of bright yellow gum wrappers, all small and confined beneath him.  He continued folding, obediently, while George Harrison serenaded the sadness of the moment.

When they arrived at the auditorium, Jared and Amy separated from mama Carousel.  She went to find a seat, while the two teenagers went to find The Squad: a group of about 25 young girls, each equipped with her own succulent, slippery pussy, ready to be tongued by men twice her age.  Amy graciously introduced Jared to the rest of the cheerleaders, all of whom were polite and vibrant.  The girls were in various stages of glam, enduring the onerous process of becoming dolled-up for the big show.  They appeared to be striving for a similar, unified look, which involved scrupulously-curled hair, complete with bows and ribbons, and a sharp twinkle of makeup.  The color scheme was green and purple (in case you care to form an accurate picture in your mind), with interspersed fragments of black and white adorning their outfits.  Amy introduced Jared to her fellow cheer mates.  He was polite and shy.  Gave them all a bashful, uncomfortable hello.  He was too shy for Amy's liking, although she wasn't fully cognizant of this at the time.  But upon meeting him, the girls all knew it.  They took one look at him and thought, 'This is the guy that Amy is regularly fucking?  This timid little boy?'  They knew it wouldn't last.  They'd seen her freakish tendencies in full splendor, and Jared was not up to the task. A woman like Amy, like many women I've known, require a rollicking type of dirty, beat-down fucking that I am incapable of providing. This type of woman would come to define a certain insecurity of Jared's. She embodied a sense of feministic intimidation that freaked him out, completely. Lucky boy, managed to get Amy right on the cusp of her transformation. He'd be her one and only nitwit, before she became a fully-realized whore. There's a certain breed of woman that I admire, but cannot touch. And I wonder about the men she allows. The rough-and-tumble men to whom she opens her legs. The bearded and strong, tattoo adorned, motorcycle men. I wonder what separates us. Levels of testosterone? Upbringing? Christianity? I don't know. But I've always felt that while I'm siting alone in my bedroom writing this tale, Amy, and the legions of women like her, are out there getting fucked by that man. That type of woman and that type of man, enraptured in the pornographic, earth-shattering, sweat-drenched, high-decibel fucking, which I'll never know. And I'll learn to cope, muttering to myself, 'It's okay, I get my kicks elsewhere.' Except I know all too well that the kicks I'm getting ain't the same sort of kicks. For damn sure. Tapping the keyboard does not equate to tapping dat ass.

But of course, in this moment, Jared remained entirely oblivious to the impending insecurities that would haunt him for the rest of his life. No, such thoughts were nonexistent. In his mind, during this divine span, he and Amy were the perfect couple. Their love would endure forever. She was his dream girl and together they shared the simple handholding warmth of human love. Jared was, and has always been, a romantic. And to the romantically inclined among us, true love is the key to all of life's uncertainty. To be in love…is all.

Jared drifted off into a daydream. Eventually, he returned to the present moment, where lovely ladies surrounded him. His heart swelled and he laughed nervously.

Afterwards, the group went to find their pre-designated seats in the auditorium. The gals gathered together, all resolute and brimming with energy. A full-fledged show of force, ready to out-enthuse the many among them.

Once the competition began, they observed their fellow competitors with an emotive cornucopia of appreciation, envy, respect and hostility. They ferociously scrutinized the other squads. Every move was critical.

Jared failed to grasp the beauty of cheerleading. To him, the routines seemed eerily similar and cluttered. Not to mention, without fail, the musical accompaniment always consisted of an obnoxious remix of the latest shitty dance tracks currently infecting the airwaves. Dumb girls seem to love these songs. Dumb girls and their obese, trailer trash moms (for the record, Amy's mama was not fat). Knowing that he would be sitting through an endless barrage of pubescent shimmying, Jared brought with him a copy of Frank Abagnale Jr.'s breathtaking book, Catch Me If You Can. Having recently been enthralled by the Spielberg film, Jared felt inspired to obtain a copy of the source material. And now, the trusty paperback would accompany him to the competition, easing any boredom that was certain to occur.

The event continued. One by one, the groups performed. They danced and the audience roared. Soon, it was almost time for Amy's troop. They were signaled by an overly-enthusiastic stagehand, and at once, they scuttled away to the backstage area, leaving Jared alone among the spectators.

At this point in time, it's worth noting that Amy's mother did not sit near Jared and the ladies. It is a worthwhile mention because were Heidi to have been siting with them, in this moment, when the girls departed, Jared would have been left alone with her. This is a social interaction that Jared hoped to avoid, and blessed was he that she was nowhere to be seen. She was likely sitting alone, accumulating yeast and boogers. Oh, but what if she was with me? Maybe we could have shared a meaningful moment. Maybe we could have again discussed our mutual interest in horses. But no, she was elsewhere. And in this moment, Jared too sat alone, with a book in his hand. Much like

you, the reader.  Alone with a book.  May I ask you a question?
Are you gaining insight?  Or, are you simply distracting yourself?
      Onward.
      After sitting through a few more numbers, it was time for
Amy (and her fellow cheerleaders) to take the stage.  They began
by getting into a predetermined and intricate formation.  A still,
motionless pose.  Statuesque, yet brimming with potential energy.
The eruption was imminent.  Then, the music started.
Commence!  And all at once, Jared was transfixed.  The way they
gestured, so seamlessly, with effervescent grace, sent chills down
his scrotum.  His balls trembled.  Every movement of the young
girls' slim bodies shifted perfectly to the music, which took on a
newfound significance.  Suddenly, he wanted to fuck everyone.
They were no longer human.  They had become methodically-
engineered machinery, every small piece essential to the whole,
every pivot encompassing a commensurate purpose.  And Amy,
herself an all-star among the crowd, how she danced with delight.
Her face was bright and beaming with joy.  She spent the entirety
of the routine wiggling and giggling across the stage.  She was
glorious in that moment, and always.  I was such a lucky boy
during this period in my life.  Now, may I remind you, today we
are many many many many x $10^{23}$ years separated from this
moment.  But still I remember the way she moved, and her
captivating smile.
      In this instance, when she was finally able to release all
her pain, I finally understood.  This girl is inhibited by a somber
and deadly shroud of despondency.  It follows her everywhere she
goes.  The principal source of her wretched despair was the
disunification of her parents.  The curse of divorce, the modern
($21^{st}$ century) rite of passage, rattles the souls of the innocents,
leaving them shackled and torn.  Of course, the fighting that
precipitates a divorce doesn't necessarily help either.  Perhaps to
some, the eventual division comes as a relief.  No more listening
through the door to the sounds of mommy and daddy screaming.
      And that smile of hers, it was sure heavy.  To see it now,
unleashed and free, on full display, coincidentally revealed to

Jared the overbearing influence that kept it upside-down all too often.  Cutie, shaking that booty.

### Emotional Weightlifting

A smile lifts the burden of 1,000 years
As the sorrows of a lifetime suddenly rejoice
And rise

Reluctance is left naked
All pain a gentle wound
The worth of such reaction
Genuinely earned
The triumph after defeat
Of a lesson toughly learned

And a smile comes all too easy
To a man undamaged and new
Without the trailing winds of *what ifs?*
Second thoughts
Or sadness
A child to woeful reprieve
Purified
And clean

But his smile is weak and unmoving
Absent a force to overcome
No struggle so deserving
A difficulty
Defeated

Heavily pressing lower
Keeping it down, down, down
And incomplete

But at once
An ability achieved
When conquered
Joyfully

So if you smile
Smile huge
And let the world know you've done it!
You're indestructible
You survived

You still know how to smile

Upon their arrival at the (mama) Carousel household, Mitch was prepared with his best attempt at exuding a (discernably false) sense of eager anticipation for hearing a fully-detailed account of the day's happenings. He surely had already enjoyed a couple beers, to assist in manufacturing his illusion of interest. Alcohol has a certain way of making it easier to make believe one's sincerity. Another couple (man and woman), about the same age as Mitch and mama, accompanied him. I can't recall if they were friends or relatives. Anyway, everyone gathered around as Amy gave a rousing recitation of the day's events, with mama Carousel interspersing her color commentary throughout the telling. As had become customary, Jared refrained from contributing to the verbal exchange. Instead, he laughed heartily, whenever appropriate. This had become a common mechanism practiced by Jared whenever he was involved in a group discussion, as the presence of multiple people often caused him to choke. His shyness would take hold and he'd say nothing. However, aware that to many, silence is frightening, Jared would be sure to laugh along with the group, as necessary. The rationale behind this tactic was that although he was not contributing much (if anything) to the dialogue, he was at the very least reacting to what was being said, and making noise. Jared utilized this stratagem, and it seemed to work; or so he thought. However, he failed to account for one critical factor: that perhaps unvaried and automatic laughter by the quiet boy can be just as frightening as pure silence. Let us consider the situation from the perspective of the rest of the group (i.e., Mitch, mama and the two faceless figures). If Jared were to remain hushed during the entirety of the conversation, the gaze of the talkative would occasionally reach him. They'd see a boy, his mouth closed, but his eyes present and involved. They'd wonder, hmm, what is he thinking about? You see, when one is talkative, he is actively expressing himself and thus there is no mystery as to his inner thoughts. Rather, he's unleashing his mind out into the world, for everyone to hear. Oh! Allow us to recognize the wonder of such a statement! I'll repeat: "out into the world." Two distinct droplets of beauty emerge from this phrase: (1) At first glance, there is a contradictory tension between these two words (out & into), as they struggle to exist in the same sentence. You see, 'out' and 'into' connote distinct actions. It would appear that only one may exist in a given moment. One suggests exit; the other, entrance. However, upon further contemplation, we realize that as a result of your departure from one location, you arrive somewhere else. Thus, to leave is to arrive, in a synchronous ballet of polarity. This is eternally true. Our earth is vast, and apparently the universe is ever-expanding. You are always somewhere. Ergo, when Jared's thoughts leave his head, they enter the world, into the aptly-titled marketplace of ideas. Which leads us to... (2) To speak is to channel that which is internal, and at once, transfer it into the external realm. An idea that was confined and hidden away from the world is now revealed to all. As a result, the suffering of mankind is lessened. By communicating, we learn that we are not alone. We realize that we are all starkly similar. To most, this is a comforting thought. We are all one. But to those who dwell in the dull morass of copyright law (particularly as it pertains to the arts), individuality is king. However, championing the uniqueness of the artist is a losing battle, as not only are we mentally unified to all of humanity, we are also limited by the same finite amount of resources. Consider the fact that the human experience can be reduced to two emotions: Comedy and Tragedy. This has been tried and true for millennia. Moreover, in expressing these two emotions, we all share in access to the twelve musical notes, twenty-six letters and three primary colors from which all art is born. That's it! All art is simply the updated iteration of that which has already been. Further, art is entirely unnecessary. If the goal is to communicate, one can just as simply talk. Open your mouth and say it. Problem solved! The burden that accompanies the life of every artist is the wretched reality that they could just as easily have a conversation and eliminate the need for their magnum opus. Hours are spent crafting a piece when only seconds are needed. Speaking is pure and immediate. By the way, what page are we on? I think this notion is best expressed in the bridge to the song "El Scorcho" by Weezer. Our protagonist, a young Rivers Cuomo, admits the futility of the entire album on which the song appears (<u>Pinkerton</u>). He realizes that if he would just talk about his feelings, the album would be unnecessary. Ten songs or one conversation, the result is the same. Now, Jared's calculated decision to laugh along with the group was almost as troubling as remaining silent. The feeling that accompanies silence (the aforementioned *what is he thinking about?*) is rooted in the insecurities of the talker. It's a Rorschach test of their self-doubt. When one remains silent, our natural inclination is to attempt to guess their thoughts, in an effortless foray into mind reading. By doing so, the talker plugs in their own vulnerabilities. Again, if everyone is talking, there is no such uncertainty. Thus, silence acts as a mirror. In the emptiness, you see yourself. You hear yourself, and you begin to question yourself. It is sinister and uncomfortable, to be confronted with one's self. Jared's hypothesis that laughter would alleviate the self-reflection that normally attends silence was inherently flawed. His robust and repetitious chuckling interposed an equally unnerving query: why is he laughing? It's a rendition of the time-honored distinction between laughing *with* or *at* someone. The response is parallel. Jared, of course, was oblivious to such suspicions, and laughed along, endlessly. The ever-jolly fool.

And then, in a frighteningly odd turn of events, when mama Carousel informed the group that she had videotaped Amy's cheer routine and subsequently began to play said video, Amy excused herself from the room and, naturally, brought Jared with her. She promptly exited, before observing a single frame of the video. And for some strange reason, no one seemed to mind. "Bye kids." Jared was apparently the only one who thought it unusual that Amy opted out of watching the video. You'd think she would eagerly squat in front of the TV screen, perched and anxious, ready to relive the excitement of the moment. But perhaps she knew, as they all knew (sans Jared), that a gritty film from several rows back could not possibly capture the physical magnificence of the event. To Amy, cheering was a live activity. Mama's 8mm would not do it justice. It's only right here and right now. That's it! Once it's over, it's over forever. To watch the video now, on the comfort of her couch, surrounded by family and loved ones, would encapsulate the same lost-glory-days sadness of a grown man watching his high school football highlight reel. Each is an attempt to grasp and recapture that which has passed. Amy would rather move forward and improve, rather than water the wilted flowers of yesterday. No, her best days were still ahead of her.

Amy led Jared to her bedroom, as the sound of the video trailed off behind them. She turned on the television and inserted a DVD of One Flew Over The Cuckoo's Nest. Once the movie began (almost immediately), she unzipped Jared's pants, pulled down his boxers and grabbed his cock. Now, mind you, the door to her bedroom remained open. This was a reckless endeavor. After giving it (his dick) a few soft tugs, she proceeded to give Jared a passionate and romantic blowjob. It was a sign of appreciation. A 'thank you' blowjob, courteous and complimentary. Each suck conveyed a sense of gratefulness. Jared had been a good sport all day. He built the gum wrapper chain, he was polite to all the cheerleaders and he patiently watched every single routine. He did not complain, nor did he seem reluctant to attend. He was simply glad to be involved. Amy was full of gratitude. And so, she slurped and gargled. In this moment, Jared's penis was the largest it has ever been. Even still, to this day, it has never attained such length and girth. Amy's soft lips and slippery tongue slithered atop his cock. Sooner than later, he whispered, "I'm gunna cum." Then came that critical, glistening second that adorns all men's lives (the post "I'm gunna cum" reaction, when you find out where your cum will end up. Normally, upon the utterance of this phrase, she will cease sucking and proceed to finish you off with a hand job, aiming at the nearest towel or tissue. But every so often, rather than retreating, she will increase her pace and swallow you whole). Amy chose the latter, and devoured ever last drop. Once the euphoria subsided, Jared responded, "You're welcome."

The weak and out-of-shape. The fat. The soft and flabby. Include with this a hint of the grotesque, weeks old, lingering odor that often emanates from the unkempt and ruined, and you'll have an accurate, sensory impression of the inhabitants of The Land of Forgotten Souls. This is, after all, how they earned their moniker: the chubby, stinky girls (and boys).

Now, a common thread in the modern 'Age of Acceptance' is that true beauty remains concealed and hidden from view of casual, piddling observers. Rather, only those who are truly dedicated, those who wish to endure the grueling task of 'getting to know someone,' will eventually learn the pure essence of an individual. The instantaneous fulfillment of physical attraction is, so they say, a shallow and false mirage of the depth and complexity of a person. But is that an entirely 100% accurate statement? Can it also be said that a person's physical appearance offers various clues and overt-suggestions as to their inner traits?

For instance, consider a fat woman, in all her warm, sweaty, voluptuous glory. The existence of blubber upon her bones reveals to the onlooker that she (our hypothetical, corpulent mass of a human) harbors a crippling weakness and lack of self-control. Being overweight is the physical manifestation that she has lost all sense of supremacy and power over herself. She forever lives as a dependent of her grumbly tummy. The body has overtaken the mind. She is a weak-willed worm, debilitated by her own ravenous appetite. Let us also not overlook the inner sadness that frequently accompanies the accumulation of lard. Fat women are never happy with their lives (although, none of us are); but the fate of a fatty is unique, in that the excessive weight gain is a telling revelation of her disappointment. She never achieved that childhood dream. All those countless adolescent nights, gazing into her future and envisioning the glory of tomorrow, for naught. So instead, she eats. She gives up. She fills the void with food. She drowns her woes with grease and oil, while muttering to herself, "This will do." But what she fails to realize is that any true feeling of accomplishment is born from countless hours of struggle. It is only by continuing to endure after the initial failures that one makes their presence known in this world. Keep striving; and most importantly, work! But the fat women of this world have decided to forgo this battle, in exchange for cupcakes. She thinks to herself: rather than experience the noble triumph of success, rather than achieve the visionary aspirations of my youth (which, assuredly, will take hours and days and weeks and months and years of physical and mental exertion, in addition to the regular sacrifice of life's many pleasantries), I'll opt, instead, for the sweet, instant joy of munching on a donut. Yea, that'll feel just as rewarding. That'll comfort me on my deathbed, as I recount the journey of my life. Yes, my grandchildren will speak of me in high regard, for I ate food. (Before you mail me your used tampons, please note that the above passage applies equally to men).

Unfortunately, in The Land of Forgotten Souls, this form of morbid laziness had become the customary lifestyle for all citizens.

Alto Undershed began to wonder, instead, about the benefits of weaponry. If one is unable to craft their own body into a wartime apparatus, weapons will provide all necessary strength.

The gun has previously been referred to in these pages as a symbolic figure of loneliness. As a point of clarification, a gun symbolizes loneliness because it destroys. You see, when a conflict arises between 2 people, one option is to say 'fuck off' and cut ties with them. This prevents any sort of resolution. A gun accomplishes this 10-

fold. The problem is, eventually, there will be no one left to kill.

While gazing upon the hapless, truculent specimens, Alto proclaimed, "Let us take arms against this troublesome siege!"

If only they could've been the recipients of a divine forecast. A telling prophecy of stunning, unquestionable accuracy. The crippling truth, that all men can become greater than they currently are. In every instance, man can improve. No matter the current triumphant circumstance to which he attains self-admiration, blinded by the allure of accomplishment and the security of completed work, which stalls progress. The upward trajectory of success, however defined, has no limit. Or, if it exists, no man has ever reached its victorious summit. A cardinal truth of life is that you can always be better than you are right now. Once you realize this, you begin to eliminate all the self-imposed barriers to your long-dreamt-of favorable outcome.

For Jared, marijuana had become a false god. The holy sacrament of his failed religion. He knew this. They all knew it. They were helplessly addicted. Desperately staying high. They were either clever enough to rationalize their weakness, or mentally tough enough to ignore it altogether. All drug addicts (and let's not mince words, that's what we were) will end up regretting ever having smoked (or whatever physical act allows for the ingestion of their substance of choice). Further, I will hereby go on record as declaring that marijuana is a gateway drug. While not all will traverse its shimmering portal, it absolutely opens the door. Logically, although not all who smoke pot drop acid, all who drop acid smoked pot as a prerequisite to their psychedelic odyssey.

It's an unusual occurrence, when the first of your stoner pals finally decides to quit. The others, still deeply entrenched in their unhealthy habits, view it as a betrayal, a renunciation of all their joyous memories. From their perspective, to give up the drug is to give up on the friendship itself. Even worse, stating that you have reached the inevitable conclusion that you regret ever having smoked, is misinterpreted as a denouncement of every memory, every laugh and every day you spent together. Upon making such declaration, some become defensive, others sit quietly in a mental flood of confusion and denial.

All of this, of course, would remain an unrealized epiphany, as none of the boys had the wherewithal to overcome their chemical dependency in pursuit of something greater. No, instead they would scorch their brains into time immemorial, never realizing their true potential, as it would forever remain buried beneath the fog.

'Tis a startling, semi-translucent euphoria of boundary shattering enlightenment, the first time a toddler's butthole is greeted by the swift maneuver of an elder's pinky. No delicacy is so wrong, yet so profound. The movement of a grown man's hand within the soft crevasse of an innocent anus can never be gentle or delicate enough, so as to preserve the chastity of youth. No, for the slightest passing movement of an adult's finger within the crisp atmosphere of a young butt eliminates all childlike curiosity, as the sensation of sexual pleasure leaves the kid a trembling mess, craving more.

A finger in the vicinity of a butthole is pulled by natural force into its suctioning grasp.

Many consider the butthole to be the body's exit point. The waste disposal mechanism by which man (and woman (and trans (and silverbelly salmon))) empties the shit of several meals. From the body → out. But now, in this moment, ponder an alternative. Unless, of course, you are shitting this very minute. If you, the battered and battle-wrought reader, are reading this atop a toilet, with your ass cheeks spread and ol' grimey prickle decamping mounds of excrement, please pause and wipe dat ass up before you go on. Because, over the course of the next several sentences, I am going to attempt to persuade you that the butthole is primarily an orifice of invitation.

In any given day, a man is mostly **not** shitting. For purposes of this argument, let us designate and accept a generalization: the average human spends 20 minutes of any given 24-hour period shitting. That is 1/72 of each day. Thus, the butthole's primary function (and we will define a body part's *primary function* as the predominant purpose to which is ascribes) is to keep poop in. The butthole works tirelessly to prevent the humiliation that would otherwise result from constant leakage. Imagine the grotesque state of affairs in which every new clump of shit created within you immediately oozed out of your ass. Ah! But G-d, in his great design scheme, ensured that the butt would remain shut, intermittently punctuated by the brief and spontaneous act of defecation. Thus, the butthole emanates inward.

It was on a brisk November afternoon, the sun's warmth reduced to a desperate struggle, when Wesley Fronten first got his asshole tickled. He had been playing outside on the family-owned swing set, carelessly frolicking in the (seemingly) eternal naiveté of childhood, the family-owned slave[1] providing the requisite adult supervision, when Lucas, a nearby neighborhood pal, approached. Mischief ready to emerge. They swung together, traversed the monkey bars and slid down the slide. Typical kids, gigglin' and hootin'. Lydia (the slave) stood watch, basking in the divine grandeur of 2 white boys.

But even the high-voltage wiring of a child's imagination eventually grows tired of the predictable limits of a jungle gym.

Beneath Lucas's swollen eyes hid a compelling secret.

He had recently been the guest of honor at the home of his friend, Brett. Young Brett lived in a gated community with his single mother. After school one day, the two boys

---

[1]  Don't forget, at this point in American history slaves were commonplace.

(Brett and Lucas) walked to Brett's mother's house. As is common among single, middle-aged women burdened with the responsibility of a child, Brett's mom had become self-absorbed and laser-focused on attaining her own pleasures in life, disregarding the petulant anguish of her sad son in favor of seeking out the hardest cock she could find. "Please lord, deliver me a man who will fuck me to the point where I forget how tragically miserable I am." Naturally, this meant that Brett was often left to his own devices. Such was the case on the fateful day when Lucas was invited into this home of disrepute. Brett's mother, likely already semi-drunk, met the boys (on foot) at the entrance to the gate. They were forced to wait until a vehicle arrived, at which point the gate slowly began to open. Brett and Lucas, a rambunctious duo, latched onto the gate as it began to move and 'rode' it until they were able to enter the community. Brett's mom found this behavior to be an absolute delight. As the boys clung to the active gate, she laughed. It was a mid-western, huckleberry slugging, good-ol'-gal kind of laugh. The cut-off-jean-wearing mama who knows her little boy will one day eat pussy, and relishes the fact.

Once they entered the home, Brett's mother vanished, presumably to go drink more of her preferred alcoholic beverage. Brett guided Lucas to his bedroom and promptly shut the door. Lucas perused his surroundings and admired the toys on Brett's dresser. Brett sat on the edge of his bed, disinterested in the trite hobbies that preoccupy most kids his age. He was quiet, still.

"Have you ever had sex?" he asked, slightly nervous.

"I don't know," Lucas replied. "What's that?"

"Sex is when a boy puts his penis in a girl's vagina."

Silence. Contemplation. Disgust. Confusion.

Lucas pondered the act.

"I can confidently say no, I have never had sex."

Suddenly, Brett's face transformed. His eyes gained a menacing twinkle and he smirked with the vulgar delight

Now, as naturally becomes an unintentional obligation of the sexually abused, Lucas was ready to infect another innocent. Wesley would be his victim. It's a grotesque variation of "paying it forward." For some reason, the tainted have an uncontrollable urge to impose their torment on another. Yet in this re-creation of the seminal destructive event of their lives, the victim now becomes the aggressor. It's a carefully crafted role reversal, in the desperate hope that by becoming the one inflicting the abuse (rather than receiving it), a sense of clarity may be attained. Seeing things from the other side will offer a glimpse into the guiding motivations of the boy who touched me. Yes! That's the answer! Ever since my balls were clasped by the soft hand of a child, I've been wondering: Why?

If
I
Reenact
My
Childhood
Trauma,
The
Remedy
Will
Be
Revealed
To
Me,
Suddenly.

Of course, what Lucas failed to realize was that by fiddling with Wesley's private parts, all he would accomplish was the perpetuation of brokenness. Not only that, he'd worsen his own situation, by including a new ingredient in the mélange of mental turmoil that would haunt him his entire life: he was responsible. He was now the bad guy. The only consolation offered to victims of sexual abuse is that their virtue remains intact. The choice was not their own. In this sense, they remain pure. They may take solace in the fact that they were an unwilling participant in the act. (After all, victimhood has become a status symbol.) However, the moment they inflict such trauma on another, their mangled tranquility is vanquished. Now they have become the sinner. The villainous taker, kicking dirt onto G-d's untarnished image. Sadly, none of this is realized until after the fact. And so the cycle continues...

Darkness hath overtaken my life.
And though I may try to run,
it outpaces me.
And though I may try to hide,
it uncovers me.

I must tend to the darkness.

Lucas initiated the moment by instructing Lydia to divert her gaze. She had been sitting on a nearby lounge chair, supervising the boys' playtime.

"Don't look," he told her.

To the best of his knowledge, she complied with his request.

Lucas led Wesley to a nearby **Little Tikes playground set.** A small, enclosed cube, consisting of four plastic multicolor panels, interlocked. A contraption intended for games and giggles would now serve as the setting for a crippling, traumatic event that would emotionally shatter the two boys. As adults, neither would be able to maintain a healthy romantic relationship, and both would remain infinitesimally confused about their sexuality.

The two boys sat down inside the play place. This edifice had no floor; rather, the grass was the ground. The

why did he change it so drastically?  Perhaps it's akin to the old American folk music tradition, in which the guitar-strapped singer puts his own spin on the tried and true classics.  Sex is certainly an art form.  Now, there's no mistaking that the act in which Lucas and Wesley were engaged was certainly not sex as it is commonly understood.  But that is precisely the artistic liberty that sex allows.  One must continually up the stakes, with each new encounter.

In a generous display of the sentiment we hope is shared by all our lovers (especially those as kinky as these two toddlers), Wesley initiated an act of reciprocity.

"My turn."

The timid little tot sounded assertive, yet (given the nasty, scatological eroticism of the moment) somewhat abrasive.  He wanted to experience the secondary joy of giving pleasure, rather than receiving it.

And so, they switched positions.  Lucas pulled down his pants and laid face down on the repugnant turf, while Wesley spread apart his cheeks and sprinkled the shit.  (There's no need to pontificate and espouse here.  This section of the story is a struggle to get through.  Sorry if I'm rushing it.[2]  In fact, writing this has rattled loose a long-suppressed memory.  Do y'all realize that this is an autobiography?  Except, I just change the names and call it fiction).  Wesley licked, and the exchange was complete.

Lucas sat up and smirked.  Once the elation began to fade from his mind, he worried that Lydia may have

---

[2] Here's some literature for you: The boys drizzled specks of poo-poo onto each other's tushies.  Consider the act.  To return poop to its place of origin is a desire all men share.  All wish to go back to what once was.  To return to our adolescence, to return to our childhood, to return to the womb.  Ah!  Simpler times.  Today is fraught with worry and sadness.  Yesterday was pleasant and happy.  Things were better then.  Putting poo on a butt signifies the desire to regress and undo the mess we now are.  Of course, it is a futile exercise; but(t) for a moment, we can at least escape the doldrums of maturity.  Sexual abstraction is an elusive tactic in achieving this sense of distracted contentment.  But then, just as shit splatters forth from an anus, we too are thrown back into the reality of life, in the present tense.  We can never return to the happy-go-lucky days of yore.  What do they call it?  Halcyon days.  I've always loved that term.  Eventually, you cum.

Wesley's cock. Lucas gently pulled his head backward, sucking off the dung. Once Wesley's penis was completely out of his mouth, it fell and ever-so-slightly bounced atop his balls, as the thin coat of Lucas's saliva shimmered in the autumn sun. Literature!

Did they swallow the shit after each of these grotesque acts? I honestly don't remember. I find it highly doubtful that they would consume it. It's safe to assume they spit it out. In case you were wondering.

Next? You guessed it! They swapped roles, and Wesley was allowed the opportunity to suck shit off Lucas's dick.

Once the boys were finished with this bizarre and inhumane experience, they rose, walked over to Lydia and asked her to make them a milkshake.

"Yes, boys. Right away!"

They followed her inside to the kitchen.

Lydia often (on command) made a delicious milkshake that was referred to as a 'Rookie Magic.' This name was bestowed by the restaurant chain known as Red Robin. Lydia had perfected the recipe. It's actually quite easy to make. Simply put 3 scoops of cookies & cream ice cream and ½ cup of milk in a blender. Enjoy! She'd always serve them in these dark red, semi-translucent, decagonal cups. Lucas and Wesley gulped down their Rookie Magics. The sweet, sugary beverage obliterated the lingering taste of butthole, penis and cow shit. Yummy!

Lucas wanted more. That evening, while lying in bed, attempting to sleep, he thought about Wesley. He fantasized about the possibilities of an additional sexual encounter with his neighborhood friend. On every one of his 10 **fingers**, Lucas assigned a different activity. He mapped out their next session. A schedule of 10 acts:

1.   I lick his penis
2.   He licks my penis

Lucas began to get angry, demanding and controlling; except he conveyed it in a gentle, yet needy, tone.

"Please, just really quick."

"I don't want to, Lucas!"

He insisted.

Wesley quickly realized that if he didn't let Lucas tap it, he'd persist until he got his way. So, like all women, he gave in.

"Fine."

They went into Lucas's bedroom. He had a small couch that folded out into a bed. But this was not a formal foldout couch; rather, it was a child's version. The seat portion of the couch was just a piece of foam, folded in half. Thus, if the user were to unfold the seat, it would (sort of) become a bed. *Am I explaining this properly? Maybe I'm not much of a writer. I'm having trouble describing this couch/bed thing. How would Ayn Rand describe the fucking couch?!* It's a traditional couch shape. It is a couch. But it's smaller, for kids. The bottom cushion can be unfolded to create a quasi-bed. It's really just a piece of foam covered in fabric. Unlike a typical foldout couch, there are no metal parts, no complex mechanisms. Just a piece of foam; or, rather, two pieces of foam, with the outer fabric sewn together along one portion of the edge, creating a hinge, which allows it to fold and unfold. Can you picture it? Ultimately, it's irrelevant what the couch looks like. The significant aspect of this tale is the act that is about to transpire on said couch. You needn't be able to visualize the exact parameters of the couch. Yet I can't resist. My inability to adequately describe this couch is frustrating me. I feel like a fraud.

Okay, so when it is folded up in the sitting position, the bottom cushion(s) look like this (this is a side view):

I neglected to include it in the illustration, but the back cushion would be perpendicularly positioned on the rightmost portion of the image. In addition, also not included in the drawing are the armrests, which exist on either side (like a normal fucking couch).

Alright, now, in order to unfold it, the user would pull up from the rear of the seat. When it's in the process of unfolding, it would look like this:

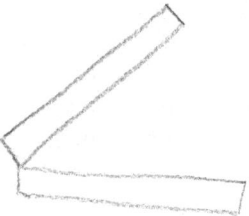

See the little hinge portion I tried to describe?

Finally, once it was entirely unfolded, á la the sleeping position, it would look like this:

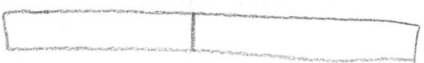

Get it? Now that you've seen it, if you feel that you could have provided a better description of this couch, please feel free to include your riveting prose below:

_____

_____

_____

_____

_____

_____

_____

_____

Wow! We're all so impressed. I'm sure you get loads of blowjobs from all the young girls who move to Hollywood with starry-eyed dreams of becoming actresses. All you have to do is whisper into your maiden-of-the-night's ear, "I'm a writer," and she's yours. She'll swallow you whole. And she's even considerate enough to spare you the uncomfortable attempt to exchange a mouthy kiss right after you've coated the inside of her skull with cum. When you're not fucking, you and her can admire all the shitty street art that adorns the cesspool of desperation that is Hollywood. All hail art! In any form! Of any quality! Please reassure me that I haven't devoted my life to a useless cause! Please remind me of the importance of art, o vapid poster pasted to a switch box!

Alrighty! Back to the child fucking.

Lucas abruptly unfolded the couch into the bed position. They both removed their clothes and stood together, entirely naked, like two angelic virgins.

They laid down, together, on the bed. Hugged and kissed. Touched each other's bodies. Lucas then slid down and began to suck Wesley off.

He would never forget the taste of penis. During their previous sexual encounter, the fertilizer overwhelmed all the other flavors. Now, with just the pure, unobstructed skin of Wesley's penis in his mouth, he was able to truly experience its unique taste.

Eventually, they decided it was time to retire. Without the grand finale of an orgasm, it's difficult to determine how to conclude such an interaction. At a certain point, the boys stopped deriving pleasure from the exchange. Their shame and confusion overtook the ticklish joy of touching privates, and they decided that it was time to cease all carnal activity. They got dressed, folded the bed back into its couch position, switched on the Super Nintendo and resumed their saved 2-player (cooperative) game of Donkey Kong Country.

And that was it. The boys never had "sex" again. They would remain friends for several more years, enjoying many age-appropriate activities together. Those two days became relegated to the status of an unspoken memory, a forbidden secret shared between the boys. In time, they lost touch. Although they lived in the same town, they ended up going to different schools. They made new friends and their lives took different trajectories. Every few years, they'd run into each other, often at a community-wide social gathering. They were polite and friendly, cordial. But their eyes held a secret. Their interlocking glance contained a tome of unresolved emotions.

I have no doubt that this experience, and my decision to suppress the memory of it (rather than confront it), has had a negative effect on my life. I'm sure it has imposed a subconscious detriment on all my relationships (which, unsurprisingly, have all resulted in failure). How can one go about life carrying the weight of such a memory?

Some 25 years later, Lucas awoke in a state of panic. The memory had burst free from its suppression and forced itself to the forefront of his mind. It consumed his thoughts. He tried desperately to ignore it, to shove it away, to forget, as he'd always been able to before. But this time was different. It wouldn't go away. Any method he utilized, in an attempt to distract himself, proved ineffective. He couldn't erase it. Why? For the past 25 years he'd been able to live with this memory, relatively at ease. Now, all of a sudden, it was inescapable. He thought to himself, 'Am I really going to go the rest of my life without ever dealing with this?' He knew it was time. Finally! He scoured the pages of the local directory and found Wesley's address. At this critical juncture in my life, I will finally tackle the beast, the gross scallywag that has been lurking in the shadows for far too long.

That evening, he wrote a letter to Wesley.

Wesley,
        The purpose of this letter is that I feel we must acknowledge the interaction we had many years ago. For most of my life thus far, I've been able to ignore it. I had convinced myself that I could live the rest of my life with this secret, and perhaps it can stay that way as far as others are concerned. But between us, I feel that we must at least acknowledge what happened.
        I hope you're okay. I hope you've been able to maintain healthy relationships. If it has caused you any negative results, then I want you to know that I'm sorry. I feel as though I instigated it. I blame myself. I often wonder why I did such a thing. I recently remembered an early event in my life in which another boy did a similar thing to me. I guess I was reenacting what I had experienced.
        Again, I want you to know that I'm sorry.
                            Sincerely,
                            Lucas

He dropped the letter into a nearby outgoing mailbox and felt an immediate sense of relief. The burden that was weighing him down for the past 25 years had finally been lifted (partially). Lucas felt as though complete closure would only come once he received a response from Wesley; and, if such response contained his forgiveness.

Several days later, Wesley received two letters in the mail: Lucas's Step 9 amends letter and a purchase order from Alto Undershed.

In the intervening 25 years, Wesley had become obsessed with guns and various other types of weaponry (but mainly guns). He had amassed an enormous collection. He even managed to make a career out of it. Yes, he was a certified arms dealer. His daily life consisted of all things guns and destruction. This was his method of hiding from the memory, hiding from his potential gayness. Any time the memory would begin to creep above the depths of his subconscious, he'd go out and buy a louder, larger and more powerful gun. Kill it!

When Wesley noticed that the letter was sent from Lucas (via the return address information located on the top left corner of the envelope) he immediately knew what it was about. 'Oh boy,' Wesley thought. 'He's finally decided to talk about it.' However, in that moment, at that particular period in his life, Wesley was not prepared to reexamine *the event*. The letter made it abundantly clear that Lucas was ready, willing and able to accept responsibility for his actions, sincerely apologize, and make restitution for any harm he caused. Wesley felt otherwise. He was not in the proper mental state to revisit and explore the parameters of that day. The memory remained buried deep, thickly caked beneath layers of marijuana resin and submerged in murky pools of alcohol, the remnants of many-a-late-night attempts to silence his mind.

In the years that had passed since their illicit tryst, he had pursued alternative avenues for dealing with his sexual befuddlement. Aside from the guns and the drugs, he had inadvertently developed a predilection for young boys. His marriage (yes, he's married) and his children (yes, he has kids)[3] are all a guise, an additional attempt to conceal the thought. It was the birth of his son that (re)triggered his pedophilic perversion. One night, while changing his son's diaper and scraping the baby poo (its distinct odor, texture and color radiating throughout his entire sensual spectrum) off of his baby balls, Wesley was overcome by a primordial urge, an irresistible neurological impulse, to exchange the sensation of touch with the tiny, naked, defenseless human being that lay spread-eagled and shit-spackled before him. The fact that it was his own son did not deter him (nor did it excite him), it merely made the whole ordeal more convenient. Wesley bent down and gently kissed his son's balls and nibbled on his penis. The pungent taste and the internal, tingling sensation that accompanied the naughtiness of this incident (the behemoth misbehavior further bolstered by the fact that mommy was quietly secluded in the next room, entirely oblivious) was remarkably reminiscent of those two fragile and immutable days from his childhood. Somehow, in some deranged acrobatic maneuver of logic, it provided Wesley with a sense of comfort and clarity. ~~To the best of my ability (which isn't saying much), I can (barely) attempt to justify his actions as follows: the sexual play between Lucas and Wesley was an experiment conducted between two boys. At the time, they were both very young and immature. Their bodies (and their lives, for that matter) were new. They were figuring themselves out and testing out their various "parts." Now, as an adult, Wesley is more aware and experienced. He is better qualified to introduce another human (here, his son) to the body's natural pleasure points. Thus, he is not a villainous monster; rather, he is a guide, a chaperone.~~ This moment served as the commencement of a frequent routine between Wesley and his son. As the boy grew older, the touching became more invasive. When he reached a certain age, he learned

---

[3] Girl, boy, girl (in that order)

to resist, to say "stop" and to fight back.  No matter, daddy always got his way.

And so began a cycle.  When that boy became a man, the tortured **and unresolved** memories of his childhood caused him to become overwhelmed at the sight of little boys (and occasionally girls).

Tender pussy
She became a wreck
She thought it was love
She needed me
It was all my fault, I let it happen

Upon the birth of his son, he could no longer contain himself.  He made a mess of that boy.  He inflicted on his own son the same mangled memories that his father had inflicted on him.  Naturally, that boy would go on to make a mess of his own.  And on and on and on and on and on and on and on and on and on and on and on and on and on and on and on and on and on and on and on and on and on and on and on and on and on and on and on and on and on and on and on and on and on and on and on and on and on and on and on and on and on and on and on and on and on and on and on and on

Another Dead Cop
Memorial Highway

How could a sweet little boy like Jared, raised in a loving household, get caught up in the scuzzy world of drugs? Was he, too, fiddled?

Equate (as I've often considered): **(1)** my intense passion re women and my extreme, distraught, post-breakup withdrawals; with **(2)** childhood sexual escapades.

My initial thought was that by having a girlfriend, it proves I'm not gay and that I can maintain a healthy relationship. Yes, despite my boyhood homoerotic-exploration, I am a well-adjusted, prototypical male. Hear me whine!

Oh, that? That was just kid stuff. Ya know? Boys will be boys. GI-Joe and asshole licking, it's all the same. Eventually, we grow up and become normal.


When the sun sets today by John Nelson
I must humbly assert myself out of situation
Where a man's modesty most certainly comes in handy
A cataclysmic wall shake of surprise
Below surges of tears, hopeless friendship lies
A mere mark of insanity and the clock has struck one
Shovel in hand, make the dig the fun
Pleasure seekers open wide, the clock has stuck two
After we bury the hatchet, what will you do?
Merrily merrily, it now reads three
A self-imposed funeral for you and me

I can't take this anymore, it now reads four
Sir, drop that thinking and remorse no more
Let it build let it build, now it say five
It would be better for everyone if you just kept it all inside
Never again never again, I can see a six
With dirty minds comes dirty tricks
I want it all to stop, here comes a seven
Skip the rest and take us straight to eleven
This is the part where I die
Where it all goes away
We pack our bags for the so-called brand new day
But in reality we're all just running away
Too scared to face the truth, there's too much to say
So we hide inside, and make it illegal
To see who we really are
Who we really can be
Throwing away all these possibilities
And dreams, where nightmares be
Be thy forbidden fruit for all to see
No more, no more, no more I say
For it all stops, when the sun sets today

In life, we have 2 options: deal with it **or** kill yourself

"The Road to Perdition awaits, my friend. The long-awaited follow-up to Sam Mendes's utter masterpiece, American Beauty, is finally here."
"Fuck yes!"
Since its 2000 on-video release, Jared and Charlie had developed a startling obsession with American Beauty. To them, this film contained a defining statement of life's truth:

The raw darkness that underlies the seeming placidity of suburban life,
&
The beauty contained within the doldrums.

# P[1]O[2]N[3]T[4]I[5]F[6]I[7]C[8]A[9]T[10]E[11]

"So, here's the plan: you, me, Amy and her rag-tag pal Mandy are all going to see <u>Road to Perdition</u> this Friday. And there, beside your sweetheart in the darkened theatre, you and her will share your first kiss, while what is sure to be the seminal performance of Tom Hanks's career flickers gently against your wrought-shut eyelids."

"Oh god, is this another scheme you and Amy cooked up? Is she confiding in you again? I thought you two had put a stop to that nonsense."

"You needn't worry, Jared. I'm just concerned. We're all concerned. You've been dating Amy for almost 3 months now and you still haven't even made out."

"Yes, I'm aware of that. I didn't realize the entire city council felt the need to weigh in on this matter."

"Your girl has needs. If you're not providing, she'll seek satisfaction elsewhere."

Fuck. It's true.

Amy might end up kissing someone else.

No.

Her lips on another man.

It can't happen.

The thought alone nearly killed him.

"Alright!"

"No pressure. After all, this is supposed to be fun, remember?"

A sudden flurry of anguish engulfed Jared's entire being. He was struck by a single, paralyzing concern.

"But," he asked, anxious to express his immediate frustration, "what if it's good?"

"Of course it'll be good. It'll be great! Marvelous! Stupendous! Spectacular! I've heard it said that kissing a girl is the first step a man makes/takes, makes & takes, takes and makes on his quest toward enlightenment."

"No, you fool. The movie. What if the movie's good?" Charlie laughed.

"Are you kidding? Come on, Jared. It looks terrible. I mean, seriously, how can you follow up the definitive examination of contemporary American life with some cops and robbers rubbish?"

Predictably, like roast beef at your mother's funeral, they never ended up seeing the dang movie. Rather, the evening's festivities proceeded as such:

> The parties assembled. Jared's mother picked them up from school and escorted them to the family household. At this point, they still intended to see the film. Somehow, with his magnanimous power of persuasion, Charlie had made 2 teenage girls excited to see <u>Road to Perdition</u>.[12]

---

[12] This seems like an appropriate moment to mention that this same group did see <u>The Pianist</u> together. As I recall, Amy giggled when the wheelchair-bound Jew was tossed from the window of his apartment. Not to tarnish her image or anything. In sharing this fact, it is not my intention to diminish the beauty of her character. Let's give her the benefit of the doubt. What 15-year-old shiksa, with a swelling cooter, wants to watch the denizens of Hollywood (and their ousted raconteur) recreate the Holocaust? No thanks.

Anyhoo, the plan was to hang out at Jared's house for a bit, eat some SnackWells (or whatever youngsters do to kick around the salt) and then go see the movie. But once they arrived and got situated in the cozy comfort of Jared's bedroom, Charlie took the reins and diverted the evening, entirely, onto a crash course. Destination: the kiss.

Charlie's grand scheme would pay off tonight.

How does one learn how to kiss? ... It's not a learned skill inasmuch as it is an innate biological function. Lip lockin' and cock knockin' are part of our DNA.

The lord hath imbued us with sexual desire to fulfill our function of reproduction. And, to provide pleasure, he/she/it/nothing cleverly placed sensitive nerve endings on and around our genitalia; thus making us want it (all the time).

There are people out there who want to fuck you (frequently). They exist. Go find them.

So tonight, Jared, a human male, will attempt to (in)gage his animal instincts and thrust-fuck her cow hump 'til her rump starts pumpin' dumps. Or something like that.

How would the events transpire? Like this:

Charlie perused Jared's music collection and selected Dave Matthews Band's Crash. He put the CD in the stereo, clicked through to track #3 and pressed repeat. He then grabbed Mandy by the forearm and rushed her out of the room. The two of them (Charlie & Mandy) retreated to a nearby bathroom and shut (locked) the door. I guess the plan was to seclude J+A and allow "nature" to take its course. **It worked.**

Jared quickly turned toward Amy (in a perfect world he would've whirled). A champion shifting of glances took place between the vicious feminine and the docile boy. She grinned, knowingly. His eyes widened, nervously. The echo of the slammed-shut door lingered in the quiet of the room, whilst the tension of their mutual expectation became almost visible in the empty space between them. She was ready to pounce, her butt twitching and shifting like a predatory pussycat that had glimpsed a helpless little mouse trapped in a suddenly unfamiliar household. And he, the still rodent, was ready to surrender.

'Welp, I guess this is it,' thought Jared. 'It's really happening. This'll be my first kiss. Right now, on this day, in this very moment.'

To ensure their privacy for the foreseeable future, Jared approached his bedroom door. He pushed in the lock, and then – anticipating failure – attempted to turn the knob, in order to verify that it was in fact locked. It was.

And for a brief fraction of a second, he stood, motionless. For he knew that once he turned around, his life would change. This bedroom had been his private sanctuary for all of his 14 years. In this room, his mother used to set out his clothes for him every morning before school. In this room, his father would bring him a glass of warm milk whenever he had trouble sleeping, and would sit with him until he gently fell back into the peaceful innocence of a childhood slumber. Now, in this room, he would experience his first kiss, with a girl he truly adored.

When he turned around, Amy was standing right behind him. She lunged. They kissed. And kissed again. And again. Once they began, they couldn't stop. Jared's reluctance and timidity immediately vanished (thanks, entirely, to the collaborative effort of Charlie's ingenuity and Amy's assertiveness). This gratuitous act – sucking, slobbering and nibbling – gave physical form to their emotions. It was easy and natural. No preparation proved necessary. We are endowed by our creator with this certain intrinsic ability. And now, having unleashed it, Jared too became animal.

The kissing continued for quite a while.  They spent the first 10 minutes standing by the door.  Upright and poised.  Thereafter, they maneuvered their way onto the bed.  Now, without the necessity of balance clouding their equilibrium, they were free to melt into a single entity.  Complete with neckin' and gropin' and growlin' galore!  Oh what fun it is to writhe…

I want to consume you!  I want to tether myself to you.  Let us fuse our body and soul together, as one.  I want to taste every part of you and lick every orifice.  Every square inch of skin must make contact with my mouth.  Every nook.  Every little unexplored area of Amy will become me.

Ah!  Words will not do it justice.  How can one describe kissing?  It is a method of communication that exceeds language.  If two humans could simply sit civilly and discuss how much they loved each other, there'd be no need to kiss.  The kiss itself is the highest form of expressing love (with several monumental exceptions; see sex).  Kissing goes beyond mere locutions.  It is unspoken.  To attempt to describe it with little letters on a page is to cheapen its brilliance.

Faintly, through the door, they could hear the muffled giggles of Charlie and Mandy, brimming with excitement.

I'm about ready to quit. I give up. I'm fucking done with this cockamamie story. It used to be fun. But now it's a burden. The excitement has fizzled out. Can't you tell? So here it is:

THE END

Regret? I often experience a recurring instance, in which I'll recall a past event and recoil at the memory. This frequently involves some sort of embarrassing interaction from the schoolyard days. The typical pants down, pee-pee dribblin' penis-in-front-of-the-class-cutie type moment that quickly becomes stored behind mama's dust ruffle, out of sight but preserved indefinitely. The traumatic secret shared and understood by a maudlin family of 4 (and the wayward half-sister who apparently doesn't deserve to know that I've sucked cock). Confess, acknowledge and ignore.

This sensation has been mentioned so often in the public forums lately that it has almost become a trope. Don't worry, I'm not going to berate you with recycled clichés. No! This involves a different category of regret. This is self-inflicted mental impairment after a multi-year clean streak. This is the catastrophic crumbling and premature end of a new nation (at once full of promise and potential).

Recently, I was afraid that I had slipped out of my sobriety by eating a (unbeknownst to me) marijuana-laced Rice Krispy treat. The next day, my mind hazy and mangled by the cruel aftermath of intoxicants (which linger much longer than we realize), I figured my life was over. I fucked up. I had been doing so well for so long, and now I completely blew it. Done. All for naught. I failed. I'll never recover. I'll never be the same. For years, my fragile and drug-ridden brain had been in the process of slowly rebuilding, one cell at a time, each neurotransmitter relearning its naturally-designated purpose. And now, with a single bite of this homemade delicacy, I was back at square one. Worse, I was erased from the world. Flushed away. I despised myself. My mental capabilities had regressed to the pre-dawn of mankind's finest achievements. The entire solar system, at once a seemingly stable (in a relative sense) and constant ballet of stone, reconfigured itself. Neptune plunged into the abyss. And I deserve death. This blessed opportunity of a human life had been squandered beyond repentance. Prepare the noose. I'm done. My existence was a disappointment. Goodbye. Oh what could've been if I hadn't smoked pot…

Being "high" is, in actuality, prolonged oxygen deprivation. As your brain suffocates, you feel euphoric. It's a false and undeserved sensation that allows the user to hoot at her own shortcomings. To love he who does not deserve love and to accept that which should be conquered.

So go ahead. Continue the ritual for years. Eventually, when it's too late, you'll realize that the damage is done. Your mind is gone. Kaput. There's no return to mental purity. And all that remains is a hollow, rotten core.

That brain of mine, it was meant for so much more. It had the capabilities. It had the means. I failed to utilize my greatest strength. Now, I am nothing. A schlub on a rub.

It's time to complete my slow-motion suicide.

But then I realized… Wait! I'm still here. This is me – present and aware – in this moment. I will move forward. My life is not over because of this incident. It will continue.

Despite my disability, I am still alive.  Repeat: Despite my disability, I am still alive.

Despite my disability, I am still alive.
Despite my disability, I am still alive.
Despite my disability, I am still alive.
Despite my disability, I am still alive.
Despite my disability, I am still alive.
Despite my disability, I am still alive.
Despite my disability, I am still alive.
Despite My disability, I am

I will regenerate as a new man, eager for tomorrow.  Because I am still me.  Here.  It hasn't destroyed my soul.  Sure, maybe it's a temporary setback.  But this is **it**.  This is, and shall now be, the story of my life.

Oh, do I have a metaphor for you!  The process of reading a book symbolizes the span of a human life.  At the beginning (page one), we start with nothing; yet an entire journey awaits us.[1]  Pages and pages and pages and pages.  As we go on reading, we collect memories and experiences and the wisdom of lessons learned.  Our life goes on, endlessly.  Our left hand grips the past, our right hand holds the future.  With each new curl-o'-da-page,

---

[1] The disquieting moment during the first few lines of every new book, in which the reader is thrust into an unfamiliar situation and must figure out what is happening.

we never know what to expect, or what'll happen next, as we continue reading toward the conclusion.

Except, in real life, the entire book is filled with blank pages. The words appear once we live them. Eventually, we accumulate a life. If it's worthwhile, from time to time, portions of our story will be revisited by our family and friends.

So to you, my dear reader,

Keep the pages turning in your life, and fill them with love and laughter and togetherness. In fact, put this book down for today. Go out and live. I'll be waiting here for you when you return.

Let live another day,
as to define blank pages.

During the midnight hours of Charlie's 13$^{th}$ birthday party, all the boys went skinny-dipping. They decided line up in the order of their respective penis lengths (with the biggest in the front and the smallest in the back). Once assembled, they entered the pool in this order. Jared was, of course, last.

"I was doing this thing where I would skateboard toward the pool, and right when I reached the edge I would kick back on the tail and the board would pop up, sorta like an Ollie, but not fully, and I'd launch into the pool. So, this time, I was going toward the water and I slipped, fell backwards and slammed my arm on the edge of the pool. I remember once I stood up my arm just fell, like the bones were no longer connected and my arm was just dangling there. The funny thing is, I told my parents I had been running. For some reason, I didn't want them to know I was skateboarding when this happened."

He sat forever,
waiting for her to appear.
She never came.

Jared joined Amy for a performance of <u>Romeo and Juliet</u> at a local outdoor theatre nestled in the nearby canyon. She drove to the show. On the way there, she turned on the CD player in her car. She was listening to The Who. 'What the fuck?' Jared thought to himself. 'Since when does she listen to The Who? She never used to listen to this kind of music before. Must be that new crowd she's hanging out with.'

Sex = surrender;
the transfer of one's power onto another

In class, as Amy was walking to her desk at the back of the room, one of her fellow classmates called out to her as she passed by.

"Whore!" she proclaimed, seemingly unprovoked.

"Oh, I'm a whore?" Amy asked, startled.

"Whore!" she repeated, having failed to prepare a follow-up response.

This exchange quickly fizzled out. There was nothing else to say. Amy kept walking and slumped down in her chair. Humiliated.

Jared was in the same class as these two ladies. He was sitting in the opposite side of the room and had witnessed the entire interaction. It made no sense to him.

Later that evening, he shared his confusion with Charlie.

"Dude, the weirdest thing happened today. The glasses nibbler called Amy a whore. Just out of nowhere!"

"Don't worry. The nibbler is crazy, she just does these things sometimes."

Kissing soon got to be so routine that it became a game; a bargaining chip to coax Jared into participating in certain activities.

The fusion of J/A in soul and spirit awoke a dormant emotion within Jared. It seemed that upon the discovery of his ability to physically express his feelings for Amy, his once balanced and finely-tuned psyche became abruptly obliterated. The Jared of yore was now unrecognizable. With one fell swoop of her puckered lips, Amy had successfully nudged Jared, thereby commencing his decent into madness. Goodbye little boy. Hello anguished and broken young man.

To Jared, laying his lips on Amy was the equivalent of branding a cow (especially when he'd kiss her squishy butt). This seal shall proclaim to the entire world that she is my personal property. No man is allowed to know her the way I know her.

Of course, Amy could not be tamed. She loved it when the neighborhood boys would give her attention. And any promiscuous ingénue knows that the best way to receive a testosterone-addled boy's attention is to subtly suggest the possibility (no matter how slight) that you'll fuck him. Hey mister! If you play your cards right, one of my many orifices may swallow your dick tonight. Yes ma'am. Whatever you say ma'am. Please let me in. Absorb my filth!

The combination of Jared's possessiveness and Amy's wild abandon gave rise to a new and unpleasant emotion: jealousy. Oh what a miserable and useless feeling. Fun fact: it's listed as the cause of death on Jared's death certificate. Yes, for the remainder of his waking days, Jared was rattled by a constant and unrelenting surge of jealousy.

In one regrettable instance (of many), Jared saw Amy hugging one of their classmates. A dubious boy named Johnny. He was poor, slightly chubby and could wail on the guitar. For some reason (and Amy is a case study of this syndrome), young ladies seem to love destitute musicians. Maybe I selected the wrong means of artistic expression. I'd love to experience eager sexuality as an accolade for my work. Writers aren't afforded the opportunity to publicly flaunt their "talent." Thus, no one (especially strangers) knows of the mountainous oeuvre we are shielding from view, when we rise from our desks and emerge from our darkened bedrooms in an often-unsuccessful attempt at social interaction. The writer has elected to imprison himself. A life sentence (ha!). Behold the musician, and how his craft demands public performance. A musician represents the mastery of man's myriad variations of the mating ritual. Simply stand on a stage and whistle a tune. Women will watch whilst waxy and wet. Then, after the show, remain in the vicinity. Those who witnessed your act have now become entranced. They will flock to you. Feed me cum! Feed me cum! Feed me cum! Feed me cum! Sooooo, when Jared saw Amy giving a hug to this Johnny fellow, the jealousy kicked in and he screamed "Stop!" A hush fell over the campus. People were (initially) concerned. It was embarrassing for all involved, once the context of his outburst was understood.

Jared's friends soon discovered that they could harness and utilize his irrationality to their advantage. Oh boy! How fun and compassionate!

A subsequent conference call between Jared/Amy/Charlie demonstrated the newfound power that both Amy and Charlie could wield over Jared. When prompted, Jared would experience an overwhelming compulsion to quash the impending torrent of lust and jealousy. Like an infected and polyp-ridden carrot on a stick, Amy and Charlie could dangle the threat of infidelity in front of him, and he'd run. Cataclysmic and screaming.

Hello?

Howdy.

Hi!

Alrighty guys.
Who's in the mood
to see Serving Sara?

(under-breath
whisper)
Again with the
fuckin' movies.

Umm… sure.

It's playing this afternoon. Come on, Jared.

It looks seriously retarded. A genuine "fuck it" movie.

(giggle)

You imbecile! It's not about the movie! The movie is only a pretext. It's an excuse for us to get together.

Oh hum, you're right. Sign me up, strap me in and whisk me away.

Look, let's make it interesting. We'll all leave from our respective homes within the next 30 minutes. We shall all walk to the theatre. This is a contest. No transportation assistance is allowed.

Transportation assistance?

Only walking. No bike, skateboard, etc.

Why couldn't you
just say that?

Never mind my
choice of words!
Here's the catch: the
first to arrive will
receive the prize.

And that is…?

A kiss from Miss.
Carousel.

What!?

Don't worry.  Just a
simple peck on the
cheek.  Nothing
raunchy.

Fuck that.  Amy,
you agreed to
this?

Honestly, this is the
first I've heard of it.

Sure.  I bet you
two rehearsed this
whole exchange
before I got on the
line.

Jared, relax.  I had no
advance notice.
Besides, it's just an
innocent little game.
Don't feel
threatened.

I am genuinely at
a loss for words.
How can neither
of you recognize
how absurd this
idea is?

Hey. Here's a
solution: win the
fucking race.

Ready?

Set.

Go.

As soon as he hung up the phone, Jared burst out the door. 'This is new,' he thought, while running furiously toward the theatre. 'My friends have become the enemy.' The concept haunted him for the duration of his trek.

Needless to say, he was the first to arrive. Pursuant to the terms of their contest, he received his whorish kiss from Amy.

So this is the new dynamic? This is our contemporary attempt at romance? Kissing his darling sweetheart, at once the epochal sunrise of his life, had now (in a mere matter of weeks) malignantly deteriorated into the dimwitted luxury of a silly carnival game's triumph. A dusty and disposable teddy bear to commemorate your efforts. An enduring struggle to attain that which should be readily available to you without condition or victory. Step right up and strangle me!

*If only I could finish writing this book, then I'd be free to die.*

Upon his return to South Forts, Nathaniel had only one comment to relay: "Gentlemen, prepare the bulldozers."

Wallowing in water
We wouldn't waste a drop
Why?
While the world willfully wastes this wondrous molecule
We will wince and whine.
Proclaim:
We'd rather destroy the world
Than acquiesce or compromise!

There was a brief moment, a super-dooper teeny-tiny miniscule blip on the boy's radar, early on, prior to the kiss, maybe a month or two into their relationship, during the beginning stages, when Amy decided to call it quits. Done. We're through.

Midday on a Saturday, she called Jared and broke up with him. Cruel and quick. Like a late-stage iteration of an ol' Zip Coon number; still shucking along, even after the nation had begun to rethink the entire premise.

"Uh, wait a second. I– I don't understand. What?"

He chuckled in disbelief, a subtle combination of amusement and terror.

"Come on, Amy. What are you– what are you saying here?"

There was a pause, as (prior to speaking) Amy carefully planned her next statement with strategic precision. Each word was painstakingly selected from her mediocre, yet sufficient, vocabulary.

Gulp. Zigzagging Siegfried Ahoy! She started.

"Although this relationship of ours has only just begun, I feel that it's time to end it."

Befuddlement quickly collapsed into anger, as Jared let loose the primitive outburst of man. The roar of domestic violence and the capacity for wretched, regretful behavior. Stupid cunt, I'll rattle your lord if you fail to serve me.

"This is incomprehensible and abhorrent!"

Silence. Breathe. Slow down. Try again.

"But… I mean, we're just getting started here. It's too early to even have an opinion yet. You– What are you even talking about? What's wrong, Amy?"

"Jared, I'm sorry. I've made up my mind already."

"Is this–? I ca– Is this for real? Like, are you genuinely sure about this? I don't see how you could be sure, but I'll ask anyways."

"Yes, Jared. The purpose of this call is simply to inform you of my decision. Don't try to convince me otherwise. And for the sake of your ancestors, don't beg."

His eyebrows wilted.

"Fucking unbelievable, Amy. What happened? There is no rational basis for you to just wake up today and arrive at this conclusion, seemingly out of nowhere. You don't even sound like you mean it. You sound like a hostage reading some anti-American diatribe written by her captors."

"Okay great, Jared!" she spoke with furious sarcasm. "Great idea! Insult me and imply that I am incapable of thinking for myself. You really know how to woo a girl."

"Ah, damn it. I'm not trying to be mean, Amy. Give me a break."

"I am."

"Hilarious."

"Thanks. Well, I've said my piece. I think it's best for us to end this conversation before you say anything else you'll regret."

"How considerate."

"Bye Jared."

Upon hearing the click of the phone line's disconnection, Jared experienced his first taste of heartbreak. He sat alone in his room, suddenly engulfed in the quiet loneliness of being single (after having had his first glimpse of genuine soul-to-soul companionship). I am by myself. She is gone from my life. She doesn't want me anymore. She is still alive. She's out there. She exists beyond my window. Outside of my reach. She'd prefer that I wasn't around. She wants me to leave her alone. Go away! But I am available. I want her. I miss her. Oh Amy…

Heartbreak is a genuine disability. It can be fatal. It can destroy a man. To give your whole being to someone, and to be refused. You are left with nothing. Broken.

No advance notice. No warning. So sudden and abrupt.

He remained eerily still for the next 5-10 minutes, paralyzed by grief, staring intensely at nothing, while his mind struggled to comprehend the circumstance. He sat, stewing in the unsettling quiet of a storm's incremental formation. What's he gunna do? How's he gunna react? This is a test that defines a man's character. How do you handle your first heartbreak?

Finally, Jared stood up. He approached his stereo and began punching the plastic display with the wrath of a net-snagged sea monster, all limbs mindlessly flailing about, in an attempt to escape the confinement occasioned by a lack of awareness regarding one's own surroundings (and, of course, the fisherman's ability to take advantage of such frailties). In this pivotal moment, when panic surpassed reason, Jared invoked his barbaric ability to annihilate all evidence of creation. His stereo (the cherished tool by which teenagers broadcast their identity) was the unfortunate target of his rage. He wailed on the thing. Pulverized it. Smashed it into fucking smithereens!

During this cathartic moment, he did not scream. Rather, he remained demonically silent, with his eyes fixed and focused on the point of impact. He noticed the painful formation of each new fracture (a false and temporary achievement).

When the fury finally subsided, he stepped back, tilted his fist upward and inspected the damage he had wrought upon himself. His knuckles were bleeding. He clutched his hand and wept. Now I am become pathetic, the destroyer of self-respect.

He sat down, awash in his grief, suspended in the dangling despondency of his newly acquired sense of solitude. The yearning soon took hold. He was unable to fathom the abruptness of her decision. Gone. So immediate. So harsh.

'I haven't even kissed her yet,' he thought.

I loathe myself without Amy. She was a part of me. I surrendered a portion of my identity in order to make room for her in my otherwise full and eclectic life. Right? And now, without her, I am left empty and vacant. Hollow be my name.

Little boy, stop this silly nonsense. A lone man is not an unfinished whole, an incomplete picture or a partial being. Rather, man is already fully formed on his own. A woman should not complete you, she should complement you. Listen! This is the rationalization of the lonely. Your self-worth needn't be dependent upon whether or not you have a woman around.

But this is a flawed argument. Let's not forget that upon seeing Adam (the divine bachelor) alone in the Garden of Eden, G-d's first thought was that man should not be alone. 'Tis G-d's grand design! Man is not meant to live his life in social isolation. The masturbating loner is an abomination. Each pump of your cock-clenched fist is a blasphemous act of defiance against The Almighty. Each self-inflicted orgasm is the culmination of a ritual practiced only by the spiritually devoid.

Now, gather around young saplings. As you'll recall, prior to the emergence of isshah, beasts and fowl were G-d's first attempt at providing Adam with some sort of living and breathing accompaniment. Fun-loving furry friends! However, as any lonesome farmhand can testify, this (predictably) proved unsuccessful (see "A Man Needs a Maid" by Neil Young. The warbly-voiced crooner longs for pussy while tilling the soil, in another classic instance of an unkempt, drugged-up folkie rock star who mistakenly believes he's a farmer. No Neil, stick to the songs and let the slaves do the grunt work. The only thing that got plowed on Neil's farm was Joni Mitchell. Heyooo!).

**Back to the Bible**. Even after surrounding him with a cavalcade of animals, G-d recognized that Adam remained sad and purposeless. Thus, a corresponding human (i.e., the first woman) was created. Yet in order to make Eve, G-d had to break Adam (remember? a rib was removed). Y'all read Genesis? Ever since this pivotal moment in mankind's evolution, man has been eternally cursed (or blessed) to need a woman in order to complete himself. Per the scriptures, a man, by himself, is fragmented and imperfect. Only a woman can restore him to the prophetic divinity of indivisible oneness that he once knew, for only a brief, fleeting moment, during his initial breath of life. She is of he. Flesh of flesh & bone of bone, both dependent upon the other. The erotically-uttered, verge-of-climax phrase "Fill me up" is an acknowledgment of the divine union of man and woman. Put dat penis in da pagina, and we become one. Let's cleave, baby!

Jared now knew the feeling. After years upon years of shameless ignorance, he was suddenly all too aware of the grayscale loneliness of wintertime; the somber, minor key tone of the days; and the un-consoled late night shivers. The misery of knowing that while you're alone and weeping profusely at the unrelenting realization that all memories of her had unexpectedly reached their expiration date, she's out gallivanting with the coolest of the cool dudes, at all the downtown hotspots you were never hip enough to know about. But I continue breathing, in my anguished and empty existence. I breathe, although we will no longer share these breaths together. Once, we exchanged the air around us. We giggled and cuddled, as you'd playfully tap my nose. Why'd you always do that? It was nonsensical, but oh so cute and playful. Today, my heart swells and I sigh whenever I think back on those memories. It's over. The solitude of this moment further amplifies your absence.

And then, the phone rang. The abruptness of the receiver's shrill frequency retrieved Jared from the depths of his downward spiral. He quickly composed himself.

"Hello?"

She spoke in a hushed, shy-Asian-schoolgirl whisper.

"Hi baby."

"Amy?"

"Yes. Are you okay?"

"Uh, not particularly."

"I– I changed my mind."

"What?"

"I was wrong."

An immediate sense of relief began to emerge from within Jared's all-too-recently mangled heart. He proceeded with utmost caution, carefully balancing his joy and excitement ("Yay, she's back!") with his confusion and concern ("But why'd she leave in the first place?").

"Yeah? I agree, Amy. I mean, I really don't know what else to say. I'm kinda confused here." He held back, suppressing his urge to proclaim 'Hooray for Rydell!'

"I'm sorry, Jared."

He was tiptoeing on a teeter-totter. One wrong move and she'll change her mind again. Be nice, but remain the victim.

"That's alright. You needn't apologize. I just don't understand. What was the point of all that?"

"I think I was just nervous. I felt scared. Ya know? To give my heart to someone. To be vulnerable and open. But during this past hour I realized that I'm ready to take a chance. With you."

"Let's give it a try, cute cake."

"I think we're meant to be together, Jared. I really do. But to love, fully and completely, one must surrender their heart to another. It requires a great deal of trust and dependence. I honestly wasn't sure if I could follow through with such a demand."

She cleared her throat. A preparatory tactic practiced by those who're about to expound on a point.

"A girl's parents provide the prototype by which she defines love, and I don't necessarily have the best example. My mama may've made a mistake by marrying my daddy, and I do not intend to replicate her foibles. It was that feeling – the stern denouncement of my broken home – that led me to call you an hour ago and break it off. But in the interim period, I realized the fatal error of my decision.

"By means of simple observation, our parents teach us lessons in 2 distinct ways: we either learn what *to do*, or what *not to do*. Repeat what works and discard what doesn't. That way, each generation becomes an improvement of its predecessor.

"In fact, this methodology applies to all of mankind. It is not solely limited to bestowals of exemplary parentage. We, as a species, learn by observation and imitation. Perhaps inadvertently, we often attempt to replicate the lifestyles of our role models, whilst avoiding the mistakes of the losers.

"Moreover, we are not exclusively limited to the passive, sideline procurements of such guidance. Rather, our ragged elders eagerly await those (all-too-rare) sacred opportunities to counsel us with cautionary tales concerning completed battles, lost and won.

"In all aspects of life, it is those who endure the experience that acquire the lesson. They are martyrs for the story's moral. Such wisdom is then handed down to the next generation, as an intangible form of inheritance we call 'advice.' A list of do's and do not's. Listen up, children!

"Everyday I observe how miserable my mommy is. I see the pain occasioned by corrupted love. I have consequently decided to distance myself from all of her avoidable faults. I don't ever want to end up like her.

"Here's my dilemma, Jared. I really like you. A lot. I fucking adore you. Okay? That is what I feel, truly and genuinely, deep within my soul. If I were to listen to the knowledge of my ancestors, I'd've run the moment I felt the first flutter of my heart. And perhaps my childlike aspiration of unquestioned obedience to the advice of my parents was what initially compelled me to break up with you. But once I hung up the phone, I was alone. I was alone and my heart was broken. I felt as though I were betraying the desires and yearnings of my own soul. Ay, herein lies the quandary. Do I honor my own adolescent whims, or do I suppress myself, in faithful allegiance to the teachings of my forbearers? Each path refuses to countenance the alternative. It didn't take me long to discover the solution. In fact, the answer is quite simple.

"To demonstrate, let's contemplate a scenario where you and I both embrace this relationship, without any hesitation. Against the advice of my mother, I dive, full-bore, into your urethral canal. Say we share a couple of decent, good-lovin' years together until our bond eventually begins to disintegrate. It's a slow but unavoidable spiral of decay. (Don't worry baby, this is only a hypothetical!) It begins innocuously; but minor irritations, if left untreated, fester and expand into gargantuan, monolithic barriers between our exposed hearts. And finally, of course, it all ends in a catastrophic and tragic downfall, leaving us both shattered and broken. Oh the humanity! I'm sure in that moment, as I'm buried in blankets and convulsing wildly, I'll think to myself, 'Dang, I shoulda listened to mommy. This all could've been avoided if only I woulda listened to mommy.' Thus, by refusing to heed advice, I end up making a terrible mistake; the very mistake my mama prophetically warned me about.  Right?  Well, now let's consider the sterility and dullness of a life lived according to incontestable commandments.  Sure, I probably wouldn't have been hurt, had I abstained from a doomed relationship.  I'd be an unblemished beauty, basking in spectral starlight.  But I would also be condemned to spend the rest of my life always wondering what could've been with that cute little boy from school.  On those lonesome nights, while I gently caress my dutifully-preserved labia (as I imagine the tantalizing and seductive way in which denim drapes atop the curve of your butt), I would assuredly doubt whether the tradeoff was worth it.  That's it!  Don't you see, Jared?  Eternal doubt is the cost of heeding advice; whereas those who endure the experience themselves have confirmed with absolute certainty that the lesson is accurate.  They can then proceed with their lives, confidently, having validated grandpa's suggestions (ultimately, that's all advice is: a mere suggestion), rather than hinging crucial decisions on their blind faith as to the veracity of such advice.  No, no, no!  I shan't allocate unchallenged trust in the life lessons learned by another.  As spectators, we are only afforded a slight glimpse, ne'er the full context, of the cumulative happenings in one man's life that generate such advice.  How are we to ever fully comprehend the grand precipice from which his learned tales are transmitted?  I refuse to live vicariously, for better or for worse.  I vow to perceive the purity of my own emotions.  When I feel joy, I will bathe in the tranquility of knowing that I am reaping the full reward of my decision.  And when I endure pain, it will yield value, only to me, as I will focus on the lesson derived from the pain, not the fleeting sensation of the pain itself.  But always, I will make my own pain and learn my own lessons."

Jared fumbled for a relevant reference.  Uhhh…

- This above all: to thine own self be true.
- Nosce te ipsum.
- Those who do not remember the past are condemned to relive it.

He was relieved.  His frightening plummet toward the unexplored depths of despair ended with a buoyant bounce on a marshmallow cushion. She gently plucked him from the emerging darkness and replenished his soul with light.

"My darling, I have no doubt that you made the right decision."

"We'll see."

He flipped. Once it was all over, as soon as the phone call had concluded, Jared was awarded with a welcome sensation: the exact (emotional) inverse from the previous hour of tumult. He forgot all about the heartache that overbore his fragile, pube-ridden anima during the brief lapse in their relationship. The stalled rotary of love's dreaded lacuna. Instead, he was inundated with the purest sense of jubilation he had ever known. Rejoice! 'Twas a moment worthy of unmitigated exultation.

At dusk, Jared was invited to accompany his sister and her friend on a walk through the neighborhood. He joined, skipping and dancing the length of the entire voyage. At one point, his sister noted that she had never seen him so happy.

He thought he had conquered the debilitating sadness of heartbreak. It was all over, for good. He had survived. And now, hand in hand, he and Amy would gently coast toward the happily-ever-after sunset of true love's attainment.

Oh child, was he ever wrong. That temporary moment of loneliness was but a brief preview of what was to come.

Not all residents of The Land of Forgotten Souls shared Patricia's timid, identity-crushing reluctance to fight. Rather, most had accumulated a lifetime of pent-up rage and unresolved daddy issues. Any authority figure was a threat, and they were seething with a frightening eagerness to quash his looming presence out of their lives. Our father, who art the scapegoat I blame for all my failures and shortcomings, your destruction will give birth to a new age. Dawn is approaching . . .

A hideous monsoon of a woman rose through the ranks to lead the assault. She had relinquished her birth name (these folks are feverishly inclined to denounce any trace of tradition in their lives; instead, everything is contemporary and devoid of substance) and was now known by her alias: Winter Tide Peach Mother Sumptuous.

The ritual naming of one's child is the first act a new parent performs. Thus, to amend your formally-bestowed title is to refuse your father from day one. Fuck you, daddy. I'll change my own diapers.

She was fat. In her idiomatic 'former life,' she had been an art connoisseur. A hopeless fan girl with no discernable talent of her own. She gained credibility by consuming the creative output of others, rather than contributing to the overloaded dumpster fire. Wait! (and withhold judgment.) This is not an insult. Not every single person must 'make art' to be worthy of life's blessings. Don't look down on her. We all have a purpose here. Not everyone is destined to sculpt shrines and compose odes. In fact, many err by mistakenly anointing themselves as artists. Ugh. This self-inflicted condemnation can extinguish the otherwise great potential of the fiercest fireball. Oh, what a waste of a lifetime, when the Sabbath is spent doodling.

### ARTIST? NOPE, TURNS OUT YOU'RE JUST A DRUG ADDICT

She had her fat little finger on the pulse of the latest trends in obscure foreign cinema. Her social mode was the ability to recommend a film you've never heard of. The more ethnic the better. She sustained herself for years with this lifestyle, as the hip indie film chick. Yea, dude. Of course her hair is black! Were you picturing anything else?

The water dispute elicited something within her. A dark and hostile force, unnecessarily aggressive and frightening, erupted from beneath the mounds of cellulite. She became radicalized, almost instantaneously. Her hair-triggered ethos clicked into overdrive, and she was thirsty for blood.

She had no known god to pray to. Thus, activism became her religion. But nothing intelligent, civil or well-organized. She preferred the chaotic tantrum method of protest, where getting arrested is the highest honor one can hope to achieve.

When the guns arrived, she salivated. Finally, a tool worthy of her rancor. A tool that could compensate for her lack of physicality.

Love songs suddenly possessed a new meaning. The tunes Jared had previously enjoyed in a passive, unattached, dangling-atop-the-surface, intrigued (but wholly unaware) sense now revealed hidden depths hitherto unknown to him; and, consequently, altogether un-traversed by his squeaky-clean sneakers. Oh... so that's what he's singing about. I too feel the yearning!

Concerning overt expressions of this feeling, the song "Your Body is a Wonderland" by John Mayer particularly resonated with Jared. Something about its concise, sweet-hearted simplicity appealed to him. The pre-chorus chord changes (i.e., when he sings "This is bound to be a while") being the definitive highlight. It's the perfect love song primer for a young boy on the brink of his first schoolyard romance. A blatant expression of love (mostly sexual) with a few easily digestible metaphors sprinkled in for good measure.

During that first summer, everyday after his European History/World Studies class, when Jared got home, he would rush into his room, sit on his bed, put on his headphones and engulf himself in the crisp tones of Mr. Mayer. He'd put that dang song on repeat. It quickly became the anthem of his heart, as lil' pumper would beat in time to da tempo.

<u>The second emotional surge of jealousy and suspicion</u>
It seemed that every year of high school, Jared and his buds would select a different location to congregate during the lunch hour. Throughout the summer session of 2002, they

decided to sit outside the main campus building, which was located directly across from the library. Got it?

So, one day, during lunchtime, Jared emerged from the library and approached his true and trusted friends. As usual, they were all enrapt in the uproarious splendor of American adolescence. Except, this time, something was off. Really off. It took Jared a moment to comprehend what he saw. At first, he was mentally unable to process the sight, like a native spotting an approaching ship on the horizon. But soon enough, the vision became crystal clear: Amy was sitting on Charlie's lap.

Naturally, an outburst followed.

"What the fuck!?" screamed the furious schoolboy.

The group's laughter fell off fast, but the perpetrators' error was not immediately apparent. They knew Jared was mad, but were oblivious as to why. To them, there was absolutely nothing wrong with this seating arrangement.

Finally, she simply asked, "What?" in a manner completely genuine and confused. Though the underlying cadence of her voice suggested she was a bit perturbed that Jared had interrupted their fun.

"Why are you sitting on his lap? Get off! That's disgusting."

She rose in reluctant obedience to her master's command.

"Oh, come on, Jared."

She approached him.

"Don't worry, we were just being silly."

He stared at Amy while his inner torment faded away and was replaced with embarrassment.

"Okay. Sorry. I just didn't know what was going on. It startled me."

"Baby, it's okay."

He looked past Amy, at Charlie, who remained seated. The rest of the guys quietly whispered to each other. Charlie nervously shifted his gaze up toward Jared.

Jared scowled.

Charlie played it off liked the stupidest country bumpkin you'd ever seen. Sorry dude, my cock must've overpowered my civilized and rational mind. You could tell he felt bad. His dumb doe eyes suggested his guilt. But he only felt bad because he got caught. I'm sure part of the thrill was how naughty it all felt.

Her ass on his dick,
Four layers of clothing between,
While Jared is nowhere to be seen.

Oops.

That evening, while listening to John Mayer, Jared couldn't connect to the music. Instead of the joys of young love, the song only conjured feelings of anger and resentment. He now heard the chorus as "Your Body is in Charlie's Lap."

He never listened to it again.

And so began the backroom dealings of Charlie and Amy. Sneaky little letters changing hands like a schoolyard drug deal. A sly, on-the-side exchange. Whispered witticisms of compassionate concern. Surely this could never evolve into an emotionally tethered, deep-rooted bond, reaching depths far beyond Jared's cursory ability to "relate" to Amy.

What can I say? He just gets me. He understands me in a way that you are incapable of grasping. Charlie and I share a similar wound. You're lucky not to know such pain.

**Every once in a while, a man must roll around in his own shit.**

Ah! Life's goodness. Despite everything, I remain grateful.

**A mistake of his own making.**

Here they sat, in Eddie's bedroom, during the weekly meeting of the failures (The Numbed Boys Club), desperately distracting themselves from the true potential of the moment. Nah, long ago they decided to forgo fulfillment and opted instead to torch their skulls of all purposeful, clear-headed ambition.

They remained stuck on one side of life's possibilities, removed from all forms of genuine sensation.

Everyday, Jared felt the tickle of addiction. It had smothered him whole. He often wondered, 'How can people live without drugs? Life is oh so dull otherwise.' In considering the void of understanding between the tripped out and the civilized, he rationalized his current lot by concluding (semi-convincingly) that all humanity is hopelessly dependent upon something; that, or they're wretchedly restraining themselves. We all feel the pull from a weakness of great allure. We can either avoid it or embrace it. This dull, halfhearted justification allowed for the peaceful acceptance of his disease.

"Put on some music," Bernardo requested, interrupting the addict's dilemma. "Have you listened to the Pinocchio song by Cursive? Dude! You gotta hear it. It's called 'Driftwood.' I'm sure Eddie has it."

Eddie had left the room (to let his dog out), leaving Jared unsupervised at his computer. While scanning the desktop for his Winamp player, Jared noticed a text file titled: Letter to Amy.

'What the hell is this?' he thought, alarmed.

He was frightened, but couldn't resist. He opened the letter and began reading.

```
Dear Amy,
     I am absolutely disgusted by your behavior
recently.  I can't believe you had sex with that
22-year-old Marine guy.  You had only just met
him!  And then, when you were telling everyone
at school about it, you were practically
bragging.  You were so undeservedly proud of
yourself.  What the fuck is wrong with you?  You
have become such a repulsive slut.  If you
```

Eddie returned, and Jared quickly closed the document, before getting a chance to read the whole thing. They never spoke of it. Jared never knew whether this letter was ever delivered to its intended recipient, or what motived Eddie to even write such a letter.

"Scan the perimeter. Establish a grid and search every last inch of South Forts. She's out there, somewhere. I know it. Must be nearby, too. How far could my little girl have gone?"

Wilbur commanded the room, his voice booming throughout the palace corridor. The legion of South Forts (his noble followers) sat listening, obediently, anxiously waiting for him to finish, as though the moment his lips emitted the final "." they'd rush into formation.

"Patricia, the Bright Princess, is missing. In fact, she's been gone for quite some time now. The Queen and I had initially decided not to share this information with anyone outside the confines of our own bedroom. We assumed that she'd eventually return of her own accord, after her casual romp reached its inevitable, naturally occurring conclusion. Once she fully flushed all the hedonistic abandon outta her system. Well, she ain't back yet. Anyone seen her lately? Hmm... Thought not. She is, instead, among the great expanse. The ode-earning, poet-blessed, ritual-devouring realm of the dreaded outside. Methinks she is consumed with delusions. I a poet, daddy. Listen to my waste. Sloppy stanzas and burnt out prose."

He approached the window, overlooking the kingdom, and began screaming.

"I know you're out there, Patricia. Still groping and grinding thy days away."

He continued addressing his hypothetically-present daughter, in a slightly more subdued tone.

"It's okay, sweetie. You're just confused. I did this too when I was your age. It's okay to fuck around and suck a dick or 2 (simultaneously). Just don't do any permanent damage. Avoid that dreaded gum rot at all costs. And above all else, preserve your mind. You can become the redeemed whore, so long as your mind remains intact during those grungy gangbangs."

He turned back to his men, slightly embarrassed. He had revealed more than he intended. Uh oh, he said his private thoughts out loud. He quickly regained his (attempted) confidence. Alrighty, back to business.

"It appears that we must now actively compel her return. Hence, you. Yes, you are to assemble a search party to locate our BP."

As he spoke, their feet shook, barely able to contain their enthusiasm. Finally, something to do!

"I am declaring this a national emergency that must be dealt with immediately. Now go, find her. I expect nightly reports of your progress."

After the figurative gavel dropped, the men rushed into formation and began scouring the landscape, leaving Wilbur alone in the conference hall. He smiled, basking in his rightly deserved sense of accomplishment.

He returned to the royal bedroom, expecting Marjorie to be happy (because of the hopeful promise his actions provided) and proud of him (because he had finally taken charge of the situation). But instead, she looked quiet, forlorn and despondent.

"Cheer up, darling. The boys are out searchin'. I'm sure they'll find her in no time! In fact, I've got an excellent suggestion for you. Howsabout you start planning some sort of welcoming parade. Nothing too garish, but something that'll remind her that she is loved and cherished by us and all her fellow citizens. Yeah?"

She was quiet, still, gazing blankly out the window. In the distance she could see the searchers, fumbling about, all clumsy and stupid. She turned toward her husband, seemingly in slow motion. Finally, she faced him.

"Do you expect me to rejoice at this occasion? Your untimely orders deserve no mention, certainly no praise. You are the leader of South Forts, for G-d's sake."

"Sweetheart, why the hostility? I've issued a directive ordering the—"

"Yes, I am fully aware of your reluctantly-issued order. It's a miracle you did anything at all. I'm the wench who prodded you into finally taking action! It wasn't a gentle nudge either. Rather, 'twas a strong whollop that finally set you in motion.

"Honestly, Wilbur, I don't understand how you've managed to rise through the ranks and attain the pinnacle position of status in our little empire. Must've been your birthright. Or maybe all that babble about privilege is true after all. Regardless, here you are. And lucky me, here I am too. For goodness sake, you are the most timid and unassertive leader this nation has ever known."

"Sweetiepie..."

"At the risk of further devaluing the writer's fledgling ability, allow me to simply list the various ways I currently feel: sad, frustrated, annoyed, confused and restless.

"It's because of you, Wilbur; because of your indecisiveness. If you haven't figured it out yet, this issue goes much deeper than the current tragedy of our missing daughter. I am beginning to question whether I can stand by you any longer.

"When I was a little girl, I used to envision my future husband. He was honest, decisive and Latino. You are none of those things!

"You never would've assembled the search party if I hadn't implicitly demanded that you do so. Instead, you likely would've sat around, relying on hope and positive thoughts to bring her back."

"Untrue, cunt! I have been heavily invested in matters of critical importance, on a grand scale. Forgive me, but when a man decides to devote himself to serving the public interest, he must relinquish all concern for the self, including, if necessary, his own family.

"I don't think you realize the full extent of the utter catastrophe that would befall this land, were our water supply to suddenly vanish. Trust me toots, when people begin to slaughter each other for a measly sip, you'll ask: Patricia who?"

"Those are the words of a monster."

"Uh, no. Those are the words of a man concerned with the nation he has sworn to serve. It's a simple numbers game, with protection of life being the king's #1 priority. Ensure his subjects can live and flourish, the rest works itself out.

"So, let's apply the formula. I'd sacrifice 1 person to save 100. Even if that 1 person was my own daughter. Even if that 1 person was you. Hell, even if that 1 person was myself. Anyone who disagrees with that sentiment has no place in politics.

"Sorry if I've been a bit preoccupied, but I've been ensuring the continued existence of South Forts. We'll carry on without her, if need be."

At that moment, she realized that their values were not in alignment. Perhaps they never had been. It's just that they'd never been put to the test before. And now, naked (figuratively), she saw the man she had married. She saw him, and was disgusted.

Oblivious, he continued.

"Our remaining resources are limited. Nearly our entire armed forces are on their way to the hippie enclave up north. What's it called? The Land of the Lonely? Something like that. You should be more appreciative. Despite our limited manpower, I've still managed to assemble a search crew to locate that little brat of ours. But instead, you've decided to take this opportunity to complain. Shocking. How about a little gratitude here? This was no easy task."

"I want a divorce."

Another riveting instance of betrayal occurred during those summer school days. And while we're on the subject, let's just get everything out in the open (we're trying to flesh out a coherent story here, after all. Every insignificant detail will be represented). Amy was re-enrolled in Spanish I. This was a required course for all 9ᵗʰ graders (or, for the high-brow imbeciles with no interest in the practical application of their primary education, French was an alternate option). Now, in proper realization of the dim-witted, white trash bitch that she was, Amy had failed her first year Spanish course. Thus, she was enrolled in the summertime repeat session. Let's do it all over again, estúpidos. Naturally, all the kids in this particular class were kinda dumb. Sheesh! Spanish I ain't that difficult.

For the summer school program, all schools within the district were combined. 𝕬𝖓𝖉 𝖘𝖔, 𝖆 𝖓𝖊𝖜 𝖆𝖓𝖉 𝖚𝖓𝖋𝖆𝖒𝖎𝖑𝖎𝖆𝖗 𝖒𝖆𝖘𝖘 𝖔𝖋 𝖘𝖙𝖚𝖉𝖊𝖓𝖙𝖘 𝖉𝖊𝖘𝖈𝖊𝖓𝖉𝖊𝖉 𝖚𝖕𝖔𝖓 𝖔𝖚𝖗 𝖍𝖚𝖒𝖇𝖑𝖊 𝖘𝖈𝖍𝖔𝖔𝖑. Now, picture this: not only is Amy in Spanish for dullards, but they're also bussing in students from the less-pristine sections of the district. Ya know, the charming and rugged po' boys. My favorite!

As luck would have it, Amy had the motherfucker of all motherfuckers in her class. Let's call him Alex. This fella takes a likin' to sweet thang Amy. Of course, we all did. They flirted throughout the summer, and (as the story goes) he approached her after class one day and simply said, "I really want to kiss you right now." She froze. Apparently, he interpreted her silence as an invitation to follow through with his blatantly expressed desires. So, Alexander the Grape went for it. He kissed lil' Amy right on the fucking lips in the fucking hall fucking way. And that was that.

Amy immediately confessed this incident to Jared. He was devastated, particularly because at this point, A+J hadn't even kissed yet. Thus, Amy's first kiss was not with her boyfriend. Rather, it was with some forgettable faggot in her summer school class. There was no romance, no passion. No! He stole the kiss. Stole it right outta her pristine, untouched lips. Violated her chastity. Such a poop head.

<u>Silly Goose: Teacher's Edition</u>
So, like, what's the significance of this story? Not the entire book, just this particular anecdote. The aggressive kissy boy. There are some recurring themes here. Compare and

contrast this event with the Marine that Amy fucked (or did he fuck her?). Both of these situations involve a dude making his intentions known and Amy putting up no resistance. Well, what's to resist? She wants it. She loves that ███. Also, Amy immediately confessed both of these encounters to Jared. But, there's also a stark difference between these 2 situations (besides the extent of the physical contact). At least with the Marine, A+J had been broken up at the time. There was no infidelity. But Alex is another story. Amy and Jared had only just begun their relationship. Why did she go through with the kiss? Also, when she told Jared about it, she didn't portray herself as an unwitting victim. She was down for the cause. Surprisingly, this was not a moment of devastation for Jared. It was more frustrating than upsetting. He was so forgiving right off the bat. Sure, he was jealous and upset, but he didn't make a fuss. Why don't you ever stand up for yourself, Jared?

He's of a particular breed of weak men. Conflict averse at all costs. Whenever something bad happens, warranting a reaction of justifiable anger, he instead swallows the bowl of shit he's been served, smiles and declares, "It's all good, man. No worries." He doesn't know how to deal with negative emotions. Rather than confronting the darkness within him, he buries it, deeper and deeper with each passing day…

Somehow, the worst sadness always seemed to occur during the summer months. Remember that seemingly crippling depression on those empty nights, knowing she's out there with someone else. She doesn't want me. And here I am, alone, left to struggle with these thoughts.

"I've got two eighths."

"So, a quad?"

"Yea dude, whatever. Sure."

"No need to get testy, my boy. Just want to make sure we're properly reducing those fractions."

"Thanks, teach! I could always use an impromptu refresher of the concepts we learned in my 3$^{rd}$ grade mathematics class. After all, you never know when it might come in handy."

"Fuck yea. I'm an pedagogical gunslinger."

They chuckled in acknowledgement of a well-deployed, Rickle-roasted ribbing. That is, until the gruesome reality of the moment set in.

"Ugh. It's actually kinda shameful."

"What?"

"Just this whole transaction. Such an uncouth implementation of those childhood lessons."

"Oy vey. Don't go there, man. We gotta embark on this voyage with an optimistic outlook. Remember? To safely cross the threshold, one must have a healthy mindset. If your mental forecast is bleak, we'll have to reschedule."

"Right, right. I'll be fine, man. Just allow me to explain why I said '2 eighths,' as opposed to '1 quarter.' I don't want you thinking I'm some sort of incompetent imbecile, Jared. Now, I had originally purchased a single eighth for you and me. Since, as you'll recall, the plan was that it'd just be the two of us taking this journey together; and, forgive me for suggesting this, but perhaps it should've remained that way. But alas, I was no swimmer, and here we are today. Anyways, you got all excited saying how Charlie wanted to join us too. And who am I to deny you? Of course he can come along. Your trusty, unthreatening companion. I should've anticipated such. And what's Charlie's response once we invite him? 'Uh, can Eddie come too?' Jesus, you guys. Inseparable. Welp, given the revised circumstances, I clearly had to get more supplies. You see, dosage is very important when taking mushrooms; or so I've heard. In order to ensure that we're all on the same level, I purchased another eighth. Hence, 2 eighths."

"Yummy mushies, I can't wait!"

Jared's response indicated that he couldn't care less about Bernardo's loquacious rationalization for his slip-o'-da-tongue. He was too excited to concern himself with such trivial matters. Up until this point, the brotherhood had been steadily enjoying a hefty intake of marijuana. Oopsie daisy, it had become a daily occurrence.

In fact, Jared had recently experienced the sad milestone that befalls the skewed life of every budding stoner: his first solo smoke. It occurred during a weeknight while Jared's mom was out to dinner with a girlfriend (Hi Judi! You made it into the book). After enjoying a pleasant dinner with his dad and sister, which consisted of takeout in front of the television, Jared announced that he was going to go for a late night bike ride around the neighborhood.

"But it's dark out."

"I know. Just wanna go for a quick ride. I'll be back soon."

"Alright…"

Thus began my life as a writer. Huh? You see, in this instance, Jared demonstrated that he would rather partake in a solitary activity than spend time with his family. Dangerous choice. What a wasted evening!

My father passed away a couple years ago. As I recall this moment, I feel a strong sense of regret. When your dad dies (or anyone for that matter), your memories of him become fixed. I will never again share a moment with him; at least, not on this plane of existence. (Here's hoping for an afterlife!) Presently, when I think about how I opted to go for a bike ride (with the ulterior motive of getting high) rather than spend time with my dad, it rips my fucking heart out. He was the most brilliant man I've ever known, and I wish I could redo nights such as this. If I could, we'd sit together, sip soda and converse. Tell me stories. Give me advice. Share with me all of your wisdom. Because one day you'll be gone and I'll be forced to endure life without you.

Honorable mentions: the time you asked if I wanted to see <u>Borat</u> with you, and I declined. What did I do instead? Got high. This was on a Saturday afternoon, when I literally had nothing else to do. Sure, I had already seen the film, but that is no excuse. And now, looking back, I wish to flog myself in disappointment. How fucking great would it be to sit next to my father and watch that utterly brilliant and hilarious movie! What a precious moment that would've been. I hang my head in shame at my decision. That film now serves as a constant reminder of my selfish idiocy.  Also, I recall the time I returned home from a recent smoke sesh with Eddie (I remember vibing hard to the lyrics of "Dodo" by Dave Matthews during the drive home), and you were sitting in your chair, quietly reading.  You said something to the effect of, "Hi!  How are you, my only son?  I love you so much.  Watching you grow up has been such a glorious experience.  From my perspective, every day has been a miracle.  Look at you.  You're sort of an adult now.  I must ask, are you properly navigating this blessed curse of life?  Are you fully utilizing all the fortunes I have bestowed upon you?  I, Richard, voluntarily decided to invite you into this world, because I was certain that the joys of life outweighed the sorrows.  So, whaddya think?"  And I didn't even stop walking.  I just said, "Hey.  Nothing much."  And headed straight to my room and closed the door.  Again, isolating myself from true glory.  A few minutes later, you confronted me and yelled, "What's the matter with you?  How come you never talk to me anymore?  You never tell me anything."  I don't even remember how I responded.  Ugh.  I was such an ungrateful, worthless piece of shit.

Note: Please, if you are reading this and your father is still alive, spend as much time with him as you can, because he is going to die.  It is a certainty.  And after he's gone, all opportunities for further communication are suddenly vanquished.  The end.  Worse still, you'll often have these little moments where you forget he's gone.  It lasts only a second; but within that brief instant you'll have the sudden urge to call him, to ask a question of critical import, or to simply say hi.  But then you'll remember.

Rather, the spoiled nitwit reached under his bed and removed the discrete lockbox containing his pipe, lighter and (of course) a lil' bag of weed.  He dropped the supplies in his pocket, hopped on his bike and rode down the road to a nearby bush capable of concealing his activities.  Jared packed a bowl, and...

Of course, he was too young to realize how stupid this all was. As a replacement for the slow distillation of learnt lessons that one acquires from a well-lived boyhood, he opted, instead, for the instantaneous conjuring (i.e., a blast of THC to the dome) of a false and undeserved sense of independence, with the slightest little hint of rebellion.

Suitably high, Jared hopped back on his bike and went for a Hofmann joyride.

This next part may seem like a dumb, uninspired metaphor; but I assure you, it is 100% true. He approached a hill and decided to ride up to the top. Simple enough. Good for you, buddy. That's a challenge, at least, requiring self-determination and the expenditure of energy. Jared thought to himself how the upward climb would represent his newfound struggle to make sense of the chaotic, shitty mess of his life.

So the symbolism goes like this: the difficult physical exertion of the uphill climb is my currently doomed, sorrow-ridden and dwindling will to live. However, once I approach the top of the mountain, I will curve sharply and ride back down. The effortless, fun and carefree descent shall represent the day I finally overcome this damned dilemma. Got it? That's the analogy Jared crafted for himself. Now, I kid you not, when Jared reached the summit and began to turn back around, he fell. He attempted his turn on the still-sloped section of the road, thereby causing his bike to topple over, right onto the concrete. He lay motionless on the ground, defeated.

Rather than interpret this moment as a warning from The Almighty that perhaps this new "hobby" of his was a potential-draining, motivation-erasing, ambition-quashing mistake, Jared (whether solo or with his friends) began smoking weed daily.

Getting high soon became a regular occurrence. An essential prelude to every activity. The only problem with this arrangement is that getting high itself eventually becomes the activity. Por ejemplo, 'Hey, wanna get high and go play mini golf?' eventually becomes, simply, 'Hey, wanna get high?'

Despite my readily apparent disdain for drug use, I'd be remiss if I didn't at least acknowledge the immutable fact that we actually had quite a lot of fun in those days. Marijuana was the perfect supplement to our nerdy fascination with the fantastical. It was genuine halfling's leaf. This culminated in the eventual development of a cute little drug-induced, roleplaying game between Jared and Bernardo. After getting high enough, they would each grab an empty 2-liter bottle and engage in a mock, medieval sword fight, complete with affected accents and Old English prose.

For a moment, smoking weed managed to fully capture (and in a way, represent) teenage innocence. That shimmering period of time where shared laughter seemed to echo into eternity, completely unobstructed, mercifully cascading through the still endless horizon of our lives. The best of times, indeed.

Nevertheless, as any drug addict in the throes of his disease will refuse to admit (and trust me, they become hostile when pressed on this. Defend the disease, at all costs!), it doesn't take long for the thrill to subside. After a few months of this routine, da ganj and the accompanying faux-enlightenment it enables are no longer new and exciting. Soon enough, the boys' stoned insights no longer contained the same fleeting significance (Hurry bro! Write this shit down. We've solved the mystery of life! Surely this will seem equally as profound in the morning). Eventually, you gotta up the stakes. The gateway beckons and you begin researching psychedelics. Jared dedicated considerable time to reading online forums devoted to recreational drug use. He read of mystical, mind-melting experiences with baited breath.

Who needs religion when you've got DMT? Skip the synagogue, suck down a burning bong load and (gasp) interrupt G-d. Jared's bookshelf soon contained the same terrible tripe that every lost soul purchases when weed no longer gets you there and you begin considering stronger substances: Cosmic Trigger by Robert Anton Wilson and The Doors of Perception by Aldous Huxley. Oh, and let's not forget the interchangeable nonsense of America's favorite loon bat, Tim Leary. Jared chose High Priest. What difference does it make?

And with that, it was time to trip.

The next day, in the early afternoon, Jared, Bernardo and Charlie met at their sacred hillside spot: Earth. They had brought with them a blanket, a bottle of orange juice, a pack of Lunchables, a stereo and a quarter ounce of psilocybin mushrooms. While Jared and Bernardo made little shroom-laced sandwiches, Charlie gave Eddie a call.

"Hey man. We're about to take them. Come meet us…Yea, we have enough for you…Well, they're supposed to last a while, so you have to take them early…I don't know, like 8 hours…Yes, we're already here…Alright, see you soon."

Charlie hung up.

"He's on his way. He said not to wait for him, that we should just take 'em now."

Bernardo handed him a sandwich.

"Bon appetite, my freak!"

All 3 boys held a sandwich in their dominant hand. They did a 'cheers' and quickly ate them. The cracker/cheese/meat combo concealed the taste.

"Wait! Before this kicks in, I feel like we should take a moment to reflect on what's about to happen here. Maybe we can each share what we hope to gain from this experience. Personally, I am ready to have the hidden forces of nature revealed to me, to touch and see the transfer of energy between all life forms, and to feel the singular, interconnected breath of this planet."

"Me, I don't really know what to expect. I guess I'm ready for whatever happens."

"Charlie?"

"Oh man, I can't wait to see some crazy shit, like talking bunny rabbits."

He started laughing with anticipation. Jared became enraged.

"Charlie, you have to stop viewing drugs in a comic book fashion. This isn't a kooky game show for your amusement. It's a spiritual quest."

Jared's outburst caused an uncomfortable tension to arise amidst the fragile atmosphere. Not a good start to the boys' first trip. Uh oh, his anger is seeping through. Fear? Maybe the drugs will bring what he has been suppressing up to the surface. You can't hide from this forever, Jared. You must confront the demon who sits right in front of you.

Anxious to alleviate the tension, Bernardo flicked on his stereo. For the occasion, he decided to play The Mars Volta's Deloused in the Comatorium.

"Dude, chill. I get all that. But I'm also hoping we'll have a good time and share some laughs."

They listened to the deceivingly tranquil opening to an otherwise masterfully chaotic album, hoping to derive new layers of sound that sober ears simply cannot hear.

*Now I'm lost*

From the distance, Eddie approached.

"Lunchables? You guys are fucking ridiculous."

"Eddie! Save us from the void occasioned by Jared's reluctance to stand up for himself. Jared, you are mad at Charlie, and deservedly so. You should be. You have every right to be fucking furious with that bastard. But instead of expressing your anger, you just keep saying everything's okay. We'll just let it ride away. No! You must deal with this now. Life ain't a non-stop, groovy celebration. Sometimes there are conflicts that must be resolved. Charlie was not a nice boy. Not at all. Give him a smack or something. I'm sure he'd willingly consent to a jab in the jaw. He'd put up no resistance. 'Please punch me. I deserve it.' This is the only feasible option. Otherwise, your unaddressed anger will erupt in odd and uncomfortable moments, such as this. Brace yourself."

*It's been said*
*Long time ago*
*You'll be the first and last to know*

"We've got more for you. Lunchables and the secret ingredient, that is."

"Let's see 'em."

Bernardo handed Eddie the bag containing the last of the mushrooms. He examined them carefully. Inquisitive. Hmm…

"You guys feeling anything?"

"No, man. Not yet. It's supposed to take about an hour to kick in."

He removed one from the bag and took a tiny test bite.

"This is fucking disgusting."

"Um, yea. You gotta conceal the taste."

Jared handed him the mostly-devoured box of Lunchables.

"Here you go."

"This is all you have?"

"That, and orange juice."

"Alrighty. My favorite childhood snack will now be forever tainted."

He made a sandwich.

"Here we go!"

*Counting the toll, counting the toll*

The first indication that they'd begun to kick in was Jared's sudden urge to explore the surrounding area.

"Hey! Let's go on an adventure," he shouted, suddenly excited, uttering the motto of the confused and uncomfortable. He quickly became restless and needed to move around, to escape the confines of the brotherhood's small, circular seating formation (especially Charlie's looming presence).

*If you only knew the plans they had for us*

Dem mushies are seeping into your bloodstream and beginning to infiltrate your brain.

Bernardo got up, too. He must've felt the same way.

"Yea, man. I'm with you."

Charlie and Eddie remained seated. They were engaged in a playful discussion. To them, conversation was not confrontation. It was a joyous form of human connection. They were high and giggly.

"You guys coming?"

"No thanks. We'll wait here. Go on without us."

They waved goodbye and set out on their journey through the community hillside. Nature, preserved. Already, something was oddly majestic about the grassy terrain, more so than normal. The splendor of this particular landscape was amplified. The settings had been enhanced, upgraded and throttled to maximum capacity. They were cheerfully high, but didn't quite realize it yet. As they walked, the varying rhythm of their footsteps against the soil sounded noticeably musical.

Alongside the path, they encountered a large metal bowl, long ago abandoned by its owner. It was dirty and partially buried beneath the brush 'n willows.

*I've lost my way*

Jared picked up the bowl and studied it closely.

"Aha, Captain! I've got it. We shall collect various souvenirs from our trek, gather the finest specimens of nature's myriad harvest and collect them in this bowl. Upon our rimshot-rattled return, we'll share it with the boys."

"Yeah!!"

Bernardo's eyes nearly bulged out of his head. They were crazed.

We were somewhere around Calabasas, on the edge of the valley, when the drugs began to take hold.

They ran around like a couple of lunatics, stopping to inspect every leaf, every little bush, every twig. It was all miraculous. Each item was another key to the Kingdom of G-d. When they came upon a sweetgum tree fruit, they lost their shit.

At one point, they found a small, blue rubber ball and proceeded to commence a friendly game of catch. The innocence of the moment befuddled them.  They played liked children.  How we used to play.

*You should have seen, the curse that flew right by you*

They soon filled the bowl with miscellaneous foliage (and the ball).  It was time to return and show their non-participating friends the bounty.


When they arrived back at the picnic site, things began to take a turn toward the darker realms of their vulnerable and unhinged psyches.  Eddie and Charlie had left, but they took nothing with them.  Thus, when Jared and Bernardo approached, they were greeted with a trash-strewn blanket.  The sky immediately filled with clouds and, in an instant, everything turned gray.  A plastic wrapper gently fluttered in the wind.  They remained eerily still for a moment, allowing bare feelings of loneliness, abandonment and decay to set in.

Finally, Bernardo attempted to break the trance.

"Where'd they go?"

"Uh, I'm not sure.  Maybe back to my house.  I don't really know."

*Who brought me here?*

Bernardo was quiet.  The sudden bleakness brought the whimsy of the prior moments to an abrupt halt.  They boys' newly warped minds struggled to process the sight.  Jared reached over and held Bernardo's hand.  He squeezed back in solidarity.

"I'm scared."          BAD TRIP

"It's okay, man."

They stood together, silently, for a solid minute, stoically staring at the picnic blanket, as the sky somehow managed to get continually grayer with each passing second.  Clouds crowded overhead.

"I guess we should pack up and go find them."

"Sure."

They returned to Jared's bedroom to find Charlie struggling to plug in the Nintendo 64.  Eddie was sitting on the floor, petting the family dog, nearly in tears, muttering something about how "He's my best friend.  He understands."  Jared and

Bernardo attempted to share their various gifts; but now, in the artificial light of his bedroom, it was just junk. The magic was gone. Their show-and-tell extraordinaire didn't go quite as planned. Eddie and Charlie were not amused. After struggling to play Mario Party, the boys decided to go to the local movie theatre to see <u>Lemony Snicket's a Series of Unfortunate Events</u>, Jim Carrey's latest immersion into the mind of a mad man. The movie perfectly encapsulated the dreary, somber tone of their first trip.

Halfway through the flick, Jared had to pee. On his way down the narrow corridor that led to the bathroom, he saw a little boy sitting in the corner. This was a devastatingly unusual and unexpected sight. What is he doing here? The boy was clearly troubled. He sat with his arms wrapped around his bent knees, pulled up tight against his chest. Upon closer inspection, Jared realized that the little boy was him. His former self.

They locked eyes.

"Uh… it… it's… uhh… Hey. Hey there."

He was dumbfounded.

"Is this real?" he inquired.

The boy spoke as though this was an entirely ordinary exchange.

"Jared, I don't know how long this is going to last. So, while I have you here, I must know, do I– or, do *we* ever confront that moment? You know what I'm talking about. Is there ever some grand resolution? Or, is the plan to just ignore it until we die?"

He was taken aback. His mind rattled, struck by a descending trombone. The cursed memory had been uttered aloud.

"Nah man, it gets better."

Jared spoke in G-dless, stoner parlance. The boy's opening remarks had cut right to the core of his most vulnerable and well-guarded secret. Deploy the defense mechanisms! Go, go, go!

"Are you sure about that? You don't seem too happy. Already, I must say, Jared, I am rather disappointed. I guess… I just always assumed we were capable of so much more. Ya know? And now, to see you... You're just blank. You are lost within yourself. I don't think you've dealt with it yet, at all. Have you?"

"No."

He hung his head.

"I'm not surprised. By the size of your pupils, I'm guessing you've decided to pursue drug use instead of actual self-betterment. Wise choice, fool."

How dare he criticize my shame-inducing habit!

"Well, it's really fun most of the time. I'm thoroughly enjoying this phase."

"Oh, I'm sure it's a blast. But that shit does more harm than good. Why didn't you listen to your parents and teachers when they'd warn us of the dangers of drugs?"

Jared laughed.

"Dude, it turns out that's all bullshit. They don't get it."

"Hmm, so that's your role now? The enlightened, bratty teen who knows more than his elders? Top notch persona you've got there. It's a safe assumption that mom and dad, and the entire school board for that matter, had your best interests at heart in bestowing such advice. I mean, what do they gain by delivering those lectures? It's for you. Jared, adults have wisdom to share if you're willing to listen. Even a kid like me knows that there's no benefit to being high, particularly at the rate you seem to be puffing. What's the point? It functions to erase the day. Especially if you wake and bake. To smoke before the sun has set is equivalent to saying: Fuck today, let's end it immediately. And where do you end up?"

"Uhh..."

"You end up in tomorrow, none the wiser. Listen, Jared, this life is finite. We only have so many days. Please, for our sake, don't waste them by being wasted all the time. Because one day you'll realize how precious time is. And this, what you're doing now, this whole lifestyle you've adopted, it's a dead end. Think of what you could accomplish if you properly utilized your time."

Jared stood, staring at the boy, as he slowly faded away. He was right. Every desperate pothead knows this to be true. They smoke to silence such thoughts.

'Better to burn out,' Jared mumbled to himself.

While the meager search party was clumsily staggering along, the entire mass of the South Forts armed forces were making their way toward The Land of Forgotten Souls, well-equipped and ready to wreak havoc.

The following summer, Amy decided to cut her hair. Super short. She looked freakish. The kind of physical appearance that beckons anal. As if to signify that her butthole was pulsating (open and closed, repeat) in syncopated rhythm, emitting a friendly and welcoming sound, like the coo of a neighborhood pigeon. A full-bloom flower inviting pollination. Asking all those who're lucky enough to be involved in such a scene, "Please tickle me. Lick and caress the outer edge of my asshole until my moans, at first gentle and subdued, become operatic crescendos. I bite my bed sheets as you dip your finger inside me. I swallow it. My digestive tract has officially shifted into reverse. With your finger pumping up and down, in-and-out, my rim expands. I'm ready for the real thing now. Put it in me."

*Sexual Deviant*

And/or, like she should be tied up and spanked. A form of (quasi-consensual) carnal punishment. Adorned in leather and sweating profusely. Out of breath and struggling to regain her composure. Engaged in that complete and total loss-of-control, ravaged, brink-of-mindlessness fucking. There she is, fully absorbed, surrendering to the physical. The type of intercourse that's so nasty it makes G-d gasp in bewilderment. "Oh dear! Y'all have deviated from My grand design."

Girls with short hair (let's elaborate. Short hair + pale skin, small in stature, skinny and clean-shaven) fulfill every man's fantasy: the opportunity to fuck a little boy. Right fellas?

When Jared first saw Amy with her new haircut, it freaked him out. He couldn't comprehend the sight. Amy, the ultimate feminine creature, was now a gross, muddy guy.

She must've suspected that Jared's reaction would be less than flattering, because when she first approached him, she had the hood of her sweatshirt wrapped tightly around her head, carefully concealing her new do. And, understandably so. A bad haircut can be debilitating. It foists a temporary slouch onto an otherwise goodly, upright soul. This crumbling catastrophe does not apply to cautiously planned and strategically deployed "trims." Nah, such cuts simply maintain the existing state of affairs (immaterial deviations notwithstanding). But a sudden, unplanned, compulsive, reinvent myself, drastic-life-revision haircut, you fuck that up and it'll take months to recover. You'll frown into every mirror. Oh hair, please grow back. Follicle stimulation ain't helping. Appropriately, it's a slow and arduous process, providing plenty of time to reflect on the mistakes we make when we embrace the false excitement of following through on a spontaneous decision. Impulse, if pursued without restraint, is the precursor to all misdeeds. And so, with all that inner torment fomenting within her, Amy nervously pulled back her hood, for the dramatic grand reveal. The soft-cottoned hood gently flopped onto her back, exposing her freshly sheared, shame-recipient hairstyle.

Jared said something rude and stormed off. Bitter, enraged, roughshod. His protector had abandoned him. Amy, the savior from and consolation for Jared's deeeeeeeply rooted trauma, the curtseying acrobat, a center stage spotlighted vaudevillian, nurturing psychological refugees in her damp, luscious bosom, was no more. Jared's secure distractor turned to reveal– no, not just to reveal, but to confront him with the very thing he'd been utilizing her to avoid. To Jared, Amy represented a warm it's-alright pat-on-the-back from on high. A clouded whisper of 'Look how well adjusted you are. You are normal. You can participate in a healthy, heterosexual relationship. You can genuinely enjoy licking pussy. It's okay. You are not impaired by your past. Don't worry about whatever may have happened when you were younger. Yeah! You were just a kid. We all share similar troubles. We're all haunted by a past memory.' Amy and her slut tendencies functioned to lift the burden, reassuring me that everything's gunna be okay. Oh but now, my cure, you have let go and removed the safety net. Woman, now reduced.

She looks like a boy and it reminds me…of him…of that day…what?…you, Jared?…this happened to you?…are you sure?…ya know, sometimes we generate false memories…did it really happen?…or, not necessarily false, but we tend to inaccurately retain certain memories, especially those long-ago forgotten memories we long to forget…downplay and exaggerate…is this real, Jared?…what're you thinking about?…little boy…a little boy's penis…I was a boy, too…Amy was supposed to fix me. But now she has arrived, embodying, in a representative sense, the very thing I'm running from. She is the boy from that day. I recognize you. I recall the sour taste of a hairless, prepubescent dick jiggling atop my tongue.

Jared actively avoided Amy for the remainder of the afternoon. Demon! Weakling, do not accuse. You instigated it.

Later on, Charlie approached Jared with a serious, angry daddy grimace on his face.

"What's up?"

"What the fuck is the matter with you, Jared?"

"Excuse me?"

"Why're you being such an asshole to Amy? She's really upset. It's just a stupid haircut. What's the big deal, anyway? It'll grow back. Actually, I think she looks kinda cute."

During that summer, Jared was enrolled in a chemistry class. A couple weeks into the course, the students were introduced to the concept of Avogadro's number:

$$6.02 \times 10^{23}$$

If I'm remembering correctly, which is doubtful, this figure has something to do with measuring the number of atomic molecules (or, moles) contained within an atom.

Soon enough, in the midst of such complex numbers, Amy and Jared were back at it, fucking profusely. He managed to overcome (rather, forget) the grim memories that Amy's haircut had conjured. However, Jared's mental anguish still managed to manifest itself in certain odd n' unexpected ways. Specifically, J+A engaged in some notable sexual shit that summer. Perhaps this was a tactic to eliminate the bad thoughts. Aggressively attack that vagina. It will prove I am a man. Swarm that pussy. Devour. Destroy. He fucked her like the little boy she was.

Amy often came over after school. They'd go into Jared's bedroom and lock the door. Private. It's worth mentioning three particular incidents from that summer:

1). Jared was required to obtain a calculator for his chemistry class. After receiving this directive, he diligently rushed to the nearest school supply emporium and purchased a TI-30XIIS. Top notch! Once home, he cut off the sturdy plastic wrapper, tossed it (the packaging) on the floor and began completing the formulas that had been assigned as homework. A couple days later, Amy came over and proceeded to give our boy a well-deserved hand job. When he alerted Amy of his impending orgasm, she aimed his cock directly at the wrapper (still on the floor), and he came all over it.

2). One particularly enchanting afternoon, Amy yanked Jared's cock outta his pants. She was hungry, with a ravenous look in her eyes, ready to gobble. Da dick immediately sprang forth a new nation, and she wrapped those thick, slippery, cherubic lips around it. Eventually…

"I'm gunna cum."

She leaned back, removing the organ(ic) speech impediment. And like a lady well-trained in the art of providing a comprehensive, dynamic fellatio experience, the moment his slobber-soaked pecker popped out of her mouth, she immediately gripped it with her hand and began jerking him off, properly utilizing the extraordinary lubrication her saliva provided.  Take note, girls!  She smiled, exuding the excited, sparkle-toned glint of a girl who knows that she is about to make her father proud (e.g., slowly approaching daddy during the early morning moments of his birthday whilst holding a thoughtfully-selected and precision-wrapped present behind your back).

"Where do you want to do it?"

He hesitated.

"Uh, how about your face?"

She didn't.

"Yea!"

And like a docile porn star, she knelt before him, genuflecting at the altar of a pressurized penis, ready to burst.  She did that slight upward tilt of her head, as though she were presenting the blank canvas of her unobstructed face for him to…ahem…splatter.

Ready.  Aim.  He shot his cum right in her eye.

"Ah fuck!"  She laughed.  Such a good sport.

"Sorry."

She closed her eyes and let him finish before rushing to the bathroom to wash her face.  When she returned, her left eye was bloodshot red.

3).  One day, she wasn't in the mood.  She was lying in bed, reading A Heartbreaking Work of Staggering Genius and reflexively rejecting any of Jared's playful advances.  She refused every worthy attempt.  Jared, his body pulsating with desire, needed her.  He wasn't going to take 'no' for an answer.  A man cannot silence his needs.  Growl, grrrr.  He took his pants off and straddled her head.  His butt on her chest, his dick right in her face.  He pressed his battering-ram-of-a-cock onto the rigid, creased meeting point of her lips, forcing his way in.  She tried to clench her mouth shut, like a baby avoiding porridge, but the strength of his cock overcame the delicate barrier of her lips.  Once inside, she surrendered.  'Alright, fine.'  And she proceeded to deliver a wife's blowjob.  Reluctant and disinterested.  I'm surprised she didn't bite it off.

Something began to shift in Patricia's ideology. A slow, gradual, fundamental change. Out on the training ground, surrounded by swaths of forgotten souls, she listened, carefully, as they'd regale her with tales of "The Plight." The hollow fortune of their tepid struggle intrigued her, and she was mesmerized by their apparent intellect. They spoke with such certainty. Their conviction was captivating. She was taught of shamed historical figures and unreported battles. The oft-overlooked and the misunderstood. Nothing was familiar. Patricia, have you heard about the Mississippi Quinceañeras of 1794? Do you know about the Zebulon Slave Revolt? The Cooper Principle? Pat, do you know who Jadwiga Ziembinski is? Pat, have you read Casual Musings on Class Warfare by Don Mayeda? She learned of new concepts, theoretical frameworks of analysis and true enemies. Institutions! Corporate interests! Globalism! Inequality! Racism!

At first, she resisted the narrative. And who could blame her? She was being told that her hometown, and all its happy inhabitants, was the enemy. None would readily accept such a suggestion. As time passed, however, she began to grasp the validity of these opposing viewpoints.

She started to enjoy it. Every diatribe (that's how these people communicate) revealed new information. Aspects of life, history and culture that she had never even heard of before. It made her feel smart, as though her ignorance was gradually evaporating with each lecture. These thoughts, these ideas, this overall mindset soon took hold. She began to see herself (rather, now, her former self) as old-fashioned, naively wedded to outdated ways of thinking, a mindless adherent to social constructs. Having been made aware of these invisible forces, she sought to overcome her newfound oppression.

It worked. She fell for it.

Well, sure, maybe she genuinely believed it; but let's not overlook the fact that she was outnumbered here. Did they actually teach her, or simply overwhelm her? The bitch was being brainwashed, and she was not properly equipped to defend herself.

Her fellow comrades, observing this adjustment in her attitude, and the feeble vulnerability by which she seemed to agree with whatever she was told (without doubt or second thought), shared with her all the appropriate reading materials, in order to further reinforce her newfound enlightenment. She devoured them.

Soon enough, Patricia cut her hair and denounced the throne to which she was the rightful heir.

# Do not disturb the sacred sleep

Deep into his trip, while gazing out at the endless surrounding landscape, Jared began to doubt the validity of drug use in the modern era. He was promised revelation, interconnectedness and fundamental order. Instead, he received chaos and confusion. Having glimpsed the other side, he yearned for the simplicity of game shows.

I dreamed **us** forever

Slowly begins our demise.
A tightly bound, spellchecked, capricious lullaby.
Talkin' déjà vu syntax.
A subtle blank stare in the face of mercy.
Piecing together the remnants of who I once was,
with not a note of aplomb.
Though I,
I've been holding this grudge since biblical times.
Oh fortune, allow sympathy!
She's just sad, don't vilify her.
Delicate tissue torn asunder.
So let blood be thy thirsty, as to bring forth the chase.
Pardon me,
may I anally fascinate you?

I'm led to believe in the sweet aging of wine,
but *forever* is always being destroyed by time.

Amy slept over, which was a semi-regular occurrence.
By this point, Jared and Amy had developed a routine whereby
she would come over late at night, they'd get high, fuck and then
fall asleep (sometimes they'd also go on a Del Taco run). Jared
would always wake her up in the morning (early enough so she
could depart before his parents became concerned as to why his
door was locked).

On one such occasion, as he nudged her awake, she
mumbled, "Nicky, no, I want to keep sleeping."

"Uh, Amy, you're... here," Jared reminded her.

She opened her eyes and scanned her surroundings.

"Oh fuck! I'm so sorry, Jared."

"Whatever. It's fine. It's time for you to go anyways."

As JARED is closing the trunk, the shot
freezes.

JARED (V.O.)
As far back as I can remember, I
never thought I'd be a pothead.

Speak up
And what do you think
Of a latent relationship

Of course
I would regret the prospect
Of converting the innocent

Oh, lusty lady
Your fingery touch drives me crazy

Stabbing my dick into your bum
And I wonder where all this shit comes from
But I don't mind cause it's all in the fun
Of the moment when I'm with this crazy lady

Flicking 'em lips
Is how I get my kicks
While I'm rummaging through my old bag of tricks
And I'm measuring the size of my dick
Just to make sure the whole package will fit

Every nip slip is important
Lick the asshole
Lick the asshole
Lick the asshole
Marmalade

And every nerve ending
Is a processed reaction
To the delicate inaction
Misbehavior
Her savior
Is around with a raging boner
Consequently a misnomer
A procedure of the game

Slitting my wrists while you're sucking my dick
I'm mangling clits at the sight of a bitch
While I'm plugging her ass with my forearm and fist
She is gaping wide a full imperial inch

As has been mentioned previously, The Land of Forgotten Souls had no standing, on-call Army. They were, of course, a peaceful people with no need to do battle, fight, slug it out, or engage in any sort of dominance establishing (or maintaining) fisticuffs. No! Absolutely not. We didn't conquer this land. We merely stumbled into our civilization. Only love, all the time. Ah, what whimsy! They weren't just conflict averse, they we conflict benign. That muscle, the muscle that rebels against tyranny and refuses even the slightest hint of injustice, had long ago atrophied and collapsed. Bred out of the gene pool in a single generation. The youngins were promptly indoctrinated into the tepid ways of mama bear. War, the ultimate culmination of an unwavering adherence to one's beliefs (no matter the cost), was a completely foreign concept to these yogurt-slurping hippies.

Despite their dire lack of preparedness, they had been doing their best to arrange a formidable battalion. King Deryk had appointed Alto Undershed and Winter Tide Peach Mother Sumptuous to lead the command. They were effectively appointed generals (or, at least, the equivalent thereof). Alto was tasked with administering and carrying out the battle plan, while Winter Tide was assigned the prominent role of obtaining and distributing the firearms.

The guns had arrived a day prior. One large crate, marked **FRONTEN & SONS**, filled to the brim with munitions. Winter Tide's boyfriend accompanied her to the train depot in order to claim the shipment. They procured a properly issued bill of lading, and transported the guns back to the makeshift headquarters.

Before we proceed, a quick word about Winter Tide and her boyfriend.

Their dynamic was that of a ferocious, fat, corpuscle-ridden woman, desperate to devise a purpose for her life, and her thin, timid, string-beaned and ultra-high boyfriend.

*Yes dear. Whatever you say, dear.* He was along for the ride, while she (wo)manned the ship.

Winter Tide was well-versed in progressive, post-modernist thought. In particular, she was obsessed with race. It was her dominant concern. Prior to the H2O debacle, she was a fierce advocate of all things race related. She fought for all minorities. The eternally oppressed, as she called them. Though it was never quite clear what her ultimate goal was. Equality, I presume? She often spoke of "raising awareness" and "starting a dialogue."

Her boyfriend, however, was white. Thus, notwithstanding the zealous social advocacy she undertook in her self-appointed role as an aggressive, loud-mouthed ally, every night she'd return to the cozy confines of her home and make a white man cum.

On Monday, October 14, 2002, Jared and Amy both simultaneously lost their virginity, together. They were each 14 years old at the time, much too young to be engaging in such prurient acts. It happened in Jared's bedroom during a sun-warmed afternoon following a rigorous day of school. It was quick. Perhaps due, in part, to the fact that Griselda had purchased a 3-pack of "Very Sensitive" Trojan condoms. These condoms came in a purple package (note: this particular flavor of prophylactic has since been discontinued, possibly due to numerous complaints of premature ejaculation, much to the chagrin of acne-faced teenage girls everywhere).

"Hello?"
"Hey Griselda. It's Jared."
"Hi! How are you?"
"Good. Um, I was just wondering if…"
"Yea, yea. What is it? What do you need?"
"Condoms."
"Ooo shit! Wow, okay, sure thing. Um, let's see. Okay, yea, that can definitely be arranged. Hmmm. [thought process]

I'll leave them in the bushes located at the top of the driveway to your parents' house."

"The bushes? Which one exactly?"

"So, like, if you're facing the house, it'd be on your right. With the little wood frame around it."

"Alright, yea. Got it."

"Okay. They'll be there tomorrow by the time you get home from school."

"Fuck yes! Thanks, Griselda. You're the best."

"Ha! Love you, Jared. Just be careful, okay? Please, and I mean this sincerely, please make sure you're both ready for this. Honestly. You don't realize the emotional impact that this is going to have on your lives. It's kinda monumental. That level of intimacy, especially your first time, changes things. There's no return from this."

Jared was taken aback. It turned out that undergirding the hedonistic, wild-abandon lifestyle that Griselda propagated, was a wise, genuine and caring soul. She was always (despite the various qualms some may have regarding the quality of care she provided) looking out for the best interests of this little brat.

This was all self-evident from her little soliloquy, right? I didn't need to spell it out. In fact, pointing it out may lessen the impact. Jay-Z always does a version of this and it annoys the fuck out of me. He explains every metaphor. Show, don't tell, hova.

"I understand. And I truly appreciate your advice. I really like this girl."

"Well, maybe you ought to wait until you love her."

"…"

"That's your decision to make. I'll get you the condoms, just so you'll have them. I trust that you'll wait to actually use them once you know for certain that the time is right."

"Fair enough. I will. Thank you, Griselda."


It apparently never occurred to Jared (nor Griselda) that there is no age limit for buying condoms. Nevertheless, this seemingly unnecessary exchange instilled a profound lesson in our young hero. A lesson he'd immediately betray.

Despite Jared's initial hesitation to initiate physical forms of affection toward his darling Amy, things progressed rather quickly after their first kiss. A few weeks before their formal consummation, Amy gave an exhaustive blowjob to a shirtless Jared, as he lay on his back, blissful. After about 20 minutes of sucking, she sat beside him and requested that he finish himself off. So, Jared masturbated while Amy watched. Perhaps it was due to the long buildup, or maybe the thrill of having a spectator excited him, whatever the reason, Jared had a volcanic orgasm. His cum seemed to launch into the sky, nearly hitting the ceiling of his bedroom, until it landed, audibly, all over his chest and stomach.

Amy was stunned. She had never seen a man cum before.

Jared was stunned, too. He had never produced such a massive, messy load. His entire torso was covered in cum.

"Whoa…" Amy whispered, as she soiled herself. The Birth of a Whore. Oh Amy, I was to be the first of many men that would orgasm in your presence. The inaugural entry in your sexual hall of fame. Ugh… I'm sure she's seen so many weird dicks by now.

Before Jared's geyser-cannon self-soak blast, the two lovebirds breached the genital-contact barrier in the cutest of ways.

It all started with the swiftest of maneuvers. While cuddled up all cozy (and likely making out, on and off), Jared gently slid his hand down the front of Amy's pants. Slowly and methodically, his hand crawled past her bellybutton and down along the soft lower-belly trail. The closeness of his fingertips to her pussy lips sent a thrill throughout her entire human form. She looked directly into Jared's eyes and smiled. Her body twinkled with delight.

This sensation, the naughty excitement of abandoning restraint and pursuing forbidden physical pleasures, was reminiscent of an earlier game that J+A used to play together (along with Charlie, too!) during their blatant 9<sup>th</sup> grade flirtations.

How to play The Nervous Game: place your hand on your crush's inner thigh, right above his/her knee. Slowly slide your hand up toward their nether region, while reciting the titular query, "Nervous?" It's a real squirm inducer.

And so here they were, less than a year later, intertwined in her bed, while Jared approached from the north. He moved down at a snail's pace until he reached the first landmark: pubic hair. He decided to take shelter here before proceeding any further. Jared gently played with Amy's pubes. Tenderly running his fingers through her hair, softly scratching the skin beneath, wrapping the hair around his finger and giving it a merciful tug, etc.

Given the gradualness of their romantic advancement, this proved to be a sufficient next step. Rather than work his way down any further (and commence the inevitable clit rubbing and finger fucking), he instead tussled her pubic hair. This excited her. She then reciprocated. She slid her hand down his pants and began playing with his pubic hair.

Jared and Amy continued this routine for a couple weeks. Camping out at the gates of paradise, too afraid to enter. They named this activity The Pubic Hair Club. Rather, the activity itself was not The Pubic Hair Club, but they themselves were members of such club, having touched each other's pubic hair (i.e., the act of initiation). They took pride in their status as members. They began referring to it by its acronym: PHC. Jared even inscribed these letters on the back of his right hand (with pen, of course; this wasn't a permanent marker type of situation), a badge of honor that he eagerly showed his friends, strategically awaiting the inevitable question, "What does PHC stand for?" At which point Jared would proudly share the news of his latest conquest.

"Hello?"
"Hi baby!"
"Well hello there, cutie."
"What's going on?"

"Not much. Just watching MTV. My fave! How about you?"

"Oh me? I'm just being a girl. The type of girl that you secretly wish you were. Black hair, straight and thin, cut at the chin. Tiny. And with a predilection for wearing skimpy gym shorts."

"Yeah, I guess you're right. I would rather be a woman. Thanks for unexpectedly causing an identity crisis that'll last for the remainder of my life. How must I go on living with these thoughts? I can confidently proclaim that I, being of sound mind, wish I was a girl. And yet, here I am."

"There are procedures and medications available for people in your situation."

"Nah. I'll just make do as a man."

"So, my parents– I mean, my mom and Mitch were thinking of going to the O.C. Fair tomorrow. Would you like to join us?"

"Absolutely! The county fair may be one of mankind's finest achievements."

The next morning, the broken-and-shattered-beyond-repair, then haphazardly reassembled Carousel family (plus one) hoped into mama's SUV, and they set off for the carnival.

Upon their arrival, the 2 couples immediately split up. Mama and Mitch went to look at the animals. To this day, I'm still not exactly sure what they meant by this. Maybe there was some sort of petting zoo there? Or a formal livestock dealer? I do recall a mention of pigs. Or, and I've never thought of this until now, maybe they just wanted some private time. I reckon there's ample bushes in Orange County.

After further research, it appears that there is a farm nearby.

While mama and Mitch absconded to inspect the local hogs and/or fuck, Amy and Jared walked the fairgrounds proper. Aside from the usual midway games, shoddy rides and shitty food, the O.C. Fair hosted various vendors hawking all sorts of excessively unnecessary goods. Whether by fate, pure happenstance or a layout mischievously devised by a well-trained marketing team, Jared and Amy (hand-in-hand) soon found themselves surrounded by hot tubs. In every direction, as far as the eye could see, were hot tubs of sundry shapes and sizes, with assorted amenities.

Jared and Amy spent the next couple hours slowly gliding amongst the hot tubs, their hands clasped tightly together. Amy occasionally did that cute little move where she'd turn toward Jared, put her hand on his stomach and give him a quick kiss. This would happen whenever something particularly cute or romantic was said. She'd suddenly become so overwhelmed with sweetness that she needed to embrace Jared in order to properly express her unhinged inner joy.

Jared and Amy carefully inspected each and every hot tub. They had a genuine objective in doing so. They were fantasizing; except, to them this was no fantasy. No! To them, this was an honest endeavor. A practical, run-of-the-mill errand for an upper-middleclass family. They were deciding which hot tub to purchase, for the house they'd share together one day. The hot tub in which they'd enjoy romantic, wine-soaked evenings together, and the hot tub their children would one day splash around in.

Jared couldn't have been any happier during this moment of domestic bliss. In his mind, their love would endure for the rest of their lives (and likely beyond). It was entirely sensible to be selecting a hot tub with her, since he had no doubt that they'd be together forever. Jared felt the comfort of certainty, of knowing the full-horizon panorama-scoped course of his future. Everything, from here on out, will be shared with you. The soft little hand I currently grip, I will hold on until we're both shriveled and decaying.

*Of course, we already know this is a flawed and ultimately incorrect assumption. But our naïve protagonist has no fucking clue. Look at that dopey smile. That irrational, undeserved and misplaced confidence. Don't you just want to shake him and yell, 'Love is not forever, Jared! This is a limited-term pursuit. We all know that Amy ain't settling down with you in the end. Sure, have some fun, get yer balls gargled and all that. Just don't expect eternity.'*

As if this endearing moment couldn't become any schmaltzier, an elephant walked by, seemingly out of nowhere (in a preemptive mockery of our current cynicism). They both froze in amazement. Amy tightened her grip.

"Baby!"

"I know."

The remainder of the day consisted of typical fair fare: milk bottle teddy bears dangling on rusted rebar, mid-withdrawal ruffians clicking switches, bandana waggin' tarantulas, the scraped-plastic booster seats of unwanted illegitimates and Mike Love.

During sunset, Jared and Amy rode a chairlift that spanned the grounds, offering a bird's-eye view of the entire scene. Jared wrapped his arm around Amy, and she nestled into him. The attraction provided an appropriate representation of this particular point in their relationship. Two young lovers, enwrapped in each other's arms, floating above the planet, lifted by their earnest devotion to one another and carried forward by an enduring dream.

Later on, they positioned themselves beside the designated meeting spot, a shanty game booth, and made out while awaiting the arrival of mama and Mitch. After sitting slouched and curled up for slightly longer than anticipated, the grownups appeared. The parties finally reconvened, having experienced 2 distinctly different days. Mitch had that sore-cock anal-afterglow in his eyes. Mama looked worn out and droopy.

During the drive home, Jared spoke up (a rare occurrence) and noted that the car was "full of love." Two new couples on the brink of a lifetime romance. Happy and complete. Welcoming every new day with enthusiastic anticipation for fresh opportunities to cross the boundaries of love's illusory limits. Springing out of bed with the joie de vivre of Broadway's latest darlings (and their ilk), who I am convinced travel via cartwheel.

Mama and Mitch exchanged a smirking glance, an unspoken acknowledgment of all the horrors that love can bring.

Sure, they were happy now, but it took a war of immeasurable casualties to reach this point. The adults in the car countenanced a statistical confidence that Amy and Jared would endure a catastrophic demise. Crazy kids, you have no idea of the torment that lurks beyond the closer-than-you-think horizon. But we needn't inform them of this. No, today let's let 'em bathe in the ignorance of young love. Ease on down the primrose path of an ill-matched relationship.

As a sign of appreciation for his unprovoked declaration, Amy discretely reached over, slid her hand down Jared's pants and tickled his pubes.

Alright! Enough with all the gradual foreplay. Let us finally fulfill the divine purpose of man. Well... almost. A couple more sexual (but not quite sex) acts.

The first time Jared ate Amy's pussy, she was completely naked, lying on the floor, right beside the mirrored and bottom-rolling sliding doors that concealed the contents of young Jared's closet. This position provided the perfect spectator's angle, allowing Jared to evaluate the sincerity of the potential pleasure that Amy derived from this act. As she tilted her head back, she inadvertently faced the mirror. Thus, whenever Jared glanced up to check in on her, he could see her face. She looked uncomfortable, and after only a few minutes, she asked him to stop.

They only attempted this particular activity a handful of times. She never seemed into it. This was entirely all Jared's fault. He never knew exactly what to do down there. What parts do I lick? And how? Do I stab my tongue inside? Do I just go nuts and devour the whole thing, like an energetic and slightly aggressive make out session? I never quite figured out how to properly perform oral sex, and I have yet to encounter a willing teacher.

Lest this passage dissuade you from pursuing me, I proudly profess that I am an excellent **finger**er.

Another example of the parties' pre-sex tomfoolery occurred on a near-monthly basis, as Amy would reluctantly allow a feverish and frenzied Jared to remove her used tampons. The protocol was as follows: she'd alert him of the impending act and he'd accompany her to the bathroom. She'd then remove her pants and sit on the toilet. He'd reach in between her legs and tug on the string, until the blood-blackened ball-o-cotton would slip out. He'd hold it for a moment, swinging, before letting go. They'd hear the gentle splash as it plopped into the water below.

This moment captures all the elements of a proper sexual exchange. An intensely intimate revelation of our private selves, coupled with a proper hint of nastiness. Oh, the unspeakable acts we share with our lovers.

And so, it was time to fuck.

Two young, unwed teenagers about to lose their virginity. Break the sacred, saran-wrapped seal without G-d's blessing, in contravention of the holy dictates. Rebellious youths, sojourners of a (thus far) existence untethered to religious edicts and devoid of a work-shopped, red-pen-spackled rough draft revised revised revised revised eventuality: a settled-dust appreciation & a learned and enlightened understanding of the precious significance this **SINGULAR LIFE EVENT** held. You were there, Amy. And so was I. 'Twas only us 2, and the flickering candlelight tickling our skin. Nude children, disrobed and disobedient. Frolicking outside of Eden, unashamed. Giggling goo goo clusters teeter tottering on the tumultuous brink of "maturity." Or something to that effect. Slow down, kids! Calm the excitement. Sex always complicates things. We should've waited. Much too early. Too young. I was not prepared to endure the burden. Oh well, there's no use regretting the completed acts of our past. It happened, regardless. My tiny dick tore apart her well-maintained chastity, unleashing a ravenous rancor of lust.

They literally have no idea how sacred this moment is. A day that'll be singed into their minds for all time. An act forever enshrined in their descending lines of ancestral heritage. Behold, the first time. Fulfillment of life's purpose. The fusion of flesh and spirit between man and woman. The premier seed dropped onto a garden soon to blossom.

They stripped off their clothing (naked) and got under the covers. Like all beginners, they started with the traditional missionary position. Amy spread her legs and Jared lined up his cock with the slit of her pussy. Prior to entry (and before putting on the condom), Jared reached down and grabbed the base of his dick. He touched the tip of his penis to the entry point of Amy's V. Rather than inserting it inside, he rubbed it up and down, on a vertical axis, against the fleshy aperture of her pussy. She became wetter with each cycle. The tension of this teasing gesture soon became unbearable.

"Ready?"

"Yea. Just go slow."

Here they were, on the verge. Both unsure what to expect. How will it feel, physically? And how will they react, emotionally? Together, my dear, we shall journey into the unknown. Jared ripped open the purple wrapper and unrolled the condom onto his dick. It was time.

He entered with the methodical grace of a brain surgeon scooping out a tumor. Every slight movement was critical. The delicate balance between disaster and salvation. He was gentle and careful, slowly pushing in, incrementally becoming one with Amy.

"Are you okay?"

"Yea."

They stared into each other's eyes and held the deepest form of contact possible between 2 humans.  She absorbed him / he penetrated her.  Fragile.

Once fully inside, Jared pulled back and slowly entered her again.

"How does it feel?"

"Good.  Keep doing that.  But stay slow."

Jared continued this move, the slow-mo hump, as Amy's hymen was quietly obliterated.  After doing this only a few times, Jared realized that he was going to cum if he continued much longer.  Instead, he tried a different technique.

To this day, I feel this is the most intimate moment that two lovers can share together.  If you are in a long-term, committed relationship, try this with your partner tonight.  Insert your penis all the way in, to the point where you don't think you can go any further, and simply hold it there.  No mean-man fury fucking, just tranquil stillness.  Then, though it may seem impossible, press in that extra little centimeter.  With all your gumption, shove yourself in, fully, past the threshold of your perceived physical limitations.  And of course, during this exchange, maintain eye contact with your willing participant.

Now, this may seem counterintuitive to those of us properly steeped in the false, filthy and disingenuous sexual exploits that occur in porn films.  We've been smearing our psyches with smut since 4th grade.  To our detriment, we were essentially taught of "sex" by watching porn.  Those brave actors, broken and tormented enough to pursue a career in the adult film industry, they were our mentors.  Through their work, they demonstrated the act of sexual intercourse to us.  Except, what we didn't realize was that porn portrays a false narrative.  Your average porn film suggests that the best possible sex consists of a muscular man forcefully and aggressively humping a dead deer with ferocious military might, while she screams uncontrollably.  Conquer that cunt!  Sure, this can be fun, especially during those nights when you wanna get filthy with it.  But I sincerely believe that the greatest sexual intimacy is achieved by staying still and focusing on depth rather than speed.  Try it.  Seriously.

And just when Amy was starting to get into it, Jared came. She observed his face while he orgasmed inside her. His pleasure amplified her disappointment. When he finished, he pulled out and immediately kissed her.

"I love you."

"I love you too, Jared."

"That was really special."

"Yea."

"Wow… that was– just… yea. That was really amazing, Amy."

He sat up and began removing the cum-filled condom, while Amy watched with fascinated interest (and slight disgust). He tied off the end and threw it on the floor.

"Are you okay?"

"Yea, I'm good."

"It didn't hurt, did it?"

"A little. But I enjoyed it."

She sat up and kissed him. They smiled at each other, unsure of what to say next. A moment of silence passed. A symbolic attestation whereby they mourned what had been lost whilst concurrently acknowledging (with humility and grace) what was gained. The carefree concerns of childhood were beginning to fade from view. The sanctity of those wild abandon bike rides was no more, replaced with the grownup obligation to preserve the wellbeing of those who allow us to inhabit their hearts.

"Remember this, Jared. Remember this day forever, as I will. You broke me. It was you. You were the boy I chose. And I have not a single regret about what we just shared together, or who I shared it with. I love you. No matter what happens between us, you will have played a pivotal role in my life. Always. You, figuratively, made me become a woman today."

"Oh, Amy. You mean so much to me."

That's it? That's all you have to say, Jared? No grandiose follow-up to Amy's heart wrenching proclamation? No soliloquy? Apparently not. Instead, Jared considered whether the tale of Humpty Dumpty was a metaphor for experiencing a drastic and unrecoverable change in one's life (e.g., losing your virginity).

Amy could tell he had nothing else to say on the matter.

"I have to go to the bathroom. Gotta inspect the damage you've wrought to my fragile clit cavern. Oh, and I must be sure to pee. I read somewhere that you have to pee immediately after every sexual encounter, in order to prevent a UTI. I'll be right back."

"Alright, darling. Go on then."

Amy hopped out of bed and hurried into the bathroom, still naked. Jared watched her bare butt jiggle with every step.

Once alone, Jared stood up, assuming perfect posture. He placed his hands on his hips and looked around his room. All his boyhood belongings shone with a new glow. Jared was proud of himself and proud of his accomplishment.

He grabbed a blue Sharpie and drew a little heart on the KROQ calendar that hung on his wall, marking the day.

Jared was afraid to throw away the sacrificial remnants (i.e., the used condom and its wrapper) in any of the numerous trashcans at his parents' house. So instead, he crumbled them together into a gooey ball and stored them in the front pouch of his backpack. To ensure that his parents never discovered any trace of their misdeed, he'd dispose of the evidence at school the next day.

The following morning, Jared shared the news with his friends in the oddest of ways. He motioned for his friend Michael to join him and Amy near one of those large, schoolyard trashcans.

"Hey you two. How goes it?"

"We are excellent, my dear pal. Just wanted you to witness us throwing something away."

"Uh… okay."

Jared then removed the condom (and its torn purple wrapper) from his backpack and tossed it in the trash, making sure Michael noticed what it was before he threw it away.

"Oh shit. Mazel tov!"

You must be wondering: who is this Michael fellow? There's been no mention of him before. Michael was Jared's best friend since 1st grade (from days of yore). Their bond had remained intact and secure throughout the years. However, when Jared started getting high all the time, they began to drift apart. Now, Michael no doubt enjoyed the occasional toke, but he was wise enough to know that a man mustn't allow drug use to define his identity (or, perhaps he was merely the beneficiary of a strict father's well-meaning discipline). Either way, at this particular moment, Jared had yet to spark his first bowl. Thus, his friendship with Michael was still pure and clearheaded. Jared purposefully chose Michael as the first of his friends that would learn of his **first time**.

When Patrick's roughened paw gripped the cool steel of the gun, something awoke within him. His inner voice, its typical status quo a dull whisper, a bashful guardian timidly guiding him through his hectic and troubled life (which, presumably would achieve some sense of stability were he to finally grab the reins and steer it toward his desired goal; this, however, presupposes that such a goal has been determined, as opposed to the aimless wander that defines him), unleashed a robust roar. He realized the horrid truth, that the natural conclusion and eventual/inevitable result of these fringe activist movements was war. Their ultimate goal, masterfully disguised as righteously deployed compassion, was always destruction. Once you've clearly defined your enemy and exaggerated the extent of their influence, they must be killed. To compromise is to surrender. We must conquer and obliterate our invented villain. You, the abhorrent masses that reside in The Land of Forgotten Souls, you declare, incessantly, that South Forts is the supreme evil in the world. You relentlessly rally around efforts to quell their supposed dominion, constantly criticize their way of life, devaluing their humanity in the process, as though they don't share your exact same values. Oh, of course not, they don't understand the true meaning of life (which necessarily implies that your G-dless paradise has somehow solved man's eternal question. And no, music itself is not an acceptable answer, no matter how hard you boogie). You think that those who dwell in material provinces lack a soul. As though success is born at the expense of spirituality. By adopting this mindset, you've managed to convince yourselves that you are humanity's enlightened saviors, sent to rescue us from the dark. And how are you implementing your plan to save mankind? Living by example. Drain your colon and show the world that perfection is attainable. Damn the skeptics! The funny thing is, no one in South Forts even knows you exist. They're deeply engaged in their own meaningful and productive lives, and have no time to so much as consider you.

He turned to Patricia.

"I can't do this," he confessed.

She returned his glance, baffled.

"What do you mean?"

He dropped the gun.

Her smile slowly drooped downward. Her little companion was quitting the lifestyle that she was now fully embracing.

"I refuse to participate in this fight."

"But, Patrick, we're in the right here. We've been given no other option. We must stand up for what is just and preserve this sacred territory. Your refusal to kill is complacency. Scratch your weakness. Rid yourself of it."

"Listen, I'm fully on board with the cause, to an extent. I believe in it, but not enough to fight for it. Violence is not necessary. Repeat: Violence is not necessary. Sure, you've convinced yourself that it is, that you're some sort of warrior who'll one day be enshrined in college dorm rooms. But you're not. You guys are pure, untethered evil."

Patrick's statements revealed that he had already begun the process of separating from the group. He no longer associated himself with these folk.

"I'm sorry, Patricia, but I am not prepared to kill for this. The second we begin carrying guns, I'm done."

She stared at Patrick, her head slightly twitching, as she attempted to contain the feelings within.

"Coward!" she erupted. "This is the moment where our beliefs are truly tested. It's easy to sit around spouting prose and to join in on the occasional protest; but if you're not willing to kill for your beliefs, they are nothing more than fragile, unenforceable dewdrops."

"If that be an accurate summation of your moral code, consider this my unequivocal renunciation of it. I knew it! All these hip jackals that preach 'peace and love,' they're all frauds. They revel in hatred. You have abandoned decency. You have abandoned Christ. And you have abandoned a worthy purpose for this life. I must go. I cannot bear to see the gleeful carelessness with which you'll readily slaughter noble men. No thanks, Patricia."

"We need you, Pat. We need all the help we can get."

"We? You speak as though you're one of them."

"Of course I am. We are. You and I have both been generously welcomed into this community."

"And I now formally reject it. All of it. I suggest you do the same. I'm going home."

"Home?"

"Yea. Don't you remember?"

"But..."

"Please don't."

"I..."

"No."

"Am..."

"Oh dear."

"Home."

"Ugh. I figured you'd recite that hackneyed phrase."

"But it's true."

"Patricia, you've forgotten who you are. You've failed to realize, or perhaps willfully ignored, the significance of your ancestral lineage. You are not new. You are not the first girl to ever experience all the pain you've endured. Your life is but another turn in the continuous cycle of humankind. You are your grandmother's breath, recirculating. Don't neglect your heritage, Patricia. Especially not yours. My dear, by the grace of G-d, especially not yours. Your origins are quite peculiar. Look at this moment. You're ready to wage war against your own family. And I know you don't believe the politics. It's not about that. It never was. We both know the reason why you ran away in the first place. It was him. John Nelson."

When one's ideals are questioned by a confrontational agitator, there are two possible responses: (1) Consider the alternative perspective. Allow it to permeate and evaluate its merits. Ponder a new way of thinking. This'll either convince you otherwise or reinforce your prior beliefs; or (2) Double down on your original stance. Not because you necessarily believe it that strongly, but because the prospect of admitting that you're wrong is the more terrifying of the two options.

To the shame of all mankind, Patricia chose the latter. She dug her stilettos into the dirt and clenched her brain, firmly, on her once-ago ill-informed and irrational decision to take up arms.

"As a little girl, I loved my daddy, as all little girls ought to. He was a source of stability. A stoic and reliable presence, ever reminding me that he had everything under control. He'd always catch me. Shall I continue?"

"We get it. You were a helpless little baby, dependent upon your parents. They took care of you, clothed you, fed you, housed you in what is unquestionably the most pristine residence in all of South Forts, and educated you."

"Aha! Yes! Precisely! They 'educated' me. Rather, they indoctrinated me. They brainwashed me. In that palatial estate, I was secluded. Isolated from the world. I lived in a bubble, protected from the hardships of genuine folk. The bruised and scraped-up workers that built this nation: the Africans that were forced to come here years ago, the Mexicans that risk their lives to come here today, and all the immigrants in between, desperate to attempt the American Dream. And where was I while they toiled away? I was in my room, comfortable, air-conditioned and Magritte-hung, peering outside as they'd sweat, the skin on their hands torn and calloused, their backs creaking from the excess of the load foisted upon them. The joyful life that my parents provided me contained a dark secret: the only way to maintain such an extravagant lifestyle is to trample on the backs of the less fortunate. We'd giggle and jump on the moon bounce supplied by the worn-out hombre, desperate for rest. We are exploiters! This system is rigged in our favor, and we intend to remain here at the top, forever. I was born into this lifestyle. Blessed, pampered and praised. But now I know the truth. Mine eyes have seen the glory of the coming of the Lord. Since arriving here, I've realized that my daddy is the bad guy. All the pleasures I was afforded in my youth came at the cost of harming someone else. The water issue is yet another example of this. Daddy will get me fresh water to drink, at the expense of tearing it from the people here. Well, not today. Today I will put an end to this vicious cycle. Today I side with Palestine. This is the crude, unspoken balance of nature. In order for one man to prosper, another must suffer. My whole life I have been reaping the benefits of this corrupt system, an unwitting recipient of the painful sacrifices of the disadvantaged. I will lead the charge against South Forts and all they stand for. And if my father shall be at the front lines, leading the assault, I wouldn't hesitate to smite him at the first instance."

"I suspect you are ungrateful for the life your father provided you. What you feel is guilt, my dear. Are you implying that you are unworthy of such riches? Because your father sacrificed a great deal, and exerted vast and grotesque efforts to provide you with the life you have; or, had. And he did so in the belief that it'd catapult you to greatness. That a daughter able to take basic necessities for granted would *think* on a different level. She'd dream, and achieve, things most never even contemplate. Not only are you now rejecting the life you've been provided, you're waging war against it. Why? To restore the balance? The nimble thread of justice tied tight round yer nipples?"

"I've made my decision, Patrick. Don't bother me with a lecture."

"You're pathetic. All of you. Don't you realize that wealth, productivity and general innovation in fields that lift all of us up are generated and maintained by men like your father? Y'all call them 'greedy capitalists.' Is that meant to be a classist slur? Those are the men pumping the heart of the America economy. And what do you contribute to this grand experiment?"

"..."

"Precisely! You contribute absolutely nothing. The desire to live in complete harmony with nature is strong advocacy for suicide."

"Patrick, allow me to simplify our stance for you. You're overthinking it. We just want to be left alone. That's it. Let us live a quiet life. Peace, exemplified. My understanding is that this is how things have been here for generations. That is, until a hostile intruder declared a right to invade and tarnish this land. It's the American way, I guess. Nothing is sacred. It's all profit. It's all resources. How can I utilize this land? Why can't we just leave it alone? Must every square mile of this great nation become a fucking mill of some sort? Allow us to bask in the beauty of nature, with no admission fee."

"Hey, I assure you that my appreciation for the glory of an unobstructed waterway is equal to that of yours. Here's where we differ: I believe we owe an obligation to our fellow men, to share in the richness of our resources. That none shall remain thirsty, if his neighbor has ample supply."

"Sharing assumes that both parties consent to the transaction."

"You consent by living in America. And your request to be left alone, though seemingly evidence of a meek humility, is actually the ultimate greed. You live amongst abundance, with a sparse population. South Forts, on the other hand, is a great population, with a limited water supply. Would you prefer they endure dehydration? How is that not the definition of selfishness, to possess a G-d-given gift and to keep it for yourself, rather than sharing it with your fellow man? This is modern life, honey. I know that river looks pretty, but we're gunna lay a big fucking pipe right through it. Good luck stopping us."

A funny thing happened to Jared after he inserted his miniscule dick into Amy's momentarily-tight, yet subsequently ever-increasing and constantly-expanding, gorged womb. He was once a strong-minded, confident and courageous young lad. His friends used to call him 'The Leader.' As a child, he seemed involuntarily compelled to actualize whatever vision currently possessed him (discipline and persistence were unnecessary; rather, he was propelled by the raw purposefulness and instinct-driven passion of a child with an idea), and he was adept at convincing the neighborhood kids to join him, properly utilizing their manifold strengths to complete the particular task at hand. His spirit inspired and excited all those around him. His imaginative direction was a contagious source of pleasure and meaning to all his friends.

After Amy, his spark faded. That vicious energy was abruptly tapped out. Expired. The at once lunatic-on-the-monkey-bars retreated into his shell, afraid of the world he once commanded.

Welp, I guess it's time to grow up now. And in order to achieve peak maturity, I must give up on every dream I've ever considered. Fuck 'em all, from the grandiose and insane to the tepid and seemingly plausible. Put down that guitar. You ain't Bob Dylan, so don't even try.

Worst of all, Jared's friends, the loyal and obedient followers of his pure and promiseful impulses, were now seen as impediments to the attainment of his crooked concept of true love. To him, a romantic relationship was an entirely private event, to be shared only between the 2 involved. The rest of the world (including his best friends) was an obstacle to be avoided. Suddenly, Jared never had time for anyone else. He'd run to Amy at the drop of a hat, even if it required him to cancel plans at the last minute. The ringleader had abandoned the circus, leaving all his adoring creatures to fend for themselves.

Finally, one day, they had enough. Whilst changing in the locker room after P.E. class, Jared's friends confronted him and unleashed a rude awakening.

*You've changed*
*You're drifting*
*You seem depressed all the time*
*You never want to hang out anymore*
*You're so possessive over her*

They were right. Every word rang true with the force of revelation. The issue hadn't been so directly articulated yet, but Jared felt it. He felt the harsh accuracy of their concerns. My goodness, what have I become? He swore to remedy the error of his ways. And in that moment, he sincerely meant it. He was ashamed of his behavior and was desperate to change.

This only lasted until the next time he saw Amy (approximately 10 minutes later). Emotion then took over and he lost all control again. Oh well...

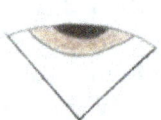

```
          When I remember
    is when I start to forget
        I, the western sea
```

The day Jared begrudgingly attended his sister's graduation from middle school marked a turning point in his life (for the worst).

Prior to the start of the formal ceremony, Jared decided to walk the grounds, as this was the same school from which he himself had graduated 2 years ago. He carried stones of sentimentality, in the hopes of recapturing some vague, long abandoned sense of childhood purity.

Inconsequentially, this was also his last day of 10th grade (from the nearby high school). Although, such occasion contained no pomp and circumstance.

Jared went to the area beside the gym, where he and his friends used to hang out during lunchtime, and where (catastrophically) he had first met Amy. Shards of broken plastic littered the ground, collecting dust. Two acquaintances from Jared's school (same age, same grade) stood there suspiciously, as though they were concealing some sort of illicit behavior. Undoubtedly, they also had younger siblings graduating from middle school that day (otherwise, why would they be there?). Jared approached, happy to see some familiar faces.

"Hey guys. What's up?"

"How d'ya do, Jared?"

"Good, good. It's nice to be back here. Conjures up lots of fond memories."

"Sure, I guess."

The two boys snickered, beholden to their mischievous minds. They belonged to a deviant cohort at Jared's high school that began drinking and drugging early on. The first clique to descend down the desperate tube of despair. Deprive thy brain of its function, and embrace the sensation. They adopted this lifestyle without a moment's hesitation. It was apparent in their manner and appearance: glazed eyes and a mellow fascination with the mundane.

Jared and the brotherhood had yet to venture into the abyss. However, for the past couple months, Eddie had been desperately pestering Jared, practically begging him, to get high together. But Jared refused every time the activity was suggested. Eddie's weak advocacy went as such: "My neighbor gets high. He told me that sometimes when he smokes, he'll just sit there and stare at the wall for hours. And he says it's a blast! Like, you don't have to do anything. If you're high, you can just *be* and it's the funnest thing in the world." No thanks, man.

"Do you smoke?"

"Uhh, no."

"Do you want to?"

In this moment, a combination of despair and excitement (plus a hint of wild abandon) compelled Jared to respond in the affirmative.

"Yes. Yes, I do. Actually, would you be willing to sell me some?"

"Of course. How much you want?"

"Um, I'm not really sure how this works. Like, what is the recommended dosage?"

"You're adorable, Jared. $20 for a gram. That should do the trick."

Jared excitedly purchased the little bag of weed, which in hindsight probably weighed no more than ½ a gram, and stuffed it in his wallet.

"Thanks guys."

"For sure. Enjoy."


Off in the near-distance, music sounded. Jared hurried over to the lawn, strewn with folding chairs and proud families. He sat beside his parents and watched the ceremony, as the school principal droned on.

"...Before each of them lies endless possibility. There are chances to be undertaken, and brilliant days ahead. Each of these children has been given the opportunity to flourish in G-d's garden of freedom. How can they best make use of this gift? Hopefully, each boy and girl here will be wise and confident in his or her decisions. Let them be strong-willed and a good friend to all. May they gain strength from life's bitter conquests, and return from its battles unscathed. Why is this important? Why is this important? Why is this important? Why is this important? Why is this important? Why is this important? Why is this important? Why is this important? Why is this important? Why is this important? Why is this important? Why is this important? Why is this important? Why is this important? Why is this important? Why is this important? Why is this important? Why is this important? Why is this important? Why is this important? Why is this important? Why is this important? Why is this important? Why is this important? Why is this important? Why is this important? Why is this important? Why is this important? Why is this important? Why is this important? Why is this important? Why is this important? Why is this important? Why is this important? Why is this important?

"Eddie?"

"Hey man. How was K-----'s graduation?"

"It was delightful. Real inspiring and shit. Anyways, doesn't matter. Sooo, guess what."

"Uh, what?"

"While I was there, I ran into Ricky and Blake."

"Yea...?"

"Annnnnnddddddddd they sold me a lil' bag-o-weed."

"Dude! Are you serious?"

"Haha, yep."

"Oh shit! When are we doing this?"

"You free tonight?"

"Hells yes! Come on over."

After a spirited and celebratory family dinner, Jared's father dropped off his son at that ne'er-do-well Eddie's house. Supposedly, the boys would be resuming one of their many goofed out hobbies (e.g., video games and/or "jamming"), for another unthreatening and wholesome night. Ah, such polite, well-behaved kids.

"Bye, Dad."

The boys skipped their usual lighthearted introductory remarks. No time for such trivialities! Right away & w/o delay, Jared showed Eddie the little baggie. They examined it carefully, excited and a tad nervous as to the capability of its contents.

Naturally, they had yet to procure a device to enable the inhalation of their burnt offering, sideswiped from The Almighty's abundant cache. As luck would have it, Eddie had been instructed in the methodology of crafting a pipe out of an apple (that same troublesome neighbor taught him). Two stabs with a pencil and they were ready to go.

Eddie suggested that they walk to an overgrown patch of bushes on a hill down the street from his home. The plants formed a little cave in which young adolescents could engage in taboo activities, concealed and protected from the prying eyes of neighborhood elders. Once there, the boys placed a pinch of cannabis atop the apple core.

"Ready?"

"Yes sir."

"Well, it's been nice knowing ya!"

"Cheers, old sport!"

And so, they began puffin' da pipe, suckin' down smoke, choo choo choom. It tasted pleasant, aromatic and pungent.

Yumyumyumyumyum.

Spiraled toadstool footprints planted on tongue.

Enter the mind.

Eddie immediately began giggling uncontrollably at everything and nothing, like a nascent diva breaking through the sharp-toothed façade of an ashamed queer.

Jared, however, felt nothing.

Curse the soil!  I want to get high.  Today, mama.  Now!

They ended up smoking the entire bag.  By then, Eddie was deep throating every phallic object in sight, while Jared's upturned turnip brain vacillated between disappointment and regret.

hahahahahahahahahahahahahahahahahahahahahahahahahahahaha
hahahahahahahahahahahahahahahahahahahahahahahahahahahaha
hahahahahahahahahahahahahahahahahahahahahahahahahahahaha
hahahahahahahahahah you don't feel anything? haha
hahahahahahahahahahahahahahahahahahahahahahahahahahahaha
hahahahahahahahahahahahahahahahahahahahahahahahahahahaha
hahah Jared, this is insane! hahahahahahahahahahahaha
hahahahahahahahahahahahahahahahahahahahahahahahahahahaha
hahahahahahahahahahahahahahahahahahahahahahahahahahahaha
hahahahahahahahahahahahahahahahahahahahahahahahahahahaha
hahahahahahahahahahahahahahahahahahahahahahahahahahahaha

"No.  Nothing."

At a certain point, Jared gave up.  Maybe I'm immune; or perhaps I didn't do it right.  Oh well.  I guess this weed thing just ain't for me.

Eddie finally composed himself enough to evoke a tinge of clearheaded sincerity.  He wiped the cum off his chin and ventured to console his landlocked buddy.

"Come on.  Let's get out of here.  Maybe a change of scenery will help."

Jared attempted to stand up, but was physically unable to.

"Eddie!"

"Yea?"

"I can't feel my legs!  I'm serious.  I can't feel my legs."

And then, upon Jared's utterance re the status of his sudden disability, Eddie lost control.  Jared's temporary paralysis was apparently the funniest thing he had ever heard.  He became full-on Elton John, effortlessly shimmying back and forth.

"Eddie, I can't get feel my legs!"

Ha ha ha ha ha ha ha ha

After a hearty 5 minutes of non-stop laughter (from both parties), Eddie offered his encouragement. He reached out his hand and helped Jared up.

It's worth observing, from a clinical standpoint, that the first intoxicating effect Jared experienced was the loss of feeling in his legs. Druggies tend to vindicate their disease by claiming that they are on some sort of spiritual quest (a layman's damned soul attempt to reclaim Israel anew). That the true nature of the world is being revealed to them, assisted by the mind-expanding capabilities of the various substances that are carelessly pumped into their bloodstream. Thus, they boldly declare that their feelings are not being suppressed; instead, when high, their feelings are enhanced and amplified.

You have to be truly deranged to believe such babble. In this moment, Jared was numb. Heya kiddo, do you like this feeling? Or, rather, this lack of feeling? Apparently yes, since the remainder of Jared's life would be devoted to the pursuit of complete mental and physical annihilation, fumigating his brain of all divinity.

For instance, on the night of Jared's first solo smoke, he got high to escape the feelings of sadness that had been plaguing him ever since Amy left. He was certainly not summiting Sinai. No! Our boy wanted to dampen the purity of his emotions (albeit unpleasant ones). Turn off, tune out, whatever the fuck.

After Jared regained his balance (with Eddie's careful assistance), the freshly minted stoners commenced their trek back to Eddie's house. Eddie walked a few paces ahead, leading the way, while Jared sheepishly followed, staring down at his feet, in the defenseless stance unintentionally utilized by all depressed cowards. He carefully measured the precision of each step, ignoring the world around him.

When Jared finally looked up, his vision erupted into a magnificent display of natural wonder. It appeared as though he was wearing rainbow diffraction glasses, in which every light source emits traces of the color spectrum. Rainbow patterns spun counterclockwise around the streetlights that lined the hill during their upward expedition. He was amazed. He felt that childlike sense of joy where one is catapulted into the moment. Tomorrow and yesterday are obsolete.

They spent the remainder of the night wandering around the community, giggling. It was an experience that forever sealed and further fused together the close bond between Jared and Eddie. No matter what happens between us (for we may drift apart in our later years), we will always have this moment. Our first time, shared together. It is, in effect, the friendship equivalent of losing one's virginity.

DANGER! HE ENJOYED IT! DANGER!

He will assuredly partake again and again and again and again and again

Later on, while lying in bed that night and trying to fall asleep, Jared was troubled by the prospect that "the high" may have caused permanent brain damage. His mind remained a scattered mess. The feeling was not going away. He struggled to obtain quiet.

'Fuck,' he thought. 'I'm ruined. I will never be the same. I smoked weed once and I'm already a dimwitted burnout. Oh shit. Maybe it was laced with something. Oh god, I'm a fucking idiot.  My brain, my precious brain!  What have I done!?!?'

To relieve his panic, he decided to quiz himself.

Let's see…

'Avogardro's number is $6.02 \times 10^{23}$.  Yes!'

And so, this became Jared's mental life raft.  Whenever he'd get too high (such that he believed he'd never regain his sanity), he'd recite Avogardro's number.  This provided a sense of civilized comfort, a reminder that his mental faculties were still functioning.  As long as I can still remember it, I'll be okay.

John Nelson was a poet.
I shall scatter his poems among these pages,
and he will live on.

And then, in the sudden darkness of Jared's desolate bedroom, while he sat, en solitude, desperately grasping for a purpose to his rapidly deteriorating life, the phone rang.

"Hello," he answered, in a tired, hopeless whisper.

"Hi Jared."

The soft tone of her voice pierced through the dull vacancy of this moment. The sound waves, crisply transmitted through the receiver, gained physical form, practically knocking him over with their might.

He had given up. Thought he'd never see Amy again. She's gone. Out fucking Nick, the mystery man. Why would she ever contact me again? She's living the quintessential fresh and fragrant, full of youth, taut and tone, hot girl's life. Simply enter a public place and men will flock to you. They'll dazzle you with fun outings, in the hopes that you'll show your appreciation in the desired way. IT ALWAYS INVOLVES HIS DICK! For a young high school boy and his young high school girlfriend, the most threatening of all "other guys" is the older guy. Nothing is scarier than a guy that has already graduated, for he lives a reckless and liberated life. Jared and Amy both must've been about 16 at the time, and Amy was now dating a 19 year old. Whoa! *We met at the Coffee Bean. That's where all us rebels hang out on Friday nights.* Understandably, Jared had lost hope. She'll never return to me. Why would she? She's riding that monstrously large "old guy" cock. He drives a truck, he's out of school, smokes cigarettes, tattoos and sunglasses, etc. Why on earth would she ever want to return to a shriveled little shrimp? The adjustment was brutal. Jared's bedroom became an unholy sanctuary, where he worshipped the out-of-reach Amy. He'd literally sit by the window, davening to his fraudulent savior, praying that she'd show up unexpectedly one day, having realized that they're soulmates. O my innocent, fill the frame and return to me! When she (of course) failed to arrive, he instead envisioned the wild sexual escapades that she was likely engaged in with this Nick fella, while he cried to himself. The visual manifestation of this obscene act broke Jared's soul. How do I go on living? She was the love of my life. We were meant to be together. Everything has fallen apart. This isn't supposed to be happening! What the fuck is wrong with you? You have abandoned us.

"Amy! Hiya. How is everything?"

"I'm good. I'm– I'm good. Just wanted to say hi."

"Oh… okay. Well, that's sure nice of you. Yea, well, hi there."

"Listen, so this guitar is tuned now but I have no idea how to properly play it. Would, uh, would you be wiling to maybe teach me how…?"

"Sure! Yes, of course, Amy. That'd be a really cool thing for us to share."

"Are you busy tonight?"

"No, no plans. I was actually just pickin' a tune myself before you called."

"Ha! Really?"

"Yes ma'am. A real hopeless yearner, too. I tell ya, the lyrics to these old folk songs, holy shit, they're fucking devastating."

"Oh… uh, well, I'd love to hear some, I guess. So, is it okay if I come over?"

"Now?"

"Yea."

"Absolutely, Amy."

"Great!"

"Hey, would you mind parking around the corner though? I just don't want my parents to see your car. It's nothing personal, honestly, I–"

"That's fine, Jared. I get it."

"Alright, thanks."

"Okay. Well, I'll see you soon."

"See ya!"

Jared was stunned. From the moment their phone call ended, until Amy's arrival, he stared at the wall, slack jawed and amazed that the goddess of his lonely religion was to reveal herself, momentarily. How dost thou prepare for the messiah's return? Apparently by remaining motionless, in shock that it's actually happening. My dear, the subject of all longing, please come before me, materialize and cleanse me of the sorrowful filth I've accumulated in your absence.

All visitors to Jared's house (rather, his parents' house) were accustomed to the procedure of arriving through the side entrance, as the back door allowed for direct access to Jared's bedroom. Guests would first pass through a little gate. The jingle-jangle of the metal upon metal opening/closing alerted Jared of an incoming visitor, like an organic doorbell.

The chime of Amy's arrival shook Jared out of his daydream. He jumped up and ran over to the door, in order to offer her a proper greeting.

"Hello Madame." He adopted a sarcastic British accent and playfully bowed.

She gave a cute little curtsey in return.

The image of Amy in the doorway, carrying her daddy's guitar, absolutely astonished Jared. She was literally glowing. This is not some literary metaphor. She was legitimately glowing. Her figure was flanked by a heavenly, radiant aura. This ocular phenomenon caused Jared to question whether her presence was real. Have my eyes betrayed me? Is she actually here, or do I see a ghostly apparition? Had his delusionary thinking degraded to the point of hallucination? He analyzed her, physically, cataloguing the image, an attempt to preserve it, were she to suddenly fade from view. She wore a sexy, thin fabric dress containing a dark, flowery pattern (a sort of gothic tie-dye) that wrapped effortlessly to her skin. Her hair had grown back, but only slightly. She had achieved the perfect length. The proper balance between too short and too long. An artful, cum gushing goldilocks.

Jared could not fathom such beauty. How. The. Fuck. is this girl in my bedroom? He was unable to contain his awe.

"You look manifestly stunning, Amy."

"Aww, thanks Jared. It's nice to see you."

"You too. It's nice to see you too," he slowly repeated.

He smiled, staring intently at the most vibrant, gorgeous and sensual woman he's ever known.

"Well, come on in."

Amy stumbled into Jared's bedroom, a little wobbly and uncoordinated. Her pristine, flawless veneer slowly started to fade. She sat down on a chair that was innocuously placed beside his bed and immediately began noodling on her guitar.

'Fuck,' Jared thought to himself. 'She's drunk.'

He grabbed his guitar and sat on the edge of his bed, directly facing her.

"I guess we should get right to it," he mumbled, disappointed.

## How to play guitar : Introductory Lesson

1. Standard tuning is EADGBe. That is, the strings are tuned to these notes.

2. The little metal bars are called "frets."

3. Chords. Let's start with some chords. Today we will learn three different chords: E, A and B7.

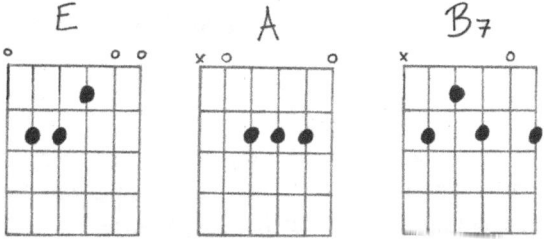

Amy genuinely seemed interested in learning how to play. She struggled to form the chords with her left hand and strummed clumsily with her right hand. Jared assisted her. He was a patient and compassionate teacher. Kept reassuring her, "Don't worry, you'll get the hang of it eventually. It just takes practice."

At one point, he reached over to help position her fingers. This was their first moment of physical contact. Finger upon finger, skin upon skin. He felt the significance of her touch, and wondered if she felt it too.

Suddenly, her cellphone rang, vanquishing all of the latent grace trembling 'neath the surface.

"Hello…Hi Nicky…I'm at my guitar lesson right now…That's okay…Yeah, I'll talk to you later…Alright, bye bye."

She hung up.

"What did he say? Is he mad that you're here?"

She laughed, defensively.

"No, not at all. He was like, 'Oh, silly goose, you shouldn't have answered your phone then. I don't want to interrupt.'"

"That's sweet, I guess."

"Come on, Jared. Don't hate him, he isn't all that bad."

They resumed the lesson, focusing on the task at hand.

Don't descend into the darkness. Think not of this man. Let's work on those chords instead. Gotta make sure each string is ringing clear. Pluck 'em, one at a time.

When Jared leaned in close to help Amy with the B7 chord, she turned and kissed his forehead. It was a quick, gentle droplet of admiration. A silent confession. The sensation of her lips making contact with his skin sent a shiver throughout his entire body. He was ecstatic. His wildest dream had come true. Jared, shocked, looked up, directly into Amy's eyes. They held this pose for a mere moment; and then, as though it were choreographed and predestined, began making out. Jared could feel his soul regenerating. My darling hath returned to me! They haphazardly put down their guitars and moved onto the bed.

Surrender. In this instant, they both surrendered to the sincerity within and pursued their unguarded impulses. A mutual desire, reciprocated. Consequence, abandoned. An honest answer to my true heart's calling. The splashed residue of untethered passion. Basketed and clean.

"I want you," she whispered.

"I want you too, Amy. Oh my god, I want you so badly. But, I just, I–"

"What's wrong?"

"Have you been drinking tonight?"

She sighed.

"It's okay, Jared. Yes, I admit I had a couple beverages before I came over. Alright? But that doesn't change anything. My feelings right now are genuine. I want you. I decided this well before the first drop of liquor landed on my tongue."

And so, having received her intoxicated blessing, he proceeded.

They made love, unleashing a massive accumulation of pent-up longing. Their fuck contained the fervor of having figured this would never happen again. The unexpected, front porch reunion between a young soldier and his hometown sweetie, after having assumed the worst (i.e., he's been blown to bits and she's blowing local civilians to bits). This eternal, elevated scene was entirely holy. A pure borne blessing. It was a real Sarah McLachlan-esque fuck. Fragile and serene. Senses were heightened. They were shaken from the daily stupor and immersed in a precious-gift-of-life, cherish-your-existence, highly emotional and tender love sesh. The reunion of 2 soulmates, after having wrongly deviated from destiny.

After they finished, Amy rushed into the bathroom. She was in there for longer than usual. When she finally emerged, she began to cry.

"Hey, what's wrong? Are you okay? What's wrong?"

Jared got up and stood by her side, in a conciliatory stance.

"I cheated on him."

"It's okay, Amy. You were drunk. You didn't mean to. It's okay. It was an accident. We just got carried away, that's all. It's not your fault."

"I can't believe I cheated on him."

He embraced her. She wept into his bare shoulder.

"I'm sorry, Amy. I knew we shouldn't have done that. I'm really sorry."

"But, Jared, I wanted you. I came over here tonight with the intention of sleeping with you. That was the plan all along."

"Well, you were possessed by a purely physical urge. Your body overtook you mind, temporarily. Fuck. I'm so sorry. I should have realized this was a mistake."

"Oh god! What is wrong with me?"

"You were drunk, Amy. Don't feel guilty." He reassured her and comforted her weeping.

"I have to go."

She retreated from his grasp and began pacing back and forth, whilst heedlessly gathering her belongings and getting dressed in a frantic, chaotic manner.

"Are you sure? Maybe you shouldn't be driving right now. You're welcome to stay the night."

"No! Are you fucking serious? Like that'll help things?"

"I don't know, I don't know. I'm not sure what to say here."

"Oh my god, this was such a fucking mistake."

"Amy, you were drunk. It's okay."

"Stop saying that! You aren't helping."

"I'm sorry."

She grabbed her guitar and rushed toward the door.

"Bye Jared."

"I love you, Amy."

She paused and looked back at him hesitantly.

"I… I have to go."

And with those parting words, she left.

Now alone, Jared couldn't help but smile. He felt as though he had somehow defeated Nick. Conquered the frightening demon of his nightmares. She's mine! She still loves me and she always will. Your insignificant little fling is over. Her heart forever belongs to me. He raised his fist to the sky and cackled like a cartoon villain.

The search party's 3rd report was delivered to Wilbur CoLaToLa, post haste. He sat at his desk, numb to the despair occasioned by the prior 2, whilst wretchedly clinging to the shallow promise that this document would somehow be different. That far-off glimmer of hope hasn't been extinguished yet!

Before opening it, he sat silently at his desk, somberly sippin' a glass of scotch (aged 12 years), mentally preparing himself for the inevitable. He engaged in the late afternoon, contemplative activity that defines the life of all elderly men: staring out the window.

### Dad is the mushroom king
Out there is the world, in all its vastness;
and here I am.
Is this where I want[ed] to be?
Have I fulfilled all of those youthful promises I made to myself?
Do my achievements outweigh my regrets?

Marjorie sheepishly entered the room.

"Well?" she asked.

"I haven't opened it yet," Wilbur responded, without diverting his gaze from the window.

"What the hell are you waiting for?"

Unnerved, he turned to her.

"It's just... I can't handle another one of these idle reports."

"Open it! Open it! Open it!"

She began jumping up and down, maniacally.

He looked over at her, disgusted by the sight. A symbolic representation of the psychic toll this whole ordeal had taken on his once happy family. My god, she's lost her mind.

"Leave me be, you repulsive wench! I will open the letter when I am prepared to bear its grim contents!"

"Open it! Open it!" she continued.

He stood, abruptly, marched over to Marjorie and slapped her across the face. Naturally, the bouncing ceased.

"What do you think it is going to say? Why do you expect this report to be any different than the rest?" he barked, further belittling her, crushing out all prospects for jubilation.

She slowly descended, droopy and hollow, into a little ball, curled up on the floor. The proper posture for a disgraced mother.

"My baby…" she sobbed.

"Get out of here, Marjorie," Wilbur ordered, knowing his words carried no authority with his newly-estranged wife.

"Who'll eat the Cornish game hens in her absence?"

Wilbur closed his eyes for a quick reprieve. A chance to temporarily escape this moment. He took a deep breath, as though the inward force could somehow absorb (and thereby quell) his impending wrath. It's worth a try.

"Marjorie, you have to leave, my dear."

"Escaped from my shelter…She leapt from my grasp…"

Wilbur shook his head in disappointment, both at his wife (for what she had become) and at himself (for what he was about to do). He reached down and pushed Marjorie out of the room. She maintained her balled-up shape and rolled down the hallway, all the while singing an obscure, unidentifiable nursery rhyme.

"Outside of my shadow…Please return to mommy…"

She eventually crashed into a cabinet, causing countless tchotchkes to fall on top of her. Now that's some genuine slapstick!

Wilbur returned to his desk, sat down, swallowed the last little splash of scotch and tore open the letter.

Nope. As he expected, the report indicated that Patricia was nowhere to be found.

'Fuck it,' Wilbur thought to himself. 'This is a waste of resources, a waste of time and a waste of mental energy on my part. I can no longer endure the emotional defeat inflicted by these reports.'

He reached for a blank sheet of parchment and issued the following command:

Cancel the search.
Join your fellow soldiers
in The Land of Forgotten Souls.

- Wilbur

On a random, inconsequential weekday, during their 12th grade year, Jared convinced Amy to ditch school and spend the day with him. His well-crafted itinerary was sure to provide a much more exciting experience than the last time they attempted this maneuver (i.e., playing hooky).

About a year or so prior, Jared had miraculously cajoled Amy into joining him for a midweek afternoon screening of the Enron documentary. He sure knew how to bore a gal! The drive home took forever. She couldn't wait to get away from him.

The night before, Jared had purchased a cheaply made (essentially disposable) badminton set from the local dollar store (to this day, I always head straight to the toy aisle). He stashed it in the trunk of his car. A Fun Thing To Do for whenever the need next arose.

"Come on, Amy. Can't we just have a pleasant day together? No discussing our 'status' and no debating whether we're lovers, friends or something in between. Let's simply enjoy each other's company. Okay? Is that too much to ask for?"

"My heart has already abandoned this relationship."

"Jesus Christ! Can you please cut it out with the dramatics? Did you not hear anything I just said?"

"Jared, I have a quiz in my English class tomorrow, anyways."

"Are you kidding? Since when do you give a shit about your grades? Listen, if you're going to make up excuses, at least try and be convincing about it."

"Okay, fine. What do you have in mind?"

"It's a surprise!"

"Oh gee, I can't wait. Another doc you're going to pretend to understand?"

"No... Our objective is fun, and nothing more. Got it?"

Their first stop was at the local park where, as a boy, Jared used to have T-ball practice. Per the schedule, they played badminton. Although Amy was reluctant to participate at first (thinking it to be a stupid, childish activity, unbecoming of her current distinction as a mature, hymenless pot smoker), once they started smacking that shuttlecock into the sky, she couldn't help but giggle cheerfully at the ineluctable pleasure this game elicited. That bright, gleaming smile of hers burst through the lame, veiled attempt to conceal the genuine happiness she felt.

The 2 sickly and wing-clipped (former) lovebirds were, at once, engrossed in the physical brilliance of sport. It was the first sense of playful innocence they'd experienced in quite a while; perhaps since before sex dictated the boundaries of their relationship. She hustled to return his volleys, yelping and hooting with each toilsome swing.

Jared acquired a false sense of hope. He began to believe that everything would be okay. Yea! We can work it out.

Their next stop was the beach. They cruised through the canyon, with the windows down and **those songs** playing on the car stereo. The songs that provide the soundtrack to these seemingly insignificant-and-futile but ultimately profound-and-treasured chapters in our lives; which, when heard decades later in a supermarket during a dull Monday night grocery run, immediately transport us back to those moments of pure, unlimited potential.

Here I find myself, weeping in the breakfast aisle.

They explored the hip, fauxhemian beach scene, fully embracing every aspect of it. The admirable homeless, the liberated sex queens and, of course, the unapologetic acceptance of drug addiction (culture excuses criticism). After getting lunch at a dingy beach grill, they took a stroll down the boardwalk. While walking, they casually and without mention, held hands. It was a sweet and comfortable gesture, mutually desired and achieved. The warmth of home, restored. They spotted a head shop (one of several) and Jared announced that he desired to purchase a pipe. Upon entering the dark, cavernous, paraphernalia enclave, they were greeted by fantastical black-light posters, designer bongs and the deep rumble of reggae music. The stoned-out shopkeeper (a mid-20's rambler) emerged from the back room and immediately recognized Amy.

"Hey girl!" he zonked.

'Fucking hell,' Jared thought to himself. 'Of course she knows this asshole.'

"Hiiii," Amy bashfully replied. "Aren't you Chris's friend?"

"Yes ma'am. At yer service."

'She probably fucked this guy. And I don't know who Chris is, but she probably fucked him too.'

"So, how can I help you two?"

"Oh, I'm just browsing, but he wanted to get a pipe."

"No, that's okay. I don't want anything."

"What? Jared, you just said you wanted a pipe."

"Yea, but I don't really need to get one today or here or–"

"Lemme help you out, man. No pressure. If you ain't interested, it's all good. But while I've got ya here, check out this little fella."

He reached into the display case and pulled out a glass-blown pipe, decorated with swirls of blue and red.

"This is a good starter. Nothing fancy. Classic style. Hits smooth, too."

Jared picked it up and examined it closely.

"I… I actually kinda like this one."

"Yea, it's pretty."

"Watch this, you guys."

The stoner dude took the pipe out of Jared's hands and threw it on the floor. Jared and Amy both gasped. To their surprise, the pipe landed on the wood-planked floor, unscathed.

"Sturdy as fuck. If any of y'all are clumsy, there's nothing to worry about."

Jared bent down and retrieved the pipe.

"Well?"

"Sure. I'll take it."


That evening, Jared and Amy got high together. They packed a bowl in the new pipe and smoked it in the backyard of Jared's (parents') house. They laughed together. Euphoric. Exhaling plumes amidst the far-off twinkle of neighborhood lights. Afterwards, they went inside. Their unrestrained and amplified sexual urges inspired them to take a shower together. Sure, why not? Jared cranked up the hot water and they undressed, slowly, while steam filled the room. Once fully nude, they gently kissed each other (a friendly 'good luck' sendoff) and stepped into the shower's enveloping warmth. Without any design or methodology, Jared sat on the floor and Amy straddled him. Their actions were the product of unmitigated impulse. They started making out. Soon enough, Amy began grinding against Jared's then-erect cock, the cushioned edges of her pussy gliding up and down its taut undercarriage, while she moaned with delight beneath the warm waterfall. Unable to resist any longer, Jared slid into Amy. Entered her, fully. She took him in, whole. While thrusting herself on top of him, she screamed. An uncensored, crystalline expression of the ecstasy she felt (as though every vein in her body were quivering, and she, fully liberated, was able to savor the entire lotus plant, let loose and unashamed). The shower walls echoed with her raw cadence. This whole spectacle was overwhelming for Jared. As a consequence, he came. Amy felt the heat of his load rushing into her womb. This sensation further catapulted her into a deeper state of sexual nirvana. She orgasmed, heavily, and they both melted into a gooey puddle of aftermath. Once the madness subsided, Amy gave Jared a forceful kiss on the lips. She then stared directly into his eyes and proudly proclaimed, "I love you."

The next morning, in the clarity of a new day (and the system reset that is sleep), Jared panicked. Oh no oh no oh no oh no oh no oh no oh no oh no oh no oh no oh no oh no oh no!

He grabbed a scrap of paper and wrote:

> Dear G-d,
> Please don't let Amy be pregnant.
> Sincerely,
> Jared

He retreated into the backyard and lit the note on fire. It burned quickly, and he was forced to drop it (for fear of singeing his fingers) before the flame consumed the entirety of his communiqué. Concerned that this would hinder proper delivery, Jared meticulously ensured that every remaining portion of the page (and most importantly, every little letter) had been sufficiently engulfed. Once satisfied, Jared watched the smoke float up to the heavens.

### *My child, your prayers will be answered*

This is a letter that I need to write
should have written a long time ago
I feel that there is a conversation
we must have
I don't even know
how to start it, but I feel like
this letter is the best way
I hope that this letter will
be the beginning of a healthy
conversation
I don't even know how to
address the issue or what to say
Ever since it happened, I've been trying
to forget.  I've gotten pretty good
at ignoring it, forgetting it
But lately
I think about it and I
say to myself
It's time
It's time I confront this
once and for all
I'm not sure what to say
or even how to say it
I think it would be healthy
if we had a conversation
and talked about it
For now, I think it's important
for me to apologize
I need to say that I'm
sorry.  I
was the instigator
I'm responsible
I'm sorry that you've had
to live with this memory
I'm sorry if it makes you
uncomfortable

"Hello?!"

*What the fuck?*

"Hello. Is anyone there?"

*Oh no. It's him. Why is he answering her phone?*

"Hellooo?"

"Hi. Umm, is Amy available?"

"Jared? Is that you?"

"…yes."

"Listen man, she doesn't want to talk to you right now. Alright? Bye."

"I just want to–"

<click>

Over the drone of the dial tone, Jared continued.

"I fucked her, Nick! I fucked her! Can you hear me? I fucked her! She still loves me."

> The noble battalion marched toward
> The Land of Forgotten Souls,
> ready to pulverize any dissidents.

In the midst of her ruinous concessions, a subtle tinge of hope revealed itself, casting aside all the dreaded uncertainty of the present moment. The drunken sincerity of her words apprised Jared of a singular, unshakable truth: their love would endure, forever. His romantic aspiration for tomorrow's close-cuddled sunrise/sunset (take your pick) had been revived.

This all became abruptly apparent when Amy called Jared and made the following request: "Can I come over? I want to show you my new haircut."

Of course, he acquiesced. However, he regretfully informed her that his entire extended family was currently at the house for some sort of celebration.

"That's okay. I just want to stop by. I won't come inside or anything."

Amy pulled up in her Toyota Supra.
Jared was outside waiting for her.

"Hop in."
"Where are we going?"
"Don't worry about it."
"But my fam–"
"Jared, we won't be gone long.  Just get in."
He begrudgingly entered the car.
Once situated, he was able devote his full attention to evaluating Amy's new haircut, which, of course, was the entire purpose of the present meeting (right?).
"Damn Amy, you look… uh, you're… you are so fucking hot!  I don't know how else to describe it.  You're just a total hottie right now."
She laughed, flattered.
"Thanks, Jared."

This day, in this moment, is how I'll always remember Amy.  This was peak Amy.  Her hair had finally been perfected. Her skin was milky and youthful, and she wore a white tank top with cheer shorts.  This is the version of her that is ingrained in my mind.

She turned onto a little side street, not far from Jared's parents' house. It was clear that she wasn't exactly sure where she was going. Just cruising around, aimlessly. She parked near a plant-covered hillside, at one of the few semi-secluded areas in the neighborhood (i.e., not directly in front of a house), and shut off the engine.

"So, what's up?"

She took a deep breath to calm her nerves.

"Nick and I broke up."

She said it so matter-of-factly, without any emotion.

"Oh! Really?"

"Yeah…"

"That's, um… I'm not sure if you're looking for sympathy or something, but I gotta say, that's great news, Amy. I guess, I don't know. I'm sorry if you're sad about this situation, but I'm not the one to–"

"I want you to fuck me, Jared. Right now."

"Uhh…"

She unbuckled her seatbelt and slithered into the backseat.

"Come on!"

Jared followed, without objection. He climbed on top of her and they started making out, intensely. Right away, she began removing Jared's pants.

"I don't have a condom," he announced, between kisses.

"That's okay. I brought one."

She slipped off her shorts and they fucked right there in the backseat of her car, in broad daylight, while the debut album by The Yeah Yeah Yeahs blasted from the stereo. It was superficial and abrupt. The entire lovemaking session occurred within the duration of the song "Tick." Nonetheless, Amy seemed satisfied. She had achieved her objective, however terse.

She then dropped Jared off at his parents' house and he rejoined the family gathering, all smiley and elated.

I knew it. Everything is going to be okay.

Alto Undershed stood at a podium and set forth the battle plan.

The strongest, most intimidating souls (a mere total of 20 people) were to stand guard at the border. Fortunately, there was only 1 road that led into the territory: the dirt canyon that bisected Hopler's Tea Trimmer (a plantation maintained by Theodore Hopler, the fella that devised a method for cutting the abundant, often obnoxiously-overgrown tea plants that flourished in the region). As such, they knew precisely where the South Forts armed forces would be coming from. This strategy was intended to frighten the incoming aggressors, and to potentially provide for a final attempt at peaceful negotiation.

As for the remaining 7,480 or so of the population, they were to link arms and form a human chain along the river, with guns strewn discretely behind their backs. Once the transport vessels (tanks, bulldozers, etc.) got too close for comfort, they were to open fire.

Interestingly, Alto thought it prudent to incorporate music into the combat preparations, as a means of riling up his soldiers.

The battle hymns of his measly republic consisted entirely of reggae music. Now, to those of us who equate reggae music with tropical island getaways and Mai Tais, this may seem counterintuitive. How on earth could the mellow vibe of reggae compel warriors to fight?

Easy.

Reggae is about revolution.

Please be sure to remind every ganja tokin' college kid of this.  Especially those with the audacity to wear green/yellow/red beanies.

Reggae music is unquestionably the most sacred, socially conscious and politically radical music ever to exist. It is capable of toppling Babylon through sheer sound waves (see rhythm, melody and lyric).  No other musical form is as powerful.  Every emergent hippie eagerly extoling the transformative force of music (typically in the form of dainty, lovelorn folk tunes) must recognize that only one singular genre has the proven ability to shake the world.

Amy invited Jared to attend a classical music concert at the Hollywood Bowl (with mama and Mitch, of course).  The Los Angeles Philharmonic was to be performing Ludwig van Beethoven's Symphony No. 9 in D minor, Op. 125; arguably the finest piece of music ever composed.

The morning of the show, while talking on the phone, Jared and Amy got into an argument about something.  The precise reason for their disagreement has since been forgotten. Regardless, this fight escalated to such an emotional height that Jared ended up throwing his phone at the wall, destroying it.

Jared's father, having heard the commotion, hurriedly entered his bedroom.

"What's going on in here?" he asked.

"Nothing, dad.  Just Amy stuff," Jared responded.

"Huh?  Well, what was that sound?"

"I… I kinda got carried away.  I threw my phone.  I'm sorry."

Jared pointed at the shattered remains.

Jared's father glanced over at the broken phone, and then turned back to face his visibly distraught son.  The weakling, derived from his loins.  Rather than offer a sense of warmhearted sympathy (for instance, on a prior occasion, when Jared was remorseful for having accidentally struck his best friend in the head with a golf club, his father told him "it's okay to cry.") or a sense of macho man camaraderie ("women are so crazy, right?"), he proceeded to berate him.

"You brat! What are you so upset about? Honestly, do you realize how fortunate you are to have such a privileged and sheltered life? With all I've provided you... show a little gratitude, Jared. Or, at the very least, have some respect for yourself."

"Dad, I–"

"I just don't get it. You can do anything, Jared! Literally anything you want. And yet, how are you making use of the unlimited opportunities you have?"

"I didn't mean to–"

"You're sitting in your room, having a little tantrum and throwing your phone at the wall because of some stupid girl? Unbelievable. You have no idea how close you are to having your life become a real struggle. Because once I'm gone, you're on your own. And I'm not going to live forever; especially not with my health."

"I'm sorry, dad. I don't know what came over me. I appreciate all you've done for me. I swear to G-d, I do. I'll clean this up right away."


Later on, Jared used another phone to call Amy. He apologized (again). She forgave him (again), and they attended the concert. Midway through the show, Amy wept. In part because the music moved her so, but also because she felt guilty.


"In honorable tribute to the natives upon whose land we now stand," Alto spoke, "we must all scream the following battle cry before opening fire on the enemy:

Cam Lé Ö Tesh rá. Tū Züme, Tū Züme.

This phrase is the last surviving excerpt of their ancient language. When these words depart from your lips, it will be as though our ancestors are here with us. After all, it is on their behalf that we are fighting. May their legacy forever endure!"

Jared and his friends began watching porn (like, carnal beast porn) at a severely young age. Must've been in 4<sup>th</sup> grade. This is due, entirely, to the graciousness of Griselda. Not only did she provide the boys with a bevy of magazines, she soon began distributing VHS tapes, too. Now, at this point in their maturation, Jared and his friends were not yet at the masturbatory stage. Rather, they would sit and watch the films, politely, from start to finish, with their hands at their sides. In one particular scene, the male protagonist "pulled out" and came all over the back of the recipient female lead (they had been engaged in the doggy-style position prior to his climax). As droplets of thick white goo chaotically splashed against her skin, Jared and his friends exchanged confused glances. What is that? I think it's sperm. But that doesn't look like sperm. Where's the tail?

Eventually, one of the boys (likely Charlie) discovered masturbation. This precious intel was immediately shared with the group. Soon they became a symphonic league of young masturbators. Of course, Jared's house became the desired destination for sleepovers. Not because he was exceptionally fun to be around (at least, no more or less than the rest), but because once his parents went to bed, it was time to press play. The boys would strategically position themselves in separate sections of his room, so as to retain some semblance of privacy. They'd cover their little dicks with blankets and it was off to the races. An impending orgasm was signaled by an uptick in heavy breathing (near panting) and an increase in pumping speed. Finally, the post-eruption moments were audibly recognizable. You could hear the squishy sound of cum-on-the-cock, as the masturbator would inadvertently self-lubricate himself during the final spurts.

Jared, being the youngest of his friends, was not yet sufficiently developed enough to achieve orgasm. While watching porn, he'd masturbate along with the rest of 'em, but he never experienced the grand triumph.

Finally, late one evening, after the porn viewing party had concluded, the boys decided to engage in a more age-appropriate activity; namely, watching The Tonight Show. With everyone's focus diverted, Jared took this opportunity to again attempt to achieve the pinnacle of puberty. Slowly and quietly, he started tugging on his dick. Soon enough, he got hard. He continued, gently and discreet. Something about this method increased his arousal (as opposed to the domineering assault he'd endeavor while watching porn). And so, Jared finally came, for the first time ever, while Jay Leno interviewed Hugh Grant.

Fulfilled and empty, Jared and his friends all slept like naughty little angels.

At 5:00 a.m., the radio turned on. It was tuned to an obscure AM station.

"Some local news for you this morning. It appears that a few elementary school students were up to, uh, no good, to say the least. Yes, a group of third grade boys were caught sucking each other's penises during their classroom's designated reading hour."

"Yikes!"

"According to the students' teacher, she noticed suspicious movements happening in the corner of her classroom where the group of boys were clustered. When she approached, she observed one of the boys with his head on the lap of one of his classmates, with the, um, receiver's t-shirt being used to conceal the actions of the... delivering party."

"Gadzooks! Sure gives a whole new meaning to the term delivery boy."

"When confronted, the boys, 4 of them in total, confessed to taking turns sucking on each others' penises. It is unclear where the boys learned of such behavior. Their parents were immediately contacted and the children have been mandated to undergo counseling."

"Ya know, I gotta admit, this story is kinda amusing at first, but in all honesty, this is a serious issue. Child-on-child sexual abuse is a real problem. It's traumatic."

"Ah, come on! These kids were just messing around here. Part of being a kid is experimenting, even sexually at times. We all played doctor when we were younger."

"Sure, but this is beyond casual curiosity. This is an instance of sexual molestation, plain and simple. I assure you that at least one of those kids is a victim of sexual abuse, as we commonly understand the term (i.e., with an adult agitator). The school responded properly to this incident. Therapy is critical here. These children have no idea how traumatic this is. It'll haunt them later in life and manifest itself in unexpected ways."

"Jeez! I think you're overreacting a bit. Again, I think these kids were just goofing off. They definitely crossed the line of appropriate classroom behavior, but there's no need to send them to therapy. This is part of the problem, we're all becoming so sensitive–"

Jared turned off the radio. He glanced about the room. Everyone was still asleep. It appeared that no one else had heard this ominous broadcast. No, his friends remained ignorantly adrift in the victimless void of a cum-crusted, boyhood slumber party.

There they stood,
20 strong,
the bravest (forgotten) souls available,
tasked with preventing the scourge,
heroic in their deed,
mighty – yet frightened, nervous and unglued,
theirs was to be the ultimate sacrifice,
the unanticipated opportunity
to embody their ethical mantra,
WE STAND, EMBOLDENED, AGAINST YOU!

The enemy approached.

They clutched their rifles,
and howled, unleashing the wrath within.

Not a single shot was fired,
their non-violent tendencies got the best of them.

Instead, the South Forts military proceeded on their trek toward the river and, without a moment's hesitation, ran over the entire feeble brigade that stood guard at the border. It was unclear whether this was a deliberate act of warmonger bravado or if they simply didn't see the pathetic little congregation. Either way, all 20 were mowed down with the careless ease of weekend lawn maintenance, marking the first casualties of this wretched fight. Onward!

"Please, Jared!"

"Ugh, I don't know, Amy. I'm really not interested in doing this."

"Come on! If we are to make this work, you're going to have to help out with these types of events."

"I don't even understand what I'm supposed to do."

"It's super simple. You and I will be stationed at one of the game booths together. We just collect tickets and run the game. I don't know what the rules are yet, but how hard can it be?"

"Yeah, but it's at your church, too… Churches make me uncomfortable."

"What the fuck, Jared!? It's not like I'm asking you to accept Christ here. You're not going to burst into flames because of this. Hell, we aren't even going to enter the church. The carnival takes place in the outer lawn area."

"But…"

"If you seriously want to get into a discussion about theology over a fucking children's carnival, I'll gladly engage."

"Sure. Whaddya got?"

"I was being sarcastic, but okay. For one, we worship the same G-d. You and I (and our respective religions) simply disagree about the fulfillment of a certain prophecy set forth in the Old Testament."

"And that is?"

"The coming of the messiah. We believe that he already arrived. Meanwhile, you're still waiting for someone better to come around. Typical."

"It was not Christ! The temple has not been rebuilt, peace has definitely not been restored, Israel's existence is beyond fragile–"

"Jesus was prevented from completing his work because he was executed! His mission was thwarted. Don't you dare cite his failure to achieve these conditions as somehow demonstrative of his lack of divinity! External forces got in the way."

"Alright! Shit. I'm sorry I mentioned it."

"Well, don't get me started then. This church is a special place for my family and I. Irrespective of my, um, improper lifestyle, I still love it there. I feel a sense of comfort and spiritual restoration whenever we go. Plus, it would really mean a lot to my mom if you helped out."

After a long, pensive pause, Jared responded.

"I'll be there."


Jared and Amy were assigned to manage a game booth at which children would be handed a stick with a nail on the end of it. The lil' participants would then be directed to poke, and thereby pop, a balloon (one of many) on the opposite wall of the booth. Each balloon contained a prize, which the kids would then gleefully retrieve. It's not even worth calling this a game. There was no skill or strategy involved. You'd select a balloon and stab it. That's it. Also, the safety of this particular activity was questionable. Oh well, the kids seemed to enjoy it. And, most importantly, it was clear that Amy genuinely appreciated Jared's assistance.


After the carnival ended, Jared and Amy helped Amy's mother (and several other volunteers) in dismantling the various game booths and cleaning up the luncheon area. When they finished, Amy suggested that she and Jared wait in the car, while mama Carousel continued her lively conversation with all the fellow churchgoing parents.


They sat in the car, Amy in the passenger seat and Jared in the seat directly behind her. Amy decided to leave the passenger-side doors open, to allow a slight breeze to pass through the compartment. Temperature control. She sat backwards, facing him.

"Oh! I wanna show you this song."

"Sure…"

Amy turned on the car's CD player and clicked through to the desired track. Suddenly, a long held organ tone sounded (always a good sign!). During the next 3-4 minutes, Jared listened the most beautiful song he had ever heard in his life. It was a majestic, tenderhearted ballad full of hope and reprieve. He was moved. His heart swelled.

"What is this?"

"It's called 'The Eternal Flame of Love' by Fischerspooner."

Strange, Jared thought. Amy had shown him this band before, and he was not a fan. Actually, the prior songs had profoundly upset and disturbed him. His first impression was that this band embodied the shitty, hyper-sexualized electronica music that Amy now listened to. Empowered slut anthems! But this song was different. Very different.

"I love it!"

She kissed him.

"And I love you, Jared."

I never heard that song again. To this day, I have not been able to find this particular song. I've scoured the track listings for all of Fischerspooner's albums, and there is no such song.

The full might of South Forts crossed over the horizon.
At once,
visible.
It was a terrifying sight.

Had they not been wholly absorbed in their delusions,
the entirety of the human chain would've known,
right then and there,
that they didn't stand a chance.

South Forts' strength was too great.

But they held tightly together,
as one.
Courageous.
Though their task was undoubtedly doomed.

At one point, Amy was taking violin lessons with some older, French fella. She had confided to Jared that this guy made her uncomfortable. He was creepily flirty with her and often made inappropriate, sexually suggestive comments. His conduct crossed the line when, on a particular occasion, while Amy was exiting the room, he slapped her ass. Once Jared learned of this incident, he was livid. "That mother fucking piece of shit! I am going there with you next week, and I am going to rip his fucking head off! Who the fuck does this guy think he is? How dare he touch you! Amy, this is horrendous!"

As promised, Jared accompanied Amy to her next lesson. When the Frenchman opened the door, Jared's heightened machismo vanished, and he again became the shy, quiet, undeservedly polite little boy.

"Ello Amy! And who is this?"

"This is my boyfriend, Jared."

"Jared! Pleasure to meet you!"

"Hello, sir."

They shook hands, cordial. And that was it. No brawl. No confrontation. Nothing.

"Please come in, young man."

"Actually, I saw there's a newspaper stand down the road. I think I'm gunna go hang out there until the lesson is over."

"Sure, sure, whatever you wish."

Monsieur Violin enthusiastically closed the door, leaving Jared (Amy's supposed protector) outside the room.

This pathetic instance became a dominant, recurring theme in Jared's life. He'd frequently announce some sort of grand action he planned to undertake, usually involving a bold, valiant gesture; however, when it came time to act, he'd shrink into his shell and hide away from his promise. Niceness, at the expense of honor.

"I'm leaving, Patricia. That's my cue," Patrick said, pointing at the approaching army.

"You're really going to do it, huh? You're honestly going to abandon us? In our time of need?" she responded.

"Precisely now. I will never use a gun to resolve a conflict. It's as simple as that. Matters of law and politics exist in the realm of ideas. If you cannot reach a consensus through logic and argument, and instead find it necessary to force your position upon someone with weaponry, I'd say you're advocating an unconvincing policy."

"Who's the idealist here? Please, as justification for the morality of our decision, let me refer you to every war in human history. I'm sorry, Patrick, but oftentimes language isn't enough. It's an unfortunate truth, but sometimes violence is necessary. That's my simple statement for you. Humans are ugly, selfish creatures. If you believe otherwise, well, you are unworldly beyond measure."

"Look, it's clear we don't agree on this. I get that. But I'm not trying to stop you from fulfilling your purpose here; or, at least, what you, through some drug-addled midnight-epiphany connect-the-dots fallacy, think your purpose is. I'm not trying to stop any of you. Go ahead and kill! Have at it. This is a personal decision for me. I am going to excuse myself from this menagerie, but I ain't standing in anyone's way."

Patricia gave up. In a way, she respected Patrick for his decision. She was impressed with his certainty of belief. Indeed, she envied this about him. He held true to his moral code, no matter if it upset his companions.

"So, I guess this is it."

Patrick bowed his head.

"It has been an honor serving you, Patricia. You entered my life during a very difficult time, while I endured a solemn transition, cast out on a fortuitous exile. My master and I had separated, right before I met you. I didn't run away. It was an accident! I swear I didn't intend to leave him. I just wanted to explore the town a little more. Most of the time, I was cooped up in the house, and whenever he'd take me for a walk, we'd traverse the same well-worn path. I just wanted some excitement, some adventure. I felt an unrelenting compulsion to leave. *Go forth, to a land that I will show you.* At first, I desired to visit the nearby, unfamiliar areas; though I planned on returning home, I assure you. But once I got my first taste of the wild unknown, I couldn't help myself. I thought, alrighty, one more street, then I'll return to him. This pattern persisted. On and on and on. Once I finally decided to go home, I didn't know where I was. I was lost, Patricia! I didn't know how to get home. I didn't mean to leave him. I spent weeks trying to retrace my steps. It only seemed to take me further away. Just when I thought all hope was lost, and I was ready to quit, fixin' to lay down and die, you appeared. You were... broken in the same way. Or so I thought. We really made a good team, Patricia. You helped me learn to embrace my circumstance. Your presence suggested 'Let's keep going!' And that is exactly what we did. We continued the exploration I had set out for. I learned to love the road, the travelin' life. Accountable to no one. Freewheeling! Except, that's not a sustainable lifestyle. At least, not for me. Because no matter had hard you're living, you can never escape what it is you're running from. Or, in my case, what I was trying to find. These heartaches exist within us. They follow us everywhere."

He turned to leave.

"Where will you go?"

Patrick responded, with his back still turned to her.

"To find him. And ya know, maybe I'll die before I ever see him again. Oh well. Until I do, I ain't quitting."

"I'm going to miss you terribly, Patrick. Good luck."

"Thanks, Pat. It's interesting. When we first arrived here, in this town, I nearly forgot. I forgot about him. And I forgot who I was. I was fully committed to this scene, for a moment. Now, as I prepare for my departure, I thank G-d that a small speck of dignity remains in me. Enough to propel me onward."

He began to walk away.

"Wait! Before you go, I want you to have something."

She sprinted toward Patrick and stood in front of him, blocking his path. She then reached into her satchel and removed John Nelson's journal.

"Here. Take it with you."

"What?! I can't take this."

"Please, I want you to have it. You deserve it, Patrick. Oh, you have no idea!" she wailed. "You helped me learn to finally accept John's death. It was a harsh and difficult truth to endure at first, and I was doggedly defensive; but, ultimately, you allowed me to forgive myself for what happened. I'm not a bad person. Sure, I was a terrible girlfriend. That is certain. But he was sick. It wasn't because I was evil or anything. I was just a dumb kid. And I was horny as shit. I was working out my own issues. I didn't think he'd actually..."

"I accept your offering. I will preserve his journal and his words, forever. Farewell, Patricia. You have been a true blessing."


"I don't want to overwhelm you or anything, but my church is having a talent show next week and... I... kinda... signed you up for it."

Jared laughed, pleased.

"Really? That sounds awesome!"

"Yes! Oh joy! I'm so relieved. I wasn't sure how you'd react."

"I would be honored to contribute my mediocre talent to this show."

"So, on the sign-up sheet I wrote that you'd be singing a song; and playing guitar too, of course."

"Perfect. That's my shtick."

"Any songs in mind?"

"I think I'll write an original, specifically for this occasion. You know, really get excessive with some biblical imagery."

"Okay. Just make sure it's child appropriate."

### Noah's Rock

Here comes a great big wave
To wash all your troubles away
Just when you thought you were safe
He's got another trick

I need 2, 2, 2, 2, 2 of every animal
I need 2, 2, 2, 2, 2 of every animal

You better watch out
You better be careful
Or they're all gonna know
It's your ark they want to ride on

Noah's Ark, Noah's Ark
Oh how I want to ride Noah's Ark
And if they don't pick me
I'll be swallowed by the sea

Please don't eat me grandpa
After the world ends
After we're all washed away
In the end

Jared played the song for Amy (an intimate, private performance). She loved it. She was nearly moved to tears. Not because the song itself was anything special, but because it was obvious that Jared had put a lot of effort into writing this trifling number. This gesture signified his devotion and commitment to things that were important to her (and which she knew were outside of his faith-based comfort zone). Amy felt content. Jared had sufficiently demonstrated his trustworthiness. He was a well-qualified lover.

The day of the talent show, he bailed. Again, Jared made a promise and then retracted it at the last minute.

"I just can't do it."

"But, why?"

"I'm sorry, Amy. I just can't. I really don't feel like it."

"That's not a valid reason. I was counting on you, Jared. I've been telling people about your song. They're really excited to hear it."

"Amy, please. I'm sorry."

"What's wrong with you? Why would you do this to me?"

"I'm not doing anything to anyone."

Jared knew he wasn't going to perform at the show well in advance of this interaction. In fact, he knew he wasn't the second he agreed to do it. So why'd he say yes? Because it's easier to be agreeable in the moment (and postpone the letdown) than to say how you really feel (when the truth will be a disappointment). The conundrum here is that he ends up disappointing Amy even worse than he would have had he just said no from the outset. Had he said no originally, she would've had ample time to find a replacement and to overcome his decision. Instead, by telling her yes (though he never truly meant it), he allows her to accumulate an emotional stockpile of anticipation and excitement, only to cause it all to come crashing down, ever so suddenly, in an appalling display of deceit.

Jared was a no show. In his place, Amy played the violin to a crowd of confused, disinterested onlookers.

*Adonai,*
*please forgive me for failing to act when action was necessary*

### Memorable Movies

Harry Potter 2 – Jared and Amy saw it together. The movie had already been out for a few weeks, so the crowds had dissipated. They sat in the back row. Halfway through the film, Amy started giving Jared head, right there in the theatre. One of the ushers came rushing over to them. "Knock it off, you two. Come on, keep it clean."

Daredevil – Amy and Charlie saw it together, on Valentine's Day. "I don't understand. Why are you guys going together?" "I asked you if you wanted to see it, and you said no." "Well, it looks fucking stupid. Had I known you would go and invite Charlie instead, I'd have said yes." "Sorry, Jared. It's too late now. Charlie and I are going." "Is this a date?" "What?! No! Charlie and I are friends, Jared. We were friends before you and I started dating, and we're still friends. We're going to see a movie. That's something friends do together. Don't you trust me? Honestly, I don't understand why you're making this into such an issue." "Because it's Valentine's Day." "Okay… Well, for one, you recently delivered a full-on lecture as to why you don't recognize Valentine's Day as an official holiday." "Neither does the state." "And more importantly, you didn't make any plans for us. I get that *you* don't think it's a real holiday, but I do." "I hope the theatre burns down."

March of the Penguins – Jared and Charlie saw it together.

> "Amy!"
> "What?"
> "I need to see you tonight. I have something very important to tell you."
> "Not now, Jared. This isn't a good time."
> "Please. I've had a revelatory experience!"
> "What? Alright… um, sure. I'll be free in about an hour. You wanna come by then?"
> "Fantastic!"

"Call me when you're outside, okay? I'll come out and meet you."

"Okay."

Jared was at her house exactly 60 minutes later. As instructed, he called her.

She answered, promptly. No hello, no greeting, just a hurried "I'll be right out."

She emerged, looking slightly worn and distraught.

"Hi!"

"Hey. Sorry, my grandpa's not doing too well. I think it's best if you don't come inside tonight."

"Oh dear. I'm sorry, Amy. Uh... Is he going to be okay?"

"I have no idea. Doubtful. I mean, he's really old and he's starting to lose– I, I don't really want to talk about it. It's not pretty in there."

"Fuck. I'm really sorry."

"It's okay, Jared. Come on, let's go somewhere. I could use a momentary repose."

"Yea, okay. Have you had dinner yet?"

"Not really. I don't know. I don't remember."

"Well, do you wanna get something?"

"Sure. But just something quick. I don't feel like sitting in a restaurant right now."

"Del Taco?"

"That'll do."

And off they drove, to Jared's favorite fast-food eatery.

"So what's this urgent news you have? Let's get right to it. I'm damn curious."

"Well, okay, so I just saw <u>March of the Penguins</u> and–"

"Are you kidding me? This couldn't wait?"

"Amy, listen! This is serious. Going in, I had no idea what I was about to experience. I thought it'd be a charming little documentary about penguins."

"Yes, I believe that is how it's advertised."

"Right. But it's so much more than that."

"Really? Are there giraffes in it too?"

"Stop joking around. It had a profound impact on me."

"Alright, sorry. Sheesh."

"The movie is about us, Amy."

"What?"

"There's this one scene where they describe how the penguins practice monogamy. Once a penguin chooses its mate, they stay together for the rest of their lives. And there's this one shot where two penguins are leaning against each other in an embrace. It was during this when I realized that **love is real**. It's not a unique human fabrication. No! All G-d's creatures experience love. Our love, too, is real. It really reaffirmed my feelings for you, Amy. Not that I needed a reminder or anything. I swear I saw us in those penguins. It was you and I."

"That's actually really sweet, Jared."

They placed their order at the drive-thru intercom (Jared: 2 hard-shell tacos and nachos; Amy: a beef burrito). While waiting in line to retrieve their dinner, Amy's phone rang.

"Oh shit."

"Who is it? Is it your mom? It's probably about your grandpa."

"No. It's Nick."

The life drained from Jared's body.

"Don't you dare answer it!"

Too late.

"Hello?"

Jared leaned over toward Amy's phone.

"You're a fucking asshole!" he screamed.

Amy was horrified.

"I'm sorry. I have to call you back," she mumbled.

Amy hung up her phone and snarled at Jared.

"What is wrong with you? That was so insanely rude. I cannot believe what just happened. What the fuck are you thinking, Jared?"

"I hate him."

"No, really? I didn't notice," she sarcastically replied. "Still, it's common decency. That was– wow, Jared. That was a new low for you. I'm like, ashamed to be with you right now."

"Oh, calm down. He's a big boy. I'm sure he can handle it."

They got their order and left. Jared steered his car back toward Amy's house. They ate their meals in silence. When they approached her house, she spoke up.

"Hey, can we actually drive around a bit more? I don't feel like going back in there yet."

"Of course, Amy."

"Have you ever driven the canyon?"

"No. Where's that?"

"Here, just keep going. I'll guide you."

Amy led Jared to a dark canyon road that curled through the base of the nearby hillside. About halfway through, Amy asked Jared to pull over. He obliged.

"I know how you feel about the whole Nick situation. But, I already told you, we broke up. Don't worry about him, Jared. He's not a part of my life anymore. I'm yours."

To express her newly-restored allegiance to Jared, she proceeded to give him a blow job, while the scent of cheap Mexican food lingered in the air.

They approached. Calculated and direct. Unflinching in their assignment. The soldiers led the final charge, followed by the demolition crew and thereafter the construction workers (all with their respective equipment.

Humongous and cruel). In addition, the members of the short-lived search party had by now joined the procession. The disparate warriors assumed their battle stance. They were ready, resolute and determined to destroy.

On the opposing side, The Land of Forgotten Souls' ramshackle fleet stood still, arms linked, terrified. Many pissed themselves. Some defecated. Once the South Forts army was close enough, they...

[Insert Battle Scene]

This is a love story.
Descriptions of war have no place here.
Needless to say, South Forts was the victor.

Patricia, though thoroughly deluded, displayed genuine courage during the fight. She never backed down from her skewed, misinformed and warped principles.

Ultimately, I regret to inform you that she perished.
Nearly the entire population of The Land of Forgotten Souls was wiped out during the conflict.
The casualties were untold.

"If you were forced to spend the remainder of your life on a deserted island with only one other person, who would it be?"

**Grandma:** That's easy. My sister (G-d rest her soul). How about you?

"I'd pick Amy."

**Grandma:** You must be joking. Amy?! Jared, how could you say that? I know there's technically no wrong answer to these types of questions, but you are plain wrong here. Family is the only correct answer. Family is much more important than some dumb girl.

"Yea, but I plan on repopulating."

After the smoke cleared, the army began their return journey (save for a select few that stayed behind to patrol the area), while the workers began the process of damming and rerouting the waterways.

Jared's acid trip:

1.  Immediately after taking the dose (one droplet, carefully dripped onto a candy), I went for a walk in the woods with my (also soon-to-be tripping) buddy. We encountered a plant with leaves shaped like hearts. "They're edible, you know," he informed me. I picked one and took a bite. "It tastes bitter." We both erupted into hysterics. "How perfect! It's shaped like a heart and it tastes bitter."

2.  We arrived at a pristine lookout spot and decided to smoke a bowl. Up until this point, I didn't feel anything. I took a hit, still comfortable. I thought to myself, 'If I can think about it, while tripping, I know I'll be okay.' You see, I'd been hesitant about taking LSD, for fear that it would unlock a certain long-suppressed memory. Were that to happen, I didn't know how I'd react. While we were smoking, I thought about the incident. Once I did, my mind shifted. I envisioned my buddy and I (in our blue and red hoodies, respectively) waving our arms in an interlocked pattern.

3.  Fully tripping now, we properly enjoyed ourselves, like giggly little goons. We played guitar (super mellow) and went for a bike ride to the nearby marsh, where we sat and watched the birds for a while. Eventually, we decided to get dinner. We went to a Philly cheesesteak stand (a local favorite) and ordered the titular dish. While sitting at the outdoor patio, awaiting our meals, we quietly listened to the following 3 songs (which were being played from the restaurant's sound system): "It's My Life" by Bon Jovi, "Spirit in the Sky" by Norman Greenbaum and "Another One Bites the Dust" by Queen. These songs perfectly encapsulated this moment in my

life.  The music communicated a divine prophecy, summarizing everything I currently felt and everything I needed to know, moving forward.

4. We then went to a party, attended by all the neighborhood rapscallions.  We, along with everyone else there, made an effort to drink as much beer as possible.

5. Now winding down, we returned home and watched Garden State.

6. Finally, before retiring for the night, we decided to smoke one last bowl together.  After a joyous, stoned recap of our day, I said "good night" to my fellow explorer.  I then retreated to my bedroom and listened to Pet Sounds on headphones, while lying in bed, with the lights off.

*Stretch Marks* Charlie once informed Jared that he was nervous about hooking up with girls, because he had stretch marks around his dick region *Stretch Marks*

Sometime in the mid-aughts (2004, to be precise), a band called The Killers became quite a presence on the national music scene.  Their introductory jingle (i.e., the first of many tunes to be played on nearly all the local radio stations) was entitled "Somebody Told Me."  This song, in all honesty, was just okay. Nothing special, really.  After hearing it, Jared was unmoved, but curious.  Their sound was uniquely distinctive (nighttime music). He remained patiently intrigued to hear more of this band's work. Amy, however, dove full-bore into Killers fandom (yay androgyny!).  She scooted her plumpy butt to the record shop and picked up a copy of their CD (which, like, still, what an incredible debut!).

Shortly thereafter, the song "Mr. Brightside" began making the rounds.  Jared heard it (for the first time) on the radio one day while driving to Eddie's house.  It floored him.  The lyrics conveyed a raw, bone chilling expression of the angst he felt while envisioning Amy getting fucked by Nick.  He needed to hear it again, for never had a song so accurately tapped into his inner torment.

Once he arrived at Eddie's house, before going inside, he immediately called Amy.

"Hey. You have The Killers album, right?"

"Yeah."

"Do you think I could borrow it?"

"Sure."

"Like, now?"

He was frantic.

"Jared, come on. What's going on? Are you alright?"

"I'm serious, Amy. I honestly just really wanna listen to it. I have to!"

She sighed.

"You heard 'Mr. Brightside,' didn't you?"

"Yeah."

"Oh dear. I knew this day would come."

"Well here we are! Thanks for making that song so relatable!"

"Jared, stop it. Don't be an asshole. I never–"

"Can I please just borrow it? Amy, that song spoke to me! Okay? I need to hear it again. It soothed my soul! After all you've done, at the very least, can you please just let me borrow that CD? It will help to heal my shattered heart."

"Alright, fine. If you must. I'm at my dad's house now, but I'm about to leave (to head over to my mom's house). Can you come now?"

"Yes."

"Okay. Hurry, please. I'll be waiting outside."

Jared informed Eddie of their mission. He reluctantly obliged, confused as to the urgent necessity of this endeavor.

*You don't understand, man!*

They (Jared = the anxious driver; and Eddie = the unenthused passenger) approached Amy's dad's apartment complex. There she was, standing by her car, holding the CD. They pulled up next to her. Jared rolled down his window.

"Hi boys."

"Hey."

"Hi Amy."

"Here you go. Enjoy it, I guess."

She handed Jared the CD and started to walk away.

"Wait!" he called out.

She turned.

"What, Jared? I have to go."

"Can I have a kiss?"

"No! Goodbye."

She got in her car and drove off. Jared watched solemnly as she disappeared from view. She had 2 bumper stickers on her car. One was an American flag. The other read:

"If not for love, then why?"

As stated in the fine print, this sticker was printed in the territory formerly known as The Land of Forgotten Souls.

Jared and Eddie sat quietly in the car for a minute. Jared sulked, internally regressing deeper into himself, engulfed in the sadness of rejection. Eddie felt uncomfortable and was unsure how to acknowledge what had just transpired.

"Uh, that was kinda weird. I thought you guys broke up. And isn't she dating someone else? I'm really confused."

"She broke up with him."

"But… are you guys back together or something? Why'd you ask for a kiss? That was fucking bizarre."

"I don't know, dude. We're not officially back together, but we've been hanging out again."

"Hanging out?"

"Yeah, well, I've been going over to her house (and she's been coming over to mine) late at night. It's become more frequent lately."

"Are you guys, like, hooking up? I assume that's what happens during these evening encounters."

"Yup. We usually just get high, have sex, cuddle for a bit and then leave."

"Dude! How long has this been happening?"

"I'm not exactly sure. Maybe like a month or so."

"Holy shit! I had no idea. I thought you 2 were done for good."

"Not quite mi amigo. If anything, it feels like we're slowly getting back together. Two lovers, once torn apart, are returned."

Later that night, after getting sufficiently stoned, Jared and Eddie took a drive through the canyon. They rolled down the windows and blasted "Mr. Brightside," on repeat.

Elsewhere, Jordan and Adam demerged from the thickets of an untenable narrative device, having thus far been integrated into a single character.

Patrick hid out in the brush for the next several weeks. His plan was to remain unseen and unnoticed until the last remaining workers and patrolmen left town, at which point he'd begin his return journey. To pass the time, he'd sit at a proper vantage point and observe the ongoing construction. He marveled at the ingenuity of modern engineering. It was truly a sight to behold. Oftentimes, he'd become transfixed by the precision necessary to achieve such a magnificent feat. On one such occasion, while nearly hypnotized by the process before him, his trance was unexpectedly broken.

"Man has sure exhibited his dominion over nature," an unfamiliar female voice spoke.

Patrick, frightened and stunned, quickly scanned his surroundings and assumed his attack stance. To his surprise (and potential delight), a young bitch was sitting beside him.

"Hey!" he growled. "How long have you been sitting there?"

"Whoa. Calm down there, fella. I didn't mean to spook you. The name's Julia."

"I didn't ask for your name. Listen, I have no interest in making friends here. Get lost."

"Well ain't you a charmer."

"I mean it. Once that aqueduct is finished, I'm getting the fuck out of here."

"Is that so?"

"Need I repeat myself?"

"Well, honey, if that's the case, you're not going anywhere for quite a while."

"Why's that? What have you heard? What's the estimated completion date?"

"Oh, it'll probably be another 2 months, at least."

"Goddamnit!"

"I wish he/she/it/nothing would, sugarplum."

No response. Patrick stared off into the distance and watched the workers. He attempted to mentally preoccupy himself, but he was unable to focus anymore. It took great effort, and he failed. She had corrupted his state of meditative tranquility.

"Two more months, huh?"

"Yes sir. You're sure gunna get lonely sitting here all by yourself that whole time."

Again he looked out at the workers. It was pointless.

"I'm Patrick."

The best mini-golf course in South Forts was not actually in South Forts. If you were serious about your putting, you'd have to make the schlep up north to Castle Land (otherwise, sure, South Forts had a smattering of shitty, poorly maintained and overcrowded courses).

One weekend, the brotherhood committed themselves to making the drive. The overall theme of the park (which should be obvious from its name) was a definite draw for Jared and Bernardo, who were at this point deep in the midst of their fantastical role-playing battle game thing.

After arriving (at the end of their longer-than-expected trek) and strategically selecting the most secluded and covert parking spot available, they all smoked up in the car (of course), the beforehand ritual to nearly everything they ever did. Feeling emboldened in their marijuana use, they brought along a bong for the occasion (and a half-filled water bottle). They gulped down compressed loads of percolated smoke, intentionally obliterating their brains. A one-way express-lane catapult-launch into the next realm. Once they felt sufficiently good and baked, they were ready to enter Castle Land.

The game commenced. The boys took great joy in its fundamentals, an applied exercise in physics and angular propulsion. As they methodically traversed the course, Jared and Bernando gradually (and irresistibly) transformed into their playful characters: two medieval warriors engaged in an endless, make believe battle. The surrounding environment's decorative landscape highly influenced the imaginative sense of immersion that this activity required.

While playing through the holes, the castle (#18; par 3) loomed ominously on the horizon. The last remaining remnant of a once proud kingdom. Local legend has it that this was once a fully functional castle for a town of reclusive, self-sustaining wormy folk. Kids often heard stories about the fate of this befallen people. The tales varied in the level of tragedy and failed heroicism that occasioned their demise. Now, all that stood was a single wall, the rest having been destroyed long ago in a great battle. For aesthetic reasons, the owner/manager of Castle Land had recently restored the toppled walls, in order to achieve the illusion that a complete castle adorned the golf course.

When they approached the castle, Jared and Bernardo were overwhelmed by the sight. For months, they had been pretending to be ancient cavalrymen on some sort of noble quest. And now, here they were, in the shadow of a full-size castle. The real life pinnacle of their enduring fantasy. They unsheathed their swords (i.e., the colorful putters) and stood proud, opposing each other.

"Betrayer! Approach if you are wiling to endure the brunt of my might."

"I fear no man! And I'll smite any who convey such threats toward me."

"Oh! I doubt thou speaks in certitude."

"Behold this moment!  You shall remember it as the fulfillment of all promised tasks.  I will never retreat from you."

"Nay!"

"Accomplice!"

They simultaneously screamed a loud battle cry and charged at each other.  Their swords flung through the air, clinking together with every swing.

Charlie and Eddie simply stood and watched, amused by the playful delicacy of their fight.  The bond among the brotherhood was so strong that they were forced to invent nonsensical conflicts.

Sport = a pretend battle rooted in friendship.


"Your Majesty, I fear this is no cause for celebration."

"Are you kidding me?  We destroyed them with nary a dent to our own forces!  Sounds like it was almost too easy."

Wilbur was elated.  His movements contained a considerable splash of light-footed confidence.  He was practically dancing around his chambers.  An entire assembly had gathered for a debriefing session, and to share in the good news.  The room held a festive air.  Though no music was being played, it felt as if a symphonic blast of triumphant melodies were sounding.  A ripe ringin' tune, ricocheting off of crystalline chalices, brim-filled and tilt-shifted, as the victors rejoiced.  Drunk & happy conquistadors, accomplished and proud.

"Yes, yes that's all correct.  Construction is underway, and they failed miserably in their efforts to stop us."

"So...?  Come now, my confidant.  I'm taken aback by your sullen tone.  What's the matter?  We won!"

"Your Majesty, please forgive me for dampening the mood here, but a member of the formerly-appointed search party has requested to speak with you.  He... there's something he wishes to share with you."

Wilbur stopped. Still and motionless. Silent.

"Oh... Certainly. Let him in. Let him in at once."

A young man entered, slowly. His head hung low.

"What's this about?" Wilbur asked, harsh and impatient.

"Sir– Your Majesty, I..."

"Speak up!"

"I just... I could not believe my eyes."

The young man began to cry.

"Explain yourself! What is this about?"

"I saw her there. Patricia. It was her. I'm certain of it. But she... she stood in linked arms with the enemy. I don't understand. It all happened so fast, so sudden. I yelled. I tried to inform them. Honest. But it was hopeless. We exerted such aggression. Oh, Your Majesty, it was brutal. I called out a ceasefire. But I was too late. We... I don't know quite how to say this. We... we killed her."

After several minutes of silence (yes, you read that correctly), Wilbur spoke to his gloom ridden, pessimistic advisor.

"Is this accurate? Has this been confirmed?"

"Yes, Your Majesty. We do not yet understand why, but she was indeed fighting alongside them. I can assure you that we are all as shocked as you are. And, of course, our condolences to you and Marjorie. Given the, uh, unexpectedness that the Bright Princess herself would be standing on enemy lines, we naturally hadn't planned on scouring the population to carefully identify each and every individual before we... killed them. No. Rather, when they drew their guns, we destroyed them all. The urgency of the moment did not allow for careful vetting of the opposition. Collectively, they were all a threat, and we acted to eliminate them. Including, regretfully, Patricia."

Wilbur approached the young man from the search party.

"You saw her?" he inquired, in an eerily calm, hushed timbre.

"Yes."

"And you tried to alert the commanding officers?"

As Wilbur spoke, he got closer and closer to him.

"Yes. I did."

"But it was too late, huh?"

"Alas. There was not enough time. The whole thing transpired in an instant. And I am but one man among many. My voice was drowned out in the anticipation of war."

Wilbur turned around and addressed the others in the room. He clasped his hands behind his back and slowly paced along the edge of the arched half-circle that had formed among the spectators.

"Gentlemen, before me stands the would-be hero of South Forts. A brave warrior who saw her, but did not speak up. Can you imagine the glory, had you not only vanquished The Land of Forgotten Souls, but also saved my daughter in the process? This young man... he saw her. He saw her. In the line of fire, he saw her."

Wilbur rushed back to him.

"Remind us all again, what did you do?"

"Wh– what?"

"Tell us what you did once you saw her."

"I called out to my commander. I told him not to order the attack."

"You did?"

"Yes, Your Majesty."

"You expect me to believe you?"

"I am being forthright."

"You shy little pipsqueak! I doubt you said a fucking word. I'm envisioning the entire scene now."

Wilbur gently tapped the young man on the shoulder and mockingly spoke in a reserved, near-whispered parlance.

"Uh, excuse me, sir, I think that's the King's daughter over there."

Wilbur's henchmen laughed.

"And then BANG! She's dead. They're all dead."

The abrupt dichotomy between Wilbur's quiet impression and his ear-piercing scream stunned everyone in the room. They communally gasped in fright. Wilbur placed his hand on the young man's cheek, and continued.

"Well ain't you just the sweetest little quiet neighborhood boy. So polite, so friendly."

Unceremoniously, Wilbur removed a pistol from his waistband and shot the young man in the head, point blank.

"Listen here, everyone! Let this be a lesson to you all. The virtuousness of the quiet man is a myth. Quiet men (and women too, I guess; though we expect less of them) have done more damage to our species than the handful of true evildoers. You see, the quiet man fools us all into believing that he's just minding his own business. He's coolheaded and poised. In all aspects of his life, he is neutral. No, my friends. He sees all and hears all, but does nothing about it. You! We see you watching from the sidelines. You're not invisible! We notice you, freakboy! This world is not a show for you to observe. You must participate. You're a part of it, whether you like it or not."

He stood above the young man's body.

"This waste of life right here is a prime example of the reprehensible acts that are implicitly authorized by quiet men when they fail to intervene during conflicts. My daughter was killed because this piece of shit has social anxiety or something. Fuck that. May he rot in hell."

Late one Saturday eve, during the first semester of their 12$^{th}$ grade year, Jared and Eddie sat together in the soothing splendor of Jared's (parents') backyard, and passed a pipe. With each puff, they became more fuzzy and unguarded. It was to be a cheery, inconsequential night. They'd simply share some laughs and say farewell.

Then, seemingly unprovoked, Eddie made a vague, but impassioned, inquiry.

"Dude, oh my god, can you believe it about Charlie and Amy?"

Jared was confused. Sure, he had already heard all about their fateful make-out nipple-suck. Charlie had confessed this misdeed prior to <u>Return of the King</u>. But this was old news by now. Why was Eddie bringing it up again? And why was he so worked up about it?

"Yeah…"

"I don't know, man. It's so fucked up. If I were you, I would've killed them both."

'That's a little harsh,' Jared thought. 'But sure, okay, fuck 'em.'

"I– uh, yeah. I guess so. I mean, it's definitely messed up. I agree."

"I just can't comprehend how you're so calm."

Jared simply shrugged and took another hit.

Within a matter of days, Patrick and Julia were fucking, profusely. But this warn't 2 strangers in the woods compensating for their own loneliness by touching genitals. No sir! This was lovemaking, in every sense of the term.

Prior to their physical flesh rubdown, they formed a deep and meaningful emotional bond. Julia commenced their soul bearing share session with this: she was a local gal, born and raised in The Land of Forgotten Souls. Her master was slain in the great battle. In recalling their many precious memories together, she began to weep. It was, after all, still a fresh wound. The healing had not yet begun.

And with that abrupt glimpse of her hastily over-exposed vulnerabilities, Patrick felt compelled to reciprocate, somehow. He clumsily told her all about Patricia. Their short-lived yet filled-to-the-brim misadventures. A flash flood, cup runneth over, whirlwind of high-drama, full-fledged tumult. *The only style of relationship I've ever known.* He also shared of his current plans to journey south, and his purpose in doing so; i.e., he sought to return to the master he had long ago abandoned

(whether his desertion was inadvertent or not is beside the point). Suddenly, Patrick caught himself. 'Oh dear,' he thought. 'Should I be telling her all this? Can I trust her to preserve these tales in confidence? Or, like a true bitch, will she end up using them against me when she needs to knock me down a peg?' He wondered whether they had yet reached that stage in their relationship where one can freely share their darkest, most closely guarded secrets.
MOLESTATION!
DON'T SIMPLY SKIM THE SURFACE OF YOUR TRAUMA.
DIVE IN AND GRASP THE DEPTHS OF YOUR DESPAIR.
ONLY THEN CAN YOU TRULY VANQUISH THE ENEMY WITHIN.

To reveal such truths is to trust, completely. But, which influences the other? Do you reveal once you've attained the trust? Or, do you attain the trust by revealing?

He opted for the latter progression. If I share my pain, we are sure to grow closer. And it worked. Once he opened up (emotionally), she opened up (physically). Hence, the aforementioned fucking.

Soon enough, Patrick was an open book. He eagerly told her about his brilliant, newfound idea, which arrived unexpectedly like an obvious-all-along, right-in-front-of-his-face epiphany. He was going to build a boat and sail down the aqueduct to South Forts. Julia was supportive and encouraging of his dreams and desires (like a proper girlfriend should be).

Every night, when the workers retreated, he would sneak onto the construction site, rummage though the refuse bins and gather parts for his ship. He'd then haul his plunder to a strategically selected, semi-secluded spot near the edge of the riverbed, where he'd begin piecing it all together.

Julia offered to help out, but Patrick insisted that it was a solitary activity for him only, and that if she were to become involved, her presence would taint the whole operation, causing it to crumble. Stay away! The purity must be preserved!

Late one evening, after returning from his workshop, Patrick joined Julia in their makeshift bed, where she had already retired for the night.

"Hey Julia, are you awake?"

"Yeah," she replied, half asleep. "How'd it go tonight?"

"Oh, it was fantastic. I'm nearing completion already. I can almost see the finish line. Just a couple more weeks or so and I'll be ready to cast off."

"That's great, Patrick. I'm happy for you."

Julia effortlessly fell back into her slumber, while Patrick stared at her. He had more to say, but struggled to conjure the words. After a momentary pause, he spoke up.

"When, uh, so, when I travel south, do you... um, would you like to come with me?"

She opened her eyes and smiled wide.

"Patrick! I would absolutely love to!"

He gave a nervous laugh.

"Well, alright then. Good to know, since I've already made it a 2-seater."

"Aww, honey, you did? That is so sweet! My heart has officially melted. Ya know, I didn't want to bother you about this or anything, but lately I was starting to worry about what was going to happen once you finished. Like, I fully support you working on this boat and all, but I couldn't overlook the fact that your final objective ultimately involved you leaving me. So, like, how excited could I really be about this whole thing? I've really been enjoying our time together, Patrick, and I certainly am not looking forward to it ending anytime soon."

"Julia, my dearest, I would be honored if you'd join me on my– no, *our* journey."

She tilted her head toward the sky and howled.

"Shhh! Be quiet. Are you crazy?"

"I'm sorry."

She winked at him, and then howled again.

Patrick laughed, and joined her in howling.

After a few minutes of this they both collapsed into their bed, fulfilled and excited for tomorrow.

"Well," she spoke, "I guess this is as good a time as any to tell you. Uh, you might want to make a little extra room in the boat."

"Huh? What do you mean?"

"I'm... I'm pregnant."

Of course she is, that's her whole purpose in this story.


"Hello?"

Jared answered the phone, cautiously and concerned. It was unusual to receive calls at this late hour.

"Hey Jared."

"What's up? Is everything alright?"

"Yeah man, all is well. I was just wondering if I could come over tonight."

"What? Dude, it's almost midnight."

"I know, I know. But still, can I? I'm supposed to be staying at my dad's house this weekend and I really don't feel like driving all the way out there right now."

"Uh, well, it's sorta, um... so, Amy is here, and–"

"That's okay. I don't mind."

Jared was slightly dumbfounded. He figured that the mere mention of Amy would shoo away any potential visitors.

"Oh, really? I thought– okay, hold on a second."

Jared covered the transmitter and whispered to Amy.

"Do you mind if Charlie comes over?"

Her face conveyed a look of fright, except it was subtle. Jared didn't notice.

"Now?"

"Yes."

"Sure... Yeah, that's fine, I guess."

Jared lifted the phone back to his lips.

"Come on over, man."


Charlie arrived (through the side entrance, of course). He, Amy and Jared had a pleasant chat. The content of their conversation was superfluous and needn't be recreated here. It does nothing to move the plot forward or otherwise advance any character development. But wait! Perhaps it could be one of those cool slice-of-life scenes, where everyone's talking about normal, everyday things. So realistic! Or not?

For no reason, in the middle of this mundane moment, Jared excused himself.

"I'm gunna take a quick shower," he announced.

He then rushed into the bathroom, turned on the shower and disappeared.

Without Jared around, Charlie seized this opportunity to discuss matters of great importance.

"He still doesn't know, does he?"

"No..."

"We have to tell him."

"When?"

"How about tonight? Right now."

"No! Please don't. I'm not ready yet."

"Come on, Amy. You keep saying that. When will you ever be ready?"

"I'm not sure. Soon. Soon I will be. But not tonight."

Julia gave birth to 5 puppies. The first to emerge from her womb was a young male. Patrick snatched him up, immediately (before the remaining 4 plopped out). He held him and proclaimed, "I shall call him Patrick. And may his son, and all the first born sons of my heirs, from generation to generation, be named Patrick."

Patrick and Julia, and their 5 puppies, were soon living the quintessential, domesticated life (in the traditional sense). Julia assumed the role of a stay-at-home mother, while Patrick would head to the office, daily (or nightly, rather), to work on his boat.

Of course, this routine didn't last very long, as the completion of the boat coincided with the completion of the weaning period for the newborns. Within a matter of weeks, it was finally time to set sail.

In the interim, Patrick and Julia, together, had made the difficult decision to leave 4 of their puppies behind. There simply wasn't enough room on the boat, and it was to be a risky voyage through treacherous waters. No use putting all of their lives in danger. Thus, only Patrick Jr. would be accompanying them. As for the remaining 4 puppies, they were to be left to live out in the wild.

"Be good, my babies. I'm sorry I won't get to see you grow up. Just know that mommy and daddy love you all very much. Goodbye."

It was a matter of necessity. See <u>Of Mice and Men</u>.

The (now) family of 3 climbed aboard.
"Ready?" Patrick asked.
"Hit it!"

The great make believe swordfight at Castle Land went on for much longer than it should have. Although it was plenty amusing at first, the entertainment value of this spectacle wore off fast. Eddie soon gave up watching it and walked over to get a closer look at the castle itself. He noticed that above the doorway to the sole genuine wall was an inscription, carved into the brick. It read: Cam Lé Ö Tesh rá. Tū Züme, Tū Züme. This was apparently the ancient language of the indigenous peoples who inhabited this land, long ago. The meaning of this phrase has since been lost to time.

Upon learning of Patricia's death, Marjorie planted a garden in her memory. It was to consist entirely of tulips, Patricia's favorite flower. This would serve as a shrine/remembrance-area/gravesite, since she was deprived of the opportunity to bury her daughter.

Marjorie and Wilbur lived out the remainder of their days never fully understanding why Patricia abandoned them, or why she joined forces with the opposition. It became a wellspring of marital strife (one of many), as each felt the other was responsible. The only source of comfort came from afternoons spent aimlessly wandering the garden, which they called Tulip't Villé.

Oh, and in case you're wondering, they never went through with the divorce. Instead, they resigned themselves to endure their loveless, war-torn marriage until the bitter end. It's better than being alone, I guess.

During one of those carefree summer nights, while Jared was schtupping Amy, her cell phone rang. The display indicated that Charlie was calling.

"What the fuck?" Jared asked. "Why is Charlie calling you?"

"Umm, I have no idea," Amy responded, entirely innocent.

"That is really fucking weird, Amy."

"Yeah, I agree. I don't know what to tell you."

"Are you going to answer it?"

"No. It's probably just an accidental call."

"I'm going to answer it."

"Jared, don't. Come on. Fuck me."

With no one left to care for them, the 4 puppies commenced a multi-generational transition back into wolves. Wild creatures.

Jared always felt that people were mad at him. Friends, family, acquaintances, colleagues and even strangers, they all had something against him. They all loathed his very existence, with downward facing disdain. Everyone he ever interacted with secretly despised him. You're pathetic! Shame on you!

Don't you see why that is, Jared?

When you were a boy, you did a bad thing; but you were never punished for it. Ever since then, you've lived as a disgraced fugitive, haunted by this stultifying memory. You carry an enormous sense of guilt, which manifests itself in the false assumption that people are angry with you.

*That is an accurate summation of my lifelong burden.*

Now that you've identified the cause of your insecurity, how can you remedy it?

You must make amends. Either by seeking forgiveness from the direct victim(s), or by assisting similarly-situated persons.

To begin, you must acknowledge what happened.

No more denial.

No more hiding from your past.

Confront it!

Stand face-to-face with the monster you once were.

Admit fault.

Accept that you are not blameless.

You are flawed.

You are impure.

And you may very well be someone's enemy. You may be hated, for good cause. But remember, that is only one person (or a small handful, at most). By refusing this fact, you've instead distributed your guilt. You've spread out your sorrow among all. This is why you think everyone is always mad at you. They're not! Not *everyone* is mad at you, Jared. But *someone* is. And that is where you must focus your energy. You must mend the soul(s) you've ravaged. Make peace with those you've wronged, if they'll let you. Or (if they refuse), tend to the needs of others in equivalent predicaments. Slowly, the burden will lift from your shoulders and you will no longer project your remorse onto those who already love you.

# No matter

# what you do,

# you'll always make

# the wrong decision.

**Disclaimer!** The character of Charlie is no more. Miraculously, he has been split in 2. Just like that. Actually, this whole time, Charlie has been a composite of two separate people. Thus far in the story, it has been sufficient to combine these 2 fellas into a single character. However, in order to fully appreciate the emotional brunt of the following scene, they must be thought of as distinct and separate persons; that is, Jordan and Adam.

The grand finale starts now:

We were all hanging out in Ms. Selke's class, generally goofing off and futzing around like we always did. It was during "block period," a free hour that occurred twice a week, in which students were encouraged to catch up on homework or attend impromptu review sessions in their more challenging classes. For those of us without such commendable academic ambitions, Ms. Selke's classroom provided a place to commiserate, talk and mostly just fuck around for an hour. She was our film teacher. Also taught creative writing and remedial English. Needless to say, her classroom wasn't a hotbed of intellectual rigor. As a consequence, this became our spot. Naturally. We'd gather here twice a week (on Wednesday and Thursday) and spend these hours mumbling and bumbling about.

So, during one of these seemingly normal, mundane, nothing special, unspectacular block periods, my dear friend Michael approached me. He appeared concerned, as though he were devoutly worried about something. Of course, I had no idea what that something was.

Truth is, he had been entrusted with a secret. A secret that was gleefully whispered among all our friends (sans me). A pale-inducing parable of ghostly betrayal. Apparently, everyone already knew this story except me. Yet I was the **one person** who deserved to know more than anyone else, as no one would be more profoundly affected by the news. Michael understood this. He had no intention of preserving the secret. Rather, upon hearing this tragic tale, he rushed right to me.

"Hey, we gotta– we have to talk. I have to tell you something," he said, urgently.

"Okay…" I responded, confused. "What is it?"

"Let's go outside."

"Huh?"

He pointed at Jordan, who had been apprehensively listening to this exchange.

"You too. You're coming too," Michael commanded.

Jordan was angry. He knew exactly what this was about.

Michael led us out onto the balcony area that adjoined the building. I followed, obediently. As did Jordan, reluctantly.

"What's going on?" I asked.

Immediately, I could sense a heavy layer of tension between the two of them. This must've been a continuation from a prior scuffle.

"Don't do this," Jordan pleaded. An inner wrath was beginning to emerge.

"Tell him!"

Michael angrily stared him down, while pointing at me.

"Tell him! Tell him right now! Tell him!"

I stood there silently, entirely dumb, while they argued.

"Michael, what the fuck are you doing?"

"Tell him!"

"Why are you doing this?"

"Tell him!"

"This isn't your place to be doing this."

"Well you shouldn't be keeping secrets from your friends!"

"What the fuck is going on here?" I interjected, finally. "What are you guys talking about?"

Michael did not speak. Rather, he held Jordan's gaze and waited, allowing the coy culprit the courtesy of confessing himself.

"I can't. Not like this, not like this."

Jordan headed for the door. Retreat!

"You coward!  Don't lie to your friends."

Jordan, full of rage, turned and reversed course.  He advanced toward Michael, in an ineffectual attempt to physically intimidate him into ceasing this entire conversation.

"What are you gunna do?  You're gunna fight me?  You're the fucking bad guy here," Michael mockingly observed.

Realizing this, and acknowledging its accuracy, Jordan left.  He cowered away.  Upset, frustrated and ashamed.

"What is going on?" I asked.  "Please, just– what the hell is happening?"

"Oh man, I didn't want to be the one to tell you this, Jared.  But you deserve to know."

"Yes…?"

"Well, so, a couple months ago, Adam and Jordan went over to Amy's house together and they–"

"What?!"

"Some sexual shit happened.  It's weird, man."

"Okay.  I've heard enough."

I had to cut him off.  Mute the entire exchange.  I legitimately could not handle another word of this story.  I knew exactly what he was telling me, and I didn't need to know any more.  With that brief but dense statement, my worst nightmare had come true.

The timing couldn't have been worse.  At this point, I had finally begun to get over Amy (to the extent that was at all possible).  I was learning to accept the fact that we weren't together anymore, and perhaps never would be again.  As part of my coping process, I took refuge in the loving embrace of my friends.  They had the keen ability to console the debilitating torment and sorrow that I felt whenever she was away (and, worse, likely in the arms of another).  While she'd be out with this Nick guy, my friends and I would laugh together like joyful, banged-up ruffians.  It helped quell the pain.  But now, the people I'd been relying on to rescue me from my despair had turned out to be its main cause.

I left. I had to. I rushed downstairs and frantically wandered around campus, aimlessly. I didn't know where I was going. I must've been looking for her; but she was nowhere to be found. I started thinking about **it**, imagining what happened. I envisioned the whole scene. My sweet little Amy was on her knees, with Jordan and Adam standing on either side of her. She alternated between jerking one of them off, while sucking the other's dick. The whole thing was a sloppy, fucked up, filthy mess. She was slobbering. Spit was dangling from theirs dicks. In the chaotic frenzy of the moment, her drool was being smeared against her cheeks and dripping onto her shirt. Eventually, it was her turn. Adam threw her on the bed, pulled off her shorts and started slurping away at her pussy. Every so often he'd venture downward and give her asshole a quick but deliberate lick. She loved it. So naughty! Mmm, yeah, gimme another flick. And Jordan just watched, casually masturbating to the sight before him, staying hard for whatever happened next. They fucked her. Oh come on! We all know they fucked her. Of course they fucked her. They had a legitimate, porn-quality threesome. No! Please no!! Oh my god, Amy! How could you do this to me!? A three-way with my best friends!!! Jordan was lying on his back while Amy rode his cock, aggressively grinding and wiggling, gold-hatted and high-bouncing, her moans muffled by the mass of Adam's dick getting jammed down her throat. They switched positions. Now Amy laid on her back while Adam thrust his thickened cock deep into her. She turned her head to swallow Jordan's dick, as he knelt before her, positioning himself right next to her mouth. Finding this arrangement to be less-than-ideal for sucking cock, she instead gave him a hand job. This allowed her to freely howl with delight, with no obstructions blocking her vocal cords. She made no effort to subdue her rapturous moans. This was unrestrained, full-volume fucking. And just beyond the thin walls, Amy's grandfather was slowly dying in the next room, listening to his precious little granddaughter getting nailed by 2 skeezeballs. Atta girl! Next... Did they? Could they have? Is it possible? Do you think they attempted double penetration? Holy shit! They fucked her in the ass, too! No, oh dear god, no. Say it ain't so. Ooo, fuck yes. Ahh! She nearly wept. The sensation was beyond anything she had ever experienced. She received both of them, fully. It caused her to squeal. And of course, at the end of everything, they came (simultaneously) all over her face and chest. She loved it. She loved getting as filthy as possible. Swimming in cum. She milked every last drop out of them. *We did it, Jared. We fucked her harder than you ever could.*

I was making myself sick. I could no longer endure life. I had to go home. To effectuate this decision, I ran to the nurse's office.

"I need to go home. I'm going to throw up," I announced, emotionless.

"Well, hello there, young man. Not feeling well? You can rest here on one of these mats until you feel better."

The gentle old nurse lady was oblivious. She had no idea that my head was swirling with images of my best friends double-teaming the love of my life.

"No. I need to go home right now," I continued, stern and resolute. "I'm going to throw up. I'm very ill. I'm very ill right now. I need to go home."

She could tell something was wrong with this boy, mentally.

"Okay. Let's just call your parents first, okay? We need to get parent approval if you are under 18 years old."

"Sure, whatever."

I called my mom. She answered, panicked and worried.

"Are you okay?"

"Mom, I'm going to throw up. I need to come home."

"Oh no! Okay, sweetie. Go on home. You have my permission. Get some rest."

Before I left, I returned to Ms. Selke's room. My objective was to simply retrieve my backpack and then leave unnoticed. While in there, I saw my friend Andrew Algebra (remember him?) asking Bernardo whether he already knew about *the incident*.

"Yeah," Bernardo responded. So fucking chill and laid back about it.

I grabbed my backpack and ran out of the room. I was startled by what I had just witnessed. That quick interaction devastated me. What the fuck? Bernardo knew all about this? How long had he known? And why didn't he tell me? I couldn't believe it. He agreed to be complicit in the secret. Shhh, don't tell Jared [giggle giggle].

I left. Although I didn't see him, Jordan watched me leave. So the story goes.

I got in my car and drove straight to Amy's house. Her mom answered the door.

"Hi Jared. What are you doing here?"
"Is Amy here?"
"No. She's at school. Isn't she at school?"
"Uh, I'm not sure. I haven't seen her today."
"And why aren't you at school?"
I squirmed away.

I got back in my car and called Amy.
"Hello?"
"I heard about you and Jordan and Adam," I told her.
She sighed the sigh of all sighs.
"I know. I don't really know what to say right now, Jared. I'm so sorry."
She informed me that she had left school too, though I'm not sure why. We arranged to meet at a nearby parking lot area.

When I arrived, I saw that she was already there, sitting in her car and staring idly at the nearby hillside. I parked right next to her. She hesitantly got in my car, anxious and unsure as to what was about to happen. How was I going to react? We sat in silence for a moment, both of us unsure how to start this difficult conversation.

"I know something happened with you guys."

"I'm sorry, Jared. I really feel so fucking awful about this whole situation."

"What is wrong with you? Why would you do this?"

"I don't know. I'm sorry, okay? They both came over and we kinda got–"

"Stop! Please, Amy. I'm not ready to hear this."

She agreed to come over, so we could talk it out.

I drove us to my parents' house. I parked down the street. While walking toward the house, I noticed a little blue rubber ball resting against the curb. I picked it up and threw it at the ground as hard as I could. It bounced into the air with the opposing force of a space launch. We looked up, to follow its trajectory. The sun blinded us.

Cast down upon rows and rows of bottled-up spirits,
I, in my most cursed nightmares,
would be fit unable to conjure up a more hideous vision.

During such an unpleasant transition,
days and days and days and days – Blast!
My mind, which more closely resembles a defeated battlefield,
drops from my eyes.
                    Drop
                            from
                                    my
                                        eyes.
Greet my sorrows with a gift.
A BALL.
This ball. This ball that I throw down so hard,
comes up so high.
This ball
this ball
this Ball
This Ball

It is me.

As I hit the haunted ground,
where once an egg hatched populations of joy
I SCREAM
I CRY
I bleed, I bleed

But I shall climb this endless staircase,
with cast'ed arm and bandaged wounds.
Into the sky,
into the sky.
Into the sky.

       We entered my bedroom. She sat on the bed and I sat down next to her.

       "I don't really know what else to tell you right now, Jared. It's too fresh, and you don't seem to wanna actually discuss what happened."

       She was right. I had no interest in hearing about their illicit tryst. Instead, I just sat there, my head in my hands, tugging at my hair and sulking.

       "I'm sorry," she whispered this time.

       She reached over and began rubbing my back, like a mother nurturing a terminally sick child, trying to conjure hope for recovery. But she knew it was hopeless. We were doomed. We were among nuclear wreckage at this point. A sunken vessel. Still, she made an effort to console me.

       I sat up and turned toward her. She looked so sad, so defeated and helpless. There was nothing she could do. The damage had been done.

       I scooted backwards and laid down on the bed, facing the wall, with my back to her. I began to cry, quietly. I couldn't contain my grief anymore. I yearned for the past, for the days when we first met. We used to be pure. I was bashful. You'd lick my ear. O, but that innocence, now, so suddenly destroyed.

She laid down behind me and wrapped her body against mine. We cuddled like fallen angels, defeated by love, our hearts ravaged.

"How could you do this to me?"

She stopped responding to my rhetorical accusations. Still, I could sense her remorse. She was emanating waves of guilt. For so long she had been living with a shameful secret, hoping to keep it concealed forevermore. And now, having had it revealed (against her wishes, mind you), she sought to solace the victim.

The sensation of her touch aroused me. It shouldn't have. Of course not. She was the source of my pain. Furthermore, she had been tainted in the worst sense imaginable. Any sexual desire toward her should have been, at once, extinguished. Gone. But I was unable to resist Amy. Even in this, our darkest moment, I still wanted her.

I turned around and faced her. She wiped the tears from my eyes. I leaned forward and kissed her, gently (at first). She paused, surprised. Then, she too kissed me. It happened naturally. This was, after all, a familiar activity for both of us. Soon enough, we were making out. It was tame, yet wholly passionate. I got on top of her and started kissing her neck. She began breathing heavily. I reached down her pants, past her pubic hair, and slid my fingers inside her. She stopped me almost immediately.

"No, Jared. We can't do this."

"But…"

"No! Stop, Jared. This is a terrible idea. Stop!"

I complied with her demand, and exited her.

"I know, I know. You're right. Ugh. What was I thinking?" I muttered.

"I think I should go. Will you take me back to my car, please?"

We sat in silence during the (luckily short) drive back to her car. After I parked, she got out of the car and stood there, looking at me.

"Well?"

"I'm really sorry about everything, Jared. I still care about you deeply and I feel horrible right now. This is all such a fucking mess. I just don't know what we do, moving forward. Maybe we should take some time apart, to sort all this out."

I said nothing.

"Okay, well, I guess, bye Jared."

"Goodbye forever."

She paused for a moment, taken aback by the statement, and then closed the door.

It was the last thing I ever said to her.


That night, rather than do anything productive or worthwhile, I opted for distraction. I decided to lock myself in my room, turn off all the lights and play Rainbow Six 3 (for PlayStation 2). Funnily enough, Jordan had recently got me this game for my birthday, and I had yet to play it. At the game's start menu, I was prompted to type in a name for the save file. Without any hesitation, I wrote: Amy Carousel.

The game itself was quite cathartic. There was a story of some sort, I'm sure of it, but I wasn't paying any attention to the narrative. Rather, I simply wanted to run around shooting people. This actually provided a genuine emotional release, albeit one rooted in violence and death.

I envisioned a scenario: What if, on the day of the threesome, I had shown up at her house, unannounced? Like, I just came over, maybe with a bouquet of flowers, to surprise her. Who knows? And then, I'd see Adam's and/or Jordan's car(s) parked out front. 'Huh, that's odd,' I'd think to myself. I'd approach her window. The curtain is drawn, but I could faintly hear sounds of sex. I'd slide open the window and pull the curtain aside to reveal my darling Amy getting utterly trampled by cock. Maybe they wouldn't even notice me at first, they're all so absorbed in the physical pleasure of the moment. Lollygagging and rim-splitting fun! Finally, one of them would glance up. Horrified. Eyes bulging. "Oh shit!" I'd jump in through the window. They'd quickly dismantle themselves. And

I'd kill all 3 of them.  Slaughtered.  A massacre!  Most likely with a gun.  Maybe I'd have a sword with me.  Slice 'em up.  Or, like, what if I just became a fucking wild animal and tore them all apart with my bare hands (and teeth).

      The phone rang.  It was Jordan.

      "Oh man, I'm so fucking sorry, Jared."

      I could tell he was crying.

      "It's okay, Jordan," I said, in my dull, half-dead tone.

      Except, it wasn't okay.  No, not at all.  But I was a wimp, unqualified to handle this situation.  I was not prepared to confront him, to let him know how I truly felt.

      "I feel so horrible."

      He started sobbing.

      "It's okay Jordan, really.  Don't worry."

      *Wait.  Why the fuck am I the one comforting him?  He deserved a fist to the face.*

      "Do you know everything now?  Did you talk to Amy about it?"

      "No, I– we talked a little, but she didn't really tell me the details."

      "Jared, I have to tell you.  Alright?  I just gotta get this all out in the open."

      "Uh, sure Jordan."

      "I… I had sex with her."

      My heart sank.  I felt stuck in one of those falling nightmares, the kind that normally causes you to instantly wake up (in a panic).  Except there was no reprieve here.  Reality had become a terror from which there was no escape.

      "Oh.  Yeah, well that's what I figured," I replied, gloomy and hollow.

      "And Adam was there, too."

      "Did he… also?"

      "No, no.  They kinda fooled around a little, but he didn't have sex with her or anything like that.  Actually, while I was with her, he sat in the closet and watched us."

      "What?"

"It– yeah, I don't know, man. This was all such a fucking mistake. I'm so sorry. I can't believe we did this. Honestly, ever since this happened, I've felt like such an asshole. You don't deserve this, Jared. I just can't belie–"

"Adam watched from the closet?"

"Yeah. But he's not entirely innocent or anything. They've had their own thing going on for a while now."

"What are you talking about?"

"Well, whenever he used to go over there to watch <u>Lord of the Rings</u>, they'd hook up. She'd give him hand jobs. I don't know what else, but yeah…"

There was nothing else to say. Somewhere within my muddled memories of this day, I recall him also telling me that **the event** had occurred during the previous summer (i.e., approximately 2-3 months before the current revelation). He made sure to remind me that although I was sleeping with her on a regular basis during that time period, I was not officially dating her (and thus, there was no infidelity involved). He also disclosed that I was at her house the night before (and possibly even the night after) he fucked her.

"Were you ever planning on telling me?"

"No, Jared. Honestly, we weren't. That night, afterwards, we made a pact to never tell another soul about what happened, especially not you. It was for your own benefit."

My entire world shattered. The pristine Lladro of my former self had been knocked from the mantle. It now lay broken and fragmented on the floor below. Everything was a lie. It was an altogether horrendous, foundation shaking realization, the discovery that my trusted confidants (and my darling, beloved Amy) had been hiding a ruinous secret. A multi-layered, Barnum & Bailey betrayal of the utmost degree.

I had been keeping her love letters. Every single one. By now I had amassed a decent collection of her pink-penned soliloquys. They were full of typical teenage gushiness. Rabid litanies of emotional excess (promises of forever, and the like). I took the folder (in which they were housed) outside and dumped its contents onto the ground. I struck a match and burned the letters. The entire pile lit up like an unholy sacrifice to a demented god. I watched it smolder. This didn't help at all. The vision, and its symbolic significance, meant nothing to me. It was not (as I had hoped) a healing, ritualistic purification of my soul. The cleansing of all things Amy. No. Rather, in that moment I realized I'd never recover from this. Despite the flame, my pain remained.

Shit. It's all shit. My life is over. I give up. How will I ever move forward? It's impossible. Things will never get better. This is the end. I'm fucked. My grandma always used to say, "This too shall pass." Well, here I have found an exception.

I snuck into my dad's office, unlocked his file cabinet (I knew where he hid the key) and removed a wooden box from the bottom drawer. I carried it to my bedroom.

I opened the box. Inside was my dad's .357 magnum.

I hastily scribbled out a note.

I made sure the gun was loaded.

I cocked it, and put it in my mouth.

The taste of the metal on my tongue was oddly familiar. As I wrapped my lips around the barrel, I suddenly experienced complete sensory displacement. I was flung back to a moment from my childhood. A suppressed memory, all but forgotten, revealed itself, like a nefarious, thrash-about intruder barging into my otherwise meticulously maintained and shipshape, serene little home, forcing the prompt confrontation of a shameful remembrance, buried deep beneath my falsified, happy-go-lucky veneer.

I was there, again, reliving that appalling incident. I saw him. I saw us, together. We touched each other.

I realized, oh, there is a much deeper source to my pain. All this time, I've been weeping about Amy, the cutie pie from high school. But the sadness I feel (which I erroneously attribute to her), this intense, suicidal impulse, is rooted in something much greater. It isn't about Amy at all, you fool.

Did... did that really happen to me, too? Was I that little boy on the playground? Yes, it was me. And I thought I could go the rest of my life without ever mentioning this. When I was 5 years old... No! As an attempt at distraction, I dove into a hyper-sexualized relationship with an unabashed slut. I thought, alright, this feels healthy. I'm having sex like a regular boy. I'm normal! Look at me! Look how normal I am! Right? That's not the solution, Jared. Of course not. If anything, my sorrow, my faux-heartbreak over our adolescent parting, is really my mourning the loss of my distraction. Because now I'll have to deal with it. Now there's nowhere left to hide. And I'd spent years hiding. I hid with sex and I hid with drugs. My attempt to isolate the thought, deprive it of oxygen, ignore it and hope it'll fade away, has proved unsuccessful. Memories do not simply disappear when neglected. No, they infiltrate other aspects of our lives. Their presence is felt one way or another. Sure, I managed to bury it for a while (decades!), but it was always there, underneath layer-upon-layer of fear, cowardice and diversion.

So what am I to do? Should I apologize? I already tried this. I tried talking to him, but he didn't want to talk. I offered to send a letter instead. He didn't want a letter either. He ignored me. I don't blame him at all. When I was 5 years old... Shut up! Now what do I do? **I don't know what to do**. I was the aggressor. It was my fault. He's innocent in this situation. Why should he have any interest in listening to me? When I was 5 years old... Stop!

I envy victims of sexual abuse, because they at least have the chance to overcome their trauma. They are not responsible for their circumstance. Not at all. They are helplessly thrust into it, against their will. But in my situation, I am the villain. I have no redemption arc.  I have no triumph.  I have nothing to conquer.  I have no one to blame; and worse, I have no one to forgive.

I am a horrible person.  I don't deserve to live.  I ruined a precious little boy's life.  ~~I taught him how to ride a bike and then molested him.~~  **I don't know what to do.**  We were only children then, both of us; but I was slightly older.  He looked up to me, like a big brother.  And I took advantage of him.  I violated his trust.  When I was 5 years old… Ah!  That taste.

"Fuck it."

I pulled the trigger.

*A man's life cannot be adequately evaluated until it is complete.*
*Until it reaches its unwelcome end;*
*when all of the seemingly limitless potential suddenly becomes finite,*
*and all of life's vast possibilities are,*
*at once, exhausted.*

Jared awoke in darkened room. He could barely discern where he was. From the limited available light sources, select portions of the space were illuminated, but only slightly. It looked as though he were on an abandoned soundstage of some sort.

Suddenly, a song began to play. A real fun time bopper. Super upbeat and joyous! Horns were blasting, drums were smashing and the bass was grooving.

Then, the lights came on. All of them. Simultaneously. Jared became engulfed in a cacophony of twinkling beams. Glowing strips of neon shot forth from all directions, and incandescent bulbs, which appeared to protrude out of every surface, flashed and circulated chaotically.

He saw too that the walls were painted in bright, cheerful colors. Spectacular! He was awash in pure awe, overwhelmed by the scene unraveling before him.

Next, he heard a raucous applause. He turned and saw an enormous audience, watching him. The crowd of spectators appeared to extend on and on into eternity.

Jared quickly figured it out. He was on the set of a game show, positioned at his podium and ready to play.

A voice sounded. "Ladies and gentlemen, please give a round of applause for your host!"

The host emerged. Some random, unrecognizable kook. He looked like a fucking clown.

The audience went wild.

"Welcome everyone! Oh, thank you! Thanks. You're far too kind. Come on now. Settle down folks. Okay. Today's contestant is…"

He glanced down at the notecard he had been conspicuously holding.

"…Jared. It, uh, only says your first name here. Tell us, Jared, what's your last name?"

"I don't have one, sir."

"You don't have a last name?"

"No, I don't. And it's too late to give me one now."

"Well, okay then! Are you ready to play, Jared?"

"Umm, what? Yeah, sure, I guess so. I don't really understa–"

"Alright! Let's get started. Round One. Now, to begin, we're going to show you a series of customized license plates. Your task is to interpret what they say."

"Okay…"

"Ready? Set. Go!"

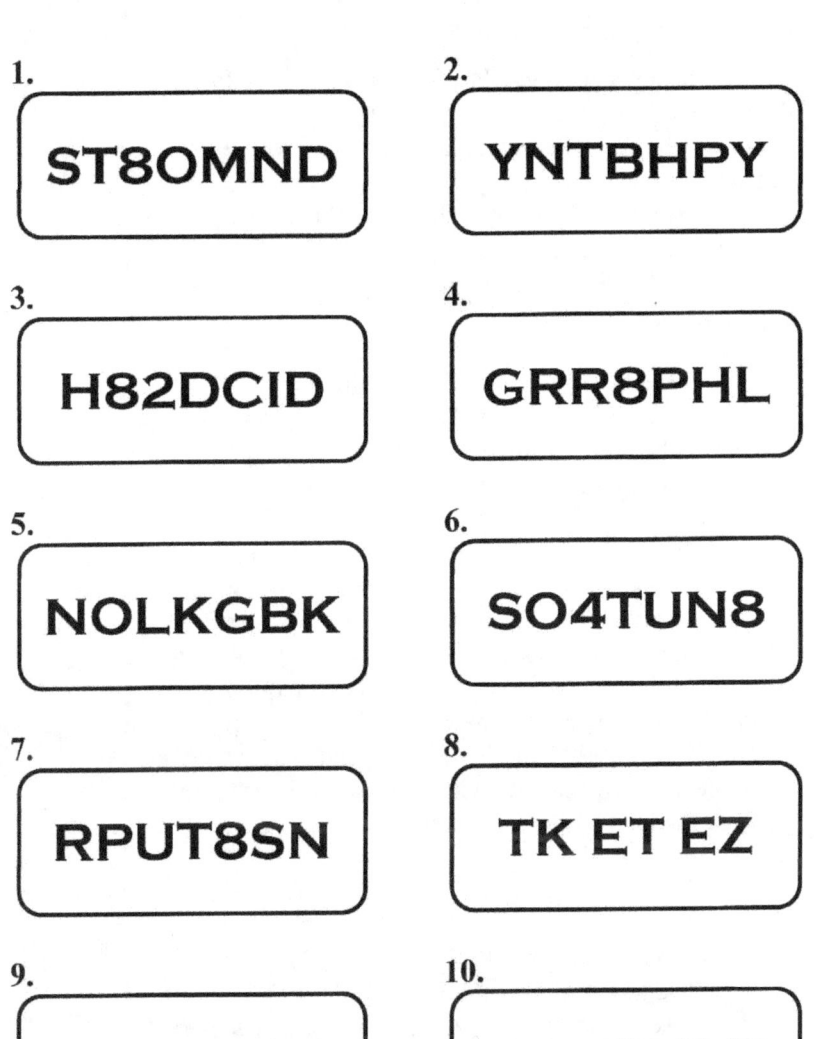

**1.**

ST8OMND

**2.**

YNTBHPY

**3.**

H82DCID

**4.**

GRR8PHL

**5.**

NOLKGBK

**6.**

SO4TUN8

**7.**

RPUT8SN

**8.**

TK ET EZ

**9.**

CZEC M8

**10.**

USNZULZ

"Congratulations, Jared! You've successfully completed Round One!"

"Thanks," he mumbled in response, totally flummoxed by this whole scene.

"Shall we continue?" the host asked, eager and anxious to move the show along.

"Sir, before we proceed any further, I'd appreciate an explanation."

"Of...?"

"Of where I am and what's going on!"

The audience laughed at the clueless fool. They knew something he didn't know.

"Oh Jared, silly boy, we're just playing a game here. What more is there to say?"

Frustrated and confused, Jared quickly realized that attempting to engage in a proper, rational conversation with this man was a futile effort, as he was devoid of sincerity. He was one of those intriguing, mysterious guys (the kind that women are often inexplicably drawn to, at first, but then quickly become annoyed with, due to their impulsive behavior, poor communication skills and hyper-independence, which leaves lovers feeling worthless and insignificant). Instead, rather than milking the host's obnoxious persona, Jared figured that he might as well just play along.

"Uh, nothing, I guess. Forget it. I rescind my inquiry. On with the show."

"That's the spirit, kid!"

The host smirked at him.

"Okay. So, tell us, Jared, what brings you here?"

"Are you kidding? I just told you I don't know what is–"

"You killed yourself, did you not?"

The host's cheery disposition disappeared instantaneously and was replaced, instead, by a solemn, harshly abrupt and confrontational temperament.

Jared became remarkably quiet and forlorn. He retreated into himself, deeper and deeper inward, attempting to hide away while still remaining physically present.

"Jared?"

"Yeah… yeah, I did."

"The next question, necessarily, is: why?  Why did you do it?"

"Um, it's difficult to answer that.  I mean, lots of reasons, I guess.  Well, mostly one.  One thing in particular brought me here."

"And that is…"

"A girl.  Amy Carousel.  She has become my legacy, in a seriously pitiful way.  But, it's true.  I hate to admit it, but it's true."

"What happened?"

"Well, I guess you could say that our entire relationship was a fucked up disaster right from the start.  Sure, we had plenty of good times, but it was mostly a mess."

Jared finished speaking, but the host remained silent.

"There is one particular incident, which I only just learned of, that finally did me in," Jared divulged.  "She, uh, she…"

"It's okay, Jared.  You can tell us.  We're here for you."

"Huh?"

The host gestured toward the crowd and explained that everyone in attendance had endured a similar, traumatic life experience to his own.  They were all broken spirits, at one time, who had finally pieced themselves back together.  Now, having learned to overcome the anguish that fatally tormented their former selves, they were tasked (voluntarily) with passing on their newfound wisdom to others.

"Go on, Jared."

"Well, heh, it's kinda funny, actually.  I don't even know the full story.  Only the overall gist of it was revealed to me.  And then I ran away.  I couldn't bear to hear any more."

"Oh dear.  We're all so sorry, kochanie.  Are you comfortable sharing what you know with us?"

"Sure.  It ain't much, but I'll tell you.  My… uh, my… Wow, it's sorta hard to say this out loud."

"Take your time, Jared."

"My best friend slept with my girlfriend, while my other friend watched from the closet."

The audience gasped, groaned and whimpered.

"Go on."

"That's it. That's literally all I know. Jordan fucked her while Adam watched from the closet. But that was enough for me. I didn't need to hear any more. Nor did I want to. Upon finding out this information, I wrapped my lips around a loaded gun and…"

His words trailed off into quiet contemplation.

"I'm curious, Jared, why you didn't endeavor to learn more about this incident before deciding to end your life."

"I guess I was scared to hear the rest. I didn't need to hear all the dirty details of that day."

"Surely there are more details."

"What?"

"There's a full story from that day. For instance, how they ended up at her house and how the events transpired."

"Yeah, of course. But what's to be gained by hearing all that? I was already sick to my stomach from the conclusion. Why bother hearing the whole story?"

"Because, my child, when we hide from the truth, we become slaves to our own subconscious. You see, if we elect to avoid the full story, our mind will fill in the blanks, regardless. Except, we will imagine the worst-case scenario. We generate a falsehood, informed by our own insecurities and fears. Come on, Jared, we've all done it. All of us imagined the wild fuck-a-thon when we learned of our partner's infidelity. Yet, what we come to realize, only after it's too late, is that the truth is often not nearly as horrific as our conceptualized version of the events at issue. So, with your permission, I'd like to show you that day, from their perspective."

"No! Fuck that. Absolutely not."

"Jared, I insist. This is for your own good. In order to genuinely forgive (that is, after all, our goal here) you must glimpse the scene from their point of view."

"I'm not ready to do this."

"Jared, you will never be ready. But that concept (i.e., your ever-sought-after 'readiness') is an excuse you will utilize to forever delay this moment. I can't let you suffer any longer. Please, Jared."

"Fine… Tell me the entire story of that day."

"Fantastic! Please direct your attention to the video screen and pay attention. You may be pleasantly surprised."

Okay, so basically what happened was, um, I was over at Jordan's and we were just hanging out. I was sitting at his computer, and he was lying on the bed. And I said, "You know what? The next time Ashley comes on AIM, I'm going to tell her I want to fuck her in the ass."

Now, don't get me wrong, I wasn't sitting there thinking this was actually going to happen. It was just a dumb shit idea. And Ashley hardly ever went on AIM.

Literally five minutes later, she pops up.

So, I'm like, well, I fucking said I was going to do it. But then I thought, okay, I'm not going to say "I want to fuck you in the ass." That seemed a bit much.

What I did say was...

Riddler9:  Hey, how's it going?
Ashpipe23:  Good. What's going on with you?
Riddler9:  Just hanging out with Jordan. Playing games and shit.
Ashpipe23:  Okay.
Riddler9:  I really want to have sex with you.

And I just assumed what would happen was
that she'd be like, "Okay, well it's not
going to happen," or that she'd simply laugh
it off or something like that.

The only thing she said was...

**Ashpipe23:** Okay. Come over.

That was her immediate response.  Jordan and
I were like, "Whoa, what the fuck!"

**Riddler9:** I'm at Jordan's.

Her reply?

**Ashpipe23:** Bring him.

And that was it.  That was the entire
conversation.

**Riddler9:** Alright.  We'll be over soon.

Let's go!

[Thus spoke Jordan...]

We both climbed in through her bedroom
window, because she didn't want her mom to
know that we were there.

So we're in her room, just sitting around.
She had put a red scarf over a lamp.  It was
moody.  Adam and her were on the bed and I
was on the floor.  I was not involved right
away.  She was wearing those green booty

shorts and a thin tank top with her nipples poking through it.

She was ready.  There was intention.

In the innocent and immature way that we were, Adam said, "Let's pretend we're in a movie, and you can film us kissing."  And then they both just started making out on the bed.  I put my fingers into a square and panned around.

She took her shirt off.  He sucked on her nipples a little bit, but then she put her shirt back on.

Adam looked over at me and said, "Come up here."  I went on the bed, and they were like pretty much making out on me.

I think I touched her, maybe.  I don't know if I licked.  I didn't kiss, if I recall.  I could tell right away that she was not interested in me.

So they're still making out, and things are escalating.  It had evolved into heavy grinding; like, dry sex or whatever.

Then, Adam pulls out the single condom.  He stood there for a second, holding it and looking at it.

"This doesn't belong to me," he said. "This is your moment.  Jordan, you should take this."

Now, I hadn't experienced any of these things yet.  I was still a virgin at this point.

I took the condom, and looked at it.  I said, "What about Ryan?  This isn't a good idea.  I'm nervous.  I'm scared."

"It's okay," she said.  She wanted to get laid.

I ripped open the condom.

I asked Adam, "Should you leave?"

"I'm going to go sit in the closet," he replied.

He got in the closet and closed the door.  Of course, he left it open just a crack, enough for him to peek out and watch us.

She takes off her shorts and lays down on the bed.  I didn't even take my pants off all the way.  I don't think I was naked bottom down.  I'm pretty sure I just pulled them down to my ankles.  Her shirt and my shirt were still on.

She laid there.  I got on top of her.  Missionary position.

And I could not get hard.  I was trying to put the condom on, but I was not hard.  So I'm trying to jerk off and she did not help me at all.  I was struggling.  The condom was sorta on, and I was trying to put it in

her.  Just trying to get my dick hard
enough.

"I can't get hard.  Can I have a blow job?"
I asked her.

"No."

Eventually, I got hard enough and got it in.

She was not into it.  Nothing.  Emotionless.
No kissing.  It was totally mechanical.  No
moaning.  No excitement.

I was humping away.  Going at it.  I
specifically remember that I started
dripping sweat on her.

Fuck, I am so unsexy.  This is so hard to
do.  I cannot do this.

This must've gone on for about 20 to 30
minutes.

"Hey guys, are you going to keep going?
Because nothing seems to be happening," Adam
said.

"I can't finish.  I can't cum," I announced.

I kept trying, but I wasn't staying hard.
So I pulled out, took off the condom and
threw it away.  Adam exited the closet.  I
put my pants on.  And we left almost
immediately.

Ryan, you have to understand how weird the whole thing was. There wasn't anything to say afterwards, like, everything had been said. It became fucking clear, she wasn't into it, she didn't want it, I was awkward as fuck about it, I didn't know how to react to it and we all just wanted to get the fuck out of there.

I climbed out of the window first and walked away.

As Adam was starting to climb out the window, Ashley said, "Wait, hold on."

He paused.

"I wish it had been you," she said.

He turned back around and climbed out the window, upset and disappointed.

"I'm sorry," he replied. "I gotta go."

And we left.

This was a weird fucking moment, dude. It was dumb.

For your peace of mind, I want you to know that we didn't come out of this being like, "Yeah! We fucking did it!" We came out of this embarrassed and feeling like we shouldn't have done that. It was weird. We didn't want to upset you. We figured that we shouldn't mention it, ever.

```
It was not triumphant.  It was not
rewarding.  It was so awkward and stupid.

We didn't feel good about it.  We felt
ashamed.
```

      The video faded out.
      "And there you have it.  The complete story of Amy
Carousel, in its entirety.  Every gory detail of that day."
      Jared stared off into the distance, stunned by the
revelatory confessions.
      "Well?" the host inquired.
      "I… I just assumed it was crazy porn sex.  But, in reality,
it was actually quite pathetic."
      "Yes!"
      Jared began to laugh.
      "Like, seriously pathetic.  I'm almost disappointed."
      "Jared, I told you so!"

      Why didn't he tell me himself?  It took the insistent
urging of Michael (bless him) to finally expose the truth.  I was
glad I finally knew.  Some ascribe to the notion that ignorance is
bliss.  Ya know?  There're plenty popular sayings that espouse
this theme.  'What you don't know won't hurt you' also comes to
mind.
      I sincerely believe that the truth shall set you free.
Always opt for authenticity, even if– no, *especially if* it'll hurt,
because that's the stuff that actually matters.  Yes!

      I shall strive to live an honest life.
To stand naked before G-d, whilst enduring the shame.

      "Thanks for playing, Jared.  We're done here.  You're
free.  The burden has been lifted.  Your soul has been cleansed.
You are restored to absolute purity.  No longer will lies and
suspicions permeate your mind.  You now know the truth.  Sure,
you may still react with anger or sadness (or the myriad other so-

called 'negative' emotions), but such reactions will be rooted in reality. You won! You beat the game. Goodbye, Jared."

Jared could now close the chapter on Amy, once and for all. The girl that haunted him for so long had finally been released from his memory. He no longer feared the mere mention of her name. He had emerged from his hiding place and was learning to embrace the world, in all its terribleness.

"I don't have to be afraid anymore," he said to himself.

He started to walk off the set, toward nowhere in particular, while quietly singing the chorus to "Poor Little Fool" by Ricky Nelson. Then he stopped. Something didn't seem quite right about this moment. It felt undeserved, in a sense. A hollow victory.

He looked at the host and the audience. They hadn't moved. They all politely smiled at him, in unison.

'Do they also know about... it?' Jared wondered. 'The, uh, *event* from when I was a boy. Strange, the host never mentioned it. He must've known, right? Yes, of course he knows. He knows all. He's like some sort of celestial being. A metaphorical messenger. So then, why? Why didn't he say anything? Is that it? He's just going to let me go now? We didn't discuss my childhood trauma! What happened to my epiphany? I guess some things in life go unresolved.'

Can that be? No! What an unsatisfactory finale! Where's the resolution? The denouement? Jared, do something! Fix this!

'Sure, we can (and should) attempt to seek amends for all our transgressions. I tried, but my efforts were unwelcomed. I can't force his forgiveness. Perhaps I must carry this particular guilt a little while longer. Today I have obtained closure regarding Amy, yet another sorrow still exists within me. Oh well. So much for a happy ending.'

"Thanks, bye," Eddie muttered. He had finished eating his piece of carrot cake.

"What? You're leaving?" shrieked Tiny. "I thought we were laying the foundational stones of a lifelong friendship here. Every minute we've spent together was building toward something special; or so I thought. Please, I've already devoted a significant portion of my life to you. Your exit would indicate that I've been wasting my time."

"Hey, little fella, not every relationship is meant to last a lifetime. Yet still, we always gain something from the people we share our days with, even if only briefly."

"Save that sappy shit for someone worth a damn! I know you're just trying to escape without any guilt. You'll forget about us the minute you turn your back."

"Listen, I appreciate your hospitality and the wisdom you've shared, but I must go. My friend is in trouble. Whether you wish to harbor any resentment is up to you. You knew this was the deal all along."

Eddie started to go, but Tosie grabbed onto his leg.

"Wait! If you leave now, it's all over for us. What then was our role in this story?"

"Does everything have a discernable purpose that is one day revealed? Every street name? Every bird? Not necessarily. Many little moments go unexplained. It is the grander picture of our lives that we will one day understand, not every insignificant detail. Give it time, my friends."

Eddie limped away.

We all share a similar pain in our own way.
We're all goofballs.
We all "feel" in the cycle of being loved and unloved.

Bernardo awoke in an unfamiliar room. He was on a bed. The hallway light shone through the open doorway, brightening an otherwise eerily dark chamber.

Henry Fronten sat on a rocking chair beside the bed, unarmed.

"You're up," he observed, in a dull, matter-of-fact, monotone grumble.

Bernardo sat up and immediately reached for his crotch, hoping the recent memory still lingering in his head had been nothing more than a bizarre nightmare.

It was covered in blood-soaked bandages.

"What the fuck did you do to me?" he screamed.

"You made a sacrifice," Henry spoke. "Recall, if you're able to, all you've given up to reach this point. All those you've pushed away, and the forgone life experiences. Then ask yourself: was it worth it? The maybe family will never be. Your wife has been discarded. And your children, the cute little girl with pigtails and the rambunctious boy, are now gone. Their potentiality is extinguished. A scar is forming. It is the souvenir you will receive instead. Young man, your cock provided some much-needed sustenance to my boys. Our gratitude is unbounded."

"I don't even understand how this happened. What came over me? I must've been lost in the moment (as they say), or something to that effect. Everything happened so suddenly. I didn't realize there'd be life-altering consequences to my decision."

A human silhouette appeared in the doorway.

"Let's go," it spoke.

"Eddie?" asked Bernardo.

Mr. Fronten stood up and slowly approached the unknown intruder.

"Sir, I'm going to have to ask you to leave my home at once," he said.

The sound of a shotgun being cocked filled the small room.

"No…" Mr. Fronten whispered.

Eddie held the shotgun. He aimed it directly at Mr. Fronten's chest.

"Bernardo, let's get the fuck out of here."

"Help me up, man. This guy's a psycho. My dick is gone!"

Eddie saw the bandages. It looked like Bernardo was wearing a bloody diaper.

"What the fuck? Are you insane? What the fuck is wrong with you?" he asked the old man.

"Listen, put the gun down and I'll explain everything. Just put the gun down first, okay?" he begged.

Eddie walked over to Bernardo's bedside, without dropping his aim. He held the shotgun in his left hand and helped Bernardo up with his right hand.

"Come on. Let's go."

Bernardo hobbled out of the room. Eddie followed, walking backwards, his aim fixed on Mr. Fronten.


Bernardo stopped at the door to the bathroom, which housed the four Asian boys. He opened it.

"Leave now! Hurry! You're free!" he yelled.

They glanced up at him, startled and confused. They had long ago lost hope of ever being rescued from their circumstance. This situation was so unfamiliar to them that they were unsure how to react.

"Go!" Bernardo again yelled.

They slowly stood, one by one.

"Wait!" Mr. Fronten shouted from the other end of the hallway. "My boys!"

Eddie stood guard between Bernardo and Mr. Fronten.

"Not so powerful anymore without your gun, hey?" Bernardo said. "Your tool of influence is gone. Look at you! Now you're nothing more than a sad, repressed old man, with some seeeerious unaddressed issues."

The boys filed out of the room.

Henry fell to his knees, and wept.

Eddie, Bernardo and the 4 boys stood together on the front porch of Henry Fronten's home.

"Thank you," said the youngest son.

They all 4 bowed and then scattered off in separate directions. The speed with which they moved was non-human. They scurried away like quick-legged rodents. In a matter of seconds, they were gone from view.

"I love you, buddy," said Eddie. "Let's get as far away from here as possible."

As they commenced their journey home, Eddie and Bernardo each shared their respective stories. Thereafter, they were quiet for several reflective minutes.

"I wish I would've told him sooner," Bernardo said, breaking the silence. "Maybe things would have been different."

"What?"

"I should have said something to Jared. Had I told him, maybe his reaction wouldn't have been…"

"This again? Don't blame yourself for what happened, Bernardo. You were completely uninvolved in that whole situation."

"Exactly! That is precisely why I should have stepped in, as a neutral party, and told him."

"I mean, it wasn't really your place to tell him. It didn't concern you."

"I don't know, man. I held onto that secret. I knew the whole fucking story for like, at least a month before he finally found out. I was an accomplice."

"And how'd you feel when you first heard about it?"

"I felt bad. I felt bad for Jared. Personally, I thought the whole situation was pretty damn funny. But I just knew how devastated he would be if he ever found out."

"So you wanted to tell him because you felt he deserved to know, or because you didn't want to feel guilty about keeping a secret from him?"

"I guess a little of both."

"The latter justification is entirely selfish. When relieving one's guilt will destroy another's life, it's best to keep quiet."

BARK

"Hey!"

BARK BARK

"Holy shit! Is that…?"

Eddie reached into his pocket and retrieved the folded-up flyer that Rupert Podemsky had given him earlier that evening. He studied it for an instant.

"Dude, it's him."

They carefully approached the dog.

"Here, boy. Come here. Here, Patrick."

Patrick sheepishly obeyed. He crawled toward Eddie and Bernardo. They crouched down to greet him, and exchanged friendly rubs, hair ruffles and kisses.

"Come on, boy. Let's get you home."

Can
you
keep
a
secret?

Can
you
tell
a
lie?

Can
you
tell
the
difference?

"My sweet darling! Oh, beloved angel! The yish-ka-bibble catapult of my dreams! An upturned tubulum aimed toward the sky! O hallowed howler, scratch-ragged scrappy laroo! Belvedere moon strap, pickpocketed and unwoven! Thoroughly marshaled meat cleaver skadunk! Rigamortis sandwiching three-peat! Thatched roof sunrise canopy! The aesthetic rinse baroque marathon! Tactile tiddlywink archdiocese! Breakfast usurper! Hangman's lockbox, jitterbugging boom toon! Reminder of the long-distance wedding! Rebel rouser, stark and uncouth! Horse-driven magpies! Crumbling loaf! Magazine clippings! Eastern aurora, flickered buffoon! Sandbagging seafarer, traversing clustered crescents! Patchwork pox! The potable knapsack of Gilgamesh! A lonely baroness's sequestered inheritance!" Rupert gushed.

He then knelt down in the doorway of his parents' home, overcome and exhausted, having purged himself entirely of every pet name. Patrick was jumping for joy, his tail wagging wildly, while he licked Rupert's face, uncontrollably.

Eddie and Bernardo proudly observed this exchange of loving expressions.

"My precious pup!" he went on, his eyes filling with tears. "Where'd you guys find him?"

They chuckled.

"Now that's a tale that'll take ages to tell. Suffice it to say we found him in the forest up near Hopler's Tea Trimmer."

"I can't believe it. Patrick! Ahh! How can I ever repay you guys? Please allow me to tender a monetary reward. It's the least I can do."

"No, no, no. That's not necessary. Honestly, Rupert, it's fine."

"I insist."

"Look, I appreciate the offer; but I, along with my buddy here, refuse to accept any money for this deed. It's worth it just to see how happy you both are together. We've reunited two trusted companions. Knowing this, and bearing witness to it, is more fulfilling than any exchange of cash."

"That's very noble of you both. But please, I must confer a token of my gratitude. Something."

"It's fine."

"I've got it!" he yelled, suddenly struck by a realization.

Rupert ran inside. He returned a minute later, carrying a journal.

"When I first encountered Patrick, some eight years ago, he had this with him. It was a journal that belonged to a young man by the name of John Nelson. He lived here about 200 years ago. Legend has it that Patrick's great, great, great, great, great, great, great, great, great, great grandfather was the first to receive this journal. Since then, it has been handed down, from generation to generation, to be carried by the firstborn son of each litter, each of whom was, appropriately, also named Patrick."

He rubbed Patrick's head.

"This little fella here is Patrick XIII."

He handed the journal to Eddie.

"Rupert, this is a seriously significant, ultra-meaningful family heirloom. We can't deprive you of this. The tradition must live on!"

Rupert nervously clasped the back of his neck.

"Well, you see, I didn't learn of this whole arrangement until after it was too late," he explained.

"Huh?"

"We, uh, we snipped his balls off."

Bernardo nearly fainted.

"Guys, I want you to have it. Prior to this moment, I had already begun to assume the worst. I started to believe that my dear pal was gone forever. But here he is! You've returned him to me. It's almost as though he has been born again. It only makes sense that you keep it."

"Wow," said Eddie. He bowed his head in humility. "It shall be observed and remembered for always. 'Tis a special honor you have bestowed upon us this day."

He opened the journal and began absently flipping through it.

"What's all in here?"

"Poems, mostly. I must warn you, John Nelson was a severely depressed individual. It's pretty bleak stuff. I was actually able to do a little research on him. The registrar here has a really odd report on him, if you're interested. So, turns out, he ended up killing himself when he was only 17 years old. He was apparently the first to ever do so in this town's history. He became somewhat of a local antihero. Scientists studied him. They did this barbaric experiment where they ate part of his brain and started hallucinating. Fucking weird, man."

Rupert reached over and flipped the pages nearer toward the end of the journal.

"As you'll see, the last 1/3 of it is blank. John Nelson killed himself before he ever finished it."

"Finished it? It's just a bunch of poems."

"No. No, it's much more than just a random assortment of poems. I've studied them. There's an interconnectedness to it all. My theory is that there was a story being told here. Had he finished it, it would've all come together in the end. But instead, we're left with this, unfinished and incomplete. He couldn't handle the pain of his life; and art, with its seemingly infinite potential, failed to lift his spirit out of despair."

"What a fucking shame."

They stood quietly for a moment, in solemn tribute.

"Anyways, it's yours now. Thank you, Eddie. Thank you, Bernardo."

Rupert went inside (followed by Patrick) and closed the door.

Eddie gripped the journal. He stared at it, seemingly upset and almost angered by whatever it evoked within him. He gave the journal to Bernardo.

"Here," he said. "You can keep it. I have no concern for the delicate ruminations of a guy that committed suicide."

An untold number of nights later, Bernardo sat alone in his bedroom and read through John Nelson's poems. Each of them. He read until he reached the blank pages that suggested "the end." Then, as though he were guided by divine will, he kept going. He carefully turned each and every empty page, ensuring that he wasn't overlooking any hidden and/or misplaced writings. When he arrived at the last page, he discovered one final note left behind by John Nelson.

Friendship and Forgiveness (a note of supreme optimism)
by
John Nelson

Everyone truly loves to be alive. Even the most depressed
individuals are thankful for the gift of life. If only they could step
out of their damaged selves and view life for what it really is.
Because this is it! This is your only goddamned chance!
Breathing and thinking, the power of the mind. Never stop asking
why, and soon you will learn all the answers. THINK about it.
Underneath all human sadness is humor and hope. It is up to us,
whether (through great effort and sacrifice) it will eventually
surface (and thereby liberate us) or (through neglect and self
sabotage) suffocate (and thereby defeat us).

Conquering sorrow is easier said than done…

Everyone has a memory from their past that they ignore and try to
forget ever happened. There are certain instances that, when
remembered (often during solitary moments of maddening quiet),
make us recoil in terror.

We all wish that such event never occurred. We yearn for a do
over, to go back and change things. Then, we'd be perfect. We
would be free of our greatest hindrance.

We THINK: If only I hadn't  [insert trauma here] . If I didn't
have that thought weighing me down **every second of my life**
(whether I'm aware of it or not), I could accomplish all my
fantastical goals. But instead, I'm being held back by a shameful
secret. This is why I'm unable to dance. I can't *let myself go* – so
to speak – because of it. It's always there, resting atop my mind.
An inner voice, constantly whispering, "You're not allowed to
experience joy. You don't deserve it."

Except, we are all imperfect and fucked up in our own unique
ways. We're all carrying our own regretful memory. This is

precisely what makes us who we are. It is how we cope with our desolation that defines us. Life is (and will always be) a struggle, no matter what. True character is demonstrated in how we deal with our burdens.

Do we let it destroy us? Or do we overcome it?

We must go on living.